FRANK RACIOPPI

Starting From Now

A Blue-Collar Romance Novel

"No matter how hard the past is, you can always start from now."

Seneca

Contents

Foreword

Starting From Now is a novel about redemption, set in a fictional home improvement store in Franklinville, NJ, called HomeMaxx. Long-time employees Jack Marsalis and Lashay Jones try to ignite a romantic relationship that may be smothered by the secrets both carry with them.

Acknowledgments

While the act of writing may be a solitary exercise, publishing a book is entirely a team effort. I am fortunate to have a talented and supportive team surrounding me. Thank you to Jim Driscoll for the developmental and copy editing. Thank you to Allison Cangelosi for the book cover design. Thank you to George from LMS Publishing for selling my books at festivals, indie bookstores, conventions, and markets. Your hustle and selling prowess are noted and appreciated.

Chapter One

"**H**omeMaxx does not allow pets in the store unless they are guide dogs or certified service animals."

Jacob Snow only felt slightly guilty about dropping off their cat in the woods.

After all, he told himself, his wife Ava had just found out she was pregnant. His father explained that cats carry toxoplasmosis, a single-celled parasite that can infect humans. His dad said that humans are often infected by being near the cat box or, worse, cleaning the cat box.

Since they adopted the cat from the Clayton Animal Shelter two months ago, Ava has been caring for it because she was the one who wanted the cat.

Jacob wasn't a cat person. He wanted a dog, but he wanted to wait until they had kids so the dog could grow up with their child, just like Jacob did with Scout, his German Shepard. Now that Ava was pregnant, they could get a dog soon.

The scary part was that Jacob's father told him that the parasite could affect the baby. Last week, Jacob decided that the cat—Ava had named it Cali—had to go. It took an entire week to convince Ava that it was necessary. Jacob spent that week employing strategies to convince Ava that Cali had to go.

First, he tried logic, explaining toxoplasmosis, but that didn't work. Ava answered, "Then you take care of the cat litter and box until the baby is born."

Then Jacob tried to scare Ava, reading the possible effects on the unborn baby if it contracted toxoplasmosis. Even when Jacob embellished the possible health effects, Ava wouldn't budge.

Jacob thought of asking his father to talk to her, but Ava didn't like his father, calling him bossy and overbearing. Jacob always defended his father, explaining that, as the head of a large private equity fund, he had tremendous responsibility and was used to telling people what to do.

By Thursday, Jacob was frustrated and ready to yell and threaten. Thankfully, Ava's mother stopped over at their townhome to see Ava. Since Ava hadn't gotten home from a work meeting yet, Jacob spent the time convincing her about the dangers of toxoplasmosis. Ava's mother, June, was one of those parents who identified dangers everywhere.

Escalators. "Don't take them, Ava. Your hair could get caught in them, and you'll be crushed."

Uber or Lyft: "I've seen Dateline. Most of the drivers are serial killers."

Toaster ovens: "They'll short circuit and catch fire, trapping you in your bedroom where you'll be burned to a cinder."

People you don't know: "Most strangers will either rob, rape, stab, shoot or torture you. Talk to no one you don't know well."

Once Jacob explained toxoplasmosis to June, Ava's mother did the rest. By Saturday, Ava relented under the onslaught of her mother's doomsaying.

Ava's one condition was that the cat, Cali, would be returned to the shelter in Clayton so another family could adopt the feline.

Jacob readily agreed, although he had no intention of following through. He didn't want the animal rescue center people to look down on him because he had returned a cat they had just recently rescued.

In Jacob's mind, cats are resilient. He read this article about feral cats taking over some island in the Pacific and killing all the other animals there. Cali would survive. In fact, Jacob reasoned that he was doing Cali a favor by releasing the cat off a main road, Delsea Drive, so an animal control officer could spot the feline and capture him.

Jacob and Ava lived in a three-bedroom townhome in the Aura section of Elk Township in South Jersey. They had grown up in the area and met at Rowan University in nearby Glassboro, where Jacob studied business, and

Ava majored in graphic design.

Ava had cried when she put Cali in the cat carrier they had bought. Jacob kept the receipt so he could return it at Petco. Cali whimpered a bit as if she knew something bad was happening.

Jacob was surprised at how quiet the cat was when he drove from Elk Township, made a few turns, and drove down Delsea Drive in Franklinville. Jacob drove his Tesla S down Delsea Drive below the speed limit as he scanned the area for the best place to let the cat out.

He knew he couldn't let anyone see him, especially the police. He didn't think he'd be breaking any laws, but it'd be embarrassing. He drove by Fries Mill Road on the left, where his old high school was, and then past the HomeMaxx store.

The home improvement store was a weak sister to Home Depot and Lowe's, but it had stayed in business here for over twenty years since Jacob was a child.

Right past the store and an open farm field was a lawyer's office that looked like a Victorian home. Jacob turned onto Leonard Cake Road, surrounded by a thick mesh of trees. Jacob thought it was a perfect place to drop off the cat.

No witnesses.

As Jacob pulled over onto the side of the road, he felt a twinge of guilt and a teaspoon of regret. Cali was a cute cat. Unlike some cats that are aloof and spiteful, Cali loved to snuggle with them on the couch. Jacob knew next to nothing about cats, but Ava's family had a long history with cats in their household.

Cali was a Calico cat. Jacob thought Calico was a breed of cat, but Ava had explained, "Calico cats are named for their coat color, which resembles calico cloth that was once imported to England from India. One calico may display the usual combination of vibrant orange, black, and white, while another can feature a more subdued shade of cream mixed with blue. In feline genetics, the latter is known as a 'dilute calico.'"

"You'll never see two Calico cats exactly alike," Ava had told him when they were at the rescue shelter and she spotted the Calico.

On the ride home from the shelter, Ava explained that "Calico cats originated from Egypt. In ancient Egyptian culture, Calico cats were worshiped. Japanese fishermen used Calico cats in boats to protect them during storms."

"Calico cats are renowned for their spunky, assertive personalities," Ava said. "You'll like this, Jacob. Calico cats are generally independent cats that don't require constant attention; the calico is also sweet, loving, and loyal. It will readily bond with a single owner but enjoy the company of an entire family, too."

"That's us, Jacob," Ava had said as she hugged him. "We're Cali's family now."

Jacob didn't shut off the Tesla because it made no noise. He slid out of the driver's seat, went to the passenger-side front door, and opened it. The black cloth cat carrier sat on the seat, with the front mesh facing the dashboard.

That's good, Jacob thought. He didn't want to look at her. He might change his mind.

Jacob grabbed the carrier by the top handle and carried it through the woods about 40 feet. Then he looked back at his car and realized that, with the new seasonal foliage grown in, he was hidden from any prying eyes.

Jacob knelt on his right knee and opened the front part of the cat carrier so Cali could come out.

He waited a few seconds, but the cat didn't appear. Jacob, nervous about getting caught, bent over and looked into the cat carrier. Cali had squeezed herself into the back part of the carrier.

It was like the cat knew what was happening.

But how could it, Jacob reasoned?

It was just a cat.

Jacob tried to coax it out.

"Cali, come on out," Jacob urged, trying to suppress his instinct to yell.

Cali, however, did not move, her opal eyes glistening in the April sunset.

Jacob cursed himself because he should have brought cat treats to entice Cali from her carrier.

After two more minutes of begging and making what he thought were cat sounds, Jacob's patience hit a wall.

Jacob stood up, picked up the cat carrier, facing the opening toward the ground, and began to shake it.

Jacob shook it hard a few times and heard the cat's nails dig into the cloth, trying to remain inside the carrier. After a few tries, Jacob suddenly tilted the cat carrier upward and then downward, and that dislodged the cat.

Cali fell onto the underbrush and righted itself onto its legs, shaking its head as the cat tried to regain its balance. The cat seemed stunned, so Jacob took off running with the cat carrier toward the car.

When he got to the Tesla and turned around, fearful that the cat had followed him, Jacob looked hard into the thick woods.

He saw no movement, no animal, no cat—just trees and bushes budding in the mid-April spring growing season.

He felt relieved. He had done it. He tossed the cat carrier into the back seat and entered his car. Jacob took a deep breath, glad that he had made this problem go away.

As he turned left onto Delsea Drive toward home, Jacob began to work on his story of how the drop-off at the Clayton Animal Rescue Center went. Jacob knew he needed specific details to make the story more believable.

He decided to tell Ava that the rescue center woman said they had a family to adopt Cali right away, and she'd be gone by tomorrow. This way, he decided, Ava wouldn't feel guilty and show up at the rescue center to visit Cali.

As Jacob solidified the details of his story, he felt better and less guilty about ditching the cat.

He had to do it.

The cat will be fine.

The cat froze as she watched the human run away and then disappear in some metal cylinder that moved faster than any prey Cali had seen.

Alone in the underbrush, Cali used her senses to evaluate her situation. Sunlight would disappear, and the temperature would dip to a level where shelter was needed. Her vertically shaped black pupils opened wide to draw in light, and her wide-field, expansive peripheral vision enabled her to spot several mice tucked away near rotted logs. To her left, two squirrels darted back and forth between two oak trees.

After identifying her food sources, Cali located water in a low area about 150 yards to her left. As a final check of her situation, she scanned for other predators who could be a threat.

Squirrels, field mice, chipmunks, rabbits, and birds didn't concern her. They existed as her food supply. Cali would reserve a watchful eye for the family of raccoons about 200 yards away because Cali instinctually knew that a hungry raccoon could be a foe one day. A skunk popped up its head about 100 years to her west. Cali made a note to avoid the animal's burrow. Skunks avoided other animals, including cats, but if startled, could spray her and cause a lot of discomfort.

As Cali assessed her situation, her ears located sounds from a human-made structure about 500 yards to her northeast. Her ears detected the faint sound of human voices and human-made machines.

Cali knew that human structures offered her plenty of shelter and hiding spaces. From her two previous owners, she recalled how humans had so many small, secluded spaces in their enclosures. Cali loved closets, the pantry, even inside the lower cabinets in their eating area, and especially under their elevated sleeping mats.

As Cali's senses absorbed the sights, smells, and sounds of the nearby human structure, she made a decision. She would find shelter in the human structure and hunt for plentiful prey in these woods.

Cali scanned the area for danger and moved carefully through the woods. When she came to the asphalt open area where humans in fast-moving machines presented the danger of injury or death, Cali waited until the area was clear of humans or their machines.

She ran across and into the open field, arranged in rows that stretched for several hundred yards. She ran along one row for safety and quickly made it to the human structure's rear.

The sun was lower now but still had time to remain in the sky.

Cali waited at the edge of the field.

As darkness set and light slipped away, she crept slowly along the dirt, her body elongated and almost slithering like a snake.

When Cali came upon a hard white surface, she knew that she had entered the outer edges of the human structure. It was quiet here, with only a dim light above to scare away the darkness.

Cali was patient. She waited until darkness blanketed the area. Then, she moved stealthily toward a metal structure with braided metal that seemed to keep people out and things in.

Like stalking prey, Cali got low to the ground and moved deliberately until she found a break in the metal braids. She wriggled through easily.

Cali's eyes drew in as much light as possible to make out details in the dark. After searching quietly for a short time, Cali found a box turned upside down with a small hole gashed in one side.

Cali squeezed into the box and assessed her surroundings. The box was about twice her height and four times her length.

There was plenty of room to relax and sleep safe from potential predators. It was cozy and comfortable here, and she liked enclosed spaces.

During the day, she could move through the field and stalk prey in the wooded area.

Cali closed her eyes as she curled into a ball, preserving body heat.

This is my new home.

Chapter Two

"**A**t HomeMaxx, we treat employees like their family.**"

Jack Marsalis walked into the Franklinville, New Jersey, Home-Maxx store like he owned it. He didn't. He only worked there. It was 8 a.m. on a Monday morning in mid-April, and the store had light customer traffic.

The double doors opened automatically, and Jack glanced over at Darla Campanna, who stood at the desk of the Returns department.

She was a 40ish woman with blonde hair that resisted any shape. She was heavy and apple-shaped, with a roundish, comely face and inviting smile that seemed to soothe people. Darla had reading glasses suspended from a gold chain around her neck.

Jack said, "Good morning, Darla. Those glasses around your neck make you look like a nun who didn't make the cut."

Darla smiled, all cheeks and white teeth, and responded, "Screw you, Jack."

"Thank you, Darla."

Next to the Returns desk was the Customer Service Desk, where ten-year employee Christine Berrino cross-trained Lauren Garcia of the Paint department.

"What the hell was that all about?" Lauren asked Christine.

"Oh, they do this every morning," Christine answered.

"They must really hate each other," Lauren said.

Christine chuckled, adjusting the full-length wig on her head.

"Actually, they've been the best of friends for years," Christine told her, leaning closer like it was a secret.

"Years ago, Jack found that Darla's then-husband was beating her up. One night, when he came to pick her up, Jack went out and had a little talk with him."

Christine used air quotes when she said "little talk."

Lauren smiled.

"Did this talk include his knuckles hitting the asshole's face?" Lauren asked.

Christine returned the smile.

"Look at him," Christine said. "Think Jack can take of himself?"

Jack was about five foot eleven inches with broad shoulders and thick arms. He has a fast-paced walk as if he were headed to a fire. His walk always had a purpose to it, and his arms and legs moved in unison as if Jack had total command of his actions, which he did not. Jack was muscular with corded forearms and a wide back. The only concession to age and lifestyle was the paunch that's been spreading gradually near his beltline. Jack resisted going from 32 to 34-inch jeans, so they were tight around his waist.

Jack had thick, brown hair flecked with grey streaks and a thinning patch on the back of his head. His scalp was close to being revealed in the next few years. Jack had adorned himself with a neatly manicured five o'clock shadow like many men today. He trimmed it every morning. When he had a home, he loved to cut the lawn. This beard trimming was his substitute activity. Even his eyebrows were trimmed neatly, and lately, he's had to trim hair in and around his ears. Jack thanked his lucky stars that he hadn't been afflicted by a hairy back like his father, who looked like he wore a thick shag rug on his back.

The tribulations of life had attacked Jack's handsome face. His deep brown eyes had lost a spark that had been there in his youth and young adulthood. Despite that chronic sadness, Jack's eyes were perceptive, roving, assessing, and sapient.

Jack walked down the aisle with lawn equipment and chemicals to his right and banged a left toward the Plumbing department where he worked this week. Jack had been working at the store for 15 years and had so much experience that he could and would work in any department in the store.

This week, it was Plumbing; last week, it was Tools and Hardware; and next week, it will be the Kitchen department.

As Jack approached the Appliances department, he spotted two angry faces – a man and a woman about 50 with matching scowls. Jack didn't need 15 years of experience to know something was wrong.

The woman spotted him and then said something to her partner, probably her husband. Jack noticed he shrugged. Then he knew they were here because of the woman.

Jack thought he'd be proactive and ask if they needed help, but the woman beat him to the punch.

"Excuse me. Excuse me," the woman called out, irritation pouring out of her tone.

"Yes, how can I help you?" Jack asked, forcing a smile onto his face with the same intensity he had to hold in his farts when customers were nearby.

"My husband and I asked this young kid who works in this department to help us buy a new washing machine, and he said he would. Then he was called over the PA system to come to the office and never returned."

"We've been waiting for 15 minutes," she emphasized.

Jack noticed the husband stood behind the woman and nodded with little enthusiasm.

Jack was pissed. Not at this couple. But when customers got shitty service in the store. His store.

"I'm sorry about that, and I'm here to help," Jack said. "Now, why do you need a new washing machine?"

"Ours doesn't work anymore," the woman shot back as if Jack had asked a dumb question.

The husband unexpectedly piped up.

"Our washer, which is 12 years old, is a top loader Whirlpool and has been bouncing all around for the last few months."

"It's shot," the wife insisted. Then to Jack:" I've been tellin' him this for months."

Jack nodded his head at the woman but then addressed the man.

"What have you tried?"

"I watched these YouTube videos about the washer not being level," the husband replied. "Try to level it several times."

"He's probably not doing it right," the wife said. "So, we need a new washer."

Jack turned his body toward the husband but focused on the wife.

"Your washing machine has dampers," Jack began. "They work similarly to the shock absorbers on a car. These dampers restrict the drum's movement as it washes an unbalanced load."

"So what," the woman replied.

"Janice let's hear the man out," the husband spoke up.

"Over time, the dampers get damaged from excessive wear and tear," Jack explained. "When they go bad, your washer looks like it's doing the Macarena along the floor."

The man laughed and asked, "How much would it cost to fix if we had a repair guy come out?"

"About 250 dollars," Jack said. "I can recommend a good repair company. It's called Dave's Appliance Repair. He'll take good care of you. Tell him Jack from HomeMaxx recommended him."

The man smiled, and the woman's face relaxed.

"We'd sure like to save the money on a new washer," she said, smiling now.

Jack wrote something on a Post-It Note and handed it to the wife.

"Here's Dave's number," Jack began. "The second number is mine. Please call me after your washing machine is fixed and let me know how everything worked out."

"Thanks, ah..." the man answered.

"It's Jack," Jack answered. "Glad I could help you both, and again, I apologize for your problem."

The couple walked away smiling and waved as they turned the corner into the row with the paint cans. As they disappeared, Jack heard a young male voice.

"Thank God they left. That woman was a shrew."

Jack turned around. Two newer employees who were supposed to be working in the Appliance department, Justin and Trevor, chuckled like six-grade boys who had just heard a poop joke.

"Jack, that lady was a B I T C H," Justin said. He was rec league basketball tall with shoulder-length black hair. Jack figured he was going for the Timothee Chamelet look to attract young women.

The other kid, both in their early 20s, was Trevor, who stood several inches taller than Jack with a sturdy body sculpted from bench presses, squats, and thousands of bicep curls.

Tyler, the store manager, hired them in February after both had graduated college—Justin from the University of West Virginia and Trevor from the University of Tennessee. Both young men had been living with their parents in nearby affluent Washington Township.

Tyler told Jack that at their job interviews, they admitted they just wanted jobs to get their parents off their backs.

"We're so desperate for people that I had to hire these entitled little pricks," Tyler told Jack. "Since Black Cobalt bought HomeMaxx and cut the starting hourly rate by 20 percent, we have struggled to hire anyone. Sometimes, I think they want us to fail."

Jack had advised that they be assigned to the Appliance department because "the appliances sell themselves. All they have to do is complete the orders." Tyler agreed, but the two had sold a few appliances.

Recently, Jack had heard multiple complaints from customers that no one was in the Appliance department. It wasn't a leap to figure out that the two were hiding from customers.

It certainly wasn't the first time that new employees thought they could get out of work by hiding from customers. Jack remembered the retired cop they hired last year for the Tools department. He thought he could wander the store during his shift and regale other employees with tales of him being a supercop in rural Franklinville, NJ. After several warnings, Tyler fired him and brought Jack in as a witness. Jack recorded the ex-cop on his phone, threatening both of them by predicting that the current Chief Of Police in the township would be citing them for the most minor of violations because he was being fired.

The retired cop was banned from the store. The Chief Of Police was contacted, and he didn't take kindly to his name being used to threaten a local business.

"So, the customer was a jerk," Jack began, trying to control his anger. "There are plenty of jerks in this world- customers and employees. You deal with them, not hide like little kids."

Justin rolled his eyes. "Chill out, man. This is just some crappy part-time job."

Jack stepped closer to Justin and lowered his voice.

"I'm guessing that your mommies breastfed you and Tristan until you were in middle school."

"It's Trevor," Trevor tried to interject.

"No one cares," Jack said without looking at him and staying locked on Justin.

"Now, I realize that you two had brand new BMWs when you got your driver's licenses, both went to expensive colleges on your parent's dime, where you fucked around for four years, and now, you're back at home, collecting an allowance and working here just to get mom and dad off your backs."

"Actually, I only have a Lexus ES," Justin said.

"I don't give a shit," Jack returned fire.

Jack pointed to the different departments in the store.

"We need these jobs," Jack said. "You see Luther over there?"

Jack pointed to a sixty-ish Black man who walked with a limp and stood near the Flooring department.

Justin and Trevor nodded.

"Luther was the senior chemist at the Sunoco Refinery in Philly for years until he had a stroke on the job and couldn't work there anymore. He's been here since the store opened 24 years ago. Luther over there has worked in every department and knows more about the store than the fuckheads in the Corporate Office. "

Jack paused to take a breath and tried to control himself.

"Luther does not come to work thinking this is an unimportant job. He knows that there are no unimportant jobs. He's also seen hundreds of assholes come and go who think they're too good for the job they have."

"We're sorry," Trevor said.

Justin didn't speak. Jack noticed that Trevor met his eyes, but Justin looked around.

"You're not the manager. Tyler is," Justin said, defiance seeping out of his tone.

Jack had been down this road before.

"You're right, Justin," Jack said. "But any employee can report another for smoking pot on the premises. Say, in the back near the dumpster."

"Jack, please. I'll work hard," Trevor implored.

"Won't we, Justin?" Trevor asked as his larger, more imposing frame suddenly loomed over his friend.

Justin smiled and said, "Jack, we're 22 years old, and this is our first job. We're still learning, and we could use more training."

Jack returned his smile, slapped Justin on the back a little too hard, vise-gripped Trevor's hand, and said, "Boys, glad to help. We'll start with training this afternoon when it's slow in my department."

"Great," Justin and Trevor said simultaneously.

As they walked away, Jack felt a hand on his shoulder.

It was Luther.

"Jack, I saw you talking to those spoiled brat white boys. Please tell me you didn't use me again to motivate them."

Jack returned the smile and said, "Luther, I could tell you that."

As Jack walked toward the Plumbing aisles, he turned and said, "But I'd be lying if I did."

Chapter Three

"**At HomeMaxx, we pay above the competition for your position.**"

Lashay Jones smiled as she continued to reorganize the Garden department in HomeMaxx. From November to mid-March, Lashay worked in the Paint department with Lauren Garcia. She enjoyed working there, helping customers pick paint colors, mediating marital spats over paint color disagreements, and talking with customers about how to develop a paint strategy for their entire home.

Lashay started at HomeMaxx 14 years ago at the Mantua store. Two years ago, she transferred to the Franklinville store, and she told everyone it was because she had found a mobile home to rent in nearby Newfield. After years of living with horrible roommates, Lashay was excited to get her own place.

Lashay enjoyed working at this store. The employees were friendly but not busybodies. She didn't want anyone digging into her past.

The customers were from nearby rural or blue-collar areas, so they could empathize with people like her who worked for a living.

The manager here, Tyler, tried to care about his employees despite pressure from the Private Equity bosses who wanted to squeeze every penny out of the place. The Mantua store manager used to leer at her and get inside her personal space when he talked to her.

Lashay had bronze skin that was neither black nor white. She was tall, about five foot ten, with a lean frame that was only interrupted by a protective layer of fat, as she calls it, near her navel. Her hips were narrow, her butt unobtrusive, and her breasts nicely proportioned to her body. She had black, shoulder-length hair that was straight yet inclined to turn curly based on the vagaries of the weather. Her blue eyes stood out, people told her, sparkling like carefully cut gems. The creepy store manager from Mantua used to whisper to her that "he could get lost in your eyes."

Lashay was careful not to piss him off, but she always gave him that dead stare to send the message, "Keep the hell away from me."

Throughout her life, she's had to deal with racists who comment, "You must be part white because of your blue eyes." As a teen and young adult, she would respond with anger and vitriol.

Her mother had met her father at a car show where her mother worked as a model. One mistake drowned in vodka and poor choices left her mother pregnant, and her father disappeared into the graveyard of one-night stands. To this day, Lashay doesn't know who her father is or what he is. Black? White? Criminal? Millionaire?

As a 48-year-old woman, she used those blue eyes to stare at any verbal assailant and insult them silently with her pupils. After nearly fifteen years at HomeMaxx with mostly male customers, Lashay had gotten accustomed to the questions about her eyes, her mixed race, her height, her marital status, any moral weak spots, and her thoughts on open relationships.

While she loved the Paint department, Lashay had a thing for the Garden department. She liked to be busy, and this department was hopping from April until Labor Day. She liked being outdoors and enjoyed flowers, plants, and gardening. Even though she rented her mobile home, she had planted bushes, perennials, annuals, and herbs around all four sides of the trailer.

Today, she organized everything along the back fence that overlooked the driveway, which, in turn, overlooked the farm field. She had humped all the old stone bags, from pea gravel to river rock, to the correct pallets, and swept all the rock from the broken bags. Usually, Lashay would find a lot of mouse pellets around the bags and near the plastic wheelbarrows. This year, however, there were no signs of mice.

Strange, she thought. *It's almost like there's a feral cat around.*

As she rearranged the wooden fence posts, she spotted movement near one of the boxes of plastic garden edging.

She squatted still and watched, trying to hold her breath.

Out popped a cat from a hole in the side of the box. It was small, maybe a year old. The cat had spotting of black, orange, and cream over its body, with a black streak between the eyes and a white section under its neck and chest.

Lashay thought the cat was a Calico, which isn't a breed so much as any cat with a combination of black, orange, white, and sometimes cream. As a child, Lashay wasn't allowed to have a dog or cat because her single mother didn't have the money. When Lashay was married, she and her husband had a blue Persian cat. When she finally found a place without roommates at the mobile home a few years ago, the landlord didn't allow pets unless you paid an extra $1000 security deposit and an extra $150 a month.

Lashay scraped by with her HomeMaxx pay, so a cat or dog was out of the question. She still fondly recalled how her Persian would sit in her lap and purr. Even when her problems started, Simone was always there by her side, on her lap, or sleeping in bed with her.

This cat chirped at her. It wasn't a meow but more like a deeper bird chirp. Lashay thought it was an "I'm hungry" call. She bent down and moved slowly toward the cat. As she approached, the cat didn't move but chirped a few times.

Carefully, Lashay used her right hand and gently rubbed under the cat's neck on her white tuft of hair. The cat responded by purring and then wrapping herself around Lashay's leg.

Lashay picked up her HomeMaxx phone from her belt clip and dialed.

"This is Jack in Plumbing."

"Jack, it's Lashay," She said softly, not wanting to spook the cat.

"Lashay, why are you whispering?" Jack asked. "Home Depot hasn't kidnapped you, have you?"

"Hahaha," Lashay whined. "You need to find new jokes, Jack."

Then louder, Lashay said, "I found a cat in the back by the fence in the Garden department. I need help."

"I'll be right there," Jack said.

While she waited, Lashay picked up the cat and cradled it. The cat sunk into her arms and hugged her forearms.

It seemed like it took a long time, but Jack came trotting through the self-opening doors and spotted her with the cat near the back fence.

"I brought some supplies," he said as he put down what he brought.

"Oh, the cat is cute," Jack said.

Without hesitation, he reached and stroked the cat along its right flank, and the cat's purring got louder and deeper.

"Jack Marsalis, cat whisperer," Lashay teased.

Jack bent down to show her the items he brought with him.

"I found a shallow plastic storage container about the size of a cat box," Jack said.

"Too bad HomeMaxx doesn't sell cat litter," Lashay said.

"Got that figured," Jack answered.

He went over to the bags of play sand stacked on two pallets by the fence. He picked up one, pulled a utility knife from his back pocket, slid open the top, and poured the sand into the box. He then smoothed it out and made a hand gesture that went along with "Ta-da."

"Impressive, Dr. Pol," Lashay teased. "What else do you have?"

"Used a flat paint container and filled it with water," Jack said as he lifted up the upside box where the cat had found a home. He placed the water on the concrete, took a lawn chair pillow he had also brought, and put it down on the concrete.

"His new bed," Jack said, proud of himself.

"Jack, you're like a survival expert," Lashay said.

"Were you ever on that TV show Naked And Afraid," Lashay teased.

"That's the wrong show," Jack mocked. "I was on the show Afraid of Being Naked."

They laughed in unison like they did a lot these days.

"How do we know if it's a boy or girl cat?" Lashay asked.

"I think one of the few things you told me about your past is that you had a cat," Jack said.

"Sue me, Marsalis," Lashay mocked. "I've forgotten."

Jack smirked and lifted the cat's tail, causing her to chirp and squirm in

Lashay's arms.

After looking under the tail, Jack said, "It's a girl. You see, girl cats have something that looks like an upside-down exclamation point, while male cats have something that looks like a colon."

Lashay chuckled and said, "Jack Marsalis, you know your –"

"Don't say it," Jack admonished her.

"Cats. I was going to say," Lashay returned verbal fire. "Get your mind out of the gutter."

"What are you going to do with the cat?" Jack asked.

"I want to keep it here at the store."

Jack placed his right hand on the side of his face.

"Whew, that's a tall order."

Lashay's features turned resolute.

"We can bring it to the Clayton animal shelter," Jack said. "It's close, and I heard they take good care of the animals and find them homes."

Jack stared at Lashay holding the cat and melted. Lashay had been at this store for two years, but she worked the evening and weekend shifts for the first year, so she hardly ever saw Jack.

In the last year, after she was assigned to the day shift, Jack and she became close platonic friends.

Lashay had hoped that Jack would ask her on a date, but then she thought about her past. What would he think of her?

Maybe they should just keep it in the friend zone. Safer that way.

Lashay knew Jack also had a dark past. Rumors flew that Jack had been in prison and had been fired from an important job.

Would they have the same relationship if Jack found out about her past?

Lashay doubted it.

Lashay had periods when she allowed herself to get close to Jack, and then she became very cool toward him for a week or two before gradually warming up again.

What would he think of me if he knew?

She repeated that question in her head multiple times a day. Sometimes, she'd lie in bed and picture her and Jack together. Then, as she'd bask in the glow of that imagery, she'd see Jack discovering her past and walking out on her.

She had suffered that imaginary pain for months.

There was silence until Jack said, "Okay, Lashay, I'm in. Operation hide-a-cat in a home improvement store is on."

"Let's meet for lunch at the food truck at one," Lashay said.

"It's Wednesday," Jack said as a smile broke out his entire face. "Hump day. Carlos is serving camel today."

"Anybody ever tell you that your jokes suck," Lashay asked.

"What did the fish say when he swam into a wall?" Jack asked.

Lashay rolled her eyes.

"What did the fish say when he swam into a wall," Lashay answered.

"Dam," Jack said as he walked away and laughed out loud.

"Jack, even the cat doesn't think that's funny."

Chapter Four

"**A**t HomeMaxx, we invest heavily in training our employees.**"**

"Jack Marsalis, please report to the manager's office," Darla announced over the store intercom system.

Jack had just finished with a customer who needed a new set for his toilet tank. After 15 years, Jack had gotten to know many of the people who came into the store. He worked hard to remember their names and personal details. Jack had used a memory palace to do that, linking names and personal details to items in the store.

For example, Paul Celano co-owned Cecil Marine, a boat sales and service business in Williamstown. HomeMaxx sold topside boat paint, so Jack remembered the PA in paint and linked it to Paul.

Paul, a friendly and engaging man, always encouraged Jack to try boating, even though, on Jack's salary, he couldn't even afford the mandatory life vests.

"Paul, how about a boat with a no-payment and no-interest clause that lasts for 30 years?" Jack would always tease.

Paul would always reply, "Jack, how about I get a deal where I can buy anything I want from HomeMaxx and then pay it back in 30 years?"

"I don't think HomeMaxx would go for that," Jack would always respond. "Let's call it even."

They'd laugh then shake hands, and Paul would return every few weeks for everything from bungee cords to weed killer.

After hearing his name, Jack cut down the aisle between Flooring and Window Treatments. He pushed open the door to the hall where the restrooms, employee lockers, and employee breakroom were located. Once through the door, you had to make a sharp right to get to the restrooms, employee locker room, and breakroom. To the left was a solid wood door with no sign on it.

Jack opened that door and walked into a small office with three women seated at desks against three of the four walls. They glanced at Jack and then went back to the computer monitors.

"Hi, Jack. Hi, Jack. Hi, Jack," they welcomed him.

"He's got a new hire in there," Ellen Cleary, the finance administrative assistant, told him. It was an early warning system, so Jack didn't walk in on Tyler and make a joke.

Jack and Tyler Rodgers, the store manager, had come to the store 15 years ago. Jack was new to HomeMaxx, and Tyler was new to this store, having managed a store in Vineland for five years.

The store never did the business that stores in Washington Township or Deptford did, but they were located in more affluent and densely populated areas. Richer people in those South Jersey towns had more money to burn. In Franklinville, nearby Clayton and Newfield, blue-collar workers lived more modest lifestyles with paltry bank accounts and sizable credit card payments. Jack grew up here in South Jersey, the poorest and least populated section of the state. Not that South Jersey didn't have its affluent towns such as Haddonfield, Moorestown, Washington Township, and exclusive communities along the Jersey shore such as Avalon, Strathmere, and Stone Harbor.

HomeMaxx was founded by Gary Beaufait, a general contractor, in Western Pennsylvania in 1974. The Beaufait family gradually expanded the business; by 2014, it had 800 stores in the U.S. That number was dwarfed by Lowe's, which had 1,700 stores in the U.S., and The Home Depot, which had more than 2,000 stores nationwide.

HomeMaxx concentrated its stores in suburban and rural areas, focusing its product mix and services on the middle-class consumer. As a family-run business, HomeMaxx didn't have the financial pressure that oppressed Lowe's and The Home Depot with its stock analysts, quarterly earnings calls, and greedy shareholders.

HomeMaxx paid no more than its two larger competitors, but it instilled a family atmosphere in the company and its stores. Employees tended to stay longer at HomeMaxx. It seemed like the relief from reporting profit and loss figures to shareholders made working at HomeMaxx a more congenial experience.

Every year, some members of the Beaufait family—brother Biff, brother-in-law Bruce, cousin Rusty, Aunt Bonnie, and even Grandma Becky—visited stores so that each store received a visit from a family member.

Jack's favorite was Phyllis, Gary's wife. She was business savvy, remembered every employee's name after being introduced, and asked smart, probing questions. Jack recalled how Phyllis visited their store in 2017 and 2019. At the second 2019 visit, she approached Jack, "Hi Jack, Phyllis Beaufait. Remember that conversation we had two years ago about selling auto products? How's that going?"

In 2017, Phyllis listened intently as Jack lobbied to sell auto cleaning supplies in the stores. A year later, HomeMaxx began selling them, and they sold well.

After two years, she remembered Jack's name and wanted to know what he thought about the new product line.

Sadly, Phyllis passed away from breast cancer in 2020, and Jack thought that signaled the downfall of the company. After COVID, business at HomeMaxx never picked up to pre-pandemic levels, and staff shortages increased because almost all businesses desperately needed employees. Then, in 2021, HomeMaxx was sold to a private equity fund, Black Cobalt.

Jack thought Gary Beaufait and the rest of the family would never have sold if Phyllis was still alive.

Once Black Cobalt took the reins of the company, everything changed.

For the worse.

Since the sale, Jack and all the other HomeMaxx employees had witnessed a single-minded goal of more profit. The road to greater profitability seemed to be lower costs, fewer employees, and decreased service levels. Employees who left were not replaced, and the store had the lowest number of employees since 2015.

Of course, prices on most products had increased even if the suppliers had not raised their costs.

Jack knew Tyler wasn't to blame. He was only the store manager. Like Jack and all the other HomeMaxx employees, he did as he was told - or he was gone. Jack knew that. He had been a manager once.

Jack immediately hit it off with Tyler, and they maintained a solid relationship over the last 15 years. They still disagreed and argued. Jack usually got upset over the lack of enough staffing to help customers or hiring people who knew nothing about the department where they were assigned or did not want to learn about the product sold in that department.

Once the winter gave way to more temperate weather, Jack had promised Tyler he'd help him put down pavers to enlarge the backyard patio area at his house. Tyler planned to add an outside pizza oven, a 65-inch OLED TV, and enough backyard furniture to accommodate a small wedding.

They had started the project a few weeks ago and were still preparing the area for pavers by raking, tamping, leveling, and then more tamping.

Jack thought Tyler was about 50 years old, which is that dangerous time frame in a career when people are perceived as either too old or overpaid to hire. Tyler owned a beautiful colonial home in nearby Williamstown in the affluent Hunter Woods development community. Tyler's wife, Pam, was a short blonde with an alluring smile that even curmudgeons who watch the news 24/7 couldn't resist. Tyler and Pam had two daughters, Morgan, who attended Cornell University, and Taylor, who went to Carnegie-Mellon University.

Tyler confided to Jack that he and Pam were stretched paper thin financially because they were trying to pay for two college tuitions to avoid oppressive college loan payments for their daughters.

One afternoon on an unusually warm March day, when they had pulled the sod and leveled the area for the pavers in the backyard, Tyler confessed, "Jack, this Black Cobalt is destroying HomeMaxx. They sold the land that all stores sit on and own and pocketed billions of dollars. Now, each store has to pay rent and still make a profit. Our store was barely profitable before that. Now, we're losing money. I think they're going to close stores later this year."

Jack had stopped raking and tamping when he heard that. The idea that he'd be out of a job again jolted him.

"Don't say a word to anyone, even Lashay," Tyler emphasized.

"Why would you mention Lashay?" Jack answered defensively.

Tyler stopped raking and said, "Jack, come on. You like Lashay. She likes you. It's obvious to me and everyone who works at the store. Darla asks me once a week if you guys have boned yet."

Jack had laughed and shook his head in disbelief.

"If Lashay knew my past," Jack had begun to say but faded off.

"Jack, Lashay has a past, too. We all do to some extent. You don't let the past dictate the future. You, you know, start from now."

"That doesn't make any sense," Jack had responded.

Some employees didn't care for Jack's close relationship with the store manager. It didn't bother Jack that some employees bitched about it because Jack felt he separated work and home relationships. In fact, Jack and Tyler went toe to toe when Tyler hired the two entitled college morons to work in the Appliance department.

Privately, Tyler confessed to Jack that working as a store manager for this private equity fund, Black Cobalt, felt like walking on hot coals.

"Jack, it's the same mantra," Tyler had told Jack. "Cut costs. Maximize profit. These people are crazy."

The door to Tyler's office opened, and Tyler stepped out.

"Jack, great timing," Tyler said, holding a frozen awkward smile.

Jack spotted someone in Tyler's office in what Jack called the hot seat because prospective employees sat there for their job interviews. Jack could see the person over Tyler's left shoulder. He was young, probably about 19 or 20, with long, shoulder-length black hair. He stood up as Jack approached and revealed his deep brown eyes and lithe frame. Jack assessed the kid as being stronger than he looked and sneaky quick.

"Noah, this Jack Marsalis," Tyler said like he was introducing an act at the circus.

"Jack is most senior and one of our best employees," Tyler poured it on thick. Jack knew that Tyler wanted him to mentor the kid, not just give him a tour and drop him off at the department where he was assigned.

The boy shook his hand and met his eyes. *That's a good sign.*

"Hi, I'm Noah," the boy said. "Nice to meet you, sir, and happy to be here."

Jack noticed that the boy's voice was high-pitched. Unlike those two jerks in Appliances, this kid had excellent pronunciation.

Jack did his obligatory speech.

"Noah, welcome to HomeMaxx. We're like a family here. We take pride in what we do and focus on our customers."

Jack had repeated the same first line to hundreds of new employees over 15 years. Sometimes, Jack could tell if employees would make it here. People came to HomeMaxx for different reasons.

Some did so because they needed a job, some because they needed money, others because they believed they could do as little as possible and still get an adequate paycheck, and still others because no one would hire them.

Jack assessed Noah with a keen eye sharpened by years as a manager working with people. He was almost always right about people- except when he wasn't, which had destroyed his life.

The boy's brown eyes were alert like a falcon, scanning, assessing, and sensing threats. Jack noticed that the palms of his hands were calloused with dirt in the palm ridges. The boy was accustomed to physical work.

Most important was the boy's posture, which resembled that of a competitive sprinter – forward-leaning, on the balls of his feet, and ready for action.

This was someone who could work hard, had worked hard, and would work hard.

Tyler interrupted Jack's assessment.

"Noah is being assigned to Lumber. We need someone good there."

As Tyler's words flowed out, Jack noticed that his intonation and body language screamed, "Don't say anything about Gus."

Jack understood. The reason the store had been understaffed in Lumber was that long-time employee Gus Burdette was a dick to most new employees. Actually, Gus was a dick to the long-time employees.

Gus Burdette was about six foot four with a crewcut and a large bald spot on the back of his head. His features were as prominent as his size. He had large ears, a beak nose, thick eyebrows with a mind of their own, and a forehead that appeared more square than rounded.

Gus had one of those resting faces that says, "I could break your neck like snapping a twig."

Before coming to HomeMaxx 12 years ago, Gus worked for a concrete driveway company for 25 years, smashing concrete with a sledgehammer or a jackhammer. He was let go 13 years ago when his wife was first diagnosed with ovarian cancer, and he began missing work to care for her. He was hired by HomeMaxx 12 years ago in the Lumber department and has been there ever since.

Gus was always irascible and a stickler for detail. The Lumber department had a high turnover, but Gus did the work of three people. Since his wife Betty died 11 years ago, he'd only gotten worse.

Jack returned Tyler's words with narrowed eyes that said, "What the fuck are you doing?"

To Jack, placing this young kid with Gus in Lumber was crazy. The kid would probably quit in days, even though Jack sensed that the kid had something special about him.

"Okay, Noah, ready to head to Lumber?" Jack said, straining to smile.

He felt he was leading early Christians to the lions to be torn apart.

"Yes, I'm anxious to start work," Noah said.

Jack noticed the boy said "yes" instead of "yeah." He thought it was a clue that Noah was from a close-knit, conservative family. As Jack led him past Window Treatments and Wallpaper and made a left into the main aisle toward Lumber and Building Materials, he recognized that Noah kept pace with him. Jack had done that to many new employees, speed walking to see if they would stay on pace with him.

Noah did that without effort.

As they approached Lumber, Jack got a vibe that Noah might be gay. He didn't know exactly why. He wished that Lashay was here. He never understood how, but the woman had gaydar that was 100 percent accurate. He didn't know how she did it, and Lashay wasn't giving up her secrets.

If Noah Fernandez was gay, then his stint in Lumber at HomeMaxx might be minutes long instead of hours or days. Gus Burdette's son, Michael, was gay. Gus was the master of life contradictions. The first person to stand up against people bullied or oppressed, Gus was also a raging homophobe.

When Gus's son, Michael, graduated college, he announced to his parents that he was gay. Gus immediately kicked him out of the house over his wife's protestations. Then Betty got the cancer diagnosis, and their lives were tossed into chaos, turmoil, and pain.

Jack visited his home several times after his wife, Betty, had passed away because Gus uncharacteristically began missing days at work with no call. Jack found him in his house, which looked like a bomb had exploded inside. Jack and a few of his co-workers, including Tyler, helped Gus clean up his house, teach him how to handle his budget now that Betty was gone, and find some semblance of order in his life.

Gus had experienced run-ins with employees from other departments at the store who were openly gay. Gus had this habit of calling these employees a different fruit name every week to torture them.

Tyler had told Gus in no uncertain terms that if he used the words faggot or homo, he'd be fired on the spot. Jack knew this job was all Gus had left in his life.

His son Michael had returned for the funeral, and Jack had to break up a fight between Gus and Michael at the repast luncheon. Gus insisted on calling him Mike because he thought it sounded like a manly name. Michael flew home to Denver after the funeral and had never returned. Jack had given Michel his number to stay in touch, and every few months, Michael would text Jack and type, *"Is he still a SOB?"*

Jack would always text back, "I think he's mellowing. Why don't you contact him?" Then radio silence after that text.

As they approached the Lumber department, Jack spotted Gus lugging a pressboard plank that needed two people to carry. Gus placed it near the register, and when he turned, Jack was there.

"Jack, what do you want?" Gus demanded.

Jack tried to maintain a smile.

"Gus Burdette, this is Noah Fernandez. This is his first day at HomeMaxx."

Jack added as a veiled threat, "Tyler, the store manager, wants you to train him and make him successful."

Jack's eyes burrowed deep into Gus's scowl.

"Hi, I'm Noah," Noah said, extending his hand.

Jack watched as Gus evaluated the outstretched hand, ignored it, and said, "Noah is a fairy name. You're not a fairy, are you?"

"Gus," Jack warned him.

Gus's body language relaxed, and he said, "All right, Noah. Let's see if you make it until lunch."

Jack was going to warn him again, but Noah cut in, "Look, I get it. You already don't like me for some reason. But I need this job badly. And I'm going to stick it out. So show me what to do and how to do it, and I'll be fine."

Gus looked at Noah and then at Jack.

"The kid has balls," Gus said to Jack.

"So, take care of him," Jack challenged. "There's not a lot of people dying to work here."

"Let's go, Noah," Gus said as he turned toward the cutting saw in the back corner.

As Gus walked away with Noah trailing him, Jack heard Gus say, "I think you're one of them. So, this week, if you make it a week, I'll call you mango. Get it, mango. Because you're a fruit."

Jack walked away, shaking his hand, thinking how people could fuck up their lives with all their own bullshit.

People's lives suck because of what they did to themselves, not what other people, life, or the world did to them.

Chapter Five

"**A**t HomeMaxx, we hire regardless of race, color, national origin, sex, and religion.**"

It took until almost one in the afternoon before Lashay and Jack could arrange to have lunch at the same time. Lashay looked forward to their lunches together. She assumed Jack did, too.

He never said no when I asked, and he's also invited me to lunch plenty of times.

The food truck was parked in front of HomeMaxx on Wednesdays and Fridays near the grills on sale. Carlos, the Guatemalan man who owned and ran the truck, apparently parked at a Home Depot and Lowe's the other five days. Lashay liked Carlos. The man worked seven days a week, was always smiling and helpful, and had prices that Lashay thought were too low.

The food truck had a large sign along the driver's side that read, "Carlos's Authentic Mexican Food." Lashay asked him about this.

"Carlos, you're Guatemalan," Lashay began. "Why the authentic Mexican food sign?"

Carlos offered her his biggest smile and, in accented English, said, "No offense, Miss Lashay, but Americans think all people south of their border are Mexican or close enough that they don't need to worry about it."

When Jack came out of the store, Lashay sat at the only picnic bench out front. This one was only a year old. Last summer, Jack and Gus built a new one from the kit on the shelves, and they threw away the old one, which was afflicted with splinters and so much instability that no amount of shimming would even it out.

"Carlos, how are you?" Jack said as he nodded at Lashay.

"Mr. Jack, Miss Lashay, you are my favorite customers," Carlos shouted.

"Sure, Carlos," Jack rolled his eyes in fake disbelief. "We heard you say that to all the Home Depot and Lowe's employees, too."

Without missing a beat, Carlos countered with, "That's true, but with you two, I mean it."

Jack glanced at Lashay and said, "Have to admit. He's smooth."

Lashay laughed and asked, "What are you having?"

Jack didn't even look at the menu board posted to the side of the window.

"Carlos, my good sir, I will have the Chiles rellenos," Jack ordered.

"He's the only non-Guatemalan customer who orders this dish," Carlos told Lashay.

"Did you ever think his Spanish is so bad that he thinks he's ordering a Big Mac in your language?" Lashay asked.

Jack and Carlos laughed, and then Jack said, "Carlos, my good sir, a gran mac, please."

"Wow, that really impressed me with the Spanish language knowledge," Lashay chided.

After ordering and receiving their food, Jack and Lashay sat across from one another at the picnic table. The table could seat six, so they spread out, leaving no room for prospective diners or HomeMaxx workers.

Lashay liked it when they were alone.

Even though there was a flurry of activity surrounding them, Lashay felt like it was just her and Jack.

They had gotten close over the last year. Very close. Everyone in the store assumed they were dating or at least screwing. They did neither. Something was holding both of them back. Lashay knew the source of her reticence. If Jack ever found out about her past, she wasn't sure what he would do. A strong inside voice said, "Jack is the kind of guy who wouldn't care."

Lashay had also heard rumors about Jack's past. Nothing concrete.

"Don't mess with Jack. He spent time in prison."

"Jack was a big boss in a company near Trenton until he got caught with his hand in the cookie jar."

By now, Lashay figured that every employee at HomeMaxx – new and old – had heard about Jack with customer service /returns clerk Darla Campanna's ex-husband.

Several years ago, Darla was being beaten up by her husband, Clyde, a general contractor, regularly. When Jack saw her bruises one morning, he walked into the lot at the end of their shift when Darla was picked up by her husband.

The story goes that when Jack approached Clyde's car, the general contractor jumped out of the car before Jack could say a word and took a home run swing with his right fist.

Unfortunately for Clyde, Jack moved left, and the punch missed. Jack hit Clyde with a right cross and then a left uppercut.

While on the ground and bleeding, Clyde swore that Jack would be fired until Jack reminded him that the HomeMaxx parking lot cameras had recorded it.

"You're going to jail," Jack had whispered into Clyde's right ear as he had reached down to grab him by the shirt while Clyde was still on the pavement.

Clyde drove off without Darla, and Jack then drove her to her daughter's house. Darla's daughter then convinced her to get a restraining order on Clyde, and eventually, she divorced him.

This happened before Lashay transferred from the Mantua store, but employees still talked about it. Like urban legends, every time this story was re-told to a new HomeMaxx employee, it grew in stature and violent details. Almost every week, Jack had to explain to a new employee that he had not stabbed Darla's husband or beat up an entire motorcycle gang to protect her.

The story did have a happy ending. About six years ago, Darla met a dump truck driver named Edgar, who doted on her with gifts for no occasion.

"Just because I love you," Edgar would say to Darla, who would recount that story to Lashay and others.

Every few months, Clyde would drive into the parking lot when Darla was leaving work to harass and threaten her. Then Jack would leave at the same time, see Clyde and run after his car, threatening to beat the shit out of him.

Clyde would speed out of the lot as fast as his 2004 Chevy Cruise would take him.

"Lashay, what should we do about the cat?" Jack asked as she returned from her reverie.

"Sorry, Jack," Lashay said, "I spaced."

"I'd like to buy the cat some food, a litter box and litter, a water bowl, and toys," Lashay said, unsure if Jack was on board with the idea of her keeping a cat in the store.

"Okay," was all he said as he ate his Chiles rellenos.

"Jack, I want a cat, but the trailer park doesn't allow them," Lashay pleaded, even though Jack had assented with no pushback at all.

Jack smiled as he wiped his face and then locked eyes on her.

"Lashay, I did say okay. I get it. You want a companion."

Lashay reached out her right hand, greasy from the food, and caressed his hand.

It was a subtle move, and neither spoke.

Just as Lashay had gotten the courage to tell Jack how she felt, a male voice interrupted them.

"Jack, Jack, 49 today so far," the voice belonged to a man at the end of his teenage years. The man/boy was about five feet nine inches tall and had long, wavy black hair that fell over his face like a window with the curtains drawn.

He wore black skateboard sneakers, blue jeans, and an X-Men black t-shirt.

Robbie Nowicki was the store's cart person, even though no other Home-Maxx had such a person. Usually, the store manager assigned employees from different departments who had downtime to collect and organize the carts.

Lashay knew the story of Robbie's employment. Jack had shared it, and it bolstered Jack's view that Tyler Rodgers had many redeeming qualities despite the fact he was HomeMaxx management. Robbie was here because his mother, Eleanor, was in the same bible study as the mother of Tyler Rodgers. That's how Robbie got the job six months ago. Robbie's mother, Eleanor, was a single mom

When Lashay asked Jack what happened to Robbie's father, he sighed and said, "The husband, now ex-husband, left her for another woman in Eleanor's Bible Study."

"I guess they were Bible humpers instead of Bible thumpers," Jack had joked.

"Jack, you can go to hell for saying something like that," she had fired back.

Then Jack's smile faded. "Been there. Done that."

Lashay watched Jack talk with Robbie, listening to his day gathering carts.

Lashay knew that Jack talked to Robbie every day, checking on him. Robbie was autistic, and no one would hire him before HomeMaxx. Robbie did an over-the-top job of organizing the carts. Robbie began in late November, and on any winter day, you can spot Robbie chasing after carts, ensuring they were all lined up inside for customers to use.

When the wind whipped through the parking lot on a frigid early January day, Robbie was there chasing down errant carts captured by the tail of an angry wind, sending carts careening through the parking lot and targeting vehicles.

In mid-February, Robbie arrived at work amid a blizzard when the only vehicles in the lot were employees forced to come to work despite a lack of customers and numerous safety challenges on the roads.

Lashay remembered Jack coaxing Robbie inside since there were no customers until about two in the afternoon, and those who did arrive only wanted two items—shovels and ice melt—all of which HomeMaxx had sold out of days ago.

When the Garden department opened in March, Robbie lined up the different carts in rows for customers. That was a big help to Lashay. When it was busy during the annual mulch sale, Robbie pitched in, loading customers' vehicles with numerous bags of mulch.

Lashay had to mentor him in accepting a tip graciously and in saying thank you.

Robbie wasn't a savant and didn't have any unusual skills. Two weeks ago, Lashay caught Harry from Tools quizzing Robbie with questions like:

"If I drop a can of Pick-Up-Stix, can you count them exactly?

"Can you count cards in AC? Want to go to Caesars with me, and we'll play Blackjack?

Lashay had chased him away, "Harry, leave him alone. He's not a freak. Let him do his job."

"Jeez, what a grouch," Harry had grumbled. "Just seeing if the kid can help me score at the tables in AC."

Lashay knew there had been a few problems with Robbie and customers in the parking lot. Robbie was very finicky about how customers handled carts.

In one incident, a woman wanting to buy all new appliances complained to customer service that Robbie was scaring people in the parking lot. She wanted Robbie fired and was threatening to "call Corporate."

Darla handled it with the woman by promising to fire him.

"I'll need your name and address, please," Darla asked the female customer.

"Why, just fire him," the woman retorted, annoyed and peeved.

Darla took a deep breath and said, "When Eleanor, the boy's mother, finds out he's fired based on your demand, she will sue you and the store. Eleanor has done this twice before and always won in court since Robbie is disabled and protected by the ADA. We provide the boy's mother with your name, and HomeMaxx evades any legal liability because you are the primary reason for dismissal. This way, Eleanor sues you and you only. HomeMaxx is free and clear."

The woman's face contorted from anger to self-concern.

Darla continued: "So first and last name please."

The woman walked out of the store.

Jack complimented Robbie on his efficiency with the carts. When Robbie wasn't that busy, he walked the parking lot's perimeter and picked up trash.

"Nice job, Robbie," Jack said. "Just remember to be nice to the customers."

"I won't forget Jack," Robbie said.

Then Robbie added, "Tomorrow, I'm wearing my Jean Gray shirt. Mom lets me."

Robbie's other obsession besides carts was Marvel's X-Men superheroes.

As far as Lashay could tell, Robbie wore a different X-Men shirt daily. Lashay never realized how many X-Men there were. There was Beast, Storm, Gambit, Polaris, Banshee. The list seemed endless.

A male customer left a cart in the middle of a row in the parking lot, and Robbie sprinted toward the cart.

"How about you and I go to Walmart in Vineland tonight after work and pick up all those items?" Jack asked.

Even after all their closeness at the store over the last year or so, this would be the first time they had met outside the store.

Lashay was sure she was blushing but assumed her skin tone masked the manifestation of her anxiety.

She had wanted this for more than a year, and now…She was nervous. Frightened. Terrified.

Lashay scanned Jack's features for any outward signs of worry or anxiety.

Like always, Jack's features were like a black hole, sucking in all the light that tried to escape from the event horizon of his emotional core.

Typical man, she thought. All closed off. Emotionally constipated.

"Great," Lashay answered, trying to keep her voice from wavering. "Pick me up at my trailer. It's located in between HomeMaxx and the Walmart. I'll text you the address."

"It's a date," Jack said, then stopped and restated, "Well, not a date date, but a date for…"

"The hell with it. See you then," Jack said as he rose from the picnic table.

With lunch just about over, Lashay picked up her trash and got up just as Jack said, "Have you given the cat a name yet?"

"Allegra," Lashay answered immediately. She had thought about it all morning.

"Like the allergy medication," Jack said, a smile breaking out across his cheeks.

Lashay gave him a soft punch to his left bicep and replied, "No, after the illegitimate daughter Of Lord Byron and Mary Shelley's stepsister, Claire Clairmont."

Jack's smile turned bright, and he said, "Mary Shelley wrote Frankenstein.

Byron's only legitimate daughter, Ada Lovelace, was instrumental in the invention of the first computer, and Byron was the model for the first vampire novel written 80 years before Dracula."

Lashay feigned shock as they walked side by side back inside the store.

"Jack, you're smart," Lashay mocked. "When did that happen?"

As they were about to part—Lashay to the left to the Garden area and Jack to the right—Jack asked, "Lashay, if a person who knows three languages is trilingual and a person who knows two languages is called bilingual, what do you call a person who only knows one language?"

Lashay rolled her eyes and waved her hand dismissively.

"I have no idea, Jack."

"An American," Jack answered and began to laugh.

"Jack, I retract that comment I just made about you being smart," Lashay teased.

"See you tonight," Jack yelled as he walked away.

Chapter Six

"HomeMaxx supports the LGBTQ+ community."

Gus Burdette didn't want to admit it, but the new kid was sharp. He listened well, picked up things easily, and was very good with his hands. When Jack first brought him over, Gus thought the kid wouldn't make it till lunch. It was past 4 in the afternoon, and Gus was impressed with him.

Gus couldn't figure out how a sharp kid like Noah could be a fruit. Then, Gus thought of his son, Mike, or Michael, as he insisted Gus call him. He was extremely talented at computer stuff. Gus thought it had something to do with design, but whatever it was, Michael always had a side business running, with him working on computer things for friends, friends of friends, or parents of friends.

Gus missed him. Michael was last home when Betty died and hadn't been back since they had a huge blow-up after the repast luncheon. After the funeral, Gus hadn't tried to reach out, and there was radio silence from Michael.

Truth be told, Gus wouldn't know what to say if he tried to mend fences with Michael.

"Michael, I think your lifestyle is warped and against nature, but let's make up."

Several times during the workday, Gus stared at his phone and Michel's contact info screen and wanted desperately to press the CALL button.

He would chicken out every time.

Gus felt the same way about this new kid. Noah was his name, but Gus called him Mango. He had already decided that if the kid returned tomorrow, he'd call him Dingleberry.

That should send him packing.

As Gus watched near the saw, the kid ran around helping several customers with a big, gay smile. Gus noticed that customers responded to him.

Once Jack dropped him off in Lumber, Gus trained him, and the kid caught on quickly.

The kid could even work the saw on the first day and do custom cuts for customers. The last kid they hired almost cut off his thumb on day one. Unlike the other losers that Rodgers, the manager, sent over here, the kid wasn't afraid to ask if he didn't know something.

"Excuse me, Gus," the kid had asked after break. "How do you make a miter cut?"

"Geez, mango," Gus had complained. "Do I have to show you everything?"

Gus noticed the kid had calloused hands with grease embedded in his fingernails like he was a car mechanic.

Then, around 3, the kid was helping a customer pick out shoe molding, and the customer, a 40-ish man in a business suit, was on the phone with his wife.

"Honey, I don't know why it doesn't start after you just filled up," the customer said loudly to his wife.

Gus watched as the kid said, "Excuse me, sir."

"Yes, what is it?"

"Pardon me for eavesdropping, but I think I may know the problem," the kid told the customer.

"Honey, hold on," the man said. "Somebody here says he can help."

"So..." the customer had said.

The kid began, "The most common culprit is the EVAP purge control valve, which is stuck open. A stuck-open valve can cause excessive fuel vapors to enter the engine, resulting in a flooded condition that prevents proper combustion."

The man said, "So what does she do about that?"

"If there's a mechanic on duty, tell him, and he will check it for you on the scanner." The kid said.

Gus watched all this, and then 20 minutes later, that same customer returned to Lumber and said to the kid, "Hey, you were right."

"Glad I could help," the kid answered.

"Here's 20 bucks," the man said, holding a $20 bill.

"I don't know if I can take that, but I appreciate it."

"What's your name?" the man asked, still offering the twenty dollars.

"Noah."

"Well, Noah, you must be a hell of a mechanic, and I will complain to the manager if you don't accept this gift from me."

Gus watched as the kids reluctantly took the money and said thank you as the man walked away.

At 4:30, the kid's shift ended, and Noah approached him rather than punch out at the time clock in the employee breakroom.

"Should I punch out, or do you still need me?" Noah asked.

"Mango, I'm not the boss, but yeah, you're done for the day," Gus answered.

Although he wanted to, Gus couldn't bring himself to tell the kid that he had an excellent first day.

Instead, Gus said, "It's okay if you want to quit."

The kid faced him, pursed his lips, and squared his shoulders. Gus noticed the kid had one of those small nose piercings on the left side.

Figures, he thought.

"Why would I quit?" Noah challenged. "Because you're calling me names because I'm gay. Like I've never had that happen before. You're just like my father. Always judging. Never seeing what is really going on."

The kid's response took Gus aback, but he quickly recovered.

"Seems to me that your father is just looking out for you and doesn't want you to ruin your life."

"Yeah, sure," the kid grumbled. "That's why he threw me out of the house."

"Sorry to ruin your day, but I will be here tomorrow," the kid said loudly as he walked away.

Gus also had to punch out soon since his shift was over, but most days, he punched out, returned to Lumber, and worked for a while anyway.

For Gus, there was nothing for him at home but a takeout or frozen dinner, watching game shows on TV, and falling asleep in his 25-year-old threadbare lounger.

About five minutes after the kid left, Gus spotted him in the parking lot. He got into an old, white Honda Civic that looked packed with stuff. Gus made a mental note of it, and when he left work in his Ford F-250 black pickup, he turned left onto Delsea Drive toward Newfield and Vineland and drove slower than the speed limit, angering the Tesla behind him.

Something about that kid didn't seem right. Why work here? HomeMaxx doesn't attract many young adults, except for those two spoiled college slackers in Appliance. Plus, the kids worked hard, almost too hard, as if he was desperate.

Why have all your stuff in your car?

As Gus drove, he realized the kid had been kicked out of his house because he was a fruit.

Just like he did with his son Mike.

Gus drove past Fries Mill Road on his right, where the new Manor Life Nursing Home had recently opened. Gus thought he'd rather be put down than end up there.

As he drove by, he spotted the kid's car at the far end of the parking lot.

"Was the kid homeless and sleeping in his car?"

Gus drove down Delsea Drive until he hit the WaWa convenience store. He pulled in, went inside, and ordered a pizza.

"I'm treating myself. It's been a tough day." He told the counter woman, who shrugged.

While he waited, Gus opened the Contacts app on his phone and stared at Mike's number. So many times, his index finger was close to pushing the call button. It hovered over the button, and then something deep inside and black stopped him, and he closed his phone.

"Number 52, pizza," the young woman with the tats and blue hair called out.

"Yeah, that's me."

Noah had formed a plan about where he would park after his first day at HomeMaxx. He knew he couldn't park at HomeMaxx overnight because the employees would see his car and possibly investigate. There was an elementary school down the street named Caroline Reutter School, but he figured the cops or school security checks the lot for cars at least once a night. Noah had gone to school there when his family arrived from Puerto Rico. Back then, Noah spoke very little English. He was teased in school incessantly, even years later, when his English was better than many regular Americans.

His father, Jose, a diesel truck mechanic, could read English better than speak it, even today. His mother, Antonella, came from a wealthy family who sent her to an academy where she learned five languages – English, French, German, Spanish, and Swedish. Noah's mother insisted he learn English as soon as they moved and worked with him daily.

Noah remembered how patient she was when he was six years old.

"Mejo, you can do that," she'd urge him.

His mother had called him several times today, but Noah didn't want to be caught on the phone by Gus, who he knew was dying to get rid of him.

Noah thought it was his misfortune that he went from a father who hated gay people to a boss who hated gay people.

"At least I know what to expect," Noah told himself as a way of coping.

Noah had slept on friends' couches the last few weeks after his father kicked him out of the house. He knew that wouldn't last more than a few days.

He couldn't get hired anywhere as a mechanic because he had no real auto mechanic experience besides working on cars for cash in his friend Ramon's garage.

Auto mechanics is the one area where he and his father bonded. He had watched his father from when he was a young boy till now, working on cars, trucks, motorcycles, and RVs. If it had wheels, his father could fix it.

His father was so proud of Noah when he decided to attend Gloucester County Institute of Technology (GCIT) in Deptford instead of college prep high school. When Noah graduated, his father was over the moon. Because it was a trade school, graduation came at different times of the year, and Noah graduated in December.

Then, the night of his graduation, Noah went to a graduation party off Grant Avenue and got hammered. He drove home about midnight with his Honda's lights off, thinking the police wouldn't spot him. He barely made it home, tried to sneak into the house, and fell on the kitchen floor as soon as he unlocked the back door.

His father and mother waited up for him, and when they ran into the kitchen and saw him spread eagle on the floor, obviously drunk, they had radically different reactions.

His mother bent down., asked him if he was all right, and then said, "I will make you my special drink to combat a hangover."

She went to the sink and opened the spice drawer, which revealed all her secret ingredients for ailments ranging from the sniffles to cancer.

His father just started to yell at him. Noah only caught bits of his angry reprimand.

"How irresponsible and thoughtless...."

"Do this to your mother..."

"Only thinking of yourself..."

"You could've had a drink here..."

"We have no secrets in this house..."

That's when Noah blurted it out.

As he regained his balance, Noah pushed back his hair off his face. Maybe Noah yelled back at his father for the first time, "Really, Papa?"

"Did you know that I'm gay?"

It was all a blur after that. His mother and father screaming at each other. His father screamed at him. His older sister came downstairs and yelled about waking her baby.

That happened months ago. His mother called him every day, brought him food, and promised to change his father's mind.

Noah wasn't going to hold his breath for that miracle.

Noah's family were conservative Catholics who believed in traditions.

They had already been shocked to their core when Noah's sister, Carmen, came home in her early senior year at Delsea Regional High School and announced she was pregnant.

Carmen was threatened with eviction, but somehow his mother was the victor, and Carmen stayed. His father remained content to glare at her, limit his interaction with her, and voice his disappointment with her moral failures.

For the nine months of the pregnancy, their house was as tense as relations between Israel and the Palestinians.

Then the baby was born.

Noah admitted that the kid was a looker. His sister named him Alejandro after their father's father. Alejandro Rivera Fernandez was his name.

Soon, "Alex" became the center of his father's attention.

Carmen's disgrace was no longer mentioned. Noah wondered if that could happen to him.

Then Noah remembered the new nursing home built next to Fries Mill Road, near Delsea Regional High School. The nursing home had shifts 24 hours a day, so cars were always in the lot. So, no one would notice Noah's Honda. When he pulled out of the HomeMaxx parking lot, he turned left on Delsea Drive and took a quick right about a thousand feet into the nursing home's parking lot.

Noah parked his Honda at the far end of the nursing home parking lot, where he figured no one would give it a second glance. Noah parked and then walked along the road to Carolla's Italian restaurant and pizzeria for food. It wasn't far, about a 10-minute walk.

Noah had hidden the cash he had saved from working on cars from other students, friends of friends, and parents of friends. He had hidden it in a metal box the size of a matchbox attached by screws to the firewall in his engine compartment.

Noah figured he had enough cash for about a month of food and gas expenses. This job at HomeMaxx would enable him to make money to subsist, but not enough to afford a place to live.

Noah ordered a pizza with extra cheese and ate the entire thing. He was so tired that he struggled to return to his car. He set back the driver's seat, plugged his phone into his portable battery charger, set the alarm for six in the morning, and then everything went dark.

Chapter Seven

"At HomeMaxx, employees are our greatest asset."

Jack rushed home after his shift to clean up before meeting Lashay. He had thought about this day for over a year.

No, not thought. Dreamed.

Jack knew it wasn't a date, but it was a date. It could be a date if they wanted it to be, and Jack wanted it to be a date. The question was: Did Lashay want it to be a date?

Jack lived in nearby Clayton, only seven minutes from HomeMaxx. Jack hadn't planned it that way. He had rented this place for more than 15 years. His small apartment was in the basement of a single-family home on Morton Street near Rite Aid. The house was an elevated ranch with blue vinyl siding and a decorative bay window on the left, looking from the street.

Behind the home was a detached two-car garage that faced the side street since the house was on a corner. Jack's entrance to his open-air basement apartment was between the house and garage. His place was small, with a tiny kitchen that contained a two-burner stovetop, a 60s-style refrigerator that made gurgling noises, and a kitchen cabinet built apparently for Hobbits. The living room re-defined small spaces with only enough room for a small sofa, coffee table, and a 32-inch TV sitting on plastic crates that Jack had fished out of the dumpster at HomeMaxx years ago. The bathroom had those old pink and black tiles from the 50s and a claw-foot tub that groaned when Jack stepped into it. The bedroom only fit a full-size bed with a dresser and a closet, which was a claustrophobic nightmare.

Jack kept it neat and clean and fixed anything that went wrong. Jack had rented it 15 years ago when he had just started at HomeMaxx. Back then, HomeMaxx's starting rate was pitiful, but Jack was fortunate that he had saved a lot due to frugality and his last job.

For several years, Jack managed a self-storage facility on the Black Horse Pike in Williamstown near Randy's Pizza. Jack made good money there and scored plenty of overtime.

In August 2008, Jack noticed a plain white cargo truck pulling in every Tuesday and Thursday, dropping off valuable items such as TVs, computers, video game consoles, and appliances. The owner of the self-storage facility, a fiftyish Italian man with a pencil mustache and a temper quicker than Usain Bolt, had cameras installed all over the place.

On Wednesdays and Fridays, Jack noticed that a young guy who loved flannel shirts with rolled-up sleeves would arrive with one or two people in the back seat of his King Cab Silverado.

They'd go to that same unit, the flannel man would open the overhead door, the people would look over the merchandise, and cash would exchange hands. The Flannel Man and his guest would load the merchandise in his truck bed, and off they'd go.

After a few weeks of this, Jack told the owner, Antonio, who responded angrily with, "As long as they pay on time, I don't give a shit what they're doing."

Two weeks later, two FBI agents with dark blue suits and matching sunglasses showed up and questioned him.

"Have you noticed a white cargo truck pull in here recently?" the taller one with the aviator sunglasses asked.

Jack told them everything that was going on.

"Can you take us to the unit where all this happens," the shorter agent with the Ray Bans asked.

"Yes, but I think you'd have to speak to the owner first?" Jack said.

Jack knew he'd get pushback from the agents, and he wanted to help them. However, he needed this job and liked it. It was easy, low-stress, and as manager, he made pretty good money.

Jack then heard a car's tires squeal as a black Cadillac Escalade screamed in the parking lot. It stopped only a few feet from the office door, and the owner, Antonio, jumped out.

"Get out of my place," he yelled at the FBI agents. "I know you don't have a warrant."

The two agents didn't match Antonio's high level of anxiety, remaining almost emotionless.

"We're going," the Ray Bans agent said. "Your manager refused to open the unit for us without a warrant, anyway."

Jack appreciated that last statement from the FBI agent. He was trying to save his ass from the owner, who yelled at the agents until they got into their Black Lincoln Navigator and drove away.

"What did you tell them?" Antonio yelled, now getting close, too close, to Jack's personal space.

"Hey, back off," Jack felt anger starting to build. "I didn't let them in and told them nothing."

The owner began a quick cool down and said as he left, "If they come here again, you call right away. Got it."

"Understood," Jack said abruptly.

Two weeks later, the FBI arrived with a warrant on Jack's off day, Saturday. Apparently, the FBI had arrested the owner's son, Ricardo, for theft of interstate commerce and had impounded everything in the unit.

Jack was grateful that he wasn't working that day, so Antonio couldn't blame it on him. When Jack showed up for work on Sunday morning, Antonio's Lincoln Navigator was already parked in the lot.

Jack knew this was a bad sign. The owner hardly showed up, no less on a Sunday morning.

When he pushed open the front glass door, Antonio was there with his hands folded.

"You're fired," Antonio yelled. "And if I find out you squealed on my son, I'll..."

Jack already had him by the neck and pushed him against the high desk that separated employees from customers.

"First, I didn't squeal on your dirtbag son," Jack gritted his teeth. "Do you want me to choke the life out of you now?

Antonio shook his head no as Jack tightened his grip.

"You owe me for last week's work and four PTO days I have coming to me. If I do not get a check for everything I'm owed by this Friday, I will find you, beat the living shit out of you, tape up your mouth shut, bind your hands and feet, and stick you in one of the units I know is hardly visited. You'll die in one of your own units."

That Friday, a check for everything he was owed showed up in Jack's mail, and he deposited it right away at his TD Bank branch in Glassboro on Delsea Drive near the Shop Rite supermarket.

Jack's landlords were this married couple – The Szczesnys, Wally, and Jackie. The couple owned a small breakfast/lunch place called Jackie's Place on Delsea Drive in Clayton. Since the couple was so busy running the restaurant and Wally didn't know the difference between a flathead and Phillips's head screwdriver, Jack happily did all the repairs on the house. The couple bought the materials and Jack supplied the free labor. Over the years, Jack had replaced the hot water heater, air conditioning compressor, dishwasher, rear windows, and attic insulation, and even picked up the living room carpet and installed hardwood flooring.

As the couple became Medicare-eligible, Jack began cutting their lawn and taking care of their landscaping.

As payback, Jack paid the same amount in rent as he did 15 years ago. It was a mutually beneficial living situation for both of them.

Jack quick-stepped it to his 2014 Nissan Altima, drove down Delsea Drive, and was about three minutes from Lashay's unit. He felt his phone vibrate in his pocket.

It was Lashay.

"Jack," she said, her voice low and sullen.

Jack knew right away something was wrong.

"Jack, I'm so sorry, but I got home and started feeling crampy and light-headed. I don't think I can make it."

Jack paused for a few seconds before responding. They had been this close before in the last year. Yet, every time, one of them sabotaged their growing intimacy. Jack knew his own demons but couldn't imagine what secrets Lashay kept hidden.

"Lashay, it's all right," Jack began, trying to disguise his disappointment with a tonal concern.

"Jack, I'll go tomorrow and pick up the cat supplies for Allegra," Lashay said. Jack realized this was her way of assuaging his dismay.

"Lashay, appreciate that," Jack answered. "But I was already driving your way. I'm near the McDonald's and CVS in Newfield now, and I'm not that far from Walmart in Vineland."

The silence lasted a few seconds just as Jack drove by Lake Road on the Newfield / Vineland border where Lashay lived in the Lake Acres Trailer Park.

As Jack passed the Telemundo building on his left, Lashay broke the silence.

"Sorry," she uttered in a low, remorseful tone.

Jack didn't answer right away.

This is never going to happen. Give it up, Jack.

"See you tomorrow," Jack said and hung up.

Once at Walmart, Jack was fortunate enough to meet Debbie, a 20-ish Walmart employee hovering by the pet section who was much too enthusiastic about her pets.

"I have a cat, a cocker spaniel, a rabbit, a ferret, a parakeet, a hamster, and four goldfish," she volunteered after Jack asked about the location of cat supplies.

Despite Debbie's never-ending tales of her pets' cuteness and Jack's continued insistence to skip her pet videos, Debbie showed him too many videos of her pets while she helped him pick out the proper cat supplies.

Jack wondered if he looked that poor because Debbie found the best deals and least expensive supplies.

"This cat litter is half the price of the brand name stuff," Debbie lectured. "But it clumps better and controls odors."

After promising to return to the store for any future cat supplies and to, in Debbie's words, "watch Sprinkles, my ferret, do somersaults," Jack drove back to HomeMaxx.

It was mid-April. Sunset held off until about 7:45, so Jack enjoyed a nice ride through Vineland, Newfield, and then Franklinville, where HomeMaxx was located. Traffic was light, and Jack drove with his front windows down to create a vortex effect of cool, spring air.

Jack had grown up in nearby Washington Township, which today was much more populated with home developments, stores, and traffic than Franklinville. HomeMaxx was located in Franklin Township, but since there was another town with the same name in Central Jersey, most people in the area called the whole town Franklinville, even though Franklinville was a small area of the township located on Delsea Drive near the skating rink, library, new WaWa convenience store, Nativity Catholic Church, and a clock shop that was only used sparingly by the owners.

The township still had truck farms that grew a variety of crops, including heirloom tomatoes, grape, cherry, and specialty tomatoes, cucumbers, corn, onions, squash, kale, lettuce, eggplants, peppers, broccoli, and herbs.

Surrounding the farms and homes were rows of pine trees that survived human development.

As Jack approached the HomeMaxx store, he surveyed the pitch pines on both sides and a cornfield nearby. To this community of farmers, small businesses, and working-class people, HomeMaxx was their place for everything from riding mowers to backyard pavers and supplies for their septic systems.

Jack stopped by the Garden department entrance, grabbed a wagon, and loaded the supplies. Jack wheeled the cat supplies past Doreen, who took over for Lashay at 5 PM till closing.

It didn't take much for Doreen to get flustered. If more than two customers were on her line, Doreen would panic. With three customers, all with plants and bushes on carts in line, Doreen was too preoccupied to notice Jack.

He wheeled the stuff to the back fence and found Allegra lounging on a seat cushion he had taken from the inside Garden department.

Jack had to admit that Allegra was a beautiful cat. Her pure white fur ran from the left of her nose down her neck and onto her lower body. A black strip ran from her nose over her head and neck. Her ears were sandy in color, and her opal, almost copper eyes seemed to judge Jack.

Her back, legs, and tail had black, white, and tan streaks.

Allegra just watched Jack set up her litter box and fill it behind the stockade fence sections. Jack then set up the cat's water bowl and dry food bowl near the supine sections of the plastic white picket fence.

Lashay had left a plastic storage container there so they could store cat supplies without Allegra or another animal getting at them.

Jack opened it and arranged the litter scooper, the wet food box, and a bag of dry food that Jack closed with a metal clip. He then put it on the top, locked the side clips so they wouldn't open, and positioned it near the chain-link fence.

Allegra sat comfortably and watched Jack complete his tasks. Jack knelt on his right knee and carefully scratched under her neck. Allegra tilted her neck back and began to purr.

"Allegra, you look like a cat I can talk to," Jack said as he sat on the storage container, bouncing a bit to ensure it held his weight.

Allegra jumped onto his lap, lay between his closed knees, and purred as he stroked her fur under her neck and along her left flank.

"Allegra, I don't know what your life has been so far, but mine has been a mess," Jack confessed.

"I lost a great job 20 years ago, lost a wife I should never have trusted, and lost my dignity by being in jail."

Jack felt stupid talking aloud to a cat. It was getting near closing, and Jack knew Doreen was overwhelmed with anything and everything, so she'd never come back here and check the area before she left.

Allegra nuzzled his right hand as he scratched softly under her neck.

"I've been starting over for 15 years, and it's been a struggle. And now, I've fallen for this woman I work with..."

Allegra jumped off his lap and then wrapped herself around his right leg. Jack took that as his signal to leave.

Jack nodded as Allegra jumped on a lidded, shiny aluminum garbage can for sale and stared at him with those copper-assessing eyes.

"You're right. I get what you're telling me. Keep working on it, Jack. It's not too late."

Jack took a few steps, turned, and saw Allegra was still fixed on him.

"I get it, Allegra. I'm down but not out."

Jack walked through the outside garden area and passed Doreen, who was too busy looking at her phone to notice him.

Chapter Eight

"**At Black Cobalt, we maximize profit through business efficiency.**"

As usual, Jack stopped at the Dunkin Donuts in Clayton on Delsea Drive at exactly 7:15. He never used the drive-thru, mostly because the line of cars stretched out to Delsea Drive.

Jack always ordered medium hot coffee, light and sweet, and a blueberry muffin. Today, he ordered a second muffin. This one was for Lashay.

Once at work, Jack sat in his car for five minutes, eating his muffin and mentally preparing himself for work. Even though his shift didn't start until 8, Jack liked to walk around the store and engage with as many people as possible.

Jack thought this behavior was a relic from his previous job as an operations manager for a massive warehouse in Trenton. He wasn't a boss anymore, but he cared about the store and the people.

Jack walked through the door and said, "Good morning, Darla. Your hair looks like a baseball helmet."

Darla smiled, all cheeks and white teeth, and responded, "Screw you, Jack."

"Thank you, Darla."

Jack punched in at the time clock in the hallway leading to the office, bathrooms, employee breakroom, and a small locker room. As Jack turned to walk back into the store proper, the new kid, Noah, came out of the locker room. The sign on the wooden door may have said LOCKER ROOM, but it was an aspirational term. The room was the size of a laundry room with only ten lockers for over 100 employees. Jack had been there 15 years and still didn't have a locker. It was like a rent-controlled apartment in New York City or Eagles season tickets. You waited for someone to die, then pounced.

Jack noticed right away that Noah had showered in the locker room. He couldn't remember the last time any employee had done that simply because the shower hadn't been cleaned in years and was filthy.

"Noah, how was your first day?" Jack asked.

Noah's hair was still wet, and he dripped on the floor.

"It was like Mr. Rodgers said it would be," Noah began. "It was hard work but rewarding."

"I like it," Noah added as an afterthought.

"If Gus's ragging gets too harsh, just let me know," Jack said sternly.

Noah's head emphatically nodded no, splashing water on the floor and Jack's shirt.

"Oh, I'm sorry," Noah said.

"No problem, Noah," Jack answered. As Noah walked past him, Jack said, "Let me know if you have any issues."

Noah gave him a thumbs up as he walked through the swing doors that separated the store from this area.

As Jack headed to the Lawn Chemicals and Equipment area, where Lashay began her day until she opened the outside garden area at 10, he wondered about Noah.

Is that kid sleeping in his car?

Jack made a mental note to talk with Gus about the kid as he turned right toward the Lawn Chemicals and Equipment area. Jack saw Lashay at the desk behind all the lawnmowers.

"Morning," Jack said as he approached, placing the other blueberry muffin on the desk in front of her.

"Morning, Jack," Lashay said, grinning as the muffin came into her view.

"What did I do to deserve a blueberry muffin from Dunkin' Donuts?" Lashay asked.

Before Jack could answer, Lashay said, "I should be buying you a muffin after bailing on your last evening."

"Lashay, no pressure," Jack said softly. "When, and if, you're ready."

Lashay responded by scanning the entire area. No one was in the area or the department behind, which was Electrical, Lighting & Ceiling Fans. For the moment, they were alone. As her right hand reached for the muffin, she leaned into Jack's left and kissed his cheek softly, her mouth lingering close for a second.

Jack's emotional barrier seemed to falter, and Lashay spotted affection in his eyes. Then, as men will do, Jack seemed to recover, packed his emotions away, and said, "Geez, if this is what I get for a muffin, what if I bring in 25 munchkins."

"Hey, Marsalis, I'm not easy. You'd have to bring at least a sausage, egg, and cheese on an everything bagel to earn a peck on the lips."

They laughed in unison, and Lashay loved their easy banter and strong connection.

Just then, Harry from Tools approached them as if he had a secret that could bring down the government. Harry had been there since the store opened. He worked in tools and hardware that entire time. Lashay and anyone who had worked there for more than a year knew that Harry knew more about tools than Tim Allen from that TV show *Home Improvement*. A lot of workers and some customers called him "Tool Man."

Harry's other gift was gossip. Harry spent much of his workday collecting, disseminating, and sometimes even making up gossip. Harry was your first and only destination if you wanted to know what was going on around the store. Lashay and Jack had spoken to him at different times and with wildly different strategies about his gossiping about their relationship.

Jack told Lashay that he explained to Harry how wrong and hurtful it was to spread misinformation about a romantic tryst that hadn't happened. He extracted a promise from Harry that he would cease and desist on all Jack / Lashay hookup gossip.

Lashay told Jack that she approached Harry one morning in Tools and told him in no uncertain terms that if he didn't stop spreading rumors about them, she would jam the largest and thickest drill bit up his ass.

Lashay thought her direct strategy worked, while Jack insisted upon his method. Either way, Harry had stopped all Lashay / Jack rumor-mongering. Lately, Harry began whispering that Lauren Garcia from Paint and Kathy Marino from Window Treatments were doing the nasty, as Harry termed it.

As usual, Harry got his facts wrong or partially wrong. Lashay knew Lauren and Kathy were intimate, but it was a throuple, not a couple. Apparently, Kathy's husband, Ron, was part of the action.

"Hey guys," Harry approached them, slightly out of breath as if he had just witnessed a fatal auto accident.

"Harry, this better be about tools and not some wild rumor," Jack growled.

"Harry, what happened?" Lashay teased. "Did you find out that someone was using one-ply toilet paper?"

Jack jumped in. "That's me. How did you know?"

"Funny, Jack," Lashay said.

"No, listen," Harry insisted. "There's a cat in Kitchen & Bath,"

Lashay looked at Jack with alarm, and Jack returned her look with 911 eyes.

"Harry, we will take care of it," Lashay said.

Lashay then went nose to nose with Harry and gritted her teeth.

"Do not say anything to Tyler," Lashay demanded.

"Harry, can we count on you?" Jack added.

Harry's hands shook when he had gossip to share. He was a short man, about 50, who looked 60. Harry had short legs and a substantial belly, making it seem that all his weight was concentrated there. Harry's black pants were always in danger of dropping since his belt was so low on his hips.

"What's wrong with you guys lately?" Harry complained.

His hands fluttered as he whined, "You're always telling me to keep my mouth shut."

Lashay was about to threaten him when Jack interrupted.

"Harry, listen to me. Keep this quiet, and I'll show you a photo of Lauren, Kathy, and Ron together this afternoon."

"Is it juicy?" Harry asked.

Jack put his hands to his face and said, "Harry, so juicy. You won't believe it."

"Don't mess with me, Jack," Harry demanded.

Jack raised his hand like he was being sworn in at court.

"Harry, I swear. I have a juicy photo of Lauren, Kathy, and her husband Ron."

"Okay, I'll keep quiet," Harry agreed. "But after lunch, I want to see it."

"Thanks, Harry," Jack said, slapping him on the shoulder.

Then to Lashay, Jack said, "Let's get over there."

As they walked quickly to Kitchen & Bath, Lashay asked Jack, "Do you really have a juicy photo of Lauren, Kathy, and her husband, Ron?"

Lashay was very skeptical, and if Jack had such a photo, perhaps she had misjudged Jack.

"Don't look at me like that," Jack chided her.

He stopped in the main aisle, grabbed his phone from his pants side pocket, swiped up, moved his thumbs a few times, and then turned the phone screen toward her.

"Look," Jack commanded.

Lashay saw a photo of Lauren, Kathy, and her husband Ron eating fruit from the charcuterie board from last year's Christmas party at Applebee's."

"It's Lauren, Kathy, and Ron," Jack insisted. "And it's juicy."

Lashay laughed so hard that two customers turned to look at her.

Jack reacted by looking like the cat that ate the bird.

"He's going to be so pissed," Lashay said.

Jack nodded with delight.

As they approached the Kitchen & Bath department, he said, "He'll be fine. Besides, I'll tell Harry about Roger from Flooring and Beth from Doors & Windows."

"What about them?"

"They're having sex behind the front doors in row 62,"

Lashay stopped walking.

"Jack, now you're as bad as Harry," she scolded him.

"Who told you that anyway?"

Jack smiled. "Roger from Flooring and Beth from Doors & Windows. Once last Monday and then again on Friday."

"They're supposed to be working hard," Lashay said.

"I'm sure they were," Jack chuckled.

As Lashay approached Flooring with Jack, they spotted Allegra rubbing against two female customers, who were delightfully cooing. The two women, who were middle-aged and bent down to caress the cat, laughed like teenagers.

"Allegra likes you," Lashay said as she approached the women.

The one in the nursing uniform replied, "I love the cat's coat. She's a Calico, right."

"You know your cats," Lashay answered. "You must have or had a cat."

"My whole life," she answered, "until last Christmas when Mr. Whiskers died at 18 years old."

Lashay instinctively frowned. "I'm so sorry. That must have been tough."

"I work across the street at the nursing home, so you think I'd be used to older humans or cats dying."

Lashay watched as Allegra jumped on the railing that held the hardwood floor samples and nuzzled her head against the woman.

"Can I pick her up?" the woman asked.

"Absolutely," Lashay asked as Jack looked on.

Lashay thought one of Jack's admirable qualities was his ability to know when to let someone else take charge of a situation. He was unlike most men who thought they knew better and were comfortable only when they were in charge.

Jack did mansplain at times. He couldn't help himself.

After all, he's part of a group that's been in charge for at least 10,000 years.

Lashay also knew that Jack had once been an operations manager, so he was competent enough and comfortable giving orders. Here, Jack smiled at the women, who didn't seem to mind looking at Jack.

As the woman in the nurse's uniform held Allegra, who purred even louder and deeper, she said, "You know, I wish we could bring cats into the nursing home. Those people would love them."

"That's a great idea," her companion chimed in.

After the woman put down Allegra, who took off immediately for appliances, Lashay leaned into Jack and said, "Tyler is going to find out. What are we going to do?"

"Are you saying the cat's out of the bag?" Jack chuckled.

"Jack, if you ever attempted stand-up comedy, the whole audience would definitely tell you to sit down," Lashay retorted.

Jack smirked and waved goodbye to the two women, who admitted they were browsing since neither had any money.

Lashay watched as Jack's smile disintegrated after the women left. His eyes looked left and right as if he were sorting out ideas in his head.

"I have a way that Allegra's presence in the store can help."

Lashay looked skeptically at the man she desired but was so frightened he would reject her when he found out.

"I can't wait to hear this," Lashay teased.

Gus watched as the kid worked hard through the morning break. As Noah helped a woman with some molding, loaded her cart, and guided it to her SUV, Gus couldn't help but wonder if the kid had slept in his car last night in the nursing home parking lot.

It wasn't that Gus cared. He didn't, he told himself.

The kid has a deviant lifestyle, just like Michael. Birds of a feather.

After the morning break, which the kid worked through, Gus went to use the forklift to load some plywood sheets for a customer. The customer had backed up his Ram pickup to the overheard door, and Gus turned the key on the forklift.

It cranked and cranked but wouldn't turn over. Gus sat on it for a few seconds, thinking of what to do. He tried again but with no success. It was still cranking but not starting.

We have the old manual jackstand. It's a pain in the ass but could get the job done.

"Mind if I take a look at it?" Noah was there and disrupted his thoughts.

"Avocado, this is a forklift, not a Ferrari," Gus said. "It's propane. You can't fix it."

"Can I at least try Mr. Burdette?" Noah asked.

Gus slipped out of the seat and made a hand gesture that said, "Have at it." He stood behind the forklift with his hands on his hips and scowled disapprovingly.

Noah went right to work.

He disconnected the hose to the LP tank, turned on his phone light, and looked inside the hose.

Noah said, "I'm checking the double O-ring in the hose connection that screws into the propane tank. There is a sealing O-ring that belongs in the tank fitting. Sometimes, the O-ring gets stuck in the forklift hose connection."

Gus looked on as Noah fished inside the hose, then reconnected it to the tank and said, "Try it now."

Gus sat down in the forklift seat, turned the key and it fired right up.

"Nice work avocado," Gus said, trying to contain his appreciation and surprise. "You people can do more than be florists and dress designers."

Gus noticed that Noah didn't react when he walked away.

Gus had two thoughts.

"This kid wouldn't break easily and quit, and this kid is damn good."

Tyler Rodgers hated these conference calls with Corporate even more since Black Cobalt bought the company. This store was the least profitable of the stores in the area. HomeMaxx had stores in nearby Deptford, Washington Township, and Berlin, and all those areas were more affluent than the Franklinville / Clayton / Newfield area where this store was located.

What the store had was consistency. Those other stores had very profitable months and then months of lagging sales. At his HomeMaxx, sales were consistent thanks to the farmers, small business people, and blue-collar residents who were loyal to the store.

What those assholes in Corporate didn't get was that the store's customers didn't buy at Amazon and Walmart even though it was a little cheaper – and at times, a lot cheaper – because they were loyal to the store. When it rained here two years ago in July, over 13 inches in two hours, Tyler had Jack and Lashay give Franklin Township cases of bottled water because power was out for days. He lent all ten of their portable generators to the town for emergency services.

And the people in the area recognized their commitment and repaid it.

But now Black Cobalt cared about nothing but what the numbers on an Excel spreadsheet told them. Every month, these conference calls went the same way. Black Cobalt execs would demand to know why the store wasn't profitable and what Tyler was doing to make it more profitable.

Black Cobalt had already raised prices on so many items that customers were now complaining and, for the first time, going to Walmart and ordering from Amazon. Tyler had been forced to cut staffing by ten percent in the last year, which hurt service, employee morale, and customer loyalty.

Every meeting went the same way, like a sitcom rerun. Some young blonde guy stood in front of a screen with an Excel spreadsheet displayed and then asked questions about the numbers.

"Why was foot traffic down 12 percent in February?"

Tyler wanted to scream, "Because it's February and cold out with several days of snow that month. You jackass."

But he didn't.

"In February 2022, your net profit was 11.8%. Now, your store shows an operating loss of 11.2%. Why?"

Tyler wanted to scream, "Because you assholes sold the land the store is on to one of your holding companies, and now we have to pay exorbitant monthly rent. Also, because you jerks take two percent from the store's top-line revenues for a 'consulting fee.'"

But he didn't.

The meeting lasted an hour and went exactly like every other monthly performance meeting in the last two years.

It was only at the end that something unexpected happened.

On the Microsoft Teams screen, an older man, about 60, appeared for the first time. He had black hair combed back, oily skin, deep-set eyes that had the blackness of shark eyes, and a pen he twirled in his right hand.

Everyone in that room at Black Cobalt was silent. Tyler, nervous and on edge, sat up stiff in his chair.

The camera panned in on that man.

"Tyler, My name is Bernard Snow. I live in Logan Township, about 45 minutes from your store."

Tyler knew this wasn't good.

While the man paused, Ellen Cleary peeked into his office and pointed at Harry Keller from Tools, who was standing behind her. Tyler knew that Harry had some gossip he couldn't wait to spill.

His hands were out of the frame, so Tyler used his right to signal NO to her, and she shut the door. Harry probably had more news on the throuple, and frankly, Tyler didn't care, as long as these three people did their job, which, so far, they had.

"Tyler, I am going to be blunt with you," Mr. Snow said as if he were doing Tyler a favor.

"It is mid-April now, and if your store does not return to profitability by June 1, Black Cobalt will close the store by October."

Tyler was stunned, not because what he said was unexpected but because his worst nightmare had become a reality. Tyler didn't want to think about all the employees who would lose their jobs: Jack, Lashay, Ellen, Gus, and even Robbie, the cart kid. Instead, he thought about the college tuition payments he owed to Cornell and Carnegie-Mellon by July 1 for the fall semester.

Would Morgan and Taylor have to take out student loans? Millions did. His daughters were fortunate, but he still wanted to give them the best chance possible for success.

What about the backyard renovation Jack was helping him with? They were only putting down pavers now, so the cost wasn't substantial, but when Tyler bought the outdoor grill, pizza oven, and top-shelf furniture, the cost would be about $20,000.

Tyler was jolted back to reality by Mr. Snow.

"Obviously, you must keep this a secret; otherwise, employees will be leaving as soon as the news gets out."

Tyler was still trying to form words.

"Do you understand?" Snow demanded a response.

Tyler put his hand down at his side below desk level and made fists.

"Yes, I understand," Tyler said, almost numb.

"You must understand, Tyler, that profitability and return on investment drive business decisions. We at Black Cobalt have a responsibility to our investors."

Mr. Snow folded his hands and leaned forward into the camera lens.

"Any questions," Snow asked.

Tyler squeezed his fists tighter. He wanted to tell the rich bastard to go fuck himself, but he thought about Pam, Morgan, and Taylor. And then Jack, Lashay, Harry, Darla, Lauren and all the others.

"If we do not make our profit goals and we have to close the store, will we offer severance to our employees? We have a loyal staff with some people working here more than –"

Snow cut him off. "Rodgers, we are not a charity. Employees will receive no severance, and you will not be able to tell them that the store is closing. They will come to work on October 1, and the place will then be padlocked with a "THIS STORE IS PERMANENTLY CLOSED" sign."

These people are monsters.

Snow must have seen the disappointment and disapproval on his face because his last words were a poor attempt at fake optimism.

"Tyler, that's not going to happen because you can turn the store around by June 1. I have complete confidence in you."

Then the screen went black. So did Tyler's soul.

Chapter Nine

"**B**lack Cobalt seeks to invest in companies that we believe will generate a lot of cash over a relatively short period of time."

Robbie Nowicki wasn't usually scheduled to collect and organize carts in the Franklinville HomeMaxx parking lot until mid-afternoon because that's when customer foot traffic grew. Jack found him near the Garden department, trying to organize various Garden carts. At the other end of the store, there were two types of carts—the regular shopping carts and the carts with two high bars for plywood, drywall, or custom wood cuts.

However, there were multiple carts in the Garden department, including one for flowers and another for bushes, trees, mulch, and stone.

Robbie was obsessed with keeping the carts organized by type. He would line them up outside the Garden department entrance, which was a chain link swinging gate, so customers could easily access them.

Jack checked on Robbie because he tended to harass customers who didn't return their carts to the cart return area. That always bothered Jack, too, but customers paid the bills and gave them jobs, so he just accepted their nonchalance about leaving carts all over the parking lot.

Robbie would confront customers, sometimes for good reason, but his approach was unnecessarily antagonistic.

"You have left a cart in the middle of the parking lot. Another vehicle could strike it, and a person could get injured." Robbie would say.

"All customers should return carts to the cart return area," Robbie would say.

"You are lazy by leaving the cart in a parking space," Robbie would say, although Jack had worked with him enough that he rarely said that anymore.

"Robbie, how are you doing today?" Jack asked him as he wrangled carts from the return area, which was a cage with two lanes.

"Jack, I have already organized 57 carts since I began at two PM," Robbie answered.

It was a bright, warmer-than-normal mid-April day with a cloudless sky. A slight breeze from the west blew through the parking lot.

"Nicely done, Robbie," Jack said. "Are you being nice to the customers?"

"Jack, you would be proud of me," Robbie began, a smile spreading over his face like a full solar eclipse.

"I helped Mister and Misses Cartwright load all 20 bags of mulch in their 2023 Hyundai Tucson because Mr. Cartwright did not want to get his new pants dirty."

"Robbie, that's excellent service," Jack reassured him.

That was the reverse end of Robbie's behavior. He would get tricked into helping customers load merchandise into their vehicles when it wasn't necessary. These repeat customers understood his limitations and took advantage of him. In February, a customer bought an A.O. Smith 40-gallon water heater. The customer got Robbie to help him load it into his pickup truck since these tanks weigh about 150 pounds before they are filled with water.

The customer somehow convinced Robbie that it was his job to come with him in his pickup truck and help him carry the water tank to the second-floor utility closet in his house in Vineland.

No one at the store noticed until Eleanor, Robbie's mother, arrived at 4 PM to pick him up. Frantic, after not locating him, she found Jack, and they searched the store with no results. Just as Jack was ready to call the Franklinville Police, Robbie walked in the store's front door.

"Robbie, we were so worried," Eleanor had said as she hugged him.

Jack, perplexed and concerned, asked Robbie, "Where were you? We looked all over the parking lot and store."

Blissfully unaware of the commotion he had caused, Robbie replied, "Oh, Mr. Nixon said I had to come with him and help him carry his hot water tank to the second floor of his house and help him install it."

"Robbie, please don't leave the store or the parking lot," Jack instructed, trying to conceal his genuine concern.

"If a customer asks or tells you to do that, you come to Mr. Rodgers, the store manager, me or Lashay." Jack had said, trying to remain calm while his mother kept saying how scared she was that something bad had happened.

Later, Jack looked up the purchase information on the computer and found the customer's name and phone number. Jack called him and tried to be diplomatic when explaining what a jerk he was, but Mr. Nixon replied nonchalantly, "Hey, I tried to give the kid $50 as a tip. He wouldn't take it. He said some guy named Jack told him that customer service was the most important thing in the job."

Robbie has been improving his understanding of customer interactions with the carts.

"How are you doing when customers don't put the carts in the return area?" Jack asked.

Robbie smiled at him. "I remembered what you told me, Jack."

"That's great, Robbie," Jack answered, then got worried and asked, "What did I say?"

"I tell them Jack says they should put the cart back in the return area, but it's alright if they don't because they are customers."

Jack patted him on the back.

"Getting better, Robbie," Jack said. "Let's work on that response just a bit, okay?"

"Whatever you say, Jack," Robbie said. "One day, I would like to be like you."

Jack smiled at that and thought about how Robbie could aim much higher.

"Thank you, Robbie. That means a lot to me."

Tyler Rodgers checked his vibrating cell phone and saw that his wife Pam was calling. She never called the office landline because she claimed that HomeMaxx was listening in. While Tyler always discounted her theory, some niggling doubt about HomeMaxx never left him, even after all these years at the company.

"Hi, hon," Tyler greeted her. "What's going on?"

"Tyler, I just talked to Katherine, who rents us the Seas Isle house every June," Pam said.

"Don't tell me she gave away our week in late June," Tyler said loudly and then realized that Ellen could hear him through the walls.

Tyler and Pam had been renting the same home in Sea Isle City at the Jersey Shore for the last ten years since the girls were still in elementary school. The house was right off the beach at 29th St. and Landis Avenue. It had five bedrooms and four baths, and the front deck had an ocean view.

Although the house wasn't new, and the appliances and furniture were dated, Katherine gave them a reasonable rate because they had been renters for so long and always left the house in pristine condition.

Tyler remembered how he and the girls would body surf together for hours.

For people in South Jersey, Philadelphia, and eastern Pennsylvania, the Jersey Shore had a wide selection of beach town vibes. There was gambling, nightlife, and bachelorette parties in Atlantic City. About 10 miles south, Ocean City offered a family-friendly town with legendary pizza, a quaint boardwalk, and eight miles of shoreline. Sea Isle City sandwiched between Ocean City and the mega-wealthy towns of Avalon and Stone Harbor, was meant for people who didn't have their own accountants, didn't also own a home in Florida, and was ideal for families who had scratched and saved their way to almost-upper-middle-class.

"No, we still have our week," Pam reassured him.

A knock on his office door deflected Tyler's attention, and he said, "Hon, hold on a minute, please."

"Yes, Ellen," Tyler said loud enough for her to hear.

The office, like the breakroom, locker room, and restroom, was haphazardly constructed with thin walls and interminable water leaks.

Over the years, he had developed a reliable routine with Ellen.

Nobody just walked into his office unless Ellen approved of it. Everyone knew that, and Ellen set them straight immediately for new employees, vendors, or others who did not.

Ellen opened the door just wide enough for her to poke her head in.

"Tyler, I'm sorry, but Harry insists on talking with you," Ellen said, rolling her eyes so only Tyler would see it.

Tyler was immediately angered, but he tried to control himself. That was the tough part of being a boss—or a good boss—you *could not let your emotions take control.*

"What does he want that is so critical that he has to interrupt an important call?" Tyler said.

Ellen then turned back toward Harry, who was in the outer office. He heard him say something about a cat.

"Harry says a cat is wandering through the store," Ellen began, "and Jack knows about it."

"Tell Harry I will check into it when I'm off this call," Tyler said as he gave Ellen the waving sign with his right hand, *which meant get rid of him.*

Ellen nodded and closed the door. Tyler heard Harry raise his voice, and then Ellen raised hers. A door opened and closed.

She had gotten rid of Harry and his silly office gossip. Tyler shook his head even though no one could see it. Harry had been here for so many years but made everyone else's business his business.

Sometimes Harry was valuable because he'd pass on gossip to Tyler about a disgruntled employee or some conspiracy theory about how HomeMaxx was going to screw the employees.

Tyler recalled that Harry's shining moment was when he finally found out that Lauren Garcia from Paint and Kathy Marino from Window Treatments were in a throuple with Kathy's husband, Ron.

Tyler, while shocked, thought it was their personal business, and he was convinced it would blow up in their faces. So, he used Harry to monitor the throuple in case their weird sex circle affected their job at HomeMaxx.

"Sorry, hon," Tyler said. "It was just Harry with some silly store gossip."

"We have a Harry at the realty office," Pam said. "Violet. The woman gossips about everybody."

"Harry's harmless and a good worker," Tyler replied. "So, about Katherine?"

"Katherine called me this morning and said she's getting too old to be a seasonal landlord and wants to sell the house. Tyler, she's offering us the first crack at it and at a reduced price."

Tyler could hear the genuine enthusiasm in her voice. Pam had been a realtor for 20 years and knew real estate. This Sea Isle house had been an integral part of their dream. Buy this house, renovate it, or tear it down, then rebuild it, and then move there when they retire. Morgan and Taylor could come and stay when they start their families.

Tyler should have been as excited, but Black Cobalt's ultimatum about store profitability had smothered his positive view of their future. Tyler had explained to Pam about Black Cobalt and how he thought the private equity firm was only interested in sucking as much profitability out of all the HomeMaxx stores and then closing the chain.

Tyler had explained to her weeks ago over a very nice glass of Merlot that the store would never achieve that level of profitability, especially with the monthly rent charges and the consulting fees paid to Black Cobalt.

Tyler and Pam had been sharp enough to pay off their mortgage and save and invest wisely. But they were paying the tuition of both daughters to top-level universities. Morgan needed a car because her 2012 VW Jetta was breaking down almost monthly, now with 250,000 miles on the vehicle. Taylor had a Honda that was close to vehicular hospice.

Tyler chose his words carefully now.

"That's wonderful. But I just had a meeting with the Black Cobalt people. Things are not looking up."

Pam was silent for several seconds. Tyler assumed that she was gauging the situation. Pam didn't panic, which was one of many things he loved about her.

"What are we going to do?" Pam asked.

Tyler could hear fluctuations in her voice in just those six words. She was scared but trying to remain in control.

"Pam, I know I've been tight-lipped about my HomeMaxx position. I didn't want to scare you or the girls. But here's what happened on the call."

Tyler detailed the call with the Black Cobalt people and their demands.

Pam listened without interruption. When Tyler finished, she asked, "Is there a chance the store could make its profit target?

Tyler paused, trying to assemble the chaos of his thoughts.

"Is there a chance? Yes, I've got good, no great people at the store. Jack, Lashay, Gus, Darla, Ellen, even Harry."

Tyler took a breath, swallowed the saliva that sloshed around in his mouth and said, "Pam, I don't think it matters. Black Cobalt thinks of HomeMaxx like a piggybank," Tyler began. "They empty coins from the piggybank every day, and when there are no more coins in the pig's belly, they're going to slaughter the store for bacon."

"I will tell Katherine that while we appreciate it, we just can't swing it financially," Pam said, disappointment flooding her voice.

Tyler had avoided this because once he said it, there was no going back. HomeMaxx had been his home for 25 years, but now, he needed a new home for his career.

"Pam, I've been talking to a guy named Sid Nelson from Excell Hardware. They're looking for a Northeast Region manager."

"You're just telling me this now," Pam objected.

"It was just talk," Tyler said. "I've had job offers before; you know that. We're not there yet. After this call, I will call Sid and go to the next level."

"If that's all right with you?" Tyler added.

"How did you get so smart?"

"By listening to my realtor wife," Tyler answered sweetly.

"Suck up," Pam said. "all compliments are accepted, even if they are designed to make up for your screw-up."

"Is this how you talk to your clients?"

"Psst," Pam said. "Rodgers, that's how I sell so many houses. I threaten them."

Tyler laughed as he leaned back in his office chair.

As his laugh subsided, Tyler said seriously, "Find out when Katherine is selling. If it's in the fall after the summer rental season is over, tell her to ask us before she puts the house up for sale. You're the realtor. She can save the realtor fee by selling to us."

"You're sure?" Pam asked.

"By then, the store will either be closed, or I'll find something else in management or – "

"Or what?" Pam interrupted.

"Or I'll be working in the Kitchen & Bath department at Home Depot in Turnersville."

"Tyler, you don't look good in orange."

Tyler chuckled, and as he said goodbye, Pam said, "What about Jack?"

"What about him?" Tyler asked.

"Are you going to tell him about the Black Cobalt ultimatum and the store possibly closing in October?"

"If you confide in him, he could tell others," Pam said, her voice encoded with a warning.

"Jack can be trusted, and if we are going to meet that profitability goal, then Jack Marsalis will be the man who can help us achieve it."

"Jack's a born leader," Pam admitted. "It's too bad what happened to him."

"Jack knows he fucked up. Twice. He's been clawing his way back ever since."

"It doesn't seem fair," Pam said. "Life should have a reset button."

"Mistakes are a fact of life," Tyler began. He paused, took a breath, and then said, "How we respond and react to our mistakes counts."

Gus Burdette didn't know if he should be mad or glad. The new kid, Noah, turned out to be a dynamo. He could fix anything and worked as hard as or even harder than Gus, and the customers loved him.

This is who Gus had pleaded for from Rodgers for years. Somebody in Lumber and Building Materials who could work as hard and as smart as him.

The problem was: his savior was – how was he supposed to say it these days? LGBTQ? Or was it LBGTQ? Oh, hell. The kid's a fruit.

Noah created echoes of his son Michael. He remembered when Michael was born, and he was so happy he had a son. Gus had such big plans for his son.

They'd throw a baseball in the front yard and maybe go to an Eagles game together. Gus would teach him about concrete—how to mix, pour, and cure it.

Gus didn't know Michael was different until he sprung it on him and Betty at his college graduation. It was like Michael had conned him. Gus thought gay men were supposed to like flowers, dresses, and cooking.

Michael loved to watch football with Gus; he played high school soccer and volleyball; he even enjoyed helping Gus with his concrete side jobs.

After his college graduation party was over, and they were cleaning up the backyard, Michael sat them down and said, "I have something to tell you because I think you deserve to know, and I love you too much to keep lying to you."

Gus still vividly recalled that moment. He and Betty sat next to each other on the folding chairs they had borrowed for the party. Gus squirmed with anticipation, but when he looked over at his wife, she remained still and calm.

"She already knows," Gus remembered telling himself at the time.

As Michael took a few gulps of air before speaking, Gus's mind raced through scenarios.

He got a girl pregnant. He's on drugs. He's not going to college.

"Mom, Dad," Michael had begun. "I'm gay."

While everything before Michael said those words was crystal clear, everything afterward was still a blur. There was yelling. Betty was crying. Then Michael was crying. Still, Gus was yelling. Threatening.

So many times, during a workday, Gus would stop, take out his phone, go to his Phone Contacts, pull up Michael's number, and say to himself: "After Betty's cancer diagnosis, that was the worst day of my life."

Then, when Betty died and Michael came back for the funeral, Gus had the opportunity to make amends or, at least, try to establish some relationship with his son.

Instead, Gus allowed his disappointment and disgust to take control of his emotions, mouth, and body language.

That's when he feared he had driven Michael away for life.

"Gus, Gus," he heard a voice and then someone snapping their fingers in his face.

When Gus focused, he saw it was Geoff, a carpenter with his own business who had been coming here for years. He and Gus shared scorn for weirdos – people with tattoos, piercings, and anyone who dressed flamboyantly. Included in that contempt circle were gay flamers, transgender pervs, and those non-binary nutballs who couldn't make up their mind who or what they were.

Gus fought the instinct to be irritated that Geoff had snapped his fingers in his face and said, "What's up, Geoff?"

Gus didn't have to be a mind reader to tell that Geoff was pissed off.

"Jeez, Gus," Geoff began his rant. Gus now noticed that Noah was loading two-by-fours into Geoff's F-250. He was about 20 feet away.

"You should know better than have some young fag loading my truck," the carpenter grumbled.

Gus didn't respond immediately. He watched as Noah loaded the carpenter's entire eight-foot truck bed with his wood. The kid surely heard what Geoff had said, but he didn't look up or didn't slow down.

Something in Gus stoked the embers of his anger.

"Geoff, you've been coming here a long time," Gus began, his voice rising in volume as his anger brewed.

"You're a loyal customer, and I always enjoy talking to you, but if you ever talk about the kid like that again, I'm going to stick one of those two-by-fours up your ass."

Before Geoff could protest, Gus interrupted, "He's loading your truck by himself, which he doesn't have to do. Now, do you have a complaint about the service he provided?"

The carpenter fumed and went nose-to-nose with Gus. The carpenter's eyes burned with rage, and Gus stiffened his body and clenched his fists in case he had to defend himself.

Geoff was taller than Gus, with a wiry frame and taut muscles that belied his age. Gus's scorched eyes announced to Geoff that he wasn't backing down.

Then Gus heard a voice.

"Mr. Stanger, everything is loaded, and I made sure that the wood is secure in the truck bed. Can I help you with anything else?" It was Noah. Gus noticed his voice was compliant and dutiful.

The carpenter relaxed his body and turned away from Gus and toward Noah, who averted his eyes as if the carpenter was worthy of that respect.

The carpenter stood between Noah and Gus, glanced at both, and said," No, thanks for loading by two-by-fours."

As he headed to his truck, the carpenter turned toward Gus and said, "Gus, see you next week when you're in a better mood."

He laughed as he grabbed the door handle, and Gus forced a smile.

"Hey, Geoff, what did the carpenter do after a one-night stand?" Gus asked.

The carpenter shook his head and said, "I give up, Gus. What did the carpenter do after a one-night stand?"

"Made a matching one for the other side of the bed," Gus said in a deadpan delivery.

"Gus, the only thing worse than your mood is your jokes," the carpenter said as he got into his truck and took off in a puff of diesel exhaust.

When he drove off, Noah said, "Thank you."

Gus had rekindled his anger.

"Hey, avocado. How did Geoff know you were a fruit?"

Noah stepped closer. He pulled up the sleeve of his grey long-sleeve shirt and revealed a small rainbow tattoo about the size of two quarters near his wrist.

Gus threw up his hands in disgust.

He stepped forward and said at a volume level much lower than his typical booming voice.

"Avocado, why do people like you always feel the need to advertise their lifestyle? Isn't that what you call it?"

Noah didn't respond to Gus's disgust or words but uttered, "Still, thank you, Mr. Burdette."

Gus took a breath as if Jack were trying to teach him to control himself with stupid customers. He took two and felt the pressure release.

"You're welcome," Gus said. Then, as he walked away, Gus added, "Noah."

Chapter Ten

B**lack Cobalt focuses on ROI, KPIs, EBITDA, and Cash Flow."**

Jack answered the phone in Plumbing with his standard, "Plumbing, this is Jack."

Jack was one of the few people who could work in almost every department except for Window Treatments and Paint, and that was because he had no eye for design or color.

"Jack, it's me," Lashay said. Her tone evinced concern and anxiety.

"Lashay, are you all right?" Jack responded.

"Can you get away for five or ten minutes?" Lashay asked. "I want to talk about Allegra."

Before Jack could answer, a tall, blonde woman in a blue business suit with high heels and brilliant white teeth said, "Sorry. Can you please help me?"

Jack smiled and nodded, then said to Lashay, "I'll be down in five minutes."

Jack hung up and said to the customer, "Yes, mam. How can I help?"

Her attractive features hid behind a mask of suppressed anger.

"My husband is a jerk," She said.

"At HomeMaxx, we can't fix jerk husbands," Jack said, "But can I interest you in a new vanity or toilet bowl?"

"Very funny," she answered, trying to contain a smile.

"So, tell me, what's happening in your bathroom?" Jack asked.

"That's a little personal," she chided him, now relaxing and allowing her soft features to appear.

"It's the toilet in the master bathroom. It keeps running. Sometimes, if I jiggle the handle, it stops. Other times, it still runs."

"Okay, let's try to zero in on the problem," Jack said. "Have you removed the tank top and looked at the guts of the toilet?"

The woman rolled her eyes. "Of course. I'm not useless like my husband."

"What did you see inside the tank?"

She thought for a few seconds as if she were recreating the image in her brain.

"It's like the chain gets trapped under that flapper thing-e," she explained.

Jack nodded. *This was good news for the woman.*

"Do I need an entire toilet tank set? And if I do, can I install it, or do I need a plumber?"

"I can't afford to take off from work," she pleaded. "It's close to our earnings call."

"Can you come over by this toilet here?" Jack asked.

Jack walked over to a row of toilets and went to the fifth one in the line. Last year, he had installed an entire toilet tank set inside the tank so that he could explain to customers how the system worked. It wasn't hard, but the visuals helped.

Jack took off the tank top and said, "Look in here. See the flapper attached to the chain connected to the flush handle?"

The woman peeked in carefully as if she was going to see something graphic.

"I think what's happening is simple to fix," Jack began. "I think your chain is too long and is getting caught under the flapper when it closes, causing the toilet to run."

"That's why jiggling the handle works only sometimes," Jack added. "Because sometimes that action dislodges the chain from beneath the flapper."

"That sounds much better than spending a lot of money," the woman said, her body relaxing and her eyes fixing on his.

"So, what do I do?" She asked Jack.

Jack pointed to the tank kit again.

"Remove the chain S hook from the handle arm and shorten the chain. Then flush with the tank top off and watch. You may have to adjust the chain, but you'll know when it's right."

Jack closed the toilet tank top to signal that they were done.

The woman flashed him her bright white teeth.

"Thank you so much. You saved me money and time. I'm sorry I didn't buy anything, though."

Jack waved her off as he prepared to head to the Garden department and Lashay.

"Have a good day, Mam," Jack said as he began to walk toward Lashay's department.

"I'm sure you wouldn't treat your wife like my husband treats me," she said.

"What's your name?" she called out as Jack walked down the back aisle.

Jack didn't answer as he turned the corner toward the Garden department, where the pesticides, lawnmowers, and outside furniture were displayed.

"Sorry," Jack said as he spotted Lashay. "Customer needed help with a toilet."

Lashay chuckled and said, "That sounds weird on several levels."

"Just one of the many benefits of working at HomeMaxx," Jack smirked.

Lashay stood behind a counter with lawnmowers surrounding her. Customers buzzed around but not near her or asking for assistance.

"I'm guessing you're worried about the cat roaming the store and Tyler finding out or a customer complaining."

"I am," Lashay confirmed. "What do you think we should do?"

"I don't want to lose her," Lashay added.

"Hey, where are your bird feeders?" a male customer yelled halfway down the barbecue grill and birdseed aisle.

"At the end of this aisle, make a left, and they're right there," Jack said. "There's a spring sale right now."

Jack turned back to Lashay. Her features revealed a strange brew of emotions from fear to anger.

Jack leaned in over the counter.

"Lashay, Allegra will be all right. She's not going anywhere," Jack reassured her.

"I've got a plan," Jack added, those four words bristling with determination.

Lashay's face relaxed, and a smile forced its way to her cheeks and mouth.

"Tomorrow, I'm working over at Tyler's house all day. We're laying the pavers and then adding the paver wall. I know Tyler getting pressure from those asshats at Black Cobalt to jack up the store's profitability."

Jack slid his left hand across the counter and touched the fingers on her right hand. They moved slowly, carefully, and with a tenderness that diluted her anxiety.

"We're going to get the media here to write a story about a cat in a home improvement store, and people are going to come to this HomeMaxx to see the cat."

"And buy stuff while they're here," Jack concluded.

Lashay's fingers found Jack's palm and caressed it.

It's a good plan if we can accomplish it," Lashay said.

"Jack to Plumbing," Kelly from the office announced to the entire store.

"Got to go," Jack said. "I'll talk to Tyler. See you Monday."

Their hands separated, and Jack thought he could still feel Lashay's long, sleek fingers touching his skin.

As he walked back to Plumbing, Jack spotted a young Black woman, about 25, leaning against a stainless-steel refrigerator and staring in Lashay's direction. As Jack passed her, the woman released her focus on Lashay and looked randomly around the store.

Jack checked on the two college goof-offs in the Appliance Department and was then stopped by a customer in the back aisle that ran the length of the store. He had that annoyed look that Jack had seen thousands of times before. He had walked around the store and couldn't find what he was looking for, and no one could help him.

"I've asked two people who gave me bad intel," the man, at least 65 with bedhead. "Where is the silicone concrete joint filler?"

"Walk to the last aisle and turn left. Immediately on your left will be the concrete joint filler," Jack pointed to the last row in the Building and Lumber.

"I recommend the Sika Pro," Jack said. It's a bit more expensive but worth it."

"Thanks so much," the male customer answered, suddenly perkier.

"Jack still knows more about this huge store than anyone else," a male voice said from behind him.

Jack turned to see a tall, thin man about 50 years old, with a perfectly coiffed full head of white hair and a neatly trimmed beard.

"Dave," Jack said, "Always good to see a worthy competitor."

Jack liked Dave Maloney, the owner of the Excell Hardware store in Washington Township on Greentree Road. Once a month, Dave visited HomeMaxx, Lowe's, and Home Depot to check out the competition. Dave was fit and trim; he was a scratch golfer, a 4.5 USTA tennis player, already one of the best pickleball players in the county after only six months of playing, a 220-average bowler in his Wednesday league, and a top Bridge player.

Jack knew him from Washington Township High School, where they met in Junior year. Back then, Jack was a sore loser in any competition and was a "win at all costs" athlete who upset a lot of people. While Jack had to work hard to excel at any sport, Dave made it look effortless.

They both lived in the Whitman section of town, so when Dave's parents bought him a car in senior year – a 1985 Toyota Celica – Dave drove Jack to school every day. They became friends, and Jack learned from Dave.

While Jack let anger, frustration, and pride fire up his emotional core, Dave showed him that his outward calm belied an inner storm brewing that was focused on a solution.

One afternoon in senior year, after Jack had stormed off after losing a flag football game, Dave met him at his car and said, "Jack, you have to stop that."

Jack responded with a sullen face. Dave stopped before opening the car doors and said, "In Freshman History, we were studying England, and I read this quote from Winston Churchill."

"I'll bet Churchill knows squat about flag football," Jack whined.

Dave ignored him. "Churchill thought success is in how you handle a situation. He said, 'The pessimist sees difficulty in every opportunity. The optimist sees the opportunity in every difficulty.'"

"I don't know what that bullshit means," Jack had said. "Open my door."

Dave still didn't open the car doors.

"When you play flag football, you see the possibility of defeat and do everything to avoid it. When I play, I see the possibility of victory or, if I lose, the chance to learn how to fix my mistakes the next time."

Jack never forgot that. After high school, he and Dave drifted away, and he didn't see him again until Dave came into HomeMaxx about 13 years ago.

Every few months in the last year, Dave would drop by HomeMaxx, seek out Jack, and ask him the same question: "When are you going to leave here and become my new store manager at Excell?"

Dave had invested wisely, bought a lot of property, held it until the time was right, and made a killing. He and his third wife, Roxanne, had bought a house in Naples, Florida, and Dave was spending more and more time there. He had even bought out a franchisee in Naples who owned an Excell Hardware store. After TrueValue and Ace, Excell was the largest franchise hardware chain in the nation. Of course, the three big boys were in their own space but were direct competitors. Excell, like Ace and TrueValue, offered friendly service, personal attention, and a quicker and easier shopping experience.

Once Jack met Lashay, Dave wanted them as a package deal – Jack as manager and Lashay as assistant manager for the store so he could spend most of his time in Florida. In recent years, Dave had hired a series of store managers who had either stolen from him, didn't care about the store, or treated employees and customers like crap.

Dave finally found an excellent store manager, and Dave was taking him to Naples to run the Florida store.

"Jack, I need a store manager, and I'll sweeten the pot," Dave said, a wry smile twisting his perfectly carved beard.

"Dave, always good to see you," Jack shook his hand. "How's Roxanne?"

"You haven't been over for dinner in years?" Dave said, ignoring the question.

When Jack didn't answer right away, Dave said, "It was my second wife, Julie, who didn't like you."

"Dave, no offense," Jack began, "That woman was a –"

Jack regained control and said, "Difficult person."

Dave laughed out loud.

"Oh, Jack," Dave tapped him on his left shoulder twice. "She hated you."

Dave's smile vanished. He looked around before he spoke, and when he did, it was in a hushed tone.

"Jack, Black Cobalt is going to extract every penny it can From HomeMaxx and close the entire chain," Dave said.

"I hear from Excell's top brass that this store won't survive the year. I need someone I can trust. Bring Lashay with you and Gus. I need good people I can trust."

Jack nodded. "Dave, I want to. I really do. But I owe Tyler, and I can't abandon him or the store."

"Or the people I've worked with for years," Jack added. "Darla, Ellen, Ted from Lighting, and even Harry from Tools. Then there's this kid, Robbie."

Dave reached out his right hand. Jack shook it.

"Jack, I'll wait because I know it won't be long."

"Dave, you've always been a good friend," Jack said. "Any Churchill quotes?"

Dave thought for a few seconds, smiled, and said, "We can always count on the Americans to do the right thing after they have exhausted all the other possibilities."

"What does that mean?" Jack asked.

"I know you'll do the right thing—eventually," Dave said as he turned toward the exit.

As he walked away, Dave turned around, walked backward, and said, "Jack, those idiots at Black Cobalt have priced everything much too high,"

"I agree, but what do we know," Jack answered, tossing up his hands in mock disgust. "We're just the workers on the front lines."

Lashay finished her shift for the week, punched out, and then walked back to the outside Garden area to find Allegra. Sunset blasted shards of sunlight into the western part of the outside Garden area. Lashay turned left toward the back fence where they had set up Allegra's food, water, litter box, and bed.

The monochromatic approaching darkness seeped into Allegra's area. Lashay struggled to see more than shadows and amorphous shapes. As she turned again, Lashay caught a thin beam of light and spotted Allegra coming back from outside HomeMaxx, dipping under the chain-link fence.

As the Calico came into her view, Lashay saw that the cat had something in her mouth.

Eww. It was a mouse. Brown and lifeless.

Allegra stopped at Lashay's feet and dropped the mouse inches from her work boots. Mice repulsed Lashay, but she had seen this cat behavior before. When she was in first grade, her grandmother rescued a black cat – they called him Martin – and it would drop killed prey at the back door at least three times a week. Martin became a neighborhood favorite because he killed mice, rats, moles, voles, and even squirrels in his nightly hunting expedition.

Her grandma let out Martin about seven at night when he meowed at the back door, and he'd return the next morning, usually with a kill. This became a daily routine until, when Lashay began second grade, Martin didn't come back. For weeks, Lashay would rush to the back door when she woke up for school, praying that Martin would be there and proudly displaying his catch. Lashay even began leaving scraps of food on the back porch in case Martin came back.

He never did.

Lashay knew why Martin and other cats would leave their prey for their human overlords. She understood that was actually quite a compliment. Cats will bring home the prey that they have hunted and killed to an area where they feel safe, comfortable, and secure. It may also be because they want to share their catch with their family.

This was Martin's way of saying, "Look what I can do."

Lashay stepped back from the mouse corpse but stopped when Allegra began to circle her leg and purr. She sat on the storage container next to her home and bed, and Allegra jumped into her lap and lay down. Her nose nuzzled Lashay's left arm, and she responded by scratching under her neck.

As Lashay sat with Allegra, she thought of her daughter Tamara. She hadn't seen her in almost twenty years, and she wondered if Tamara even remembered her because she was only a toddler when Lashay went away.

Of course, she lost custody of her daughter when everything went down. Every time she felt the urge to see her daughter, her shame prevented her from following through.

She had told herself she would not meet her daughter until she had put her life back together. As she sat with Allegra, Lashay wondered, "Have I accomplished that?"

What would she say if she met her daughter? She's an adult now? Would she ever forgive me? Who knows what poison was injected into Tamara's head about how horrible her mother was?

What if Jack knew she had a daughter? What if Jack knew her story? All of it, even the most humiliating parts. There were slices of her life that she couldn't even face.

"Allegra, what should I do?" Lashay asked as the cat purred and relaxed in her lap.

"I think Jack and I could have something, despite his bad jokes," she told the cat, who looked up at her with golden eyes. *Allegra's eyes seem to change color and shade depending on the light.*

Lashay sat with Allegra, scratching tenderly under the cat's neck and feeling the darkness swallow her.

"Allegra, I'm going to have to do something bold," Lashay said as she gave Allegra one good scratch before getting ready to go home. She needed her lumpy couch, some disgusting reality TV, and the dollar store pretzels she'd been saving for Friday night.

When she stood, Allegra meowed, jumped up on the storage container, and folded her paws under her body.

"Allegra, maybe I'll do something to get Jack's attention, like drop a dead mouse at his feet."

Chapter Eleven

Jack was grateful it was a cool mid-April Saturday morning because they had already worked hard, and it was only nine o'clock. The sweat soaking his shirt and the dull ache in his back alerted him to the fact that he was fifty years old, not 20.

He had shown up at seven, and Tyler carried the pavers from the front yard where the stone company had left them while Jack used the plate compactor to compress the gravel and level the area.

Tyler and Pam Rodgers lived in the Hunter Woods neighborhood in Williamstown, located off Fries Mill Road. Hunter Woods was a well-established residential neighborhood of single-family detached homes and was one of the more affluent neighborhoods in the area. Jack thought the homes were built in the mid-to-late 90s and guessed there were about 300 homes.

The majority of the homes were situated on approximately one-half of an acre. The average house had four bedrooms, two full and one-half bathrooms, a full basement, and an attached two-car garage. The medium living space was approximately 2,600 square feet. Tyler and Pam's house had white shingles with black shutters. The house was a center-hall colonial with a large transom window above the black front door that revealed the chandelier, the top of the stairway, and the second-floor hall to anyone driving or walking by.

They purchased it about 15 years ago when Jack and Tyler had just met. That was how they became friends beyond boss and employee. Tyler needed help with renovating the kitchen, master bath, and laundry room, finishing the basement, and installing the back deck. Those projects took Jack and Tyler almost a year, and during that time, they built a friendship with the understanding that their work relationship would not be affected.

When Tyler and Pam conceived this backyard makeover, Jack had convinced them to rent an Evolution 12.6-in x 15.7-in Plate Compactor because a level and tamped-down surface would extend the life of the pavers and keep the new back patio even.

Tyler already had a 12X16 Trex deck off the back of his home. The pavers would extend the back area another 15 feet so they could add a fire pit, pizza oven, new built-in gas grill, a gazebo with a steel roof, and outside furniture that could seat 14 people.

Today, Jack and Tyler planned to lay all the pavers and build the retaining wall on three sides. If everything went smoothly, they could finish today before it dark, about 7:30.

So far, Jack and Tyler had been too busy to talk much except about the backyard project. Then Pam walked out of the kitchen's French doors carrying a large tray.

"Boys, let's take a break for breakfast," Pam called out.

Jack had known her for years since he met Tyler. Jack always chided Tyler, "Rodgers, you are a lucky man. Your wife is a beauty and as smart and sweet as she is pretty."

Tyler would always answer, "It's life's way of paying me back for having to work at HomeMaxx for 25 years."

Jack sat at their seven-piece aluminum non-rust dining set with swivel rocking chairs. A Lazy Susan sat in the middle of the aluminum engraved faux stone dining table.

Tyler sat across from him and said, "I'm starved. Thanks, hon."

Pam put down the tray and then arranged everything on the Lazy Susan. There was a coffee carafe, three mugs, three plates with a Western omelet, fruit, toast, and mini blueberry muffins.

"Pam, I can't thank you enough," Jack said. "Although after eating all this, we may need a nap."

Pam shook her index finger and said, "If you fall down on the job, Marsalis, then no lunch."

Jack and Tyler looked at each other with an "I already know it is going to be delicious" glare.

Jack had already finished half a cup of coffee, attacked his omelet, and was eyeing the mini muffins. Tyler had rotated his breakfast, eating a little omelet, fruit, buttered sourdough toast, and even a mini muffin.

"How are Morgan and Taylor?" Jack asked Pam.

"Morgan is doing great at Cornell," Pam said. "She has one more year and will graduate with a degree in Architecture."

"That is terrific," Jack said, his mouth full of omelet and two mini muffins.

"Soon, you'll have an architect in the family,"

"It's been her dream since she was a little girl," Tyler said, grabbing the last two mini muffins. "She used to design doll houses when she was just in kindergarten."

"And Taylor?" Jack asked.

Jack hesitated to ask about her. Although she was two years older than Morgan, she was the difficult child. Jack knew from Tyler that she had struggled at school in Pittsburgh and basically wasted her first two years. Tyler indicated she had found herself and was doing well with a major in artificial intelligence.

"As you know, it's been a rockier road," Pam admitted. "Taylor was always good with computers, and she's finally found something that's motivated her, other than boys, clothes, and drinking."

"Carnegie-Mellon became the first university to offer a bachelor's degree in AI," Tyler said. "It's actually the place many say where AI was invented."

Jack heard Tyler's pride in his voice and felt jealous of this family. This is what he had always wanted. But he had screwed it all up.

"She has this older Honda that's been acting up," Pam said. "She only has a month left of school. We're hoping it makes it till she drives back home, and maybe we'll get her another car. Plus, Morgan needs a car, too."

"Tyler, that new kid you hired in Lumber, Noah, is actually an auto mechanic," Jack said. "Why don't you have him look at it? Gus says the kid can fix anything with wheels and a motor."

As Jack was finishing breakfast and wiping his hands, Pam spoke up.

"Jack, what's happening with you and Lashay?"

"Hon, that's Jack's business," Tyler intervened.

Jack wasn't surprised by Pam's question. She had been trying to set him up for years with girlfriends, other real estate agents, and even a few clients. Jack would never forget the recently divorced woman who bought a home through Pam's real estate firm in the Bateman Farms development off Hurffville Grenloch Road in Washington Township. Pam had hired Jack to help the woman unpack and arrange all her furniture and stuff that the movers had dropped off. When Jack showed up the next morning after the move, the woman answered the front door with her cell phone in his face.

"I'm live streaming this entire day in case you try something. I have four family representatives as witnesses."

Jack responded by walking to his car and driving away.

Pam liked Lashay and thought they would make a great couple, which he told Jack every time she saw him.

"Thanks for the breakfast," Jack said, as he used his napkin to wipe his face and hand and sip a little more coffee before heading back to work.

"Pam, I like Lashay," Jack began, mug in hand. "But we both have a similar problem: our pasts. I know mine, and as messy, embarrassing, and disgusting as it is, I'm ready to share with her and see what happens."

"Lashay is not there yet," Jack said. "Whatever is in her past still haunts her."

Pam started to gather the plates and mugs and arrange them back on the tray. She observed, "Jack, I think sometimes people feel the need to punish themselves to the point that the punishment is much more severe than the crime."

Jack nodded. He agreed with her. He didn't know how bad her past deeds were, but he knew that Lashay believed her actions were so heinous that he would not want to be with her.

For Jack, there was no way that was true. After prison, he had no money, lived in a rooming house with just a bed and dresser, and shared a bathroom with the entire floor. There was no way to attract a woman, nor did he have the energy to do so. It took all he had to get his life on track. After that, he had very little extra money to spend on dates.

Once he became more settled at HomeMaxx and lived in the basement of the Szczesny's house, Jack visited some of the local bars even though he wasn't much of a drinker. Two beers, usually whatever was the cheapest, could last him a few hours while he watched the Eagles, Phillies, Union, 76ers, or Flyers on TV.

Jack's favorite bars included the Lake House in Williamstown on Iona Lake, P.J. Whelihan's in Washington Township, Landmark in Glassboro, which had the best Happy Hour deal, and Village Pub near the Washington Township and Deptford line.

To Jack, it seemed like everyone unattached at these bars was searching desperately for someone without a troubled or traumatic backstory. Sadly, most had either a horrendous childhood, were victims of sexual assault or rape, had past or current drug problems, suffered from functional alcoholism, or were so stripped of compassion, empathy, and anything left to give, they simply used a person they met for a night for a few weeks.

Jack knew that he belonged to that group. He had told the story of his downfall so many times that he almost had it memorized. Jack asked himself the same question every time he recounted his fall from respectability.

How could I have been so stupid?

"I thought we had made a date earlier this week to buy the cat supplies, but she bailed on me at the last minute," Jack said without anger and with more of a note of regret.

"Jack, I have to explain something to you," Pam began.

"Jack, I know that voice," Tyler interjected. Flashing a smile, he headed back to work on the pavers.

"Men are emotionally stunted creatures," Pam began. "In trying to connect with Lashay, you have to open yourself up to her and reveal yourself."

"Are you telling him to flash her?" Tyler joked.

Without looking his way, Pam said, "Tyler, how would you like a paver on your head?"

"I'll shut up now," Tyler said.

Jack stood up, nodded at Pam, and said, "Thanks, Pam. That's good advice."

Jack walked over to the pavers and knelt, ready to lay them down and hammer them into place.

"I'll be out in a few hours with lunch. I have to show a house first in Elk Township," Pam said as she carried the breakfast tray inside.

As Jack and Tyler laid the rows of pavers, Jack said, "You are a lucky man."

"Jack, I say that every day," Tyler answered. "But, of course, she is the wife of a HomeMaxx store manager. That's quite an honor."

They laughed, and Jack said, "Sure. You're several steps up from a Family Dollar store manager."

"I can still fire you, Marsalis," Tyler joked.

"And what then?" Jack shot back. "You'd hire more of those college slackers like Justin and Trevor in Appliances."

"We're desperate," Tyler said, but without the wry tone.

They worked for several hours on the pavers, laying them down and using a rubber mallet to tap them into place. Once the pavers were all laid, Jack used a plate compactor to set the pavers into the sand bedding. Later that afternoon, they'd seal the area with a sand binding sealant to ensure the joint sand would not disappear. The sealant will also prevent the growth of vegetation between the joints and prevent stains from oil, grease, grime, rust, moss, algae, tire markings, and day-to-day spills. The sealant allowed them to clean off such stains with greater ease. Then, they began on the first of the three retainer walls. They had already leveled and prepared the ground, so this should be easier than the others.

"Jack, I've got something to tell you about HomeMaxx," Tyler said as they laid the bricks along the wall's row.

"Are you promoting me to region manager?" Jack chided.

When Tyler didn't smile, Jack knew this was serious.

"I was on a call with Black Cobalt the other day," Tyler began. "It didn't go well."

Tyler explained the private firm's demand for profitability by June or that they would close the store in October. Jack didn't interrupt and let Tyler unfold the entire sordid story. Tyler's contempt for the private equity firm, Black Cobalt, was obvious, as was his forecast of the store's chances.

"I knew the store was not one of HomeMaxx's most profitable, but I thought we always did all right," Jack said as he slid more bricks on the wall, locking them into place.

"Jack, we were always in the middle of the pack, and HomeMaxx Corporate seemed resigned to that. They knew the store was located in a lower-income area, but we always topped the list in customer loyalty."

"So, what's happened since Black Cobalt took over?" Jack asked.

Tyler stopped placing more bricks on the wall, stood up straight, took off a garden glove, and wiped his brow.

"Private equity firms, like Black Cobalt, buy retail companies and then sell the land the stores are on, usually to a holding company they own. That means HomeMaxx now has to pay an exorbitant rent to the holding company —"

"Which is owned by the private equity firm that collects the rent money," Jack interrupted.

"That's their game plan," Tyler said. "Black Cobalt made hundreds of millions from the sale of the land that HomeMaxx stores sit on and then collected money from the holding company that bought the land."

"And the monthly rent payment is evaporating the profit that the store did make," Jack said.

"Exactly," Tyler said as he reached for another brick. The first wall was just about done, and there were two more to go.

"Plus, these bastards collect a two percent dividend reinvestment fee from every store."

"Essentially, we have from now until June 1 to show a profit," Tyler said. "That's about six weeks."

Jack heard Tyler's dejection and simmering anger. He tried not to think about himself, about what he would do without a job.

The economy is healthy, unemployment is low, and I'll be okay.

Then he thought about Gus. What would he do without his job here? It's the only thing keeping him going. How about Luther, Harry, Darla, or Ellen? Where would Robbie get a job as an autistic person?

What would happen to Lashay? Jack knew being black made it harder for Lashay to find work, even today. The "I don't see color" people always claimed that racial equality had been achieved, but Jack knew better than that.

Selfishly, Jack wondered if they would drift apart if they didn't work together.

That's when he began thinking about Dave Maloney's offer.

We could work together at the Excell Hardware store in Washington Township.

But before Jack gave up and embraced the inevitable, he did have that idea about Allegra.

By one o'clock, lunch had arrived, and Jack and Tyler were dirty, sweaty, grimy, and fatigued. As if on cue, Pam came out of the French doors with a tray and a smile as large as the plates on the tray.

"Sold a house today," Pam beamed.

"That's great, hon," Tyler said.

"Congrats, Pam," Jack added.

Pam put down the tray on the outside table and surveyed the yard.

"Boys, you do surprisingly good work," Pam joked. "Perhaps you can leave me a business card, and I can recommend you to other homeowners."

As Tyler and Jack used the hand sanitizer and then sat down, Tyler said, "We only do work for extremely beautiful women."

"While your husband is an accomplished brown noser, I agree with him,"

Jack said.

Pam took the plates off the tray and placed them in front of Tyler and Jack.

Each plate contained a Monte Cristo sandwich, a cup of coleslaw, another cup of strawberries and cantaloupe, and a piece of apple pie with vanilla ice cream on top.

Jack and Tyler looked at Pam and let out a simultaneous whistle.

Jack said, "I feel guilty getting paid for this work and being served such a gourmet breakfast and lunch."

"Jack, this is your one and only payment," Pam said as she handed out the napkins and cutlery. "So, enjoy it."

"Hon, I think Jack may be overpaid," Tyler said. "I think we should take away his apple pie and vanilla ice cream."

Pam smiled and nodded, and Jack reacted by placing his hands over his plate.

"I refuse to take a pay cut," Jack said.

They all laughed. Jack marveled at how Pam had timed it perfectly. As he and Tyler had finished the sandwich and the coleslaw, the ice cream had melted just enough on the apple pie.

Pam sat down with them as they ate and said, "Have you boys talked and come up with any ideas?"

Before Tyler could say no, Jack jumped in.

"I have this idea that's been forming, and it's going to sound a little crazy, but I think it could work."

"Okay, Jack, we're all ears," Pam said as Tyler nodded and devoured his apple pie and perfectly melted vanilla ice cream.

Chapter Twelve

"**H**omeMaxx is run by a family for the families near our stores."

Gus pulled into the Manor Life Nursing Home parking lot at about ten o'clock on a Saturday morning. He had been awake for hours, cleaning up his house just as Jack had shown him, and was close to hangry.

Betty always took care of the house until she was no longer there. After she died, Gus let the house fall apart. If he were truthful with himself, he would admit that he had allowed his whole life to fall to pieces after Betty died.

Gus thought it was ironic that he worked with concrete his whole life, just like his father and grandfather, yet his wife Betty was the strong one.

Like cold, hard steel, only with a perpetual smile, natural humility, and unbreakable resolve, Betty was the best thing that ever happened to Gus.

He knew it but never said it. He couldn't. It was the nature of things. Betty managed the home, and it was always clean, organized, and a source of pride. As a mother, she was loving yet demanding, supportive yet not afraid to push Michael to what was right, even if it was difficult and painful.

Gus never knew that it was Betty who had urged Michael to tell Gus that he was gay. Michael told him in an angry, resentful voice when they battled after Betty's funeral.

"She knew it was killing me inside to keep that secret," Michael had screamed at him. "She was confident that you would understand."

"Mom always saw more in you than anyone else," Michael shouted.

"She was never the same after that," Michael bawled.

Gus hated to admit it, but his son was right. When Michael left after his confession, his wife was never the same. A light dimmed and eventually went off inside of her. Betty never argued with Gus or screamed at him concerning his behavior toward his son.

When she was diagnosed with ovarian cancer a few years later, Gus realized that the fight had gone out of her. She was already defeated before the fight of her life began.

She went through the chemo and radiation treatments and suffered stoically. When Gus began to miss work because she became sicker and bedridden, she urged him to return to work.

"Gus, this is the job you love," she had whispered one late night when the pain kept her up as she battled her own body.

"I want you to have that job after I'm gone," she told him.

As her condition worsened and treatment stopped because the doctors said, "There's nothing left to do but keep her as comfortable as possible," Gus stopped showing up for work, and they fired him after 25 years there.

When the night came that Betty's time was up, Gus had learned from the Hospice nurse how to administer pain medication. He had given her a shot after she howled in pain. A few minutes later, Betty lay motionless. Gus felt her chest to see if she was still alive.

She was. Barely.

As he leaned in close to her, Betty's eyes opened, but she seemed unable to focus on anything. Her right arm reached his left shoulder, gripping his flannel shirt tighter than Gus thought possible.

In a raspy voice, Betty said, "Promise me that you will make up with Michael."

Gus could feel her strength ebb away. He didn't answer.

"Promise. Promise," she demanded as her grip grew stronger and then suddenly went slack.

Betty was gone.

Then Gus had gone and screwed it all up by ignoring her last wish and fighting with Michael when he came back for the funeral.

They had never spoken again.

When he tapped on the window of Noah's white Honda, Gus somehow thought he was honoring Betty.

The kid was sleeping in the front seat, leaning far back. His car was filled with clothes and other items that weaved in and out of his twisted tangle of pants, shirts, underwear, and socks.

He banged hard on the window.

"Noah, Noah, wake up," Gus yelled.

The kid stirred and opened his eyes. When they locked on Gus, the kid said, "Holy shit, Mr. Burdette."

As he rubbed rocks out of his eye crevasses, Noah said, "What day is it? Am I late for work?"

"It's Saturday. Now get up; make yourself presentable if that is possible because I'm taking you to breakfast."

Noah returned the driver's seat to its upright position and rolled down the window.

"Is this a dream?" It's so real."

Gus knew that patience was a quality he possessed in minute quantities.

"For chrissake, kiwi, this is real, so let's go. I'm hungry. We'll take my truck. I can't be seen anywhere near your car."

As Noah opened his door to step out, Gus complained, "Jeez, kiwi. Why does your car smell like lamb? Are you barbecuing in your car?"

Gus got in the driver's seat of his F-250 black pickup and waited for Noah to climb in the passenger side. The truck had a lifter lift, so Noah had to step onto the side rail before getting in.

"Thanks, Mr. Burdette," Noah said. "Where are we going?"

"First, it's Gus from now on, and second, you are about to eat at a place with the best breakfast in Gloucester County."

As Gus drove onto Delsea Drive northbound, he said, "We are dining at Clayton's Silver Lake Diner."

The diner was well-known in the area for its great food and its namesake, Silver Lake, which was located a few miles away. Gus's family was born and grew up in Clayton. Gus's paternal grandfather, John Burdette, worked as a glass blower in the industry that reigned supreme in South Jersey for 100 years.

The story of Silver Lake was familiar to many long-time Clayton residents. In about 1856, Jacob Filser sold the lake that once powered the old mill to John Moore, who, along with his brother, employed hundreds of men at their glass works. With a need for housing for these men and their families, the Moore Brothers built houses and churches for their workers, and now they had a lake, too. During the late nineteenth century, the glass industry and Clayton were thriving. To top off all this new development, both brothers built elaborate mansions for themselves and their families.

In those early days, the local people used the lake in various ways. Ice houses and boat houses lined its shores. In the cold months, the lake supplied ice to the fast-growing new town. In the warm months, people used the lake recreationally for boating, swimming, and fishing and, of course, as a place to socialize. It was known that both the Moore Brothers Glass Works and the Whitney Glass Works held company picnics there. Moore Brothers and Whitney were geographically close to each other, only about three miles apart, and often shared bottle molds, orders, and probably employees, too.

In 1905, Dr. Moore formed the Still Run Boat Club, a club for bachelors and a place for local businessmen to gather. In 1907, the club built a clubhouse at a cost of $1,700, which still stands today. The clubhouse was largely financed by a rich businessman named Mr. D Linton Silver.

After a couple of attempts to broker a deal to buy the lake, Mr. Silver was finally successful in 1918. He paid $6500 for 181 acres, 81 of water, and 100 acres of land. At that time, there were 50 dwellings on the lake; they were called boat houses by their owners and valued at $25 each. After his purchase, Mr. Silver began to do maintenance on the lake and the dwellings on the common ground. The old wooden dam was replaced, and the lake was drained and cleaned. By the Fall of 1923, the new Silver Lake offered shares to its prospective buyers.

The glass works were long gone, and Clayton had seen better days. The borough of 8,000 people struggled to find a road back to prosperity. It was now a town with more liquor stores and dollar stores than churches.

Gus and Noah walked into an aluminum-skinned diner that hadn't changed much in 60 years. A server in a deep blue uniform seated them at a booth that still had the record player attached.

"My treat," Gus said as he regarded the menu. "Everything's good here."

"Thank you," Noah said as he perused the menu like a lion stalking an antelope.

"Are you sure?" Noah asked. "I haven't eaten much in days."

"It's fine," Gus waved his hand. "Besides, I am going to offer you the opportunity to make more money and afford more meals here."

The server, Bonnie, came over and took their orders. Gus had his usual—a Western omelet with breakfast potatoes, rye bread, and coffee. Noah ordered pancakes, French toast, turkey sausage, and coffee.

"Thank you again, Mr—, I mean Gus," Noah said as he sipped from the water glass Bonnie had brought them.

Gus looked over at the kid.

God, he reminds me of Michael.

While they waited for the food to arrive, Gus sipped his coffee in silence until the kids asked, "Why do you hate gay people?"

The question caught Gus off-guard. Not that he hadn't heard it before or that he hadn't asked himself that question thousands of times.

"Think you're pretty ballsy, huh," Gus demanded in a hushed tone.

He came in all the time and didn't want to make a scene.

"Mr. Burdette, Gus, I am not judging, just asking?" Noah said.

"Okay, wise-ass," Gus began. "Why do you think I do?"

Noah took a gulp of coffee and then filled up his cup from the carafe on their table. He added two packets of sugar and plenty of milk from the silver container on the table.

"With all due respect, I think you might have a son or daughter who is gay."

Bonnie brought their food: two plates for Gus and two for Noah.

"Can I get you, gentlemen, anything else," Bonnie said, smiling at Gus.

Gus returned her smile and said, "You hear that, Noah. Bonnie called us gentlemen."

With the fork and knife already in his hands, Noah launched an all-out assault on his breakfast.

"Bonnie, did you know that Gus is the hardest-working and most valuable employee at HomeMaxx?" Noah said.

Bonnie enjoyed the banter. "I've stopped by to see Gus when I'm at HomeMaxx, but he's always too busy to talk."

Gus didn't know how he lost control of the situation. He forced a smile, although it felt like he was trying to swallow mucus.

"I'll check on you both in a little while," Bonnie said as she walked to her table down the diner row.

Gus attacked his omelet. He had always been a fast eater and was scolded by Betty for years. He could see that Noah craved the food in front of him, but the boy wanted to talk for some stupid reason.

Gus just wanted to feed the boy a good meal, so he was energetic enough to help Gus with a concrete sidewalk job he had scheduled for tomorrow at the fancy development down the street from his house.

"She likes you," Noah said, lowering his shoulders and talking in a soft tone so Bonnie couldn't hear.

"Okay, kiwi, what would you know about men and women relationships?" Gus challenged.

Noah was already halfway down his stack of pancakes, just stopping long enough to pour more artificial maple syrup on the remaining stack.

"I know enough," Noah said, his mouth full of pancakes. "Dude, she stopped by to see you in the store. What woman does that unless she likes a guy? Plus, she keeps looking over here at you."

"She's probably wondering what I'm doing here with this fruity kid," Gus said.

"Now, she'll think that I'm, you know, a fairy," Gus added.

Noah scooped the detritus of his pancakes and forced them into his mouth.

"Gus, trust me. I am an expert in this subject. No one will ever think you are gay."

Gus always ate one food at a time. He remembered Betty and Michael teasing him about that.

"Okay, Dad, what's it gonna be tonight?" Michael would joke when he was in middle school. "Peas, then baked potato, then meat loaf or meat loaf, then baked potato, then peas last."

Gus finished his omelet and rye bread and now jabbed at each breakfast potato with his fork one at a time. Even though they didn't talk for a minute, there wasn't silence. Conversations from the busy diner on a Saturday morning and Noah cramming his food in his mouth and chomping on it like a beaver on a downed pine tree created an overall hum to the place.

Gus loved to come here on Saturdays, sit by himself, chat with Bonnie, and listen as people connected with each other. Noah now tore into his French toast, looking at Gus like he expected Gus to talk.

Gus nailed a particularly rebellious breakfast potato that rolled around his plate and did not want to be speared by his fork.

"My son Michael," Gus said, focusing his eyes on his plate and avoiding Noah.

"He's a . He's... He's gay."

Noah quickly finished his breakfast, cleaned his mouth with his napkin, sipped his coffee, and then folded his hands on the table.

"Are you waiting for a story?" Gus demanded.

Bonnie came over, all smiles and flirty body language. She was about sixty with dyed blonde hair that was sprayed to keep it immobile, pleasing features, and an orange wristband on her left wrist that Gus had made out before. It read. 1-800—662-HELP (4357).

Gus had discovered on a rainy Saturday when the diner was practically empty that Bonnie's son, Robert, had died of a heroin overdose over thirty years ago. He remembered what Bonnie had told him, fighting back tears that day.

"Gus, cherish those moments with your kids if you have any. It's time that is so precious."

"You boys, want anything else?" Bonnie asked as she stood near Gus.

Gus decided to have a little fun.

"You hear that, Noah. First, we were gentlemen. Now we're just guys."

They all laughed loudly and in unison. Bonnie handed Gus the check and said, "Always good to see you, Gus."

"You too, Bonnie," Gus answered, his eyes meeting hers.

Gus put down the check after Bonnie left. Noah sipped and played with his coffee cup, rotating it in a circle.

"His name is Michael. And I don't hate gay people, Noah," Gus said.

"Did you kick him out of the house?" Noah asked.

"Yeah, I did. How'd you know? Jack tell you?"

Noah shook his hand.

"That's what my dad just did to me. That's why I'm homeless. I've exhausted all my friends and family from couch surfing. I figured I'd get a few paychecks under my belt and then look for a place."

"That's a dumb plan. You'll never get enough money for the first and last month's rent and the security deposit."

"I'm kind of out of options," Noah responded.

"I know someone who may take you as a roommate," Gus said. "As long as you don't try to, you know, go all gay on them."

"Gus, have you been watching Fox News?" Noah asked. "Where are you getting this?"

"All news is bullshit," Gus responded. "I just know what I know."

As Noah finished his coffee and Gus picked up the check, he paused and said, "I don't hate gay people. I hated the fact that I wanted a son who was nothing like I got."

"I get that," Noah said.

"Is that why your father kicked you out?" Gus asked.

Noah shook his head no. "Actually, the opposite. I'm just like my father. I'm a hard worker and an excellent auto mechanic. I learned those skills from my father."

"So, why'd he kick you out?" Gus asked, puzzled.

"Because he's a conservative Catholic and very traditional," Noah said.

"I'm going to pay the check," Gus said. "I'll be right back."

Gus paid the check with cash, then found Bonnie and gave her a twenty-dollar bill on a fifty-dollar check. When she accepted the money, her smile spread out from ear to ear.

"Thank you, Gus," Bonnie said. "You're a sweetheart." Then she touched his hand ever so slightly.

Maybe the gay kid is right. What do they call it? Gaydar. Maybe the kid has it for normal people.

"Let's go," Gus commanded. They left the diner and got back into their truck.

Gus started the truck. "Noah, I do side jobs on the weekend, usually in this large fancy development called Hillbrooke Farms near my house. I have a concrete sidewalk to do tomorrow at a house."

Gus hesitated. The kid looked at him, expressionless.

"I'm getting older," Gus began, clearing his throat. "I need help with the job."

Noah didn't respond as if he expected Gus to come out and ask.

As Gus pulled out onto Delsea Drive and headed south toward Franklinville, Gus said, "Are you available to help? I'll pay you $200 in cash."

The kid broke out a massive smile.

"Gus, I'd be honored," Noah said.

"That sounds gay," Gus harrumphed.

Chapter Thirteen

The HomeMaxx Employee Manual states, "Employees who engage in consensual romantic relationships must conduct themselves in an appropriate professional manner while on company property."

Jack and Tyler finished at about six-thirty in the evening, with the fading sun still vibrant in the sky. Jack drove home feeling his muscles ache from the day's physical work, but his mind rejoiced at what they accomplished in Tyler's backyard. The pavers were laid, and the three walls were built brick by brick to frame the new yard area. Next week, they would tackle the installation of the new gas grill, the pizza oven, and the gazebo. That would take all of Saturday and Sunday.

The pizza oven was a kit that had to be built, as was the gazebo. The Rodgers were trying to have the backyard done before their daughters returned from college in mid-May.

Jack thought that goal was realistic. They still had to hook up the refrigerator, install and set up the 85-inch TV, and build and install the bar with chairs.

Jack pulled into the driveway and parked his car at the far end. He could see Wally and Jackie sitting on their swivel chairs in the backyard. Sometimes, after a hard day at the restaurant, the couple would relax in the backyard, drink some bourbon, and just laugh about their day.

Jack knew nothing about hard liquor. For years, he drank whatever was on tap and on special for Happy Hour or some other promotion. The Szczesny's were obsessed with bourbon whiskey. They had taken vacations in Kentucky and Tennessee, doing bourbon tours. When they returned, the couple would spin tales of bourbon excellence and history for hours. Jack would sip on whatever bourbon they poured for him, making sure he eventually drank it all, not wanting to offend them.

The couple would buy monogrammed whiskey glasses from whatever bourbon tour they took and then sip it in front of Jack. After their lips smacked from the bourbon, Wally or Jackie would say something like: "Jack, it has a slightly floral nose that conveys whispers of cedar and raisin in between soft vanilla notes. Can you taste the vanilla and toffee dance around subtle notes of dried fruit and white pepper?

Jack would nod politely, unable to distinguish one bourbon from another. The couple needed the distraction because they worked hard—very hard.

Jackie's Place opened at seven every morning but Monday and closed at two in the afternoon. The Szczesny's arrived at 5:30 every morning to set up and didn't leave until about four in the afternoon. The locals loved the place, and the Szczesny's, who were outgoing, unassuming people, kept the business profitable enough to last 25 years. Jack knew that the restaurant business was cutthroat and had a high rate of failure. His landlords beat those odds by being decent people who served good food at reasonable prices.

For 25 years, the couple attended St. Catherine's, the Catholic Church on Delsea Drive near the post office, every Sunday. They donated to every local charity and always bought Girl Scout cookies.

"Jack, you look beat," Wally said.

"I think you need a shot of Blanton's," Jackie snickered. "It's the best bourbon."

"We did a lot of work at the Rodgers' house," Jack said.

Wally and Jackie were about 65 years old, with grey-streaked hair, bellies that pushed forward, and aging scars from working so hard.

As Jackie poured Jack a shot, Wally said, "Jack, you had a visitor."

Jackie handed Jack a whiskey glass with ice and the amber bourbon that coated the two cubes.

"Thanks," Jack said, holding his glass out in front, then saying, "To good fortune and finding a fortune."

Wally and Jackie laughed as they always did when Jack made that toast.

Jack sipped and pursed his lips to enjoy the vanilla, caramel, and oak flavor the couple told him to expect, then asked, "Who was my mystery visitor?"

Jack watched the couple glance at each other as if they knew a juicy secret.

"It was a woman," Jackie said.

"She's black," Wally said. Then: "And very attractive."

Lashay came to my basement apartment. How? Why?

"Jack, she is definitely a keeper," they both said almost simultaneously.

"I hope that wasn't a problem?" Jack asked. In the 15 years he had lived here, he had never had a woman in his apartment. He didn't think it was respectful to the couple.

Wally and Jackie had a daughter, who was the reason the couple built the basement apartment. After attending Clayton High School, she moved to South Philly with two friends. That move began years of trying to help their daughter kick her heroin addiction.

After several aborted attempts at rehab, Kelly, their daughter, got clean, and they built the apartment for her to keep a close eye on her while she rebuilt her life. Kelly worked at the restaurant for about six months, and the dining customers enjoyed the self-deprecating humor of Kelly, who always wore a smile.

At least on the outside.

Every morning, Wally and Jackie waited at 5:25 by their Ford Explorer for Kelly to emerge from the basement door. One morning, she did not. The couple waited a few minutes and then went down the flight of concrete stairs and knocked.

And knocked. After five minutes, Wally used his keys and opened the door. When recounting what happened over too many bourbons, he told Jack that he told Jackie, "Stay here. Don't come in."

Wally found Kelly on her bed with a needle sticking out of her right arm. The autopsy revealed that she had overdosed.

The apartment remained empty for over five years until they rented it to Jack. Even after 15 years, Jack knew that Jackie would never go inside the apartment. If she needed Jack, she'd knock on the door.

The couple never discussed it unless they were drinking heavily, and Jack never brought it up. If they did, he listened, sadness overtaking him even though he had never met the troubled girl.

"Jack, come on," Wally said. "We're happy for you. You deserve somebody nice like her."

As Jack thanked them and headed to the stairs, Jackie said, "Jack, we need to tell you something."

Jack turned back toward the couple, who stood up from their swivel chairs and looked uncomfortable.

This can't be good.

The couple reached out for each other's hand.

Jeez, am I dying?

"Jack, we're selling the restaurant," Wally said.

"And we're selling the house," Jackie added, regret instead of jubilation in her tone.

Jack processed the news and immediately stopped his inner voice from demanding, "What's going to happen to me? Why did you do this to me?"

Instead, he verbalized, "Guys, I'm so excited for you."

Smiles appeared on their faces as their worst fears of Jack's negative reaction didn't materialize.

"You've worked so hard, and you deserve a break," Jack said, as genuine enthusiasm replaced the forced positivity that he projected.

"We sold to a Mexican couple who live in Clayton and promised to keep it a neighborhood restaurant," Wally told him.

"Are you also moving to a warm, sunny climate?" Jack asked, thinking he would beat them to the true bad news for him.

He was going to have to move after 15 years. He'd never be able to rent anything this cheap, but the Szczesny's were like family to him.

The problem for Jack was that his criminal background kept him from being a viable renter. He'd find an apartment, write a deposit check, and then ten days later, the landlord or management agent would call and, in a regretful voice, explain that his background check excluded him from renting here.

"We're not going to Florida, where my brother lives," Wally said.

"It's too expensive there now," Jackie added. "There are hurricanes, humidity, crazy politicians, and alligators."

"Let me guess," Jack said, possibly overamping his reaction. "New Mexico, where your sister lives."

Jackie's sister, Marilyn, lived in Albuquerque and had been trying to convince them to move there since she and her husband Kyle had retired there in 2018, right before COVID.

Jackie said, "There are new homes available in a 55-and-over community where Marilyn and Kyle live."

Wally stepped forward and reached out his hand to shake Jack's hand.

Jack shook his hand, and Wally said, "Jack, you are family. We haven't even put the house up for sale yet. We want you to have as much time as you need to find a place."

"We can help you look," Jackie interjected.

"Whatever you need," the couple said almost simultaneously.

"I'd hug you both," Jack chuckled, even though he felt like crying. Not only because he could be homeless again but because these people had been his family for the last 15 years.

How many backyard barbecues had they had together? Jack and Wally had a serious horseshoe rivalry going on for years. Jack took care of the pits with sand from HomeMaxx and treated wood he used from the store to build new pits last year.

"But I'm filthy and smelly," Jack said. "We'll talk tomorrow. I'll cut the lawn and need to put lime down."

Jack sat at his tiny two-person kitchen table, unable to move. Of course, he was happy for the Szczesny's. They deserved to relax and enjoy life. Jackie only had a sister in New Mexico, and Wally's brother in Stuart, Florida, had leaped into a conspiracy hole with wild stories of Deep State operatives and even false flag operations for mass shootings.

After a few years, Wally stopped calling his brother, and his brother Eric returned the favor.

Possibly unemployed by October. Now, homeless by maybe July or August.

Something has to go my way. Anything.

There was a knock on his door.

Jack didn't get up right away.

Chapter Fourteen

"Hiding our workplace romance is the most strenuous work I do all day." Anonymous employee.

"Hi, Jack," Lashay said as he opened the door.

He was filthy with dirt smudges over his jeans, a blue t-shirt covered with dirt marks, bits of sand, and dirt trails on his forehead, forearms, and neck. He looked exhausted to Lashay. His caramel-brown eyes dimmed from the all-day exertion.

To his credit, Jack attempted to revitalize himself in a nanosecond. He stood straighter and less stiff and managed to throw a smile onto his face.

"My landlords told me that a beautiful woman stopped by today," Jack said, waving his hand to invite her in. She stepped in but remained in the doorway.

"Really. Who was she?"

Jack's face twinkled as he said, "You, of course."

"What do you think, Jack?" Lashay tempted him.

"The woman standing in front of me is gorgeous."

"Jack, does that line actually work?" Lashay challenged.

Still brushing dirt off of himself, Jack returned fire. "There's always a first time."

Lashay had role-played this scenario of her visiting Jack's place numerous times, usually while she was in bed. She had crafted scenarios, responses, jokes, verbal teases, and even an outright confession about how she felt.

Everything suddenly melted away. She didn't know what to say. What to do.

"Tyler and I had a great day at his house. Got so much accomplished. Why don't come in, sit in my luxurious and spacious living room while I shower, and then I will make us dinner."

"Jack, you clearly worked very hard today, and you're probably exhausted," Lashay said, not moving from the doorway.

Jack's face turned serious.

"Lashay, I've thought about this day for a year."

Lashay froze at Jack's emotional exposure.

Men, including Jack, didn't do this. They were usually as emotionally frozen as Gelato.

"What am I wearing in your...thoughts?" Lashay asked, trembling inside.

"A HomeMaxx safety vest and nothing else," Jack crooned.

"You're an asshole, Jack," Lashay said, suddenly feeling like his humor had relieved the stress.

"A guy can dream, right?" Jack said.

"Then get it right," she answered. "If I were only wearing a HomeMaxx safety vest and nothing else," Lashay said, pausing to allow him to get a mental picture, "I would still wear my HomeMaxx hard hat as ordered by OSHA."

Jack laughed. "Have to follow the rules even in a dream."

"Or a nightmare," she said, sticking out her tongue.

"Now, who's the asshole," Jack replied.

Jack clapped his hands together. "I'd like you to stay for dinner. I'm going to take a quick shower, then we can chat while I make dinner."

"You sure?" Lashay said, trying to gauge his sincerity.

"I even have a bottle of J Lohr Pinot Noir saved."

"Saved for what?"

"One day, I overheard you talking to Lauren about the only kind of wine you like," Jack said. "You mentioned this wine, so I bought it at Kenny's Liquors and have been saving it."

Inside, Lashay started to shake. Her inner voice became vocal, telling her she wasn't worthy and that he'd reject her when he found out.

"You, okay? Jack asked, apparently noticing her sudden discomfort.

Lashay chased away her inner critic with a stick and said, "Come on, Marsalis. Get the dirt off in the shower and make some dinner. I'm hungry."

Jack saluted as he walked a few feet to his bed. "I've never seen you hangry. How bad is it?"

"You have no idea."

Jack grabbed some clothes from a drawer that slid out from under his bed and hurried into his bathroom. A few seconds later, Lashay heard the water running. She surveyed his apartment before she sat down.

Lashay sat on the couch and scanned the apartment. The green microfiber couch was old and worn. Jack had the red Christmas blanket Lashay had given him last Christmas folded neatly along the top of the back pillows. A coffee table painted with vanilla bean and distressed matched the two end tables that held two Rustic vintage table lamps with built-in frosted glass.

Lashay thought Jack had refinished the coffee table and the two end tables. Even though the apartment was small, the space matched her view of Jack's home behavior. Everything was neat, organized, and carefully positioned.

The small circular kitchen table with two chairs was also painted vanilla bean, and the tabletop was refinished with dark oak. Lashay was sure Luther from HomeMaxx had fashioned the pedestal base for the table. The man was a woodworking wizard.

The kitchen area had only one bank of cabinets that hung over the sink and a small butcherblock countertop. To the left of the drop-in basin stainless steel kitchen sink was a two-burner electric burner and a smallish oven below.

Lashay didn't see a dishwasher. The only natural light in the kitchen area emanated from the white door with a six-panel window inset. Jack had added faux blinds over the window for some privacy.

The apartment was painted a light blue, probably to approximate a clear blue sky. Jack had a few photos framed on the walls. As Lashay expected, each photo was framed with a black frame and a tan matte. The photos were probably his parents, who weren't smiling in any of the framed photos.

Across from the couch was a dark espresso TV stand about 40 inches high. The TV was older and was from a brand Lashay had never heard of.

To Lashay's left was a full bed with a cloth headboard and footboard. Two drawers on each side of the mattress could be accessed. The bed was meticulously made with a waffle cotton beige blanket and two pillows. Above the bed, the only other window in the place was inset, offering the only other source of natural light. The window was only about two feet in height and nearly the length of the bed.

The closed bathroom door was positioned to the left of the bed, and Lashay imagined it was as small and compact as everything else here.

The water flow from the shower stopped, and Jack yelled, "Be right out. Then we eat."

Lashay compared this place to her mobile home. They were about the same size, although configured differently. Lashay had a bank of three windows in her kitchen and windows in her bathroom and bedroom.

When her inner voice chattered about living here with Jack, Lashay shut down her internal dialogue with a brusque, "Jack will never want me when he finds out."

If he ever does, she reminded herself and felt better that her secret was safe as long as she kept her mouth shut.

Jack came out of the bathroom dressed in clean jeans, a grey, crewneck outer Banks shirt, and grey socks. Lashay noticed he closed the bathroom door.

Jack clapped his hands together.

"While I whip up dinner as quickly as possible, I have an appetizer with a nice red wine," Jack said as a mixture of a statement and question.

"Jack, you are full of surprises," Lashay said.

This was a side of Jack she had never seen. He was domestic, and she could tell he took pride in his place. That he had purchased her favorite wine in case she ever visited made her feel even more guilty that she had bailed on him when they planned to buy Allegra's supplies.

Jack opened the wine deftly with a wine opener and then took out two stemmed wine glasses from a higher cabinet he clearly didn't use often. He poured about five ounces into each glass, then took out an ice tray, twisted it, and put the cubes in a glass near her glass.

"I think I heard you prefer ice in your wine," Jack said.

Jack moved smoothly in the kitchen as if he were comfortable in this area. He went to the refrigerator and pulled out a block of cheese wrapped in plastic. Then he opened the thin pantry cabinet next to the door and took out a box of balsamic vinegar and basil Triscuits.

"This will tide you over," Jack said, smiling as he carefully but expertly cut cubes of cheese and placed them around the edge of a small plate with Triscuits stacked neatly in the center. Jack took out a jar of hot pepper jelly and a small knife from the refrigerator door. He placed the plate, the wine, the glass of ice, and several napkins on the coffee table in front of her. He brought over his glass of J. Lohr Pinot Noir and tipped his glass toward hers.

"Cheers," he said.

"Cheers," Lashay replied. "Jack, thank you. I feel guilty. You worked hard all day… "

"I'm happy you stopped by," Jack said. "I'm going to make dinner now. It'll take me about 20 minutes."

"Want me to put on the TV?" Jack asked.

"Can we talk while you cook?" Lashay asked. "What are you making?"

"Chicken rice bowl," Jack said. "If you like that. It's grilled chicken strips with white rice, chopped onions, sage, green peppers, sweet peas, corn, and a little olive oil."

"That sounds delicious," Lashay began. "I could order Mexican food at Neri's or pizza from Nick's, so you don't have to cook."

"Thanks, but you've heard me talk about cooking at work ad nauseam," Jack said. "Tonight, I prove myself."

"Thank you, Jack. And, for the record, I never doubted your culinary skills."

"Wait until I use my special razor-sharp knives and flip pieces of chicken right into your mouth."

"Jack, you're kidding me, right?"

Jack tossed her a "just kidding you" smile and continued to toil in the kitchen.

As Jack prepared and cooked, they chatted about work, Allegra, Black Cobalt, and when the throuple with Ron and Kathy Marino and Lauren Garcia would explode.

Jack asked her opinion on his idea of getting media attention for Allegra to attract more shoppers and help boost sales at the store.

"Something in the Courier Post or Vineland Journal would help," Jack said.

Lashay didn't read the local papers, but she knew those were two that still existed in this digital world.

"How about even a TV spot on WPVI News?" asked Lashay. "I love Adam Joseph. He's cute."

WPVI was the Philadelphia ABC affiliate, and Joseph had been a meteorologist there for years. Lashay loved the way he smiled so effortlessly.

"You do realize he's gay?" Jack said as a question.

"A girl can dream, can't she?" Lashay hit back.

As they talked, Jack moved around his small kitchen like a top chef at an exclusive restaurant, cutting, dicing, shaking, adding, tasting, and preparing. He set the table with the only two plates he had, apparently: Bounty paper napkins on the left side of the plate, a fork and knife on the napkin, a water glass with a Phillies logo, and honey mustard and Balsamic vinaigrette dressing bottles.

"Dinner is served," Jack said with pride.

He placed a medium-sized glass bowl with salad in the middle of the small table, then motioned for her plate. He scooped the Chicken Rice Bowl into her plate and set it in front of her.

Once he filled his bowl, Jack sat down and said, "I'm not sure if you say grace or..."

"I used to," Lashay said. "But it didn't help, so I stopped."

"Okay, then, get ready to taste the most delicious meal you've had," Jack said and paused. "Since your last meal."

"Funny, Marsalis," she joked, then tried the chicken rice bowl.

"Oh my God, Jack," Lashay said. "This is amazing."

"I am going to take some salad with honey mustard dressing," Lashay said as she reached.

"I'm glad you like it," Jack said as he scooped a few mouthfuls.

"How do you learn to cook like this?" Lashay as she alternated between the wine, the chicken rice bowl, and the salad.

"I started to cook when I was married because my wife at the time didn't cook and didn't want to learn," Jack said.

"Practice makes delicious," Lashay said.

Maybe it was the wine because, by now, they had consumed almost the entire bottle, but Lashay decided this was the time to ask about Jack's past.

Lashay had almost finished the chicken rice bowl when she said, "Jack, although we know one another at work, I don't know anything about you, your family, and your past."

Lashay's right hand froze as she wondered if she had gone too far. Instead, Jack grinned, reached over, and laid his hand on hers.

"Of course, you've heard the rumors that I was in prison," Jack said.

Lashay stammered, "Jack, I – I mean, Harry was just talking nonsense."

"It's all right," Jack said calmly, putting her at ease. "I did spend time in jail for nearly two years."

Jack reached over, took the wine bottle, and poured the remainder of the bottle into their glasses. As he set down the empty bottle, Jack's hand grazed hers.

"If I am going to tell you the Jack Marsalis story, we may need more liquor," Jack joked, but without a smile. "My landlords upstairs are bourbon fans and are good about sharing."

Jack had released her hand, but Lashay reached out and grabbed his. His hands were lined by bulging veins and calluses on the pads of the palms.

"Jack, I know you. Nothing you can tell me will change how I feel about you."

Jack took his hand back, gulped the rest of the wine in his glass, and leaned back in his chair, "We are going to find out."

Chapter Fifteen

"No amount of guilt can change the past, and no amount of worrying can change the future."

Jack was glad he could finally tell his story. It wasn't a secret. But it was to the person he cared more about than anyone else. She had to know. This way, they'd know if they could move forward or remain co-workers.

Jack knew that Lashay also harbored secrets from her past, but that was her story to tell. Clearly, she wasn't ready now.

He was.

"How far back do you want me to go?" Jack asked.

"I don't want to hear how you were conceived," Lashay joked, "But, I don't know, you decide."

"If you fall asleep, that's on you."

"Fair enough," Lashay said. "I know you grew up in Washington Township."

Jack folded his hands on the small kitchen table.

"Growing up was uneventful and not much different from other suburban kids. We lived in a Cape Cod near Whitman Elementary School, where my mother worked as a cafeteria worker for 30 years. My father was a regional sales manager for a wallpaper company, so he was on the road almost every week. I was an only child, so it was me and my Mom most of the time."

"I'll bet you wowed all the girls in high school with all the sports you played?" Lashay said.

"I played football, wrestled, and even played on the volleyball team. I was a good but not great athlete. I enjoyed playing sports but didn't love it."

"When I graduated high school, my parents wanted me to attend Rutgers University in Camden. It was close by, so I could commute, and the tuition was in-state, so it was affordable."

"And they paid for your college tuition?" Lashay asked.

"There was a condition," Jack answered. "They wanted me to have skin in the game, so I had to get a job that was at least 20 but no more than 30 hours a week during college semesters and work full-time in the summer."

"Where'd you work?"

"My mother knew the manager of the Acme supermarket that was ten minutes away from the house, so I worked there for all four years, part-time during school and full-time in the summer and during school breaks."

"How'd you like working there?" Lashay asked.

"I loved it, and they liked me," Jack said. "After I graduated from Rutgers, they actually offered me a job as an assistant manager."

"In my last year of college, my father got cancer. Throat cancer. A smoker. He died two weeks before I graduated."

"Jack, I'm sorry," Lashay said.

"I spent most of that summer helping my mother cope with my father's death. He did all the bills and took care of their finances, so she had no idea what they had, what they didn't have, or how to manage their budget. I tried to look for a job, but it was tough with looking after her."

Jack flexed his hands a few times as his grip tightened from stress.

"In early August, my mother was feeling ill and went to the doctor. They diagnosed her with stage four ovarian cancer. By Halloween, she was gone. It was fast."

"Jack, I'm sorry." Lashay consoled him.

"We didn't have a big family, so once my parents were gone, I didn't feel the need to stay around there, so I found a job near Piscataway in Central Jersey. I have a Bachelor of Science degree with a specialty in management. I got a job as a shift manager for Grove Logistics, which was a huge company that had warehouses around the world."

"Jack, I always knew you were in management," Lashay said. "You're bossy."

Jack chuckled and said, "The next seven or eight years were good ones for me. I moved up several times to become the Regional Logistics Coordinator with Grove. I bought a house in Piscataway and married Tracey, a woman I met at a bar in Edison. We married about a year later."

"Jack, it's sounding good so far," Lashay said.

Jack took a breath. He felt his chest expand and contract. He flexed his fingers again and again and again.

"Myself and another manager, Dave Rendino, who was also a friend, ran the four warehouses in the Central Jersey area. He had two, and I had two."

Jack's eyes searched for Lashay's and found them. Her blue eyes relaxed him and prompted him to open up.

"One day, Dave stopped by my office in a panic. He told me that he had done something incredibly stupid and fudged the production numbers for his two warehouses. When I reported my numbers on Friday, the company would know that he had screwed with the production numbers to make himself look better than he really was."

Jack inhaled. He didn't exhale right away.

"He asked me to wait until Monday to send my production numbers to Corporate so he'd have time to prepare a report on what he had done and then confess to everything. Dave said that if Corporate found out what he had done, they would fire him and have him arrested. Technically, he was stealing."

"But if he filed a report admitting everything on his own before they found out, they'd just ask him to resign, and he'd still be able to find work at other warehouses."

"I had known Dave for several years. We lived close to each other, and our wives were friends. I just thought I was helping him to make things right."

"What happened? What did you do?"

Jack shrugged. "I said okay. I didn't file my production numbers on Friday, which wasn't that unusual to be a day or two late."

"What happened when your friend confessed?" Lashay asked.

Jack took the last swig of his wine.

"I think I may need that bourbon," Jack said.

"That Friday night, as I was walking to my car, a police car pulled up, two cops got out and arrested me."

"For what?" Lashay asked.

Jack tried to contain himself. Even after all these years, the anger boiled up quickly and torqued him.

"Apparently, Dave Rendino went to Grove Logistics in Corporate that Friday after I delayed my production report and told them he just found out that I was altering company data and fudging numbers."

"But you had the proof that Dave was doing that," Lashay said, her tone anxious and concerned.

Jack shook his head as he relived how stupid and naïve he was.

"This may be the stupidest thing I've ever done besides voting for Trump in 2016. And only then."

Lashay tilted her head and pursed her lips.

"That Thursday, Dave called me and asked me for my warehouse productivity and inventory system password. He said he got locked out because he was so stressed."

"Oh no, Jack."

"Oh yes, Jack," Jack slapped each temple with his hands.

"I gave him the password. He's my friend. Of course, he used my password to alter all the production numbers to point the blame at me."

Jack continued: "Anyway, I called my wife Tracey, but Dave had already called her with his bullshit story that I got caught stealing from the company and changing production numbers. She immediately left for her parents' house in Princeton and would not take any of my calls."

"Oh, Jack, I'm sorry."

"Lashay, she didn't love me. She loved the lifestyle of an upper-middle-class suburban wife. She didn't work, and we didn't have any kids. Tracey did lunch, tennis, Bunco with the girls, book club, Friday bridge, then Saturday morning mahjong."

"That sounds like a good life to me," Lashay said.

"Once I got arrested, I guess she figured that lifestyle was trashed, so she ghosted me and drained all our accounts. I didn't hear from her until her lawyer sent divorce papers to sign three years later. She tried to get the house, but I had to second mortgage it to pay my legal fees, so I ended up short selling it a few years later."

"So, what happened with the charges?" Lashay asked.

Jack had allowed this part of his life to dominate his thoughts for years. How many times, even now, had he woken up in the middle of the night and ended up staring at the ceiling and reliving those moments?

He'd go over how stupid he was. How easily he had been manipulated. How he let his anger get the best of him.

"I sold and mortgaged everything I had to get a good lawyer. He got me out of county jail in Woodbury after two months. After I told him what happened, he started investigating Dave, and what he and his people found persuaded Grove to drop the charges against me."

"That's good. What happened to your friend or ex-friend? Or total jerkoff?" Lashay asked.

"My lawyer's investigator discovered that Dave was selling merchandise from the two warehouses he managed to a Russian crime syndicate. He was arrested and charged with multiple crimes."

Lashay smiled. "Justice prevailed. Is he still in prison?"

Jack pushed back his chair from the table. He spread his feet apart and clasped his hands together. His eyes focused on the cheap laminate floor.

"One night after Dave had been arrested and made bail, he came to the cheap motel I was staying at on the Pike. You know, the one across from the DMV. He begged me to testify on his behalf. He wanted me to be a character witness for him because his lawyer said it would sway the jury."

Jack shifted in his chair.

"It's all right," Lashay's voice said, trying to soothe him.

Jack stood up and started pacing.

"He kept asking, and I kept saying no. He begged, and then he begged some more. Then he threatened me. And I lost it."

"What did you do, Jack?"

"I beat him. Bad. If our voices weren't so loud and other people hadn't heard us and came to break it up, I think I would have...."

Jack put his hands in his face.

"What, Jack?" Lashay asked.

"I'm pretty sure I would have killed him. In fact, I'm sure of it."

Lashay stood up, approached Jack, and hugged him.

"You've been torturing yourself all these years," Lashay said.

Jack felt the warmth of her body and the reassurance of her touch.

"What happened then, Jack?"

Jack went limp and slid away from Lashay.

"I was arrested and charged with second-degree aggravated assault. The charge carried a four-year prison sentence and a $10,000 fine. I sold my car, whatever jewelry Tracey had left behind, my Grove Stock, cashed in my 401(k), and used the money from my parent's life insurance policy so that my lawyer got the charge knocked down to a fourth-degree aggravated assault charge, which I pleaded guilty to."

"Oh, Jack."

Jack started to clean up the table to keep his body busy while his mind raced wildly.

"I spent 23 months and 17 days in Bayside State Prison, which is in Maurice Township on Route 47 on the way to Wildwood."

"How was it?"

"It wasn't that bad. It was a minimum-security prison, and we raised and milked cows there."

"What happened after you got out?" Lashay asked.

"I never realized how being an ex-con made life after prison so incredibly difficult," Jack said.

"I decided to go back to where I grew up. I got out of prison with nothing and was lucky enough to get a room at this boarding house in Woodbury, where every person had a small room and shared a bathroom with everyone on the floor. I thought prison was bad. There, at least, you had your own toilet in the cell."

"So, what did you do once you got out?"

"I finally got a job as a markout person for this company in Washington Township. You know, the people who spray the paint and place the flags so you don't cut a cable, water, or gas line. It didn't pay much, kept me busy, and was pretty easy work. I was doing fine there until the company discovered that I had lied on my job application and omitted my prison experience."

"Was lying on your application the only way you could find work?" Lashay asked.

"This doesn't make it right, but yes. I filled out hundreds of applications when I got out of jail, but nothing. The companies never told me it was about my prison time, but I knew. So, I lied and got that job. When they found out, they fired me for lying on my job application."

"Where'd you go from there?" Lashay asked.

"I learned my lesson and included my prison time on the application and found a job as an appliance repairman with Mantua Appliance."

"Jack is a Maytag repairman," Lashay joked. Jack realized she was trying to keep it light.

"I loved that job. They gave you a truck that you could take home. I parked it in the lot of the boarding house, and every morning, I'd leave to do my repair calls. It was a great job. I liked most of the customers. I liked helping them. And it paid well, and I did okay in tips."

"I feel a BUT coming on," Lashay said.

"Lashay, I was desperate," Jack implored. "I was going to get kicked out of the boarding house, and I'd be homeless."

Jack started pacing again, and the apartment wasn't large enough to go very far.

"Jack, far be it for me to judge you or anyone else," Lashay said. "If you knew..."

Jack waited for her to continue, but she regained control. He wondered if his revelations from his past would encourage her to do the same. As tired as he was from working on the backyard pavers and retaining walls all day, this confession of his ugly past had exhausted him.

"After a year, they fired me when they discovered that I had lied about the repair certifications I claimed I had earned."

"Jack, I'm not judging," Lashay reassured him. "We all do things in our lives that we wish we could take back. "

"There are so many…" Lashay began but stopped.

"Even without those certifications, I was still their best repairman," Jack insisted.

"Then I found a job as a manager at a self-storage facility in Williamstown on the Pike. It was a great job and enabled me to move out of the boarding house, which was closing anyway, to get knocked down and replaced by an assisted living facility. I found a roommate who worked as an HVAC repair tech, and we rented a two-bedroom in Williamstown."

"How did that work out?"

"He was quiet, kept to himself, and was a great cook. He mentored me on my way to being a top chef."

"I'm surprised the chef hat will fit on top of that inflated head," Lashay joked.

"I worked there for two years," Jack continued. "Then I reported these suspicious guys who were selling stolen merchandise out of one of the storage units."

"Jack Marsalis, private eye," Lashay said.

Jack smiled and tossed up his hands.

"How did I know that the son of the storage facility's owner was the one who was selling stolen merchandise?"

"Fired?" Lashay asked, curling an eyebrow.

"That day," Jack said, his forehead cresting and falling with stressful memories.

"That's when I filled out an application at HomeMaxx, met Tyler, and found a home."

"Around the same time, I met the Szczesny's and got this place," Jack added, smiling broadly.

"The rest is history," Jack added.

Lashay stood, signaling it was time for her to leave. Jack tried to read her face for emotion, thoughts, or just general revulsion. She faced him with the kitchen table between them. Jack didn't know what to say, so he stood frozen in silence.

"Jack, thank you very much for dinner," Lashay said. "I learned a lot tonight, and most importantly, you are an excellent chef."

Jack laughed. "Wow, you are easy to please."

As Lashay turned to leave, she stopped.

"Jack, thank you for sharing. You're more courageous than I am."

"Does anything you heard here tonight change your opinion of Jack Marsalis?" he asked.

Lashay looked away as if she was ruminating and replied, "What I learned is that a man I care about suffered from rotten luck, made a few bad choices, and has busted his butt to reclaim his life."

Lashay stepped toward Jack. Her right hand touched Jack's cheek softly.

Then she kissed him. Softly, Tenderly.

"See you on Monday, Jack."

The door opened and closed. Jack touched the doorknob on the inside.

He took a deep breath.

His secret was out. Exposed.

Maybe he could really start over.

Chapter Sixteen

"**A** **cat has absolute emotional honesty: human beings, for one reason or another, may hide their feelings, but a cat does not.**" **– Ernest Hemingway**

The cat left the safety of its bed in the outside garden area along the fence to visit with humans. Since her two humans weren't there, she decided to visit other humans. She had to wait for a human to walk through the doors that somehow opened, and she scampered into the place with the high shelves, bright lights, and walls of human things.

She made her way to the area where large cans and brushes filled the shelves. She spotted two humans, male and female, looking at paper.

She introduced herself by rubbing against their legs, marking these humans as hers. She left her scent on their clothes as a sign of ownership and to warn other cats that these humans now belonged to her.

The humans reciprocated by bending down and scratching under her neck and making sweet human sounds that comforted her.

Matt and Nahtalya DiTomasso felt something around their legs.

"Matt, look at the beautiful cat," Nahtalya said.

"She's a Calico," Matt said as he squatted to get closer to the cat's vantage point.

He used the tips of his fingers to scratch under her neck. The cat responded by purring and doing a figure eight around his two legs.

"Do you think she's lost?" Nahtalya asked.

The DiTomassos knew about cats, currently owning two, Dahlin, a cream-colored cutie, and Aspen, a tabby who was shy around any humans except them.

Matt and Nahtalya were in the store trying to choose a paint color for the kitchen.

Matt came to HomeMaxx often. He was an HVAC technician for Vineland Plumbing, HVAC, and Refrigeration, and too often, his company didn't stock the parts he needed.

"I know Jack, who works here," Matt told Nahtalya. "He told me about this cat they rescued and are feeding here."

"Ah, that's so nice," Nahtalya responded as she bent down to rub the cat along its flanks. "I love Calico cats. I read up on them. Did you know that Calico cats are the official state cat of Maryland, and only two other states have state cats?"

"You're ready in case they ask about cats at next week's Trivia Night at the Main Street Brewery," Matt said, his eyebrows dancing as he spoke.

Nahtayla ignored him.

"No, it was fascinating. Due to their rare nature, Calico cats are lucky charms around the world, and adopting one can bring good fortune."

"Nat, we are NOT taking this cat," Matt insisted. "Two are enough. Besides, Aspen barely tolerates Dahlin."

By the time they finished their discussion, the cat was gone.

"Hey, where'd the cat go?" Nahtalya asked, obviously disappointed.

"Probably overheard you were planning a kidnapping and split," Matt said.

Jim Schultes checked out a new front door lock with a keypad in the hardware aisle when he felt something brush past his right ankle. He jumped back and looked down to see a tricolor cat winding its way around his right ankle and then his left.

"Hi, kitty," Jim said.

Jim was not a cat or dog person. The cat apparently either didn't know that or didn't care. The white, orange, and black cat with a sprinkling of beige on its underbelly nuzzled his pant cuffs.

"Allegra likes you," the HomeMaxx associate said.

"You know this cat?" Jim asked.

The HomeMaxx associate was short, with a substantial belly and a crooked smile. His name tag said, Harry.

"It's become like our store cat," Harry said. "It's a female, and two of our associates started taking care of it when it showed up here."

"It's strange that she's rubbing against me," Jim said. "I've been married for 46 years with four kids, and in all that time, we never owned a dog or a cat."

"Allegra doesn't know that," Harry answered. "And I don't think she cares."

"She likes you," Harry added, punctuating his words with a forced smile.

A few minutes later, in Flooring, Mike and Stacey Childs walked the hardwood and laminate floor sample aisle, rubbing the samples like a genie's lamp.

"Whadda think?" Mike asked his wife.

Stacey took her time assessing textures, wood grains, and prices.

As Stacey evaluated the floors, a cat jumped up on the shelf above the flooring samples.

Mike jumped back. "What was that?"

Stacey's features opened like a rose in bloom as she admired the tricolor cat that had presented itself to them. The cat let out a soft but plaintive meow that Stacey thought meant, "I need attention. Now!"

"It's a cat, Mike," Stacey said as she reached into the shelf, picked up the cat, and held it.

The cat began to purr and sink herself into Stacey's arms.

"What's a cat doing in HomeMaxx?" Mike asked.

"It's either a runaway, feral, or lost," Stacey said.

"The cat likes you, Stac," Mike said as the cat relaxed in her arms like a newborn hugging its mommy.

Several customers now joined Mike and Stacey as they admired the Calico cat.

A Black woman about 40 with blondish cornrows said, "Can I pet her?"

"Sure," Stacey said. "She's not mine. I don't know where the cat came from."

"I do," said Jim Schultes as he walked by with a Schlage keypad lock in his hand.

"The guy in Hardware said it's the store's cat. He said the cat showed up around a week ago, and then a couple of associates started taking care of it."

"This would make a great story for the Jersey section," the woman said to her companion, a younger Black woman with two buns and curls on either side of her face.

"You ladies from the Courier Post?" Mike asked.

"No, the Philadelphia Inquirer," the woman with the bangs and curls answered.

She spotted a HomeMaxx associate and yelled, "Hey, excuse me. Can you come over here?"

Stacey still held the cat, which seemed content in her arms.

Meanwhile, the 30-ish couple from Paint came over, and Nahtalya said, "We just saw that cat in the paint department."

"Can I help you?" the associate named Lauren said. "Everything all right?"

The older Black woman with the cornrows took out a business card from her jeans back pocket and said, "I'm Gwen Phillips with the Philadelphia Inquirer Living section. This is Audie Ward."

"I'm only an associate, so –" Lauren stammered.

Gwen Phillips waved her hand. Audie smiled to reset the tone and calm the worker's anxiety.

"Don't worry," Gwen said. "This isn't a sting from Sixty Minutes."

"But I'd like to do a story about this cat for the newspaper," Gwen said.

"Here she comes," Stacey announced as the cat leaped from her arms and began to do a figure eight around the legs of Gwen and Audie.

"This cat is too cute," Audie said as she bent down to pick up the cat.

The cat responded by relaxing in Audie's arms, laying her on her right forearm and purring.

"The cat's name is Allegra," Lauren said, visibly relaxed that she wasn't trapped in some Dateline exposé. A random thought that the news was doing an investigation into their throuple did cross her mind.

"I can give your card to Jack or Lashay, the two associates who found and care for the cat," Lauren said. "Of course, they'll have to clear it with our store manager."

"Of course," Gwen said. "Will they be in tomorrow?"

"I don't think the cat will last in the store that long before some customer takes it home," Matt DiTomasso said.

The other customers milling around – Nahtalya, Mike and Stacey Childs, and Jim Schultes – nodded in agreement.

"I'll be in tomorrow, and so will they," Lauren reassured them.

"Okay, great. Can you give me someone's number?" Gwen asked.

"I have Lashay's number," Lauren said. "You should talk to her."

"Why," Audie asked. "Her name sounds black, and we're black. Is that why?"

Everyone tensed up except for the cat.

Gwen said, "She's just messing with you."

The smiles from the customers returned, and the cat jumped out of Audie's hands and followed a tall man with overalls, a stringy red beard, and a black hat that read in white lettering, Gods, Guns, and Freedom.

"I guess the cat doesn't discriminate," Gwen chuckled.

The cat followed the footsteps of the man in the narrow aisles of the Tools department until the man felt the cat at his feet, stopped, looked down, spotted the cat, and used his boot to shoo it away.

"Get out of here, stupid cat," the man grunted.

As Matt and Nahtalya DiTomasso, Mike and Stacey Childs, Jim Schultes, Karen Garcia, Gwen Phillips, and Audie Ward looked on, Harry asked, "Who doesn't like a cat?"

"Somebody who hates everybody and everything," Gwen Phillips said.

Chapter Seventeen

"Most of us are just a few bad breaks away from being homeless." Becky Roesler.

Jack had just finished cutting the lawn on a warm April Sunday. The Szczesny's had purchased a riding mower several years ago. Jack enjoyed using it. It was a 46-inch Cub Cadet XT1 LT46 lawn mower with a 23 HP/725 cc Kohler engine and a hydrostatic transmission that eliminated shifting. Jack rode in comfort with a 15-inch high-back seat.

Wally and Jackie had left earlier in the day to kayak at Scotland Run Park in Clayton. Scotland Run Park was the largest of the Gloucester County parks, spanning more than 1,300 acres. Eighty-acre Wilson Lake offered passive recreation opportunities like fishing, boating, and nature observation. Jack had fished there numerous times and even went out on Harry's bass boat before sunrise and caught largemouth bass, chain pickerel, black crappie, and even channel catfish.

After cleaning the mower deck and storing the mower in the garage, Jack sat on the deck in a white Adirondack chair with a beer in hand. The sweat on his body evaporated and cooled him off as he relaxed in the shade. After a full week of work at HomeMaxx and working at Tyler's house all day yesterday, Jack's 50-year-old body felt a lot older.

What will happen when I'm 70 years old?

Jack had no family left. His parents had died. He was an only child, and Jack had lost touch with his parents' siblings. Would he be some weird old guy staggering down Delsea Drive in Clayton to the Heritages convenience store in a dirty flannel shirt and sweatpants on a steamy August day?

Jack thought of Gus Burdette. His wife had died, and he was estranged from his son and alienated from the rest of his extended family; Gus was in a similar situation.

In one of those strange consequences, when you think about someone, and they show up, Gus Burdette pulled up in his black F-250 Ford pickup. Jack watched him exit the truck and walk toward him. After an adult life of hard physical work, Gus's body showed all that wear and tear. He walked with his shoulders hunched and back stiff. Creaky knees forced his gait to be more of a shuffle than a stride, and too much time in the sun jackhammering and then pouring concrete had created fissures in his features.

"Gus, you old dog," Jack smiled and greeted him. "Beer?"

"You have to ask?" Gus joked as he stepped on the deck and sat in the Adirondack chair to Jack's right.

Jack had brought out a cooler with ice and pulled out a Rolling Rock Extra Pale beer in a smoked green bottle.

"Going all out, Jack," Gus said as he reached to accept the bottle. "Rolling Rock is like dollar store beer."

Gus collapsed in the chair to Jack's right.

"Hey, I work on HomeMaxx," Jack chided him. "I have to economize wherever I can."

"Tell me about it," Gus answered, clinking his bottle to Jack's.

"Finished that concrete sidewalk?" Jack asked.

Gus took a long guzzle, wiped his chin with his sweat-stained shirt, and answered, "I hired the kid, Noah, to help."

"How'd he do?" Jack asked, finishing his beer, and then he took out one more from his cooler.

I'm replacing my electrolytes.

Gus laughed and shook his head. "The kid reminds me of me when I was his age. He works hard, doesn't complain, and learns fast. You tell him something once, and he's got it mastered."

"Glad to hear that," Jack said, delighted that Noah had impressed Gus, which was no mean feat.

"Jack, you won't believe it," Gus began. "The kid noticed that the customer's Lexus in the driveway had a loose heat shield in the undercarriage. He told the customer, and with the customer's consent, he crawled underneath and fixed it."

"Geez, Gus, you better be careful. If the kid works with you again, customers may think you actually are a nice guy."

They both laughed.

As the April sun tickled the tops of the pitch pine trees, it headed inevitably below the horizon. Both men sat in silence, nursing their aging bodies.

Gus finished his beer. Even when savoring a beer to quench thirst, Gus had that "I'd like to punch you in the face" glare. Jack remembered visiting Betty as her cancer progressed. At that point, she was bedridden, and Gus had been hired by HomeMaxx about a year ago. Gus was her caregiver and doted on her.

"Can I get you water? Are you comfortable?" Gus had said.

When Betty thanked him and said no and then yes, she waited for him to leave the bedroom. Jack sat by her side in a wicker chair that Betty explained she had found in an antique store in downtown Pitman.

"He's a good man, Jack," Betty said in a hushed voice as her strength slowly ebbed away. "He's always had that mean resting face, but underneath, he's a sweetheart."

Jack chuckled. "I'm sure that's true, Betty. But Gus does a very good job hiding his more sensitive side."

Betty attempted to laugh but only managed to grin.

"I'm sure he's a terror at work to his co-workers, bosses, and customers."

Jack smiled and reached out and held her hand.

"Jack, I feel like Gus and I have known you our whole lives," Betty squeezed his hand. "I feel like I can ask that you look out for Gus after I'm gone."

"Betty, you'll get – "

Betty squeezed his hand again.

"Jack, I know what's coming. I think I'm as ready as one can be. But Gus isn't prepared. He will need a friend like you. He's tough but not strong. He pushes away those he loves because he's afraid. I talk to our son Michael several times weekly but can't let Gus know. Even since Michael told us he was gay at his graduation, Gus drove him away and refuses to talk with him."

Jack could only nod. "You can count on me."

"Maybe my death will bring them together, but if it doesn't, I'm asking you to try and do that."

"God knows how I've messed up my life," Jack said. "But Betty, you have my word."

"Hey, Jack, another beer," Gus demanded.

Jack's memory faded as he returned to the deck and Gus.

"Sorry," Jack said. "Getting old, you know."

"Jack," Gus said, leaning forward in the chair. "I know the kid's a fruitcake, but he's a good kid with a great work ethic."

Jack put down his second Rolling Rock and waited for Gus to continue. He knew what was coming.

"Listen, Jack, I hate to see the kid living out of his car in the nursing home parking lot. His plan to save enough money to rent a place will never happen. He'll never afford the security deposit, first and last month's rent, and the monthly rent itself."

"I agree," Jack said. "Noah reminds me of someone."

Gus sat up in his chair. His features tensed, as did the rest of his weary body.

"Marsalis, do not say it."

"Gus, come on," Jack replied, not matching Gus's intensity but remaining relaxed. "Noah reminds me of Michael, your son."

Jack tensed his body just in case Gus attacked him. He didn't think Burdette would react violently, but Jack knew that family issues burned the hottest.

Instead of anger, Gus voiced quiet regret.

"So many times during the day, I take out my phone and find his number in my Contacts," Gus said, remorse mixed with sorrow.

"But I can never hit the SEND button to call him."

"I get that, Gus," Jack said.

"The way I acted after Betty's wake. I don't know how he —."

"Are you afraid Michael will hang up on you?" Jack asked.

Gus finished his second bottle of beer and inspected it like a fortune teller's crystal ball.

"Jack, all those years. It was Betty. She was the one who took care of me, raised Michael, took care of the house and all the bills."

"And she worked mornings at Liscio's Bakery in Glassboro before going to the cafeteria at Hurffville School," Gus added.

Jack saw his opening. "I think Betty would want you to invite Noah to live with you."

Gus stood up. "What the hell are you talking about, Marsalis?"

"I came here to ask you to invite Noah to live with you," Gus stomped around in a circle on the deck.

"Gus, you've seen my place," Jack began, remaining calm. "Have you forgotten how small it is? Go ahead, walk around down there now. You can walk through my place in about ten seconds."

"Jack, are you going to let that kid live in his car?" Gus answered, refusing to consider Jack's idea.

"Gus, I couldn't even if I wanted to," Jack said.

"That sounds like bullshit."

"The Szczesny's have sold the restaurant. They're retiring. And moving."

Jack let that information sink in for a few seconds. Gus tossed his empty beer bottle on the deck in a plastic recycling can. He put his hands on his hips.

"When are they moving?" Gus asked.

"They say they'll give me time to find a place," Jack began. "But I get the sense they'd like to move as soon as possible. With today's housing market, someone will buy this place days after it's listed."

"Your idea of Noah living here won't work. Plus, I can't explain to the Szczesny's that I am looking for another apartment, but I just let this kid move in with me."

"Sorry, Jack. I didn't know."

Gus paced around the deck like a wild animal suddenly caged. Jack understood his storm of feelings. He had come here to ask Jack to take

Noah in and now realized that his house was the only option except living in a Honda.

Jack knew that Gus needed to work through this.

"Jack, I can't take the homo thing," Gus said as if he was pleading with Jack.

"When I was a kid in Elmer, we beat up fairies like Noah," Gus admitted.

"That was then. This is now," Jack said. "Growing up in Washington Township, I had a neighbor boy my age who had development issues. Me and Greg Hanson used to call him retard at school and flick his ears with our fingers."

"I'm so ashamed of that now," Jack confessed. "I've learned how bad that was and is. I think I knew it back then, but I somehow enjoyed torturing the kid."

"Pretty bad, huh?" Jack admitted, a wave of shame rolling over him.

Gus continued to pace, shaking his hand at Jack's confession.

"Marsalis, you were an asshole as a kid."

"Just like you, Gus," Jack countered. "You don't have to be an asshole as an adult. A much older adult, I might add."

That comment elicited a faint smile from Gus.

"But what if he tries his homo stuff on me?" Gus demanded.

Jack laughed. "Gus, stick to watching the Game Show Network and stop watching those twenty-four news networks where they spread that crap."

Gus paced faster around the table and chairs.

"I don't know, Jack. What would people at work say? If Harry found out, he'd blab to everybody in the store. People would think I'd become a rump ranger."

"Jesus Christ, Gus," Jack said, incredulous that Gus had said that.

"Don't tell anybody then. Tell Noah to keep it a secret and drive your own vehicles to work."

Gus threw up his hands.

"Marsalis, have you ever sold timeshares? I come over here to get you to take Noah in, and you fuckin' suck me into taking him into my house."

Jack smiled and leaned back in the chair. "Betty would be proud of you."

"I'm going to need another beer," Gus said. "Maybe more."

138

"I'm going to need another beer," Gus said. "Maybe more."

Chapter Eighteen

"We will provide customer-valued solutions with the best prices and offer products and services to make HomeMaxx the best choice for home improvement."

Now that April brought warmer weather, Lashay could spend her weekend tending her garden and taking walks while listening to her favorite podcasts. Lashay's mobile home park, Lake Acres, consisted of only 38 mobile homes, so Lashay couldn't walk more than a mile, even if she had circled the park three times. Lashay walked down Lake Avenue and then onto Delsea Drive, a main thoroughfare that ran 75 miles through South Jersey from Brooklawn to Wildwood at the Jersey Shore.

Since there were sidewalks into Vineland, Lashay felt safe walking for miles, usually doing three miles down into Vineland and then back. She had been doing this since she lived here and tried to walk either before or after work, depending on her shift that week.

After a few years, Lashay had come to know some of the people who lived on Delsea Drive, on the sections of the road that were mostly residential. There was a retired chicken farmer named Rooster Red, a 70ish man with flaming red hair, who regaled her with tales of when Vineland was called "The Egg Basket of America" because the poultry industry dominated the economy.

Then there was Pete Number 2, who sat in his wheelchair on his porch almost every day, regardless of the weather.

"You're looking fine today, Miss Jones," Pete Number 2 would call out.

Lashay would offer him her best smile, twist her hips more than usual, and call out, "Thank you, Pete Number One."

"I'm Pete Number Two because Pete Number One next door moved in two weeks before I did 50 years ago." Pete Number Two would clarify.

"Well, you're number one in my heart," Lashay would respond in her sweetest voice.

Lashay loved to garden, a holdover from her former life, which seemed like decades ago. She loved to dig in the dirt, plant her annuals, and nurture them to maturity. Lashay usually followed the rule that you don't plant until Mother's Day, which meant she turned the soil, added lime, trimmed her perennials that survived the winter and mulched.

As she walked into the employee locker room and punched in, Lashay rushed to the outside garden area to visit Allegra. The cat was there on a section of cedar fence, meowing as she approached.

She picked up the Calico and hugged her, and the cat responded by kneading her forearms and burying her head into Lashay's chest.

"I missed you, girl," Lashay said, as she did to her daughter before—-.

"Who's hogging the kitty," Lashay heard Jack call out.

He turned the corner, and her face brightened when she saw him.

"Did you speak to Harry this morning?" Jack asked.

Lashay thought it was strange that they didn't engage in their usual "what did you do over the weekend" banter.

Allegra jumped out of her lap and wrapped herself around Jack's jeans and his Red wing boots.

"Teacher's pet," she scolded him.

"Lashay, Harry says that the reporter from the Philadelphia Inquirer, Gwen Phillips, is here with a photographer," Jack said, his face stone-cold and serious.

"She wants you," Jack said. "She's at the customer service desk talking to Darla."

"Thanks, but it looks like you have something else to tell me," Lashay inquired.

Jack's features went dark, and Lashay recognized fear on his face.

"The CEO of Black Cobalt, Bernard Snow, and his son Jacob are here. They're in Tyler's office, and word is they are inspecting the store."

"Holy shit," was the only response Lashay could think of.

"You take Allegra to the reporter, and I'll see how I can help Tyler," Jack said.

"Now that I know your backstory. You were a big-time manager. You like giving orders," Lashay chided him.

"Get your ass in gear, Jones," Jack joked as he walked away.

She saluted him. "Yes, sir, General Marsalis."

"Don't you forget it," Jack said, feigning a stern face.

Tyler Rodgers spotted no signs of humanity in the dark, deep-seat eyes of Black Cobalt CEO Bernard Snow. The man stood in front of Tyler's desk wearing a custom-fitted black twill weave business suit with matching deep blue pocket square, gold cufflinks and brushed leather-laced Oxford shoes from Prada. Tyler had seen them once in Manhattan and walked away when he discovered they were $1,200.

Snow's son, Jacob, wore a similarly expensive suit without the protective coating of arrogance.

There's hope for this kid, Tyler thought. Maybe.

"My son and I are going to walk around the store and find out why this store is losing money every month," the elder Snow announced.

"Would you like me to escort you, Mr. Snow?" Tyler asked, trying to sound as obsequious as possible.

His inside voice, however, was screaming, "What a complete asshole. What does this guy know about a home improvement store?"

The elder Snow waved his hand to dismiss Tyler.

"No. We want to see why this store cannot make a profit," Bernard Shaw said, as Tyler knew there was no way to make a profit after selling the land the store sat on and charging the store a two percent reinvestment fee every month.

Before Black Cobalt, the store's net profit margin averaged four percent for the last decade. However, the exorbitant rent and reinvestment fee have stolen that profit and put the store in the red.

As Snow and his son marched out of his office, Tyler knew their visit today was simply performance art. Black Cobalt would close the stores in a few months, sell off all the assets, and make a healthy profit.

Meanwhile, all the employees would suddenly be jobless with no severance and a loss of their 401k plan contributions and earnings since Black Cobalt had revised the plan's investment portfolio so that employee money was in Black Cobalt-related investments.

When Snow and his son came in earlier, they didn't say hello to Ellen Cleary and didn't acknowledge her on their way out, even as she said, "Gentleman, have a great day."

Tyler stood in the open doorway of his office and looked at all three women in the outside office.

"Ladies, if I were you, I'd start looking for another job in the next few months."

Tyler closed the office door, went back to his desk,, and dialed a number on the office landline.

"Sid Nelson, please," Tyler said. "I'll hold."

"Hello, Tyler," the voice on the other line said.

"Sid, I'll take the job if you can wait until October first."

There was silence on the other end of the line, and then, "Tyler, I know that you're loyal to the people in your store. I respect that. Excell Hardware really wants you. I'm going to give you a tip that's going to help you change that date."

"That's the Black Cobalt line on the stores," Tyler answered. "They'll close the entire chain of stores by sometime in October if we are not profitable. And Sid, you know, with Black Cobalt, that's impossible."

"Tyler, here's my tip. Make your start date August first," Sid said.

"Sid, do you know something?" Tyler asked, the left hand holding the phone receiver trembling ever so slightly.

"Black Cobalt will close stores in stages and not all at once," Sid said calmly and directly. "Your store is the first to go sometime in August."

Tyler stood frozen, standing at his desk, the phone receiver to his ear.

"Tyler, still there?" Sid asked.

"I have this on good authority," Sid went on. "One of our top suppliers had dinner with Bernard Snow in Philadelphia last week. Snow had too many Jamesons and let it slip."

Tyler absorbed all this new and shocking information, unable to process it.

"Tyler. Tyler. Tyler," Sid Nelson said.

"Yeah, Sid," Tyler stuttered. "I'm here."

"So —" Sid said but more like a question.

"Yes, July 1," Tyler answered, sounding more like he was announcing a funeral date than the first day of an exciting new job as a region manager with much upside on compensation.

"And Dave Maloney will take some of my best people from the store?" Tyler asked.

Sid Nelson's voice was soothing and reassuring.

"Tyler, this is a win-win," Sid said. "Dave wants to retire and run his store in Florida. He needs good people to run his store. Dave tells me he loves Jack and Lashay and will take Ellen, Darla, and Christine, too."

"I'm in," Tyler said, still numb from this new information.

"Great," Sid said. "Welcome to the Excell Hardware family. I want you and Pam to fly to Downers Grove, Illinois, in the next few weeks to finalize everything and meet the Excell management team."

"Thank you, Sid," Tyler said. "I'll talk to Pam tonight and get back to you."

"Sid, Snow, and his son are here now, touring the store," Tyler told him.

Sid Nelson let out a hearty laugh.

"Bernard Snow doesn't know the first thing about the home improvement industry," Sid said, contempt in his tone.

"He's like a vulture, sizing up his prey before it's even dead, and then when it is, he'll pick the bones clean."

Lashay met Gwen Phillips, the Philadelphia Inquirer reporter at the customer service desk. She carried Allegra with her, who remained comfortable in her arms. In a grey business suit, Phillips introduced her to the photographer, Grady Hawkins.

"Mr. Hawkins is an excellent photographer who is anxious to capture some photos with Allegra traveling the store and interacting with customers," Phillips said.

"Hi, I'm Lashay Jones," she said to Hawkins, the photographer, while nodding toward the reporter.

"How do we make that happen?" Phillips asked.

Lashay tossed out a big smile. She caressed Allegra one more time and then put her down on the sealed concrete floor.

Allegra immediately took off for the Paint department while the reporter and photographer watched.

"I think you two better move if you want a story," Lashay chuckled.

To Gwen: "I'll fill you in while we watch her tour the store and greet customers."

Hawkins bent down, pointed his camera, and started firing.

"Today, I love my job," he said.

The three of them took off, and Allegra leaped onto the paint counter to say hello to a young couple waiting for their paint cans to mix.

Tyler had warned Jack that Bernard and Jacob Snow were on the floor. This week, Jack was assigned to Doors & Windows. He was finishing up with a man in a Philly Fanatic hat when Jack spotted the Snows coming his way.

"You don't need a new storm door," Jack explained to the man with a furry green baseball mascot on his head.

"This bottom storm closer kit will do the trick. A guy on YouTube calls himself 'The Doorman.' Search for him and find the video on the bottom closer kit. He can walk you through it. I promise you can do it."

"Thanks, man," the man replied, and as he walked away, "Go Phillies."

"Suarez is going to pitch a shutout tonight, and Harper is going to bomb one over the center field fence," Jack said.

"Mr. Marsalis," a voice behind him said.

Jack was confronted by two unsmiling faces, one old and one young, who viewed him as a lion and saw an antelope.

Jack didn't want to play any games.

"Mr. Snow and Mr. Snow," Jack said, trying to balance friendly with being obsequious.

They stood side by side, ignoring his greeting until Bernard, the older man, said, "We just came from the Tools department and spoke to Harry. Apparently, people who work here seem to have time for everything but work. One woman from Paint and another married woman from Window Treatments are in a three-way sexual relationship with one of the husbands. "

Before Jack could speak, Snow said, "And you are apparently seeing a woman from the Garden department."

Jack resisted his initial temptation to punch the elder Snow in the face and said, "Do you normally believe gossip from people you just met, Mr. Snow? That doesn't seem like something a successful man like you would do?"

"Very good, Mr. Marsalis," Bernard Snow retorted. "Tyler said you were the best employee here."

"Well, Mr. Snow, I can rattle off the names of many employees here who are very good at their jobs."

The younger Snow spoke in such a way that Jack suspected a setup.

"Can I call you Jack?"

"Sure."

"My father and I met a couple at my in-law's house, Janice and Fred. The couple raved about this worker they met at HomeMaxx, who saved them the cost of a new washing machine by explaining that the dampers needed repair."

"I remember them from last week. They're a nice couple. I also recommended the repair guy. He's the best," Jack answered.

He knew where this was headed, but he was prepared.

"Just wondering why you would do that and lose HomeMaxx the revenue from that customer purchasing a brand new washing machine from us," Jacob Snow asked, more as an accusation than a fact.

Jack knew that they had rehearsed this interrogation.

"My job is to help customers," Jack said. "It's called customer service. If I recall, it's part of HomeMaxx's mission statement."

"Our mission is to sell more products and services and make more money," Jacob Snow said, obviously learning this from listening to his father drone on about it since he was in diapers.

Bernard Snow crossed his arms, and Jacob Snow stood a little straighter.

"Actually, I agree with you," Jack began, "but our methods couldn't be different."

"Why is that?" Bernard Snow asked.

Jack stepped back three paces to the Doors & Windows computer, typed on the keyboard, made a few mouse clicks, and then smiled.

"Sure, Janice and Fred Moore," Jack said, looking at the computer screen and attempting to control his urge to smirk.

"Why would they be in the HomeMaxx system?" Jacob Snow asked. "They didn't buy anything."

Jack looked up and stared at the Snows.

"Because," Jack emphasized and then paused. "The Moores came in after their washer was fixed and bought hardwood flooring and a new dishwasher from us."

The Snows didn't respond. This was the CEO and his son. Jack knew they were accustomed to being the smartest people in the room. And when they weren't, they expected the others in the meeting to treat them as such, anyway.

Jack admitted to himself that these two were indeed sharp businesspeople who commanded respect when they spoke. Despite their moral defects, these two knew their stuff. Sadly for HomeMaxx and its employees and customers, the Snows only cared about extracting as much profit as possible from the home improvement chain.

They were like vampires who knew they were inherently evil but viewed ordinary humans as weak and dense.

"You see, gentlemen," Jack decided a lecture was needed.

At this point, he thought the store and the whole chain were doomed anyway.

I'm about to be homeless soon. Might as well add jobless.

"Customers respond to great service with loyalty to the HomeMaxx brand. Selling them something they don't need or want is really a one-time proposition. They'll discover they've been duped and never come back to the store again. Not even for one screw or bolt."

Bernard Snow had one hip pointed toward the exit when he clapped back.

"Your pet theory doesn't work because this store is losing money. Every month. Every week. Every day. Shit, the store probably lost several thousand dollars while I was talking to you."

Jacob Snow said nothing but glared at him. Jack assumed he did that a lot around his father. It was like a "That goes double for me."

The Snows turned and left the store, never looking anywhere but straight ahead.

When the doors opened, a black SUV limousine pulled up, and the two men were gone.

Jack heard a voice behind him as he watched them exit the store.

"Jack, how the hell are you?" the voice asked in a Spanish accent.

Jack turned to see a short man, roundish with a scraggly beard and shaved head.

"Luis, how are you?" Jack brightened up.

They shook hands. Jack hadn't seen Luis in over a month when he stopped for cleaning supplies for his office cleaning business. Jack had met Luis in the store about two years ago, and they began to talk. After explaining the business he was starting, Jack offered to help him register his business with the State of New Jersey, get a Tax ID, and set up his payroll and H.R. systems.

Jack had walked Luis's wife, Aldea, through all the paperwork, and she had become the master of the office.

"How's Aldea?" Jack asked.

"Wondering when Jack Marsalis is coming over for some of her famous pupusas," Luis answered.

"Love her pupusas, especially with the corn dough," Jack said.

Pupusas were a Salvadoran specialty that looked like griddle cakes and contained cheese, refried beans, cabbage, and tomato salsa. Luis and Aldea Martinez came to this country as refugees 15 years ago. They were successful business owners with three children and lived near Jack in Elk Township.

Like a lot of towns in South Jersey, Elk Township was still a predominately agricultural community. In the late 19th and early 20th Centuries, the economy of Elk Township consisted of lumbering, farming, basket making, and milling. It was particularly well known for its apple orchards. Indeed, the Lewis Mood Farm near Ferrell is credited with creating its own recognized variety of apples, the Mood apple, in 1922. This variation on the "Red Delicious" apple, later called the "Starking Delicious," was sold and released on the market in 1975.

Jack visited their home several times when he helped set up their business, LAM Cleaning Services LLC. Their 100-year-old home had welcomed two additional wings in the last decade, with the Martinez Salvadoran community chipping in the labor to enlarge and renovate it. To Jack, it was like one of those Amish house raisings, with everyone chipping in.

"Jack, when I tell Aldea I talked to you, she will smack me if I don't get you to come for dinner," Luis insisted.

"Next week?" Jack asked.

"Great," Luis said as he slapped Jack on his shoulder. "I'll text you."

As Luis walked away, Jack called out, "Luis, do you have any openings?"

Luis tossed out his biggest smile. "For you. Of course."

"For a friend," Jack said.

"The economy is good, and workers are scarce," Luis said.

"Text me a date for dinner," Jack yelled as Luis headed toward the cleaning supplies near the Paint department.

As he said goodbye to Luis, Jack spotted the same young Black woman he had seen in the store watching Lashay. This time, she stood near the rear sliding doors to the outside Garden department.

Jack thought she could probably see Lashay from that vantage point.

Why?

Chapter Nineteen

"**At HomeMaxx, we ensure that our parking lots are well-lit during all operating hours, including evenings and nights.**"

Noah's second week at HomeMaxx was much better than his first. Gus stopped calling him fruit names, although he couldn't resist making gay jokes. Noah had organized his car so he had more space to sleep at night, and he had even scored two nights on the basement couch of his old high school baseball roommate, Lorenzo Gonzales, who now lived in nearby Elmer.

It was a bright, slightly muggy Wednesday. Noah was pushing a cart to a customer's pickup truck, where he'd help load drywall sheets the customer had just purchased.

As Noah and the customer, a 50ish man with a hat with a flag on the front and the words, "I miss the America I grew up in," loaded the drywall in the bed of his pickup truck, he heard loud voices toward the middle of the parking lot by the cart return area.

As Noah finished the last drywall sheet, the customer smiled and said, "Thank you, young man. I'm sorry you'll be caught by ICE and sent back to Mexico."

Noah felt a vein at the right side of his temple throb.

"I'm from Puerto Rico," Noah said, allowing enough exasperation to slip through in his tone.

"Sorry, little buddy," the customer answered, oblivious to Noah's emotional thermostat. "Hope you don't get sent back to Puerto Rico then."

"Puerto Ricans are American citizens," Noah said, raising his voice.

As the customer grabbed the handle of the truck's driver's side door, he turned and said, "Hey, listen. I'm on your side. If ICE buys it, I'm all for it."

Noah stood still, both hands on the large cart. The voices became louder and angrier.

When Noah looked over at the cart return area in the middle of the parking lot, four young men were grabbing the carts in the area and pushing them all over the parking lot.

They were laughing and pointing at the cart kid, Robbie. Noah had said hi to the teen a few times. He sensed he was autistic or had some developmental issues.

When Noah watched the scene unfold of these college-age guys taunting Robbie, he snapped.

He yelled, "Hey," and ran toward them.

As he did, Noah had visions of the hundreds of times he was bullied in school because he was different. Punched. His books were knocked out of his hand. Wetback written on his locker in permanent marker. Or fag.

As he got closer, Noah spotted four young men who were getting into a silver BMW sedan. Noah didn't know the model but knew the car was expensive.

As Noah came with five feet of the car, all four men got out. They didn't step toward him. Noah knew if he started a physical fight, he'd be fired.

"Robbie, you okay?" Noah asked as the kid ran around, frantically trying to gather up the carts the men had scattered.

All Robbie said was, "Carts. Carts. Carts. Gotta get the carts."

Noah noticed the BMV had a Rowan University sticker on its back window.

The car's driver was tall and blonde, with a big chest and bulky frame.

"You better stop right now and cross over the Rio Grande River back to Me-hi-co," the boy ordered.

The other three laughed.

Noah decided that enough was enough. He no longer cared if he got fired. Something had tripped in him, like a fire alarm.

He had a black belt in karate, and he was about to use it on this college boy. But could he take all four?

"You better stop, or I'll put you down, little man," the blonde college kid warned.

Just as Noah was within a foot of the group, he heard a voice behind him.

"You boys better get in your rich car and never come back, or I will pound you all in the ground."

It was Gus.

Noah turned around, and Gus stood next to him, breathing fire. His normal mean resting face had been transformed into that of a crazed monster.

"I'm not afraid —-" the blonde college kid started to declare.

Gus walked up to him and bumped him until the kid had two choices. Get into the car or fight. Meanwhile, Noah turned his attention to the other three and took two steps toward them.

"I'm not afraid of you, old man," the blonde kid said as he sat in the driver's seat and quickly closed the door.

The other three followed their leader. One got in the front passenger seat, and the other two into the back seat.

Gus said to Noah, "Use your phone and take a picture of their license plate number."

The BMW screeched away and circled the parking lot.

Gus didn't move. Didn't take his eyes off the BMW. He stood, arms akimbo, face spewing hate, anger, and the desire to be violent.

Noah had taken a picture of their plate number and walked toward Gus.

Robbie was still gathering carts around the lot that the men had pushed all over.

As the BMW came toward them, it almost hit Robbie, who had to jump out of the way.

The BMW continued toward Gus and Noah, picking up speed.

"Don't move," Gus said in a controlled voice.

Noah obeyed, and the BMW veered off at the last minute, missing Gus and Noah.

A few feet past them, the BMW stopped, the driver's side window rolled down, and the blonde man screamed, "I'm going to tell my mom. She'll get you fired."

The BMW driver then hit the accelerator, and the car sped through the parking lot in seconds. Noah followed the car as it pulled out onto Delsea Drive without stopping, almost sideswiping a black SUV.

Robbie was still trying to corral all the carts when Noah said to Gus, "Thank you. I didn't have a plan to fight all four of them."

Then Noah asked, "Want me to help Robbie gather the rest of the carts?"

Gus turned toward the Building Materials overhead door at the far end of the store and said, "Fuck that. It's the kid's problem."

Gus walked back to the store while Noah headed over to help Robbie.

"Carts. Carts. Must get the carts," Robbie said repeatedly.

Ever since Gus had visited Jack to ask him to take in Noah, he tortured himself with constant mental battles in his head. It was as if Gus fought his own mind and will.

Gus's mind would attack Jack for being an arrogant asshole for even suggesting that Gus take in Noah.

Jack doesn't want to be the bad guy and say no, so he's putting it on me.

A few minutes later, Gus pulled out his phone, touched the CONTACTS button, and searched for Michael's contact information.

So many times, his index finger was millimeters away from touching the number and speaking to Michael. Would Michael speak to him? Had it been about a decade now? Was it too late? Had too much time passed?

Gus had kept tabs on Michael's life in Colorado. With Lashay's help, Gus paid for a people-finder website to learn about Michael.

Michael lived in Greenwood Village, Colorado, a rich suburb of Denver. The city had about 17,000 residents and was known for its superior school district, walking trails connecting to downtown Denver, great restaurants, and thriving economy.

Through Lashay, Gus found Michael's address and could view his house. The home was two stories and all brick. It had three bedrooms and three bathrooms, and it was on a corner lot with a large brick paver patio in the spacious backyard.

Michael was the owner of BED Digital Systems, which was a company that did computer stuff like making websites, building apps, and designing computer programs. Lashay told him it was a highly successful business.

Gus laughed at Michael's business name because BEB stood for his wife and Michael's mother. Betty Eleanor Burdette was BEB.

Why would he ever want to hear from his old man?

That's where Noah came in.

Gus figured he could make some things right by taking in Noah, a gay kid thrown out by his father.

There was a sense of justice there.

By the end of the workday on Wednesday, Gus's head was spinning constantly. Gus had already punched out and was headed for his truck when he saw Noah about to get into his white Honda a few spaces away.

For a few seconds, Gus froze. His mind fired conflicting thoughts at such a rapid-fire pace that he felt physically exhausted. He was spent from too much thinking.

He closed his truck door and walked over to Noah's car.

"Hey, kid," Gus said.

The boy turned around and smiled at Gus like he wished Michael would smile at him one day.

What the fuck am I about to do?

"Gus, did I forget something?" Noah asked.

Gus couldn't look the kid in the eyes. He checked out Noah's work boots.

They were beat up, with tears in the tops and tread worn down.

"Why do you have such shitty work boots?" Gus asked.

Noah looked puzzled but stared down at his boots.

"No money, I guess, would be the big reason," Noah answered.

"I guess I should get new ——"

"You can stay in the spare bedroom in my house," Gus blurted out.

Gus refused to make eye contact.

Why didn't I notice how crappy this kid's work boots were?

"Did you say I could stay with you?" Noah asked.

"Hey, if you don't want to, I don't really give a shit," Gus answered.

"No, no, I definitely want to," Noah said. "Are you sure it's all right?"

"No, it's not all right," Gus said, angry and resentful. "Fuckhead Jack Marsalis wouldn't take you when I asked him to last Sunday. Jerk off."

"Now, I'm stuck with you," Gus emphasized.

Gus finally looked up. Noah had tears in his eyes.

"Thank you, Gus. I can't thank you enough. It's been tough living in my car –"

"Whatever," Gus cut him off. "Just follow me home."

As Gus was about to get into his truck, he said to Noah, "Absolutely no faggy stuff at my house. No other people like you are allowed over, and if they do come over, I'll strangle them with my bare hands."

Noah shook his head. "No visitors. Check."

"And don't try any of your gay stuff on me because you may not live to regret it," Gus alerted him.

"I'll try to control myself," Noah responded.

"Follow me," Gus instructed.

"Do I get a key?" Noah asked as Gus got into his truck.

Through the windshield of his truck, Gus nodded an emphatic NO.

Gus rolled down his window and yelled, "When we get to my house, park your car in front of the garage on the left side. This way, my truck will hide it so my neighbors don't think I bought a Jap car."

"Thanks, Gus," Noah said over the engines starting.

Gus just had a thought. Something important he had forgotten.

"Noah, do not, and I mean, do not, tell anyone at HomeMaxx that you are living at my house. If you do and I find out, I'll throw your shit out onto the driveway so fast it'll make your head spin."

"Not even Jack," Noah asked.

"That know-it-all asshole probably already knows I'm doing this."

"Let's go," Gus yelled as his truck exited the HomeMaxx parking lot at a speed that exceeded the speed limit by at least 25 miles per hour.

After an especially grueling day, Darla Campanna rubbed her temples as she said goodbye to Aisha Jackson, her replacement at the customer service/returns desk. Since Black Cobalt took over HomeMaxx, customers have been getting angrier about higher prices, fewer sales associates on the floor for assistance, and tougher return policies initiated by the private equity firm.

She didn't think the store would remain open beyond Labor Day. It wasn't as if she and her husband Edgar would be in financial trouble if she lost her job. Edgar, unlike her first husband Clyde, was reliable and stable as a dump truck driver. He had worked for the same company, Medwin Trucking in Vineland, for 20 years and now had his own successful business.

Unlike Darla, who unloaded on him when she got home after a bad day with a torrent of curses and horror stories, Edgar would answer her, "How was your day?" with, "Dirty."

Although she had been married to Edgar for only six years, it had been the best six years of her life. Ever since Darla was a teenager, executive decision-making had eluded her.

When she was 14, she got pregnant and had an abortion. Back then, with a thin waist, curvy hips, blonde hair, and big boobs, she was a prime target during young male hunting season. If possible, Darla hooked up with the worst guys possible.

At 17, she got pregnant again and got another abortion, but this time, her parents kicked her out of the house the day she turned 18.

Darla was homeless for a few months and then interviewed for the job at HomeMaxx 23 years ago. The store had opened a little while back. Back then, the store manager was this older guy, Nick Barbato, who wore a full-piece wig and had hands that were magnetized toward Darla's breasts. During her first six months there, Nick would find ways to feel her boobs several times a day. Married with four kids, Nick would proposition her several times a week, sometimes driving up to her in his car as she went to her car in the parking lot, rolling down the window, and exposing himself.

She never understood that. Guys thought that women would immediately swoon over the sight of their dicks and submit themselves to the guy.

She put up with Nick because she needed the job. Darla had found a place over the garage of an older couple in Vineland. It was small, cold, and smelled like gas fumes, but the couple was nice and charged well below market price for rent, even with the gas fumes.

After a few years, Nick, the manager, moved on to younger girls at the store, and Darla was safe. About 15 years ago, she met Clyde, a general contractor who bought supplies for his business several times a week.

In retrospect, Darla realized that Clyde appealed to that bad boy image she fell for as a teenager. After only knowing him for three months, she married Clyde and moved into his house in Franklinville on Marshall Mill Road.

The place was a dump, and Darla worked hard to clean it up and make it presentable. It didn't long to learn that Clyde was a terrible general contractor who ripped people off, and drank every night, usually at Cap'n Cat Clam Bar on Delsea Drive.

When sober, Clyde had an edge to him that attracted Darla. When drinking, Clyde was nasty to men and women. When drunk, Clyde beat her. During the first few years, Clyde was smart enough not to leave any visible marks. A punch to the stomach or ribs or a kick to the small of her back. But then, Clyde's drinking got worse; he lost all of his clients, so he just sat home and drank all day, blamed everybody but himself for his problems, and beat Darla when she came home, even though Darla supported them.

When Jack started noticing her bruises at work, he'd ask her about Clyde, who was picking her up at work because they had to sell his work truck to survive. In the beginning, she put him off with excuses that were followed by false laughter to quell his suspicions.

Then, one night, Clyde came to HomeMaxx to pick her up. Jack came out, and Clyde tried to punch him. Jack threw a few punches to defend himself, but Clyde was bleeding.

Unbeknownst to Darla, Jack visited Darla's daughter Christy, whom she had when she was 21. Christy's father was a biker who left the area shortly after she was born, and she never heard from him again. Darla's parents raised Christy, and Darla had just begun to develop a relationship with her daughter when Jack talked with her.

Darla was amazed that Christy had grown to be an amazing adult. She was the high school valedictorian at Delsea Regional High School in Franklinville. She graduated from Stockton University in Galloway Township and was a Nurse Practitioner at Jefferson Hospital in Washington Township.

The restraining order got Clyde out of the house, and with Christy and Jack's help, she filed for and got a divorce. Even now, after six years with Edgar, Clyde would sometimes park in the lot at HomeMaxx and eyeball her when she left at night. He drove this rust bucket 2004 Chevy Cruise.

Sometimes, Edgar would pick her up after work, hoping to see Clyde and pummel him. But Clyde stayed away when Edgar arrived.

So when she walked out of the doors and turned toward her car parked near the cart return cage, Darla didn't expect to see Clyde.

He pulled up just as she approached her car.

"Darla, you won't get away with this," Clyde growled at her.

"Jack and your pussy husband won't be able to protect you," he threatened her as his car inched closer to hers.

Darla's hands started to shake, and she almost dropped the key fob. She hit it about ten times and jumped into her car, a 2014 Honda CRV.

Clyde drove up to her driver's side window, stopped, put his finger to his left temple, and pulled the imaginary trigger. Then, he drove off slowly.

Darla waited for his car to exit the lot and pull onto Delsea Drive. Her legs were shaking, and she couldn't breathe. She started crying in the car but pulled herself together because she didn't want Edgar to see her like this.

She was afraid of what Edgar might do to Clyde and what Clyde might do to her.

Jack Marsalis walked out of HomeMaxx's front sliding doors and spotted an older, rusted Chevy Cruise. He knew it belonged to Darla's ex-husband, Clyde. Jack stopped before crossing the car lane that separated the store from the parking lot.

His body tensed. He felt anger like he hadn't experienced in years. Since he almost killed Dave Rendino.

Jack knew he had to do something about Clyde.

He didn't know if he trusted himself to know when to stop.

Chapter Twenty

"**It is a risk to love. What if it doesn't work out? Ah, but what if it does?**"

Jack turned left onto Lake Road and went into Lake Acres Mobile Home Park. It was only a ten-minute drive from his place in Clayton. During that short time, Jack had experienced a dry throat, the sweats, a headache starting to gain strength like a hurricane in the Atlantic, and a generalized feeling of weakness in his legs.

How can I be this nervous? I'm a 50-year-old man who's been married and dated.

His landlords, the Szczesny's, helped him with his wardrobe. When he went upstairs after picking out what to wear from his mini-version of a closet, Jackie looked at Wally and said, "Do you have anything that will fit him?"

"Why? Is this not good?" Jack asked as the couple scrambled, bringing out some of Wally's shirts on a hanger, placing them against Jack, and then evaluating with a, "What do you think?"

Jack stood there in the living room, too dazed to move.

"Is everything all right? What should I be wearing?"

After several trips to Wally's closet in the master bedroom, Wally and Jackie said to each other, "We got this."

Jack took off his white dress shirt, which he tucked into his jeans. The couple replaced his brown belt with a black one. Then, they tightened the belt and pulled up his jeans.

"Put this on," Jackie instructed as she helped him. She buttoned the shirt, stood in front of him, assessed him, and pulled down on the shirt.

"Perfect," Wally said.

"Come here," Jackie commanded. "Look in the mirror."

Jack followed the couple down the hall, into their bedroom, and then toward a free-standing mirror near an armoire. He now wore a solid black button-down shirt that seemed the perfect untucked length. The black belt matched the shirt, and his jeans fit better pulled up just a bit and with the belt tighter around his waist.

"Jack, you look terrific," Wally said as Jackie emerged from the master bathroom with an aerosol spray bottle and a brush.

"Jackie, what are you doing?" Jack asked, apprehensive. He felt his parents were dressing him for his eighth-grade graduation.

Jackie was not flustered. "Jack, I am going to comb your hair and spray just the slightest amount of hair spray."

"Wait, what," Jack stuttered.

Jackie stood on a stool Wally had grabbed from the laundry room. Jackie stood on the stool in front of Jack, bobbing her head as she assessed his hair. She'd spray a spot, comb it, and do another area while mumbling, "This is good. It's getting there. It's almost there. One more spritz. We're there."

Jackie stepped off the stool and admired Jack like an artist admiring their completed canvas.

"Jack, you are going to wow Lashay," Jackie said as Wally gave him a thumbs up.

Jack stepped in front of the mirror again for a longer look. His jeans fit better, and his belt matched his shirt and shoes. His shirt now hung perfectly below his belt and form-fitted his upper body. His hair was combed to the side, with two small curls hanging on his forehead like they were posing for a magazine.

Jack had to admit it. The Szczesny's had made him presentable. Maybe even temptable.

"Jack, one more thing," Wally said as he grabbed a deep-blue spray bottle from his armoire.

Jackie grabbed it from Wally and said, "Don't move, Jack. I'll spray you."

"Jackie, with what?" Jack asked.

"Dior Sauvage," Wally said. "A customer gave it to me two Christmases ago. It's very expensive."

Jackie moved around Jack as she lightly sprayed select spots. Jack smelled the cologne, and it did smell appealing.

"It has a lavender essence with a hint of woodiness," Jackie explained.

"Now go," Jackie ordered him. "You don't want to be late."

The mobile home park was built like a horseshoe, with Lashay's rental unit on the other side. Jack wanted to get a sense of the park, so he drove in on the far side.

He drove slowly, his head moving left and right as he checked out the mobile homes. They were clearly a mixed bag of units. Some sagged and slouched from age and lack of repair, while a few glistened from attention and maintenance.

Lashay's unit was the last one on the right. Across the street, an empty unit was also there. The two units on either side of Lashay were rundown and abused. Between the properties, a rusty lawnmower and a decaying charcoal barbecue lay on its side.

Lashay's unit was smaller than a lot of their units. Clearly, it was a single-section mobile home. The tan vinyl siding was clean and freshly scrubbed. Jack figured that Lashay had power-washed it. The black shutters had been painted with glossy enamel, and the small asphalt driveway had been recently sealed.

Lashay had edged the perimeter of the unit with Belgian block stone. Inside that perimeter, Lashay had planted a variety of annuals, perennials, and bushes. Everything was trimmed and neat. Knockout rose bushes framed the concrete stair unit to her front door.

Jack took a breath and knocked. Nothing.

How long do I have to wait to knock again?

Lashay opened the door. She wore light grey tight-fitting pants with a button front. The pants matched a short-sleeved sweater with an overlapping V-neckline in a wrap look. Her sweater cut across her chest to reveal the tiniest amount of cleavage. Around her neck hung a white gold infinity necklace.

Jack had never seen her with makeup on, and she was a vision with brownish-red lipstick that highlighted her full lips.

"Wow, you look beautiful," Jack said.

She smiled and blinked at him.

"You look very handsome, Mr. Marsalis."

On the ride to the restaurant, Jack kept the conversation light—work stuff, a blow-by-blow account of how the Szczesny's had saved him from a fashion 911.

Jack still didn't quite believe they were going on a date. He had wanted this for so long, but a romantic relationship is based on what both people want. Despite their close friendship, Jack wasn't sure Lashay felt that way about him.

The danger frightened him.

There's no coming back from that kiss and this date.

If their romantic relationship never blossomed, their friendship was probably dead.

Of course, with the store probably closing in October, we wouldn't be working together, anyway.

A few days after the kiss, Jack and Lashay enjoyed tacos at Carlos's food truck.

Jack took one bite out of his fish tacos and exclaimed, "Carlos, you are amazing. These fish tacos are delicious with a little kick to them."

"Tell my wife, please," Carlos answered as he waited on Harry. "She's not talking to me right now."

"Carlos, what did you do?" Lashay asked as if she already knew he was at fault.

"Give my man a break," Jack said. "He may be in the right here."

Carlos hesitated and confessed, "I forgot our eleventh anniversary yesterday."

"You were saying," Lashay stared down Jack, who waved an imaginary white flag.

"Carlos, my advice is flowers, jewelry, an expensive dinner, or, if that doesn't work, just beg," Jack counseled.

"What he said," Lashay added.

Carlos nodded as the line of customers grew, and he focused exclusively on his business.

"If we were married, I know I'd never forget our anniversary," Jack said as he started on his second fish taco after wiping his hands.

"You're getting ahead of yourself there, Jack," Lashay said as she picked at her cheese quesadilla. "We haven't even gone on our first date."

Without hesitation, Jack said, "Lashay, would you like to accompany me to The Green Olive restaurant this Thursday night?"

"Yes," Lashay answered as she pulled apart her quesadilla. "I've heard that place has great pizza and a fantastic dessert display."

As Jack pulled into the parking lot of The Green Olive, he wondered why he hadn't asked her out before this.

All he could think of was "fraidy cat."

The Green Olive was in the retail section of Vineland, close to the decaying Cumberland Mall and within a mile of every well-known chain and fast food restaurant.

This area of Vineland bordered Route 55, which ran north and south. The highway ran about 30 miles northbound until it dropped onto Route 42, only a few miles from the Walt Whitman Bridge into Philadelphia. The "Walt," which opened in 1957, led commuters to South Philly and the Phillies and Eagles stadiums.

Southbound, Route 55 ended in another seven miles. Then, southbound vacationers could continue on Route 47 for about 30 miles and end up in Wildwood. The shore towns of Wildwood, North Wildwood, and Wildwood Crest were famous for their wide beaches, family-oriented activities, their fifties retro architecture, and its five-mile boardwalk with its ever-present trams that called out, "Watch the tram car, please."

The Green Olive was a massive place with a catering hall in the rear, a restaurant with several distinct dining rooms, and an exquisitely decorated bar. The exterior was almond-colored stucco with classic architectural flourishes like cornices, gables, and stacked stone accents.

The restaurant was a testament to architectural excess with terrazzo tile floors, stacked stone walls, and overwhelming wagon wheel-style chandeliers.

After ordering drinks – Jack a light beer and Lashay a Cosmopolitan with rocks on the side – Jack chattered about the restaurant décor, the menu, and the dessert display case they had passed on their way to their table. While Jack desired Lashay and wanted to hold and kiss her, his main focus tonight was finding out about her past, which she kept hidden.

What could be so bad that she could not share her past with him?

They ordered from a young, blonde woman named Aurora, who had a high-wattage smile. Jack ordered the meatloaf, and Lashay ordered the Chicken Parmesan.

"Last weekend, I shared about my childhood and growing up," Jack began, not sure how to frame his question. "Any chance I learn about Lashay Jones growing up?"

"Jack, I can tell you about my childhood," Lashay said. "But I will need another Cosmo before the night is out."

Jack smiled at Lashay, who sat across from him in a high-back booth, which gave them privacy.

"Deal," Jack said. "And how about a Bailey's as an after-dinner drink?"

"Why, Mr. Marsalis," Lashay chided him, "Are you trying to use alcohol to take advantage of me?"

Even though Jack knew she was kidding, he said, "I would never do that."

"I know," Lashay answered.

Jack sipped his beer as Lashay played with her glass of rocks that were melting.

"I grew up in Pemberton, New Jersey, next to Fort Dix," Lashay began.

Jack had worked as a manager for Grove Logistics in nearby Hamilton Township before he was promoted and assigned to Piscataway. New Jersey was the most densely populated state in the nation. Therefore, it was divided into North, South, and Central. Such a simple division compared to larger states like Texas and California created controversy. Some Jerseyans didn't believe in the central part. They liked the simple, two-way split.

Regardless of its designation, Pemberton was over an hour north of the HomeMaxx store in Franklinville.

"Back then, there were separate facilities for the Army, Navy, and Air Force," Lashay explained. "Now, they're combined into the common name Joint Base McGuire–Dix—Lakehurst."

"My mother grew up in Pemberton, and she was beautiful," Lashay said. "My grandmother told me that it seemed that every serviceman on the base showed up asking for a date with Aisha Jones."

Lashay took out her phone, clicked a few times, and turned the screen toward Jack.

"Here she is at 22 years old," Lashay said, a combination of pride, sadness, and regret seeping into her tone.

Jack saw a photo of a gorgeous black woman who was tall, with wide blue eyes, dimpled cheekbones, an ample chest, and a note of mischievousness in her smile.

"My grandma warned her to be careful with those service boys, especially the white ones," Lashay said. "Those white soldiers didn't want to be seen in public with her, but they weren't against banging her in some back room."

"Is your mom alive?" Jack asked to fill the silence.

"No," Lashay said. "My mother was carefree and not careful about her health, her reputation, and her future. She got pregnant. She had no idea who the father was because she had been so – so active – in that time period. She told my grandma it could have been one of ten men."

"When you look at me, it seems like my father was white," Lashay began. "But look at my mother. Light-skinned, blue eyes, small nose."

"I don't know who my father is or was. I don't know if he was white or black or brown."

Lashay finished her first Cosmo, and their server, Aurora, brought their food.

"Let's eat," Jack said, "In case this story makes you lose your appetite."

Lashay dug her fork into a healthy piece of chicken parmesan and said, "It was a long time ago, and you have to live with your history. After all, history doesn't change, just your interpretation of what happened."

"Grandma arranged for my mom to go away to family near Raleigh, North Carolina, who cared for her during pregnancy until birth. My mother returned nine months later with me, and they started living at my Grandma's house. Soon enough, my mother returned to her carefree lifestyle and started shooting heroin. After a few months of my mother's addiction and her stealing from my grandma to support her habit, my grandma kicked her out. I was just a baby, not even one year old."

"Did your grandma raise you?"

Lashay stopped eating and put down her knife and fork.

Aurora came over for the obligatory, "How is everything" but delivered that phrase like she meant it.

"Excellent," Lashay said. "Can I get another Cosmo with the rocks on the side?"

"Sure," Aurora said. "You, sir?" she directed toward Jack.

"No, thanks," Jack said. "I'm saving myself for dessert."

"Our dessert selection is to die for," Aurora countered as she walked away from their booth.

"My grandma was a strong woman," Lashay continued. "She gave me the love, direction, and discipline I needed to become a responsible adult. That poor woman lost her husband when my mother was only ten. The police shot him in Trenton. They claimed he was threatening them. But he had no gun, and my grandfather was shot in the back."

"Sorry," was all Jack could think to say.

"When I graduated from the College Of New Jersey in Trenton, my grandma attended the ceremony. She was so proud of me. Two weeks later, I came home and found her collapsed on the couch. The EMTs pronounced her dead of a heart attack."

Jack reached over with his right hand and felt for her. Lashay responded by squeezing his hand and intertwining her fingers with his.

"After she passed, I went through her things since I was her only heir," Lashay. "I found a death certificate for my mother, Aisha Eloise Jones. She had died in 1985 in Trenton of a heroin overdose."

"Can I have my hand back so I can finish my delicious chicken parm?" Lashay broke the mood.

After dinner, Aurora recommended that they peruse the expansive dessert display near the entrance and choose their "poison."

Jack relished how Lashay gushed over the dessert selection.

"Jack, look at this Black Forest cake."

"Jack, the carrot cake looks so moist and scrumptious."

After oohing and aahing like teens at a Taylor Swift concert, Jack let Lashay pick.

"We'll take the strawberry cheesecake," Lashay said.

Jack loved to see her happy and carefree, not weighed down by the secrets of her past. As sad as it was to hear, Jack knew that the story of her childhood was only the preamble.

When the cheesecake arrived, Aurora placed it on their table like it had significant monetary value. Jack waited for Lashay to take the first bite.

It was a big one.

"Oh my God, this is amazing," Lashay said so loud that other diners looked over, spotted the cheesecake, and nodded approvingly.

Jack always thought that eating dessert with a romantic interest was sensual. When devouring the dessert, people made noises, grunts, and sighs similar to two people having sex and enjoying the hell out of it.

After paying the bill and thanking Aurora for her great service, Jack drove Lashay home, arriving at her mobile home at about 8:30 pm. The lack of street lights in the mobile home park made the darkness even more pronounced.

Jack pulled up to her front door and said, "Thanks, that was fun."

Lashay leaned over and kissed him as her right hand caressed his right cheek.

"Jack, I had a great time," Lashay said, quickly exiting his car.

Jack rolled down the window. "I'll wait until you get inside. It's the gentlemanly thing to do."

Lashay didn't acknowledge him. Or move.

She stood about two feet from his car, frozen. Jack was going to ask if something was wrong, but intuition told him to do nothing.

Lashay stood about 20 feet from her front door, not moving.

Jack waited. Lashay didn't move for over a minute.

Then Lashay turned and grabbed the car door handle. She froze again for a few seconds and then quickly got back into his car.

She didn't look at him. Jack could tell that she was crying.

Jack forced himself to give her the time and space to do whatever she was about to do.

"Jack, I am going to tell you about my adult life, my married life, and my life after that," Lashay said, still looking out of the windshield.

"You don't have to, Lashay," Jack said. "The truth is, I love you."

"Jack, whatever you learn about me tonight...," Lashay began, sniffling.

"I love you. I want us to be together. I want...."

Lashay started to cry.

"Lashay, you don't have to tell me whatever it is. But I feel like you need to come to terms with your past in order for our relationship to move forward."

Lashay cupped her hands and scooped away her tears.

"After you hear this, there is a good chance you will regret those words," Lashay told him.

"Only one way to find out," Jack said, trying to transfer his emotional strength to her.

Lashay paused for several seconds and said, "I graduated with a degree in Finance. I always loved math and numbers. I got a series of finance jobs in the next two years, each with increasing responsibility. After three years, I had a nice condo and a good job as the CFO of a medical device company in Marlton. Then I met Daryll. He was a Mt. Laurel police officer. We hit it off and dated for about a year and a half before getting married. Daryll was handsome, thoughtful, and funny. He had only been a police officer when I met him for a year."

Lashay continued. "After we were married and he gained more experience as a police officer, Daryll began to change. He started to yell at me and call me names. I made more money than him, and that seemed to set him off.

Stupid me, I thought that a baby would help. You know, some men mature when they become a father."

Lashay paused as if she needed support before telling the rest of her story.

Jack didn't know what else to do, so he reached for her hand and caressed it.

"After Tamara was born, Daryll got worse. The verbal abuse turned physical, and he began to push me at first. Then he began punching me. Once my maternity leave was up and I was ready to return to work, Daryll flipped out and demanded I quit and be a stay-at-home mom. I tried to explain that we had purchased a four-bedroom colonial in Medford, and his salary alone wouldn't cover the mortgage and our bills.

"We argued for several hours before I put Tamara down for the night. After I did that, I was at the top of the stairs when he came flying out of our bedroom, screaming, and then he pushed me down the stairs.

"Oh, Lashay, I'm so sorry," was all Jack could think to say.

"He refused to take me to the ER, so I made an appointment with my primary care doctor for two days later. I still can feel the excruciating pain I was in, all while trying to take care of a baby. My doctor said he thought it was just a muscle pull. I couldn't tell him that Daryll pushed me down the stairs, so I made up this story: I tripped on the area rug in the foyer."

"So what did he do for you?" Jack asked.

"Something that made my life a living hell. He gave me Oxycontin for the back pain. That helped with the pain but not with my back, which was still in spasm. I renewed the prescription four times, and before I knew it, I was hooked.

"It went quickly downhill from there. I became an addict, seeing multiple doctors to get a script for painkillers, and when that dried up, I started selling stuff in the house to support my habit. I found a guy in Camden who sold oxys, and he became my dealer."

Jack had heard too many stories like hers. They never ended well.

"I was desperate, so I told Daryll. He exploded and beat me that night, punching and kicking me. The next morning, he dropped me off at Pyramid Rehab Center in Hammonton and told me not to come home if I didn't get clean."

"Jack, I tried. But the pain of withdrawal was so bad. I thought my skin was on fire. I shook. I threw up. I shivered. I hallucinated. After six days, I left. I didn't have any money or a phone. So, I slept in the nearby NJ Transit train station for three nights. The Hammonton police arrested me for vagrancy, and when I told them Daryll was a Mt. Laurel police officer, they called him.

"The police officer talked to Daryll for a few minutes and then put me on the phone. He told me that I had been fired from my job and that he had canceled all my credit and debit cards. His mother had taken Tamara and would care for her. If I showed up there or told anyone that he had hit me, he would find me and kill me."

"Oh, Lashay, I'm so sorry," Jack tried to console her.

"Jack, the worst is yet to come," Lashay said. "And if, after hearing this part, you are free to drive away, we can remain co-workers and nothing more. I will understand."

"Lashay, I'm not going anywhere," Jack said.

"After rehab failed and Daryll abandoned me, I was hopeless and homeless. I reconnected with my oxy dealer in Camden and started selling drugs for him. That wasn't enough for me. I needed more."

"Jack, I was desperate. I lived in this abandoned house in East Camden. I was out on the streets at night or early morning trying to sell and deal for myself."

Lashay's hands trembled in the car. Jack knew the worst was about to come out. He was prepared.

"Jack, Jack, I, I became a prostitute so I can get money for drugs," Lashay sobbed. "It was horrible. Sweaty, dirty, disgusting men violating me so I can score more drugs. That went on for two months before I was saved. The police arrested me.

I was charged with and pleaded guilty to drug possession. My court-appointed lawyer was able to get the DA to drop the distribution charge, which carried a minimum ten-year sentence. "

Jack said softly, "I'm here, Lashay, and nothing I've heard has changed my mind about loving you."

Lashay reached over the seat and hugged him. He kissed her and then dried her tears.

"Jack, just like with you, it's hard to get back once you hit bottom. I served two years in prison, got myself clean, and began to rebuild my life. I worked as a waitress for about a decade at various diners but kept quitting because the owners or the owners' sons would rub their flabby dicks on my leg, like a dog humping, and think I'd just surrender to them because of my prison record. I had various roommates during that time since I couldn't afford my own apartment.

"I had one roommate who was an Applebee's cook who thought she could steal anything from me because that woman's name was on the lease. Then there was the older grandma type in Mantua who rented me a room in her four-bedroom colonial and tried to fix me up with her loser grandsons."

"I lived out of my car in the Washington Township Walmart parking lot for a year. Then, I got a job at the HomeMaxx Mantua store, and my life began to turn around. One day, I ran into a server I worked with at the Peter Pan Diner in Williamstown.

"She had married some rich guy from Moorestown and was renting her mobile home in Newfield. The rent was dirt cheap, and the place was disgusting. It was full of rodents, bugs, discarded food, and dust bunnies the size of Bigfoot.

"Why didn't she just sell the mobile home?" Jack asked.

For the first time since she sat back in Jack's car, Lashay laughed.

"Her theory was that in case her rich husband kicked her out, she'd always have this place as a backup."

"So what happened?"

"When the private equity firm bought Lake Acres three years ago, the woman sold her place to the company. Now, I pay rent to them, and they've been jacking up the rents the last two years."

"What happened to Daryll?" Jack asked. "Do you know?"

Lashay nodded. "Daryll got fired from the force a few years later for trying to coerce a woman he had pulled over for speeding into having sex with him."

"Jones, you know how to pick 'em," Jack said.

"Maybe, just maybe, I'm breaking the mold with my latest pick," Lashay said.

"Anyway, Daryll moved out west somewhere. He left Tamara with his mother, and she raised her."

"Did you ever try to contact her?" Jack asked.

"As much as I wanted to, no. What would I tell her? Her mother was abused by her father, became a junkie, and then a hooker. And she's an ex-con."

"I'll spare her that horror story," Lashay added.

"Well, Lashay, it looks like I'm still here," Jack announced.

"Marsalis, I don't know if you're sweet or just stupid."

Jack answered right away.

"I'm sweet on you, Miss Jones, and stupid in love with you."

"Jack, I don't know if you feel this way, but for me, I sometimes wonder if I deserve a second chance."

"I know exactly how you feel and think about that, too," Jack said.

"Then I think that I screwed up my life so bad and got punished for it," Jack said. "But, just like you, I've worked hard to get back my life, my self-respect, and the respect of others."

"Even after what you told me tonight, I appreciate that you shared. I know it was awful. I've been there. But Lashay Jones, when you transferred to the Franklinville HomeMaxx, and I got to know you, I realized that you were absolutely the best thing that has ever happened to me."

"Ditto, Jack," Lashay said and then kissed him.

"Did you just say ditto?" Jack asked, amused by her brevity.

"Good night, Jack," Lashay said. "I feel like a weight has been finally lifted off of me."

Lashay got out of the car and went to the front door. She put the key in the door and turned around. Jack had the driver's side window down.

"You're a good man, Marsalis. Although, you did kind of hog the cheesecake."

Jack smiled, rolled up the window, and drove away.

He hadn't felt this good in – well, maybe never.

Chapter Twenty-One

"Approximately 2.1 million cats are adopted each year. About 100,000 cats who enter shelters as strays are returned to their owners. About 12 percent of cats adopted by people are returned to the shelter within four years."

Saturday morning was already hot and humid, and it felt like July in South Jersey. Jack had already assembled the pizza oven while Tyler worked on the Gazebo, which came in a kit.

"These instructions make no sense," Tyler vented. "The screw holes don't line up for the roof."

"I'm just connecting the gas supply for the pizza oven, and then I'll come over and help," Jack said.

"I hate these assembly kits," Tyler groused. "The instructions are bullshit."

Jack had just hooked up the gas line and fired up the pizza oven. Inside the oven, a blue flame appeared with a poof, and Jack felt the heat from the oven.

"Houston, we have liftoff," Jack said. "All we need now is the pizza."

Pam emerged from the back French doors with an uncooked pizza on a pizza board as if on cue. She held the board handle gingerly as she approached.

"Tyler, this is for you," Pam said, smiling in response to his pouting about the gazebo assembly.

Pam veered off to show the board to Tyler. She had the board personalized, and the handle read, "Pizza Chef Tyler."

"That's awesome, Pam," Jack said. "But what did he do to deserve this high honor?"

Tyler studied the inscription on the pizza board, finally breaking out in a broad smile.

"I know his employees all hate him, but Morgan, Taylor, and I kind of like him," Pam chided Tyler as she handed him the pizza board.

"That's very true," Jack piled on.

"Just for that smart ass, you're working on the gazebo after lunch," Tyler said.

Tyler kissed Pam and slid the pizza into the hot, flaming oven.

"Do you think we should give Jack a piece?" Tyler asked Pam.

Pam's eyes sparkled when she said, "Every pie has that small piece. He can have that one, I guess."

"Hey, if you feel that way, I'll just head home," Jack kidded.

"Don't you move, mister," Pam ordered. "You can have three pieces."

"Besides, we have a lot to talk about at lunch, don't we, hon?" Tyler said.

When Gus woke up on Saturday, he realized he had slept later than usual, even for a weekend. Typically, Gus woke up by six and was out of the house by 6:45 to arrive at HomeMaxx by 6:55, time enough to get coffee and talk to Jack or Lashay or ignore Harry. On weekends, Gus was out of bed by 7:30.

He checked the portable alarm clock on his nightstand. It read 8:00 a.m. Gus heard a noise in the kitchen as he got out of bed. Gus's bedroom and the spare bedroom, now Noah's, were upstairs, with a bathroom between them in the hall.

After the bathroom, Gus got dressed. He smelled something delicious. He walked down the stairs and into the kitchen, and Noah was there placing a plate of food on the kitchen table. There was a placemat that Gus hadn't seen since Betty used them for meals. To the left side was a napkin with a fork and spoon placed on it, with a glass of orange juice and a cup of coffee in front of the mat. A milk pitcher and sugar bowl hugged the coffee mug that read, "Concrete Mason because miracle worker isn't an official title."

Gus had no words. He looked around the kitchen, surveying it from a 360-degree view.

Was this his kitchen?

Everything was put away and organized, and he sniffed the bleach and glass cleaner odor.

"Morning, Gus," Noah said with a perkiness that Gus found irritating.

"I made you a Mexican omelet," Noah said, referring to the food before him as he sat in his chair. When Noah first arrived, he warned Noah that this chair was his and the lounger in the family room was his. Off-limits to Noah.

So far, the kid had followed those rules and the others he randomly made that he now couldn't remember.

"What the hell is in a Mexican omelet?" Gus asked.

"There are beans, peppers, corn, tomatoes, and onions, then it's topped with chunky salsa, sour cream, and avocado," Noah explained.

"I thought you were Puerto Rican," Gus said."Is a Mexican omelet a betrayal?"

Gus had to admit that the kid didn't rattle easily.

"Try it," Noah said.

Gus took a small bite and chewed.

Holy shit, this is delicious. I haven't eaten this good since...

Gus took a second bite and then a third.

"Gotta admit, Noah," Gus said. "This is delicious."

Noah smiled and said, "I reorganized the pantry and evicted a few mice. Then I started to work on straightening out the basement."

Gus sipped his coffee and then his juice. This reminded him of when Betty was alive. She always took care of him, even when he didn't deserve that thoughtfulness.

"I made you empanadillas for lunch," Noah said. They're in the fridge in foil. Just microwave them for two minutes."

Gus finished the omelet, using his fork to clean up scraps and consume them.

"Noah, thank you, but I eat American food," Gus said.

"Gus, empanadillas are a pastry stuffed with ground beef, peppers and olives. If you don't like it, toss it out."

Gus shook his head, not knowing what to say. He had lived alone for over a decade and had forgotten what it was like to exchange pleasantries with another person. Betty was always upbeat and solicitous, unlike him. He knew he was a grouch.

Gus decided to give it a shot.

"What are you doing today?" he asked

"I'm meeting my mom at Kohls in Washington Township," Noah began. "She's going to buy me some new clothes. Stuff I need. Shirts, more jeans, other stuff."

Gus just nodded his head that he understood.

"Want to come and meet my mom?" Noah said.

"No thanks," Gus declined, then he remembered something.

"You need boots, BAD," Gus said. "When you come back, I'll take you to Red Wing Shoes on the Pike in Williamstown. You're an embarrassment to HomeMaxx and our department with those boots you have now."

"The Pike" was the local term for the Black Horse Pike that meandered through South Jersey, starting as Route 322 in Atlantic City and then becoming Route 42 50 miles later near Philly and veering off to become Route 168 until it ended near Camden.

"Gus, come with me to Kohl's, and then we can drive to Red Wing Shoes," Noah said, enthused by his bright idea. "It's a straight shot down the Pike from Kohl's."

Gus thought for a few seconds, his resting face betraying no emotion. He remembered being dragged around with Betty as she ran Saturday errands.

"Okay," Gus said reluctantly. "But we are using my truck, and I don't want to wait while you try stuff on in the store."

"Deal," Noah said, obviously elated.

As Gus got up from the table, Noah said, "And Gus, just because I'm gay doesn't mean I don't like trying clothes on like any other guy."

Gus couldn't help it. He had to laugh.

Jack admitted that the pizza was delicious. He was stuffed. He didn't have a clue how he got the energy to complete assembling the gazebo. He knew he had to because the daughters came home from school in nine days. Next Saturday was the final preparations day, with the TV installed, the chairs assembled, and the furniture placed.

Tyler looked sleepy, too, but Pam was always alert and full of energy.

"Jack, we have some things to tell you," Pam said.

"Are you leaving Tyler?" Jack said, mocking concern. "Finally."

Tyler arose from his post-pizza slumber and said, "She was just waiting for us to complete the entire backyard renovation to do it."

"You two are not funny," Pam said, hitting Jack and Tyler with her yellow cloth napkin.

Tyler sat up and adopted his manager's voice. "Jack, the Snows are closing the store in August. They don't care about our performance. The store's revenues have increased by 11 percent in the last month. People are working harder, the cat has attracted attention to the store, and Black Cobalt's price hikes and labor cuts have helped. If it weren't for the rent the store now has to pay and their monthly fee, the store would have posted in the best single month since it's the first year."

Jack knew this was coming, but it was still hard to handle.

Shortly, I am going to be homeless and jobless.

"I won't kid you," Jack began. "I'm worried about myself, but what about Gus? I don't know what he'll do without work. Who will Harry gossip with if he doesn't have a job? How about the new kid, Noah? And Robbie doing the carts."

With that last comment, Tyler and Pam looked at each other, and Jack caught a warning flare.

"Is there something going on with Robbie?" Jack asked.

"Jack, you know I don't want this," Tyler began as Pam stood closer to him as a support system. "But some woman complained to Corporate, and it got all the way to the Snows about Robbie getting into a tussle with some college kids from Rowan."

"I heard about it from Gus and Noah," Jack said, anger erupting in his voice. "They said those college kids were taunting Robbie by pushing the carts all over the parking lot."

Jack clenched his fists. "So some rich, spoiled college kids abuse an autistic teen and get caught, and mommy demands the kid gets fired because 'God forbid if my little darlin' is not just perfect.'"

"She told the Snows that Gus and Noah threatened them and banned them from the store, and she wanted them fired, too."

"Because they defended Robbie," Jack threw up his hands and started to pace.

"I told her and the Snows NO," Tyler said. "Gus and Noah stay, but Robbie is gone."

"Goddamn it, Tyler," Jack said as anger poured out of him.

"Jack, do you think I like this?" Tyler asked, his anger boiling up. "I had to tell my mother, who plays bridge with Robbie's mother every week. My mom has been playing bridge with Robbie's mom, Eleanor, for 40 years. You're mad. My mom is mad. I don't like this either."

Jack paused his pacing and tried to halt this fight or flight response.

Solutions, Jack. It's done. Now, how can it be fixed?

Jack had an idea. He took out his phone and started texting.

"Jack, what are you doing?" Tyler asked.

"I have an idea to help Robbie," Jack said. "I just have to see if it will work out."

Pam approached Jack, took him by the hand, and placed him back in his seat.

"Now, Jack, we have more to discuss, and some of it relates directly to you," Pam said as if she were showing a home to a prospective buyer.

"Eat that last piece of pizza," Pam said. "You know you want to."

Jack sat and felt himself calming down.

I do want that last piece.

"Jack, I've been in talks with Excell Hardware from their corporate headquarters in Downers Grove, Illinois," Tyler said. "You are looking at the next East Regional Manager for Excell Hardware beginning July 1."

Jack's broad smile matched Tyler's.

"What," Jack exclaimed. "That's terrific. You deserve it, man."

"Thanks," Tyler said. "I'm excited and nervous."

Jack stood up after he inhaled that last pizza piece and said, "Bring it in."

He hugged Tyler and slapped his shoulder. Pam joined in for a three-way hug.

"Jack, this is also good news for you and Lashay," Tyler said as he smiled at Pam.

They know something that they think will make me happy.

"Jack, you know, Dave Maloney wants to move to Florida to manage his Naples store and semi-retire there. Dave and Excell want you and Lashay to run the store as manager and assistant manager. I even got it worked out that Ellen and Darla can work there. Christine is taking a job with her sister at a dental office."

Jack sat back down and shook his hand.

"Dave has approached me several times," Jack said. "But honestly, I wouldn't leave you or HomeMaxx—or Lashay, for that matter."

"But now..." Jack said, shaking his hand as if he didn't believe it.

"It's not a done deal until you and Lashay say yes," Tyler said. "So, I'd talk to her tomorrow so I can call Sid Nelson first thing Monday morning."

"And Jack, one more thing," Tyler interrupted Jack's response. "Dave Maloney is open to you, or you and Lashay, buying him out of the Washington Township store so you could own it one day."

"I can't thank you both enough for what you're doing."

Pam jumped in and said, "Jack, please. All the work you've put into OUR house for free. You acting as a second manager at the store and supporting Tyler. No, Jack, we're the ones who are grateful."

Jack was back in the group hug again until Tyler said, "Jack, there is one thing you should know. It's not bad, but may complicate your decision."

"All right, what is it?" Jack asked.

"When you talked with Bernard Snow and his son earlier in the week, you made an impression on them," Tyler said.

"I actually thought they were going to fire me because I showed them how stupid they were," Jack answered.

"No, Jack," Tyler began. "On the contrary. Bernard Snow called me the next day about you. He knows people in high places in Grove Logistics, where you used to work. Despite what happened, several executives thought highly of your work in operations. They thought you got the raw end of that deal. With that recommendation and the fact that you impressed them in the store, Bernard Snow wants to hire you as a consultant for Black Cobalt."

"Wait. What?" Jack said, a little dazed from this turn of events.

"Jack, the salary he quoted was in the 175 thousand range," Tyler said. "Apparently, Black Cobalt squeezes the companies it buys for every penny but pays its executives very well."

"Wow," Jack responded to the salary. "But what about Lashay if I did take the Black Cobalt job? Would Dave Maloney offer her the manager position at the Washington Township Excell store without me?"

Tyler and Pam looked at each other as if they had already discussed this scenario.

"No, Jack," Tyler answered. "You must be part of the deal at Excell for Lashay, Darla, and Ellen to come along."

Jack shook his head. "No, then I'm not taking it. Besides, working for those greedy assholes."

"Jack, as a friend," Tyler began. "You should take time and think about this."

"Jack, I agree," Pam said. "After all, if you work for Black Cobalt, you'd be a voice of reason and an advocate for the bought-out companies and their employees."

"Plus, Jack," Tyler said. "The starting salary as manager of the Washington Township Excell Hardware Store is $70,000. You can make over a hundred thousand more at Black Cobalt. That's a lot of money."

"Talk to Lashay," Pam urged him. "See what she thinks. Think about it carefully before you make a rash decision."

These revelations still dazed Jack. He nodded yes.

"Can we get back to figuring out how to put this friggin' gazebo together?" Tyler asked.

That comment snapped Jack out of his stunned state.

"Rodgers, I have to save your ass again," Jack said as he picked up the instruction booklet.

Noah had to admit that his mother handled Gus like an experienced diplomat. When his mom helped Noah pick out some work pants and shirts, she also convinced Gus to buy some clothes. Based on what Noah had seen Gus wear since he had worked with him, Gus's wardrobe was pre-Y2K.

"Mr. Gus," his mom had implored, "You need some new work clothes, also. Don't worry. I will help you."

Before Gus could protest, she thrust work jeans from the rack against his hips and eyeballed the fit.

"Yes, very good, Mr. Gus," his mother, Antonella, flattered him. "Now, please go try them on. Go. Go."

"You too, mejo," she commanded Noah.

Gus seemed flattered, intimidated, and stunned by his mother's fussing over him.

When they walked out of Kohl's into the parking lot, Gus said, "Mrs. Fernandez, thank you. It was nice to meet you."

Noah had not seen Gus be this polite to anyone in the short time he had known him.

"Antonella, please," his mother answered as she reached out and shook his hand. Noah thought that Gus actually blushed.

Noah always wondered why his mother had married his father. Not that his father wasn't a good man, but because his mother came from a rich and well-known family on the island. His father was a diesel truck mechanic, then in San Juan and now in Vineland.

With Gus sitting in his truck, Noah's mother said, "Mejo, he seems like a good man but lonely."

"Yes, Mama," Noah answered. "His wife died about ten years ago, and his son Michael is like me, gay. And Gus is like Papa. Close-minded and not willing to see another viewpoint."

Noah allowed his anger to show itself with that sentence.

His mother responded by placing his palm on his cheek.

"Oh, Noah, your father doesn't handle change well," She told him.

"He calls routines and habits traditions," his mother told him, her tone sad and regretful.

"He'll never change, Mama," Noah said.

She patted his cheek. "Oh, my dear son. He already has. Do you know what he did after work last week?"

"No," Noah answered her.

"He gets off at 3:30 and drives from Vineland to Franklinville. He parks his truck at the far end of the HomeMaxx parking lot, and he watches you when you come out to help customers."

"How do you know this?" Noah asked.

She hugged him and whispered in Noah's ear, "A mother knows all. It is our superpower, mejo."

"Give your father some time," his mother implored him. "Traditions are easily embraced but difficult to abandon."

"Meantime, take care of Mr. Gus," she instructed him. "You must care for him. Where is the rest of his family?

"I don't think he has any, except for a son he banished. He's also gay. They haven't seen or spoken to one another in ten years."

"Does Mr. Gus want to?" his mother asked.

"His son's name is Michael," Noah began. "Michael's phone number is written on a sticky note and adhered to the wall next to the kitchen landline phone."

His mother hugged him.

"I will stop by to see you at Mr. Gus's house," his mother said. "I will make him my Arroz con gandules. He will not resist them."

Noah chuckled and said, "Thank you, Mama. I love you."

"I love you, too, mejo," his mother answered. "Mr. Gus is doing a good thing, helping you and giving you a place to live. Now, we must return the favor and help him."

"Help him do what?" Noah asked.

"Reconnect with his son Michael," his mother answered as she waved by his car door.

Chapter Twenty-Two

"To be trusted is a greater compliment than being loved." – George MacDonald

Ava Snow felt fortunate that she hadn't experienced the morning sickness that her mother had during her three pregnancies. Instead, she had these cravings for a Dairy Queen blizzard. She made Jacob drive from Elk Township to the Pike in Washington Township to pick her up a Reese's Peanut Butter Cup Blizzard, a Cotton Candy Blizzard, and a Snickers Blizzard.

She froze two and ate the Snickers one.

As she read the Sunday edition of the local *Philadelphia Inquirer*, Ava spotted an article about HomeMaxx. The article was written by a reporter named Gwen Phillips. She became more interested and disturbed as she read the article about a Calico cat that had shown up at the HomeMaxx in Franklinville. The dates that the cat wandered into the store correlated with the date that Jacob dropped off Cali, their Calico cat, at the Clayton Animal Shelter.

Tyler Rodgers, the store manager, and Lashay Jones and Jack Marsalis, the two employees caring for her, were interviewed. Jones named the cat Allegra.

Ava felt a lump in her throat as she turned the pages of the newspaper to find where the article continued. Bordered by an ad for a mattress store, the article had two photos of the Allegra, the Calico cat.

Ava stared at the black-and-white photos—one of the cat lying down on a bath vanity and the other of the cat frozen in its walk across the PVC pipes.

That is Cali. I know it.

How did Cali get from the Clayton Animal Shelter to the HomeMaxx store five miles away on Delsea Drive?

Jacob was in the baby's bedroom, assembling the crib. She could hear him curse during the process.

"Where the hell is slot B? What's a dowel?"

Ava knew that Jacob was controlling but not as bad as his father. Ava had a lifetime of experience with controlling parents. Her mother and father have been charter members of the Micromanager Hall Of Fame for her lifetime. Ava recalled her teenage years, and they were like jungle warfare. She fought with her parents about almost everything except her choice of Jacob as a husband.

Her parents wanted her to study nursing. She fought and won the war for graphic design and now had her own successful business. When her parents and Jacob wanted her to give up the business to be a stay-at-home mother, she said, "Absolutely not."

She only gave up on the cat because she thought the animal shelter could easily find another home for the cat.

Now, she thought, *"Jacob just dropped off the cat somewhere in the woods on Delsea Drive."*

Ava stared at those photos.

Could it be just a coincidence?

No, she decided.

She stood up and headed for the baby's bedroom. She heard Jacob banging around there as he stumbled through the crib assembly process.

He stopped holding two pieces of faux mahogany wood in his hands when she entered the bedroom.

Ava drilled into Jacob's eyes.

"Jacob, I'm warning you. If you lie, I will pack up my car and move out now."

Tyler Rodgers didn't work on Sundays. He was the store manager, and that position had a lot of stress but some perks. While two of his assistant managers took care of the store, he did something he hadn't done in a long time.

Walk around the store like a customer.

Tyler had always been too busy to walk deliberately around the store through a customer's eyes. After all, home improvement stores were not designed like upscale department stores with attractive, enticing interior design, mood music, familiar smells pumped into the space, and soft lighting.

HomeMaxx followed Home Depot and Lowe's design concepts, duplicating the warehouse look with high ceilings, uneven fluorescent lighting, high metal shelves, and sealed concrete floors. No matter how carefully the home improvement companies organized their stores with abundant signage, customers still roamed the store with their heads on a swivel, desperately searching for their products.

Tyler recalled the early days when he started out after completing his University of Delaware Business degree. He was hired by The Home Depot in the Turnersville store in Washington Township.

What a struggle that was.

He had a store manager, Paul Lanza, who thought screaming and degrading his assistant managers and other employees was the ideal motivational tool.

How many times did a customer approach Tyler in those early days with a question about how to locate a product, and Tyler didn't know?

Are you supposed to be the assistant manager? Shouldn't you know?

He heard that so often at the beginning of his career it haunted his dreams or nightmares. His former college roommate had introduced him to Pam, and he was trying to launch his career and find a way to convince the smartest and most beautiful girl in the world to marry him.

There were times when the job stress, the highs and lows of any new relationship, and just trying to be an adult almost overwhelmed him.

His parents made it worse. Before he moved out two years after graduating college, they never embraced the concept of positive feedback. It was always something he wasn't doing, doing wrong or not doing as well as their friends' children.

In less than two months, I'll be a regional manager.

Still, I'll miss HomeMaxx and all the people. Harry's daily gossiping, Darla's ability to soothe the angriest customer, Jack's capacity to work in any department, handle any emergency, and pump up everyone else, Lashay's versatility, Ellen's cool efficiency, Kelly's store announcements, and even Gus's ornery yet unbeatable work ethic.

Tyler focused on the present when he strolled through the entrance doors and immediately spotted Darla Campanna, who didn't usually work on Sundays.

"Darla, what are you doing here?" Tyler asked.

Darla removed her glasses attached to the silver chain, let them fall to her chest, and said, "Christine called out. Sam called me and begged; otherwise, he would have to pull Harry from Tools. You remember the last time Harry ran the returns/customer service desk?"

Tyler recalled that Harry received 14 complaints in one day for various infractions. Most of the complaints involved Harry asking customers questions that, on the bright side, could be called nosy and, on the legal side, inappropriate.

"Thank you, Darla," Tyler said. "There'll be an attaboy in your paycheck this week."

Darla met Tyler's smile with a smirk. "Hey, boss. I'll take one Ulysses S. Grant in place of ten attaboys."

Tyler saw the cat Allegra in Paint, up on the counter, and making friends with two customers Tyler was familiar with. This married couple, Chuck and Peggy Letts, had been shopping at HomeMaxx since Tyler came here as manager. They had been retired for a few years and lived in a 55-and-over community in Clayton called Villages at Aberdeen, not far from Scotland Run Park.

"Chuck, Peggy," Tyler said, offering a smile. "Long time, no see."

The couple said, "Hi, Tyler," in unison, and then Chuck asked, "Tyler, can you level with us? Peggy and I hear that the store is closing soon. Is that true?"

Tyler had to force himself to maintain his smile despite the strange brew of emotions boiling up inside him.

"You have been loyal customers since the store opened, and I appreciate that," Tyler began, massaging his words as he went along. The couple were lovely people who had spent a lot of money here over the years.

I owe them something more than an outright lie, but the truth can't get out yet.

"Our new owners haven't kept me in the loop," Tyler said, his words picking up speed as he firmed up his nuanced response. "So I will be as surprised as you to find out what's coming soon."

The couple parsed his words and nodded.

"We'll stop by before you leave," Peggy said.

Tyler smiled and waved, appreciating the couple's insight, as he walked down the aisle with the cleaning supplies. He spotted Allegra rubbing up against a woman in a nurse's uniform. Tyler knew the Calico liked to roam the store when her two humans weren't around.

"Allegra really likes you," Tyler said.

The woman, about 50, with brown hair and a fine dusting of grey, was as thin as a piece of copper wire.

"I used to have a cat for 18 years," the woman answered. "Mr. Whiskers."

"I'm Dotty McBride," the woman introduced herself. "I work across the street in the nursing home that just opened."

"Tyler Rodgers," Tyler replied.

"Oh, you're the store manager," Dotty exclaimed. "I saw your photo on the wall near the customer service desk. I have to say that it doesn't do you justice."

While Dotty spoke, Allegra rolled over on her back so the woman could scratch her belly. The cat's eyes closed, and her body relaxed as the woman massaged her.

"Well, thank you," Tyler said, not sure how to handle the compliment. He decided to change the subject.

"The nursing home looks beautiful on the outside," Tyler said. "How do you like working there?"

"The people who run Manor Life are terrific," Dotty began as she massaged

Allegra, whose purring now reached audible levels.

"This private equity fund owned the last nursing home I worked for in Glassboro. The Carlson Group," Dotty continued. "I quit after 12 years there. When they took over three years ago, patient care went out of the window, and it was all about profits. They cut staff so low that several patients died from neglect."

"You think the government would do something," Tyler said.

"I think they tried," Betty said, her exasperation leaking out. "The Carlson Group owned the nursing home through some shell companies, so they could never be held liable."

"Since a private equity firm bought HomeMaxx, it's been a challenge," Tyler said, afraid of divulging more information.

As Allegra popped up and now snuggled with Tyler's arm, Dotty said, "The nursing home patients would love a cat like this. It would brighten their day. They wait all week for a visit from their families. This cat could bring them that love and attention they seek every day."

Tyler nodded his head. "I'm sure you're right. Luckily for the store, this cat has brought us a lot of media attention, and sales have increased. Plus, the two employees caring for Allegra have grown attached."

"If that changes, let me know," Dotty said as she gave Allegra one more slow, deep stroke down her back.

"And you should update that photo on the wall by the customer service desk," Dotty recommended.

"I think a better photo would attract a lot more women into the store, Tyler."

Tyler hoped that the blushing he felt on the inside wasn't evident on the outside.

"Jack, I need help," Lashay said over the phone. Her voice sounded nervous and on the brink of panic.

"Lashay, are you okay? Are you in danger?" Jack asked.

"No, sorry to scare you," Lashay said. "The pipe under my kitchen sink cracked, and water leaked underneath. I shut off the water supply. I'm sorry to ask, but can you help fix it."

"Of course," Jack said. "Easy, peasey. Now, take a photo of the P-trap. That's the name of that pipe. I'll stop at HomeMaxx, pick up a new one, and be over in about 30 minutes. I have something to do here that'll take five minutes."

"Jack, if I'm ——-" Lashay began.

"It's all good," Jack said. "See you in 30."

When Jack hung up, he immediately changed from his nice jeans and a black polo shirt with these casual brown shoes he had just bought back into his work jeans, Flyers t-shirt, and work boots.

He planned to get dressed up, call Lashay, and take her to lunch at the Scotland Run Golf Club on Fries Mill Road. The club had an excellent restaurant called the Highlander. Jack knew the restaurant manager, Cliff, and could get in without a reservation.

Scuttle that plan. Time for plan two.

He couldn't leave, however, without first going to see the Szczesny's. Today was May 5, the 20th anniversary of the death of their daughter, Kelly, from a drug overdose. Every year, the three of them toasted Kelly. The toast took place at 3:30 pm after they closed the restaurant on Sunday at 2:00 pm and cleaned up.

It was 3:29. Jack walked upstairs and tapped on the back door.

"Jack," Wally said after he opened the door.

He held it open, and Jack walked through the kitchen and into the family room. The couple had a bar there with at least 20 different brands of bourbon whiskey displayed, from Blanton's to Woodford Reserve and Buffalo Trace to Pappy Van Winkle.

Jackie was seated at the bar with a full whiskey glass in her hand. Wally followed Jack, picked up his glass, and then handed Jack his glass. The whiskey glasses were monogrammed with a stylized S for Szczesny.

The grandfather clock in the living room chimed on the half hour.

It was 3:30.

"Let's raise our glasses," Wally began. "And remember our sweet Kelly.

Gone from us now for 20 years, but missed as if she left us only yesterday."

They all raised their glasses, nodded to one another, exchanged solemn expressions, and then drank.

"Woo," Jack said, shaking his head. He wasn't much of a hard liquor drinker, and bourbon seemed especially bitter to him.

"It's called Widow Jane," Wally said, making that smacking sound after he drank the bourbon. "It's a small craft bourbon with a tangy punch to it."

"As always, my condolences to both of you," Jack said.

They both nodded and put down their glasses on the bar.

"We miss her every day," Jackie said. "Some people get to start over."

"Kelly didn't get a do-over in life," Wally added.

"We can't change what happened to us," Jack said. "But we can change what we do with what happened to us."

They both nodded in agreement. Somehow, Jack sensed that the couple had more to say. Usually, the three of them would drink together, and then Jack would head out or back downstairs, and the couple would spend the day looking at old family photos.

Today, something else was about to happen.

"Jack, we need to talk to you," Wally said as if he were a physician delivering bad news to a patient. Like, "I'm sorry, you have cancer."

The couple stood close to one another like they needed support.

Wally looked like he was about to talk, but nothing came out.

"Jack, we told you we sold the business," Jackie began. "That process is moving faster than we anticipated. The buyers are offering us a lot more money if we close on the restaurant by June 1."

"Well, if they are going to give out extra money," Jack said, trying to give them permission to tell him what they were about to tell him.

"The same goes for the house," Jackie said. "A young couple from Sicklerville wants to buy the house at a premium price and close by June 1."

Jack did not move at all. His face remained impassive, but his insides felt like they were riding the highest, fastest rollercoaster in the world.

"I know we said you'd have time to find another place," Wally was now able to form words. "And we are going to honor that promise to you."

"One reason this sale is perfect is that the wife has an elderly mother, and the couple wants to move her into the basement," Jackie was back in charge. "But the mother is trapped in an apartment lease until October 1. She can't move into your place downstairs until then. We have written it into the sales contract that you can stay in your basement apartment until September 30, which should give you plenty of time to find another place to live."

Jack's insides went from frenetic to calm.

That's almost five months. I can find a place by then. Maybe with Lashay.

"Thank you both for thinking about me," Jack said. "Congratulations on the sale of your home."

The couple became more relaxed. Jack was touched that they considered his needs when selling their home. It was then he realized how much he would miss them.

The couple had been an integral part of his still-evolving redemption. They gave him a home, a sense of belonging, and unconditional love that emanates from families.

"How are you going to buy a house in New Mexico?" Jack asked. "You have less than a month?"

"Jackie's sister Marilyn and brother-in-law Kyle know of a vacant home in the 55-and-over community where they live. They toured the home and checked it out, and we've already made an offer," Wally explained.

"They accepted," Jackie said. "We have to start packing up immediately."

"You can count on me to help," Jack said.

He stood up because he needed to go to HomeMaxx, buy that P-Trap, and then go to Lashay's place to replace it under the kitchen sink.

"Thanks, Jack," Jackie said. "You know you're like family."

"Feel the same way," Jack responded before they spontaneously merged into a joint hug.

Chapter Twenty-Three

"**Trauma is hell on earth. Trauma resolved is a gift from the gods.**"
— **Peter A. Levine**

Jack checked the Nissan's trunk for his toolbox and then drove to HomeMaxx. He had already called ahead to HomeMaxx, and Harry had purchased the P-Trap for him and would meet him at the front door.

As Jack turned right onto Delsea Drive, the main drag for Glassboro, Clayton, and Franklinville, he tried to focus on the task at hand and not worry about the precarious future of his relationship with Lashay.

As he drove, he checked out the Silver Lake Diner and its full parking lot with patrons waiting outside for their names to be called. Clayton borough ended with a shabby Dollar General, Kevin's Liquors that was disturbingly warehouse-sized, a rundown independent gas station with a gas nozzle as its logo, and landscaping company property that was as perfectly sculpted and maintained as the manicured lawns the company cut.

Once in Franklinville, Jack spotted Angel House, which was a pet-boarding business that had been there before HomeMaxx was built. After that, there was a strip mall with a seemingly rotating roster of stores. Currently, there was a bagel place, an animal hospital, a Chinese takeout place, and one of the few Hallmark card stores left.

Jack pulled into the HomeMaxx parking lot and up to the entrance door. Harry was waiting.

"Thanks, Harry," Jack said as he opened the driver's side window of his old Nissan. "How much do I owe you?"

"Jack, we'll call it even if you can get me a job at Excell Hardware," Harry said, worry turning into panic in his voice.

"I heard that HomeMaxx is going to close soon, and I've seen you talk to Dave Maloney from Excell. Can you help me out?"

Jack handed him a ten-dollar bill and said, "I'm happy to talk to Dave. No promises, of course. But I'm paying you."

Jack took the P-trap and pulled away, thinking the cat was out of the bag. If Harry knew or thought he knew, then soon everyone would know. HomeMaxx employees would bail for other jobs.

Jack didn't blame them.

As Jack approached the intersection of Routes 40 and 47, he turned right, and his eyes always drifted to a completely empty shopping center on the right.

He started to feel the same panic that Harry had evinced at HomeMaxx. It wasn't the first time he had felt the overwhelming sense of his world crashing down on him.

Twenty years ago, he was sitting in jail, wondering if he'd be there for ten years. His wife had not only left him but abandoned him. His job was gone. He had no place to live. No money. And he had almost killed a man he had considered a close friend.

He thought about Lashay. Hooked. Addicted. She was only looking for pain relief, not for her whole life to be destroyed. Once down the rabbit hole of addiction, she could not find the light of redemption. Darkness swallowed her mind, then her body.

Jack couldn't really understand what she went through. He could only emphasize. But he found it ironic that Lashay was so worried that he wouldn't care for her anymore after he found out about her past.

If anything, her disclosure had made Jack love her even more.

Jack had made mistakes. He trusted a friend when he shouldn't have. He married a woman to fit a lifestyle, not for love. He almost killed a man.

Lashay, however, suffered the mental and physical attacks of an abusive husband. When he injured her, her doctor prescribed pain medication that was the gateway into a descent into the living hell called addiction. Once there, her willpower had been stripped away by the drug.

As Jack turned left onto Lake Road near the sleazy used car dealer, he thought about what he and Lashay had in common. It was powerful.

They had both battled back from the edge of disaster and slowly rebuilt their lives. Jack believed that they had survived because the fire that burned inside of them burned brighter than the fire around them.

Jack knew that redemption was not a straight line but more like a maze. Right now, both wandered, not knowing where the next corner would bring them. Their long-time job was ending. Jack had a few months left after more than 15 years in the same apartment with the same supportive landlords. He guessed that Lashay was dealing with a real estate giant who was only interested in draining mobile home tenants to improve the bottom line. After all, Jack had read that yacht prices had risen 18 percent in the last two years. These execs needed that extra money to afford the largest boat in the marina.

On the bright side, Jack and Lashay seemed to have jobs at Excell Hardware, working together in the Washington Township store. Jack even had an offer for a job with Black Cobalt that would make life very comfortable for him and Lashay. Yet, he never considered that offer.

Jack had been at the bottom of the well. He saw how the deck was stacked against those at the bottom of society. Sure, plenty of people climbed out. The strongest survived. So many others, like Robbie Nowicki, the cart kid, never really had a chance.

The government could sometimes help, but there were always strings attached. And those at the top denigrated them as "takers," "losers," and "thieves." They forgot the privileges – race, class, and a system prioritized for their needs — that always put them ten yards ahead of everyone else in the race for the American Dream.

Jack pulled up to Lashay's mobile home. She was at the door.

"Thank you, Jack," Lashay said. "I've learned to fix a lot around a house, but plumbing has always eluded me."

As Jack walked up to the door, he said, "Jack Marsalis Heating and Plumbing, ma'am. You know our motto. We keep you flushing."

"You're kind of a douche, you know that?" Lashay answered.

They laughed, and Jack got right to work under the kitchen sink. It didn't take Jack long to remove the old, damaged P-Trap, install the new one, turn the water back on, and test it.

"Good as new," Jack said.

"Want something to drink?" Lashay asked.

"Do you have an expensive bourbon?" Jack kidded. "Preferably on the rocks."

Lashay went to her fridge and pulled out a plastic water bottle with a HomeMaxx label. She handed it to Jack.

"Here you go, sir. Spring water from the corporate headquarters executive washroom of HomeMaxx."

Jack twisted the cap and took a big swig.

"My landlords have sold their house," Jack said.

"Oh, Jack," Lashay said. "You are welcome to sleep in my car."

Jack laughed. "The Szczesny's worked it out that I could stay until the end of September."

"That's a relief, I'm sure. You should be able to find a place by then," Lashay said, then hesitated and continued, "On that same note, I received a letter via certified mail. My corporate overlords are not renewing my lease. I have to be out by August 1."

"You can sleep in my car," Jack said, chuckling.

"Lashay, you know you can stay with me," Jack said. "My place is small, but then maybe we can find a –"

"What, Jack?" Lashay asked.

"A place together," Jack answered.

"Even after what I told you about my past?" Lashay asked.

They were still standing in the small kitchen area. Jack stepped closer to Lashay. He took in Lashay's long, wavy black hair, soft features, cobalt blue eyes, arched eyebrows, and satiny shoulders.

"Lashay, I love you," Jack said softly. "What I heard about a woman who fought her way back from so many obstacles has made me realize that I'd like you to take a chance on a guy like me."

Jack stepped even closer, putting down his water bottle. Lashay's blue eyes sparkled like pure-cut sapphire.

Lashay then realized that there was no reason to hold back. She had confessed everything to Jack and he still wanted her.

In fact, he loves me.

I think he wants us to live together.

Lashay hadn't been this happy since —. Maybe never.

"Jack, I love you."

She kissed him softly at first, then with more force as she pressed her body up against his. Jack responded, kissing her as she felt his strong body grip her.

Lashay put her hands under his t-shirt and felt his taut back and sinewy arms. She squeezed him tightly, and Jack slid his arms under her white t-shirt, moving his hands along her back.

She had no bra on, and as his hands brushed up against her left breast, she began to seize up. Suddenly, a flashback played in her head. She was on the streets in Camden, and this white guy offered her ten dollars for a blowjob, and she told him to get lost. The man was shorter than Jack but bulkier, with a shaved head and a Swastika on his neck.

He slapped her across the face with such force that she went down to her knees, and then he was on her. It was late, after two a.m., and the streets were quiet now that the bars had closed.

As she tried to get up, he slapped her again, and she collapsed on the sidewalk.

"Black bitch," she growled.

He grabbed her by the hair and dragged her down an alley. She tried to fight him off, but he was too strong. When she tried to scream, he punched her in the jaw, and she went limp.

In some back alley behind aluminum garbage cans, the man pulled down his pants, knelt down as she lay motionless, and pulled down her jeans.

Dazed and in pain, she had no strength to fight him off. He pulled her butt close to his body and then rammed his dick into her and started to pump away as he grunted.

"That's why we are the superior race, whore," he growled into her left ear, and he used his hands as leverage on her hips to jam his dick into her.

She felt him get harder inside her and tried to push him away, but she was too weak from the blows, and he was too strong and angry.

After what seemed like hours but was only a few minutes, he leaned into her ear.

"I'm going to leave you something to remember me by."

Then he was out of her, and she thought it was over.

"Take a deep breath, bitch because here it comes."

She still recalled the intense pain so vividly after all these years. As his heavy breathing and lunging increased in intensity, she passed out.

Lashay awoke some time later. Was it a few minutes? A few hours? Her jeans were still around her ankles. She felt wet back there. It was his ejaculate.

He had left her there like a piece of garbage.

Then suddenly, she was back with Jack. She pushed his arms away and backed away from him into the kitchen sink.

"Lashay, are you okay?" Jack said.

"What's wrong? Did I do something—?"

She started to cry, and Jack didn't move, afraid to touch her.

Lashay moved toward him. "Just hold me, Jack."

Safe in his arms, Lashay remained there, using his strength to regain hers.

"Lashay, if I did something –" Jack was apologetic.

She kept her face on his chest.

"Jack, I still have trauma visions of men, sweaty, smelly men with whiskey breath, violating me and me letting them do it for money or for drugs."

Jack just held her, and Lashay felt comforted by his silence.

"Their greasy, dirty hands on me, pawing at me. Grabbing me. Some hurting me because they liked that."

"Lashay, I'm sorry you had to go through that," Jack said. "I'm not rushing you at all. It's when you're ready."

"What if I'm never ready?" she asked.

It was a question she always asked herself.

"What if Black Cobalt decides to give out huge employee bonuses? Or Harry stops gossiping? Or the throuple breaks up? One thing we both should know better than most is that life offers no certainties. No extended warranties."

"Jack, are you sure?" Lashay asked. "With you being white and me black…"

"Wait," Jack said, looking puzzled. "You're black?"

"Jack, you are a jerk off," Lashay said as she pushed him.

They both laughed.

Lashay went back into his arms.

"Jack, I still have nightmares about the time this skinhead raped me," Lashay said. "I've never told anyone."

"If it'll make you feel better," Jack began, "go ahead and tell me."

Jack desperately wanted to beat the shit out of that guy. As Lashay shared her living nightmare, Jack forced himself to control his anger. He just held her and listened.

Sometimes, Jack knew, the best thing you could do to support someone emotionally was to stay nothing. Just be there.

Lashay remained silent for a few minutes after she described what happened to her. Then she lifted her head and kissed him.

"Thank you, Jack," Lashay said. "I feel better telling someone."

"I'm sorry you had to go through that, but I'm glad you felt like you could share it with me," Jack said.

Lashay's smile returned, and she said, "I never thought I'd fall for a white man."

"And I never thought I'd fall for a cat lover," Jack teased.

"You're okay, Marsalis," Lashay said. "I don't care what they say about you."

"Ha, ha, Jones," Jack answered. "We still have a few things to discuss."

"Okay, yes, Jack," Lashay said with a dramatic flair. "I'll move in with you, but we need to find another place. Your basement apartment is not even big enough for you."

"Great," Jack said. "I'll talk to Pam, Tyler's wife. She's the best. She'll find us a place."

"She better be," Lashay said. "Let's see two unemployed people—one black and one white, both ex-cons. Good luck with that search."

Jack held up his hand and wiggled his index finger.

"Not unemployed," Jack announced. "You are looking at the new manager and assistant manager at the Excell Hardware Store on Greentree Road in Washington Township."

"What," Lashay answered, confused. "What's happening? Dave Maloney made an offer?"

"Dave is moving to Naples, Florida, and is taking his long-time manager with him," Jack said, happy to share good news for a change of pace.

"We will be the new manager and assistant manager of the store. We can also bring two people with us, which I thought could be Darla and Ellen."

"If that's all right with you, Manager Jones," Jack teased.

"Jack, I hope you're kidding," Lashay said. "You have all the operations management experience."

"We'll argue about it later," Jack said. "Dave is stopping by the store to talk to us sometime this week. He'll talk money then."

Lashay suddenly lunged at Jack, hugging him.

"Jack, I don't believe this," Lashay cried.

Jack felt so good in her arms. He didn't want to move.

However, he had to share two more pieces of news.

"Lashay, Tyler texted me today," Jack began.

"From your change in tone, I'm guessing this is not good news," Lashay said.

"No. He was in the store today. Harry knows the store is closing sometime in the next two months. That means everybody knows. Tyler texted that even a few loyal customers think they know."

"That sucks," Lashay said as she started to pace in the small kitchen.

They stood directly in front of the three large windows that looked out onto the street. The mobile home was only about ten feet from the street.

Jack noticed an older woman with a wool cap on despite the warm temperatures, walking a white teacup dog with a pink bow in her fur about her eyes.

"Why is that lady with that dog staring at us?" Jack asked.

"That's Mrs. Beesley," Lashay answered. "She lives on the other side of the park. But she's the spy for the management company. Rumor has it that her rent is half that of everyone else because she rats everyone else out."

Jack looked at the woman spy and her little dog and then at Lashay.

Without warning, he drew her into his arms and kissed her. Surprised, Lashay didn't respond at once, but her mouth locked onto his lips after a few seconds.

Lashay pushed back, and then foreheads touched. Jack forgot about the woman and her dog.

"Jack, what if I never get over it?" Lashay asked.

Jack responded by looking out at the woman who had just stood in front of the mobile home and stared at them. Jack stuck out his tongue at her. Her eyes registered surprise and scorn, and she pulled the leash hard on her dog, who yelped as they moved away.

"When I was in prison, we'd get magazines to read that were sometimes torn up and twenty years old," Jack began. "I still remember to this day reading an article about Katherine Hepburn, the actress. I know she's famous, but I have only seen her as an old woman in *On Golden Pond*. Anyway, in the article promoting the movie, she said something I'll never forget."

"What was it?" Lashay asked.

"She said, 'Love has nothing to do with what you are expecting to get – only with what you are expecting to give – which is everything.'"

"There's the answer to your question," Jack said.

Chapter Twenty-Four

"What we imagine is order is merely the prevailing form of chaos." Author Kerry Thornley

Darla Campanna was relieved. It had been over a week since she spotted her ex-husband Clyde again. She thought maybe he was on a bender when he showed up. She pulled into the lot, didn't see his beat-up Chevy Cruze, and relaxed. She hadn't told Edgar because she was afraid that he'd confront Clyde. Edgar could handle himself, but Clyde was dangerous. Like take-your-life dangerous.

As she exited her car, a car's tires screeched next to her. It was the Chevy Cruze.

Clyde jumped out of the car and grabbed her by the throat.

She choked from the pressure of his right hand around her neck.

He got within inches of her nose and said, "I don't forget. I'll never forget how you betrayed me. You're going to pay, bitch."

He released his hold on her neck.

"And very soon," Clyde threatened as he got back in his car and drove away.

Darla couldn't move. She stood paralyzed by the open car door of her Honda RAV4.

Cars pulled up behind her, and doors slammed. Still, she couldn't move.

"Darla, Darla, are you okay?" It was Jack.

"Darla," Gus said.

She didn't respond. She couldn't move. Both men walked around and faced her.

"It's Clyde, isn't it?" Jack said, and she heard the anger spill into his voice.

"Jack, this time, you and I are going to put him down for good," Gus grunted.

For Darla, her nightmare was becoming more real every day. She wasn't afraid of Clyde hurting her as much as she was the kind of trouble Jack and Gus would get in for hurting Clyde.

Lashay thought Allegra was especially attached to her today as she watered the hanging flowers in the outside Garden department. It was early, and the outside Garden entrance wouldn't open for another two hours. Allegra wrapped herself around Lashay's legs and purred.

A few times during the morning watering, Lashay stopped and picked up Allegra. She held her in her arms and lightly massaged the cat's neck. The cat had been an oasis of warmth and optimism at the time when the store and its employees with Black Cobalt and its warning about closing the store and all others in the chain.

Since Allegra had come into her life, Lashay felt past echoes in her mind. She recalled nursing Tamara, holding her, and rocking her back to sleep in the middle of the night.

How had she been so wrong about a baby bringing Daryll and her closer? Tamara's arrival had the opposite effect. As Lashay took care of their newborn, Daryll would yell, "I need my sleep."

"I'm too tired for the baby."

"Will you keep that damn baby quiet?"

The one constant that year was his rage. Lashay should have realized that the baby distracted her from focusing solely on Daryll. Tamara was too young to be affected by Daryll's physical abuse, but Lashay kept thinking, "What happens when she's older?"

"Will she also become a target?"

After her descent into addiction and then prison, Lashay could have visited

Daryll's mother and demanded to see Tamara. Her life had been smashed into a million pieces. Putting it back together took all her energy and willpower.

At that point, she didn't think she deserved to be a mother. She had abandoned her child to chase an addiction she could not control. As a Black woman, she couldn't escape the shackles of slavery. As an addict, she was a slave to a drug and a pawn for anyone who could supply her with that drug.

As Allegra jumped up on the flower display trays, Lashay used one hand to water with the hand sprayer and the other to caress her soft, full fur.

How many times had she thought about finding Tamara? A thousand. Ten thousand. What would she say to her daughter? Now 24 years old, Tamara spent a lifetime without her.

"Hi Tamara, I'm your mother. Your father used to beat me up, and so I was prescribed pills for the pain, and I became an addict and went to jail."

It had been so difficult to confide in Jack, but somehow, the revelation seemed to help her accept what happened, what she did, and what she had done to start over.

"Excuse me," a female voice behind her shook her from her reverie.

Lashay turned to face a 20ish white woman with blonde hair who was several months pregnant. She was still able to wear her regular jeans, but Lashay could tell that new clothing was in her immediate future.

"Hi, I'm Ava Snow," the woman's voice sounded friendly yet oddly formal.

Allegra remained next to Lashay, standing on the flower table and rubbing against her right hip.

"Can I help you?" Lashay asked as she would for any customer.

"I saw WPVI news last night," the woman began. "They did a whole story about this cat who lived at a HomeMaxx store in Franklinville and delighted customers in the store."

"This is Allegra," Lashay said. "Beautiful cat, isn't she?"

"She is beautiful," the woman responded, then paused. Lashay could tell that she was trying to frame her next words carefully.

"I know this may sound a little – I don't know – unusual," the woman stuttered. "But my husband and I live in Elk Township, and several months ago, we adopted a Calico cat from the Clayton Animal Shelter."

"Don't you love that Calicos chirp at you," Lashay said. She knew there was more to this woman's story, but she decided to keep it friendly.

"I found Allegra in the back by the far fence," Lashay stopped watering and pointed toward the back of the outside Garden area.

Then, thinking that this woman might try to claim her, Lashay added, "She clearly had been abandoned by its owner."

"You see, that's the weird part," the woman countered. "We rescued our Calico named Cali from the animal shelter. My husband thought the cat could endanger my pregnancy, so he returned the cat to the animal shelter."

"Are you saying this is the cat you rescued and then gave up?" Lashay asked, dropping in a healthy dose of skepticism in her tone.

"Well," the woman began, clearly struggling. "So you didn't go to the shelter and adopt her?"

"As I said, I found the cat by the back fence several weeks ago," Lashay said. "There was a hole in the chainlink section, and Allegra came in. My co-worker Jack and I have been feeding her, and we have set up a litter box for her and a comfy bed."

Lashay gave the woman a "Is there anything else I can do for you?" look and waited.

It occurred to Lashay that the woman's husband had not returned the cat to the animal shelter as promised and had released it, probably in the cornfield near the store. The woman had apparently come to a similar possibility because she said, "So I guess I should call the Clayton Animal Shelter and check on the disposition of Cali?"

Lashay recognized confusion, regret, and hurt in the woman's deep brown eyes.

"Do you want to hold her?" Lashay said.

The woman's face lit up, and she carefully picked up Allegra, who settled into her arms and purred.

"She seems so much like my Cali," the woman said as she caressed the cat, who chirped at her and prompted a giggle from the woman.

"Ava," Lashay used her name now. "Why don't you stop at the Clayton Animal Shelter and have them check Cali's adoption records."

"That's a good idea," Ava said. "It's on my way home on Delsea Drive."

After a minute, Allegra riggled out of her embrace and took off after two customers who had just entered from the inside doors.

She looked at Lashay with a sadness Lashay could understand.

She gave up a cat. I lost a daughter.

"I shouldn't have let my husband, mother, and father-in-law talk me into giving up Cali."

As she turned to leave, Lashay had a flash of recognition.

"Snow," Lashay said to the woman.

"Yes," Ava answered.

"Are you related to Bernard and Jacob Snow?" Lashay asked.

"Yes," Ava said. "Why?"

"Because they are closing this store and putting all of us out of work," Lashay said as she turned away and began misting the hanging plants again.

The woman walked away, and Lashay shut off the water and unlocked the outside Garden customer entrance. It was a chain lock holding two chainlink gates together.

As she opened the gates, Lashay stopped and stared at the parking lot. There, Robbie was gathering carts and organizing them. Robbie, who the Snows had insisted be fired after a complaint from the mother of those entitled college kids, was working again.

Lashay called Tyler on the work phone, dialing his three-digit extension.

"What's up, Lashay?" Tyler answered. His voice sounded remarkably calm, considering that Harry had blabbed to all the other employees who were lined up to talk to Tyler to find out if their jobs were disappearing.

"Tyler, Robbie is gathering carts in the parking lot," Lashay said. "Did you rehire him?"

"What, oh jeez," Tyler said, his calmness vaporized. "I better call his mother."

"How did he even get here?" Tyler asked.

"Lashay, can you possibly corral him and keep him by you and out of the parking lot?" Tyler asked. "PLEASE."

"I'm on it," Lashay said as she headed for the parking lot.

Jack hoped today would not be a harbinger of things to come at HomeMaxx. First, there were not a lot of customers, and Jack wondered if that was due to the rumors that HomeMaxx was closing. It seemed the only customers in the store were searching for Allegra, saying, "Excuse me, sir, my daughter wants to pet the cat we saw on the news."

Jack had just changed her litter box, refilled her dry food, and fixed her bed while Allegra chirped and purred. She had followed him back to Doors and Windows until she leaped onto a bathroom vanity and was surrounded by three women with expensive-looking pocketbooks.

In addition, co-workers like Kathy Marino, Lauren Garcia, and Christine Berrino held intense conversations with him about rumors of the store closing.

"Will Kathy, Ron, and I still have a throuple if the store closes?" Lauren asked him.

"Do you think we'll get severance pay for every year you worked here?" Christine asked, who had been at HomeMaxx ten years ago.

"Should I take advantage of the employee discount? We need a new dishwasher and refrigerator." Kathy asked.

Jack told her emphatically yes.

Jack talked to Luther from Maintenance, who said in his usual low-key way, "Jack, I'm tired. If the store closes, I have my excuse to retire."

As Jack walked around the store to check on everybody, he spotted that young Black woman again standing near the stacked boxes of ceiling fans and looking out into the outside Garden department.

Now that Lashay had shared her past, Jack assessed the young woman. She was about 22, maybe older, at least five foot nine, and as Jack came closer, with sparkling blue eyes.

Jack stopped near the solar garden lights display and thought about whether he should engage her.

It's not really my business. Lashay may resent it that I got involved.

His cell phone rang.

"This is Jack," he said.

"Jack, Lashay just spotted Robbie in the parking lot gathering carts," Tyler said, the urgency in his voice. "Can you help? I just called his mother, and she'll be here in ten minutes."

"Be right there," Jack said. "I'm just finishing with a customer."

Jack approached the young woman slowly. She was so focused on watching Lashay that she didn't even notice Jack.

"Hi," Jack said.

The young woman looked at him, hesitated, nodded, and returned to watching Lashay. Her body language signaled, "Leave me alone."

"I'm sorry. I just wanted to know if you are ever going to actually speak to your mother," Jack said.

That got her undivided attention. She turned to confront him.

"I don't know what you think you know, but stay out of my business," The young woman ordered.

"Fair enough," Jack said. "But you should know that your mother is a wonderful woman, and she loves you."

Now, she was fully engaged.

"Wonderful. Wonderful," the young woman said, her voice rising in volume and intensity. "She was a junkie. She's an ex-con. And she abandoned me when I was a baby."

"Who are you, anyway?" she asked, irritated.

"I'm Jack, a coworker, and I'm a friend of your mom's," Jack said, keeping his tone low and nonthreatening.

"You're Tamara," Jack said, half as a question and the other half as a statement.

"She told you about me?" Tamara asked, genuinely surprised.

"She has," Jack said. "What do you know about your mother?"

"That she became a pill addict and dealt drugs in Camden, was arrested, and did time. And she abandoned me and my father."

"That's not the whole story," Jack said. "Why don't you ask her?"

Jack realized he had gone as far with Tamara as he could without crossing even more lines. He had to call Luis and then see Robbie in the parking lot.

"Do you want me to tell her that you were here?" Jack asked. "It's your call."

Tamara hesitated, turning toward the exit, taking a few steps, and then stopped.

"Yes," she said, and she hurried out of the store.

Jack should have known that Lashay would have the Robbie situation well in hand. When he walked through the automatic doors inside to the outside Garden area, he spotted Robbie helping a couple by loading black mulch on their cart.

"Your girlfriend seems to have everything under control," Tyler's voice came from behind Jack.

Tyler moved next to Jack and they watched this scene unfold. Robbie smiled as he loaded bags of mulch on the cart, stacked neatly so they wouldn't fall when the cart was moved.

"Robbie's mother was frantic," Tyler told Jack. "She went to Shop Rite to do her weekly grocery shopping, and when she returned, Robbie was gone. She thought he had gone for a walk, which he had started to do since he was fired from HomeMaxx. She said he listened to Star Trek audiobooks while he walked. When he didn't return, she was about to call the Franklinville Police."

"Thankfully, Lashay spotted him in the parking lot gathering carts," Tyler continued. "She called me, and I called Robbie's mother."

"Where does Robbie live?" Jack asked.

"In Franklinville, off of Coles Mill Road," Tyler answered. "By the Janvier Fire Company building."

"That's a long walk down Pennsylvania Ave," Jack said. "and dangerous with no sidewalks."

Tyler looked over at Jack, and his blue eyes hovered over Jack's features.

"Jack, I've known you a long time," Tyler began. "Please tell me you have something for the kid."

"Luis and his wife, Aldea Martinez, own an office cleaning business they run out of their home in Elk Township," Jack said.

"Where are you going with this, Jack?" Tyler asked.

"They are having a problem hiring people to clean offices at night for them," Jack said. "First, because they are Salvadoran immigrants, and some people think they are too good to work for, you know, such people. Second, the unemployment rate is under four percent. Working at night as an office cleaner is not a desirable job unless..."

Tyler finished that sentence, "unless you're an autistic young adult with a penchant for cleanliness and organization."

"I just called Luis," Jack said. "They've invited me over for dinner several times. Tonight, I'm going over for a delicious taste of native Salvadoran dishes. Have Elaine and Robbie meet me there at six."

Tyler stared at Jack. "You know, Jack. It pisses me off that you could probably do a better job at managing this store than I did."

They laughed as a blue, beat-up Ford Taurus pulled up in the lot outside the Garden entrance.

"I'll talk to Elaine and Robbie," Tyler said. "Text me Luis's address unless you want to come over and talk to mother and son. After all, you should take the credit."

"No, it's all right," Jack said. "I have to talk to Lashay about something. Besides, I am Mr. Spock, and you're Captain Kirk of the Enterprise."

Jack called out as Tyler walked toward the parking lot. "Everyone knows that Mr. Spock is smarter than Kirk."

"You don't have pointy ears, Marsalis, "Tyler chided him. "Just a pointy head."

Jack walked over to Lashay, where she was checking out the couple with all the mulch bags.

"Mr and Mrs. Childs," Lashay began, "thanks for allowing Robbie to help you and for tipping him so generously."

"Happy to help him," Stacey Childs said. "He was really helping us. After all, Mike has the upper body strength of a newborn."

They all laughed as Mike Childs posed like a bodybuilder, showing his biceps.

"Mike, I'll help you load the bags into your car," Jack said. "Let me just have a word with Lashay here."

"Oh, oh," Lashay said. "You have that look. Either you have bad news, or you've done something. Knowing you, Jack, it's the latter."

Jack rubbed his stubbly face with both hands.

"I just talked to Tamara," Jack said.

Jack waited for a reaction. Lashay's eyes welled up, and her right hand tried to clear them away.

A customer pushed another cart to the checkout area with bags of mulch, perennials, and a juniper tree balancing precariously on the flat surface.

Jack leaned into Lashay and whispered, "We can talk later, but when I asked her if she wanted me to tell you that she was here, she said yes."

Lashay immediately went back to customer service mode, composing herself and saying to the customer, "Hello, sir. Did you find everything you needed today?"

Chapter Twenty-Five

"People used to think I was a monster. And for a long time, I believed them. But after a while, you learn to ignore the names people call you and trust who you are." Shrek

Noah was so nervous this morning that even Gus noticed it.

"What's wrong with you, kid?" Gus asked as they drove to work together in his pickup truck. Gus had substituted fruit names for "kid" for Noah, and that worked for Noah. After all, he had been called a lot worse, usually at school. He remembered sophomore year when someone – he never found out who – was printing out photos of naked men and slipping them through the vent in his locker. That went on for most of the school year.

Noah would never have believed it after his first horrible day at HomeMaxx, but he concluded that living with Gus was all right. Better than "all right," Noah was actually enjoying the curmudgeon. He was like a BlowPop, hard on the outside and softer, not soft, on the inside.

Noah had just finished cleaning and organizing the entire house. At first, Gus just watched him with amusement, but then he began pitching in.

"Let's throw this out. I don't need it," he'd say.

"It's too crowded in here," Gus agreed when Noah tried to change the family room's design.

Gus was ecstatic when Noah convinced him to drop Comcast cable, keep their Wi-Fi service, and sign up for YouTube TV. It saved Gus $80 a month, especially for someone who basically watched three channels – Game

Show Network, ESPN, and Noah, who was sworn to secrecy upon threat of evisceration, the Hallmark Channel. Noah would come home and find Gus sitting in his broken-down, threadbare recliner, trying to dry his eyes as the end of a Hallmark Christmas movie.

Gus's exact words were: "Kid, if you ever tell another living soul that I watch these movies, they won't find your body until they have to redo my septic 15 years from now. And I'll be dead by then."

At work, Gus was still Gus. He was rude to customers but helpful in that he knew more than them and helped them in his own rough-and-ready way. Noah had grown accustomed to staying an hour after they punched out because that was Gus.

Noah's mother began stopping over the house and bringing delicious Puerto Rican food that Gus initially disdained until he tasted it.

He'd try a few bites and then say, "Kid, what do you call this?"

"Mofongo, Gus," Noah would say.

"I like it," he answered and then ate the entire helping his mother had brought over.

Gus's favorite was his mother's Pastelon, which Noah explained was like lasagna. Noah's mother always called him "Mr. Gus" and did her best to give him a lot of attention. Noah could tell that she liked Gus and wanted the best for him.

Last week, she stopped over and said, "Mr. Gus, I ate lunch at the Silver Lake Diner with my book club. I think the server there, Bonnie, is sweet on you."

Gus's response was short and direct. "Women."

Noah had now noticed his father stopping by HomeMaxx and browsing the store, trying to make sure that Noah didn't see him. Noah had alerted Jack and Lashay to his dad's spy missions, and they had kept track of him in the store.

Jack would call on the store phone to lumber. "He's in Appliances."

Or Lashay would call and say, "Noah, your father is looking at knockout roses."

Noah didn't push him. He knew his father needed time. Noah didn't think it was right that his father had kicked him out of the house and cut off all contact. But he also knew his father was on a journey that meant a radical change in his beliefs and values.

Noah knew that transformation took time. Safe and secure at Gus's house, Noah could now give him that time. Even his sister, Carmen, had even stopped over with the baby.

Gus surprised everyone by going wild over baby Alex. Gus played with him and was so uncharacteristically free and fun-loving that Noah and Carmen grinned at each other with an "I can't believe I'm seeing this" look.

The visit ended with Gus saying to Carmen, "Alex is welcome here anytime. In fact, he's more welcome than Noah."

Of course, Noah was worried that the store was closing. Gus had told him the rumors were true.

"How about you, Gus?" Noah had asked. "Will you retire?"

"Kid, that's like asking if I want to die," Gus grumbled. "Friggin' Jack. The guy's like a matchmaker for jobs. He got the spastic cart kid a job at a cleaning service. He got Lauren Garcia a job at Lowe's in Mantua in the paint department, which is her thing, and he found me work with Edgar, Darla's husband, as a dump truck driver."

Even when things were bad, they were good, Noah decided. He thought he deserved some good fortune in his life.

That was until the phone call ten days ago.

Gus had a landline with a very old push-button phone that hung on his kitchen wall. It was this weird green that apparently was popular in the 70s. Gus didn't have an answering machine and didn't know how to retrieve his messages through the system voicemail. Most of the calls were scams or telemarketers.

Gus would answer and invariably start screaming and cursing at them, asking for their physical address so that he could "kick the livin' shit out of you."

One night, Gus had gone to bed at nine, which was his usual bedtime. Noah stayed downstairs and switched from *Family Feud* to *Elsbeth* on CBS.

The phone rang, and, as usual, Noah didn't answer it. Gus had made it clear that only he answered the phone. Five minutes later, it rang again. And again, Noah ignored it. Every five minutes, the phone and every time Noah ignored it. After almost ruining the part where Elsbeth catches the killer, Noah finally had enough.

The phone rang. Noah answered.

"Hello, who is this?" Noah asked, contempt baked into every syllable.

The voice on the other end was a middle-aged man.

"Who is this?" the man asked. He sounded young and perturbed that someone other than Gus had answered the phone.

"Is this Gus Burdette's phone?" the man asked, now sounding more puzzled than upset.

"Sorry," Noah answered, trying to put the caller at ease. "I'm Noah, Gus's co-worker and current roommate."

Silence. Then: "My dad has a roommate? In what universe?"

Noah realized that the voice was that of Michael, Gus's son.

"Oh, hi. You're Michael, Gus's son," Noah said. "I heard a lot about you."

"Did my father call me the names of different fruits?" Michael asked.

"No, but he did that to me that first few days we worked together at HomeMaxx," Noah said.

Again, silence. Then: "Wait. I'm trying to process this. Noah, you're gay?"

"Michael, I know what you're thinking," Noah began.

"I'm thinking this is a nightmare, and I'll wake up soon," Michael interrupted.

"Do you have time for me to tell you how I got here?" Noah asked.

"I have to hear this," Michael said. "Let me sit down."

It took Noah about twenty minutes to explain the events of the last month. Michael was interested in Noah's life and his banishment by his father.

Noah liked Michael right away. His voice was lower-pitched like Gus's. Michael sounded like he had it together, Noah thought.

He's where I want to be.

"My dad was a good father," Michael told him. "I know I wasn't the kind of son he wanted. You know, watching MMA fights, and beers at the VFW. He was grumpy but good-hearted."

"When he turned on me when I outed myself, I wasn't surprised more than I was disappointed," Michael said. "My mother had known, maybe even before I did. Noah, she was such a wonderful woman. Only someone like her could have put up with my father."

"Your father has your cell phone number on a sticky note next to the kitchen phone on the wall," Noah said. "Sometimes, I catch him picking up the receiver, putting his fingers on the buttons, and staring at your number. He does that on his cell phone multiple times a day at HomeMaxx."

"To tell the truth, I've done the same thing," Michael admitted.

"So, is this the breakthrough phone call I answered instead of your dad?" Noah asked.

Michael chuckled. "Actually, my partner of five years, Max, has been nagging me to call my father, and I've been ignoring him until…"

Noah took a breath. This revelation was either going to be very bad or very good.

"The Colorado Department just approved us of Human Services to adopt a baby girl," Michael said, unable to contain his excitement.

"We've been trying for three years now," Michael said. "But with the backlash on gay people these days and the bureaucracy of the government, we thought it might never happen."

"Hey, congratulations," Noah said. "Boy? Girl? Details?"

"It's a girl," Michael said, his voice softening. "Her name is Aubrey Mae. That's Max's mother's maiden name and my mom's middle name."

"That's great," Noah said. "You were calling to tell your dad?"

"No, actually," Michael said. "My plan was to let him know that I was flying into Philly and visiting my mom's sisters, Barbara and Bridget, who live in Haddonfield. They were close as sisters with my mother, and I know they'd love to see the baby."

"It was Max who convinced me to visit my father," Michael continued. "He's a therapist, so he has this insatiable desire to solve family problems."

"You were calling then to tell your father you're visiting your aunts, and could you stop by the house," Noah said. "Then you'd surprise him with his granddaughter."

"That's the plan," Michael said. "Think it'll work? You know him now better than I do."

"The other day, my mother brought over her new grandson and my nephew Alex, who's a little older than one. Your dad loved him. He played with him, held him, and made silly faces. I've never seen him that happy."

"Noah, my dad happy and smiling is like a solar eclipse," Michael said skeptically.

"That's true," Noah answered. "But a solar eclipse is so rare, it's big news when it happens."

Noah and Michael had hatched this plan for Michael's visit. Noah thought Michael approaching Gus at work, HomeMaxx, would make it much less likely that Gus would make a scene. Michel would arrive with Max and the baby, and Noah's job was to have Gus outside when that went down.

Today was D-Day. Or G-Day for Gus. Noah was as nervous as a parakeet in house full of cats.

It was 10 o'clock—arrival time. Luckily, the Lumber and Building Materials department wasn't busy. He and Gus had just loaded ten sheets of pressboard onto a pickup truck, and now just a few customers were milling around. Gus was still outside when Noah saw Michael and Max, who was carrying the baby in his arms, walking through the parking lot.

Noah could tell it was Michael because he looked like a blend of Gus and Betty, whose photos Noah had seen all over the house. Michael was over six feet tall with broad shoulders like Gus, short, light brown hair combed to the side, and soft features like his mother's.

He's an attractive man. He walks with such confidence. I need to find that confidence.

As Michael approached, Noah kept swallowing as saliva welled up in his mouth from nervousness.

"Hello, Dad," Michael said.

Gus, who had been moving some lumber to the side, looked up and saw Michael with another man and a baby.

Gus froze. His body didn't move. His face was stone.

Noah was behind Gus and thought he might hyperventilate.

"Mike," Gus said, standing up straight in a neutral voice.

Noah could tell that Michael was anxious, especially given Gus's initial emotional reaction, but he plowed ahead.

"Dad," Michael said, using his open palm to point. "This is my partner, Max, and our daughter, Aubrey Mae, who we just adopted."

"Hello, Mr. Burdette," Max said convivially.

Gus didn't respond. He turned back toward Noah.

"Did you know about this, mango?" Gus asked accusatorily.

Noah swallowed hard.

"Yes, Gus," Noah answered in a low, scratchy voice. "I thought..."

Gus turned back toward Michael, Max, and the baby.

"And they let people adopt a baby, like you two," Gus said. "That's a crime. And if it isn't, it should be."

Michael looked over To Max as if to say, "I told you so."

"Let's go, Max," Michael said as he turned and headed for their rental SUV.

Max didn't follow. He was shorter than Michael but in great physical shape, with corded neck muscles and a classically handsome face. He wore black jeans, a black polo shirt, and black sneakers.

"Mr. Burdette," Max said. "We are staying at the Hampton Inn on Route 42 in Washington Township in case you come to your senses."

Then he turned with the baby and headed toward a black Lincoln Navigator.

Gus turned around and glared at Noah. He thought Gus might punch him.

"You knew about this?" Gus asked.

"Yes," Noah answered.

"I am going to finish work today and have dinner at the Silver Lake Diner," Gus told him. "By the time I get home, you better have all your shit out of my house."

As Gus walked away, he turned and growled, "Go back to living in your car, tangerine."

When Jack heard Kelly announce that he and Lashay should report to the office, he figured Dave Maloney was there to make the formal job offer as manager and assistant manager for the Washington Township Excell Hardware Store on Greentree Road in Washington Township. He met Lashay outside the office door, and his broad smile matched hers.

"Big day for us," Jack said.

"Better get used to taking orders from me," Lashay chided him.

They walked into the outer office and said hi to Ellen and Kelly, who did not look happy. Jack figured they had heard something inside Tyler's office that had upset them. The smile from his face evaporated like sweat in the walk-in freezer.

When they walked into Tyler's office, Dave and Tyler were both standing up.

Not a good sign at all.

"You guys want to sit down?" Tyler said, pointing to the two plastic chairs in front of his desk.

"You two are standing, so I guess we will, too," Jack said.

Lashay nodded in agreement and leaned up against the far wall.

Dave Maloney looked morose, and that was a difficult task for a man who, as long as Jack had known him, was as upbeat as you would meet. Sometimes, Dave was even too false positive, as if feeling pain was not a viable defense mechanism.

"Jack and Lashay, I received a phone call from Jacob Snow from Black Cobalt. Apparently, your employee contracts have a non-compete clause of two years," Dave announced.

Maloney looked over at Tyler as if they had rehearsed this news.

"Jack, this relates to me, too," Tyler said. "My job offer as region manager for Excell has been rescinded."

Jack looked over at Lashay, who appeared stunned.

"Sorry, Tyler," Jack said. "This sucks. Is there anything we can do?"

"We can get a release agreement from Black Cobalt," Tyler said. "But I don't see that happening."

"What if I accept Snow's job offer as a consultant," Jack began, "and agree only if they release you so you can work at Excell."

"Wait, what job offer?" Lashay asked.

Tyler looked over at Jack with a "you didn't tell her" look.

Jack realized that he had screwed up. He had no intention of taking Black Cobalt's job offer. He'd never work for those greedy bastards.

But he should told Lashay. He didn't think about it. Now, he regretted not saying anything.

"Lashay, I should have told you," Jack began, regret seeping into his tone. "I never took it seriously. I'm sorry."

Jack looked at Lashay, whose face stiffened in anger.

"Jack, it's bad enough that we lost this opportunity with Excell, but for you to withhold this from me..." Lashay lectured him.

Jack said, "I'm sorry. You're right."

Dave Maloney, who had stood by when they all anguished over this development, spoke up. "Look, Sid Nelson and Excell Hardware are not sitting back and allowing Black Cobalt to screw us, and me, like this."

In one of those rare times Jack had seen Dave angry, Maloney clenched his fists and said, "We're going to fix this."

Tyler appeared much calmer than Jack, who manufactured anger inside like the electric grid on a hot August day and nodded at Maloney and his remark. Lashay still maintained an "I could stab you in the heart" glance toward Jack.

Life makes us work for everything.

Jack shook his head in disbelief.

Chapter Twenty-Six

"Change the way you look at things, and the things you look at change." — Wayne W. Dyer

Gus walked into the Silver Lake Diner before dinner and after lunch, so the place was quiet. Gus had been coming here for years, and Betty loved it. They'd go to breakfast on weekends or have a Sunday dinner here with Michael after his soccer games. It was familiar. You knew what to expect, and Gus didn't like change or uncertainty.

Gus had known Bonnie, the waitress, for over twenty years. Gus remembered that she had started working here after her husband had died in a construction accident at work. Bonnie never talked about her life but focused on the lives of her diners.

"Sam, how's the gout? Make sure you take your pills."

"Bev, what's new with your book club?"

"Have you made up with your daughter?"

Bonnie had kind words for those who needed it, supportive words for those who required encouragement, and even "kick in the ass" pronouncements for those who didn't know what was good for them.

"Hi Gus, want a booth?" Bonnie greeted him with her characteristic smile and twinkle in her eye.

Gus nodded and followed her to a booth in the back, where no other diners were around. He sat down and forced a smile, wondering why Bonnie had seated him so far away from everyone else.

"Coffee, please," Gus said.

He wanted to be alone and think. Think about how everything was so wrong. Noah had betrayed him. The kid he took in and saved from living in his car had stabbed him in the back.

Michael was back, but no different. Not that Gus thought he would be. Gus really thought that his reaction to Michael's lifestyle would change.

It hadn't.

Bonnie returned with a cup of coffee, a bowl of non-diary creamers, and a bowl of concern on her face. Gus studied her as she assessed his well-being. Bonnie was only a little over five feet tall, with a roundish body, alabaster skin with few wrinkles, and smoky, deep brown eyes. Gus wondered how old she was. 60?

"Gus, are you okay?" Bonnie asked.

She stood next to him at the booth. Concern leached out of her. Gus felt it.

"Bonnie, what do you do when your beliefs interfere with your family? With her life?" Gus said.

"Ah, I don't want to bother you with my problems," Gus said, dismissing his problems with a wave of his hand.

"You work on tips," Gus continued. "You got other tables."

Bonnie had this smile that seemed to emanate from inside of her, Gus thought. He never really noticed it until now.

"Gus, I clocked out five minutes ago," Bonnie began. "I stayed because I saw you coming in from the parking lot."

"Bonnie, why would you do that?" Gus asked.

"Why do you think, Gus?" Bonnie said as she rolled her eyes.

After Betty had died, this place was his sanctuary. He thought that was because of the diner. Now he realized it was because of Bonnie. She had been his sounding board, his therapist, and his life coach. All over coffee, waffles, and apple pie with vanilla bean ice cream when he came for dinner.

How could he have been so dense? So stupid?

"If you're off from work," Gus said, bumping into his words. "Would you like to join me?"

"I've been waiting for you to ask me that for several years," Bonnie answered as she slid into the seat on the other side of the booth.

Bonnie then made a hand motion, and another server, Joanne, came over. Gus noticed the server's smile was about to break orbit because it was so large. Gus realized that, apparently, the rest of the diner knew about...them.

"What can I get the both of you?" Joanne asked, looking back and forth at each of them like a celebrity had just rolled in.

"Joanne, I'll have a Diet Coke. Can you have Sergei make me his special eggplant lasagna? Thanks."

Joanne tossed out an easy smile. "One Bonnie special coming right up."

After she walked away, Bonnie said, "Now, Gus. Please tell me what's going on?"

"I mean, how far back should I go?" Gus asked. "This will be boring for you."

Those smoky brown eyes caught a flame and lit up.

"Gus, we're friends," Bonnie answered. "What's going on in there?"

Bonnie took her right index finger and gently touched his forehead.

Gus decided what to do.

"I think an open-faced hot turkey sandwich with cranberry sauce and stuffing would help me," Gus told her.

Bonnie rolled her eyes and said, "Men. You have only two things on your mind."

Gus began to tell Bonnie his history with his son Michael. Kicking him out after his college graduation when he told Gus and Betty he was gay. Then, having a blowout argument with him after Betty's funeral. Then, Gus had not heard from him for years, and Michael suddenly showed up at HomeMaxx earlier today.

"Gus, let me ask you," Bonnie said. "Why are you so against Michael being gay?"

Gus shrugged. "It's how I grew up. It was part of our values. I'm not religious, and neither were my parents, but they didn't approve. My father taught me what it means to be a man. And being a ho...gay, wasn't it."

"Gus, do you love your son?" Bonnie asked.

"Well, I think..." Gus stumbled over those few words.

"No, Gus," Bonnie cut in, her voice like he never heard before – strong and insistent.

"Yes," Gus replied.

"Then, Michael being gay may be against your beliefs, but is it worth losing him for a lifetime?" Bonnie asked.

"I don't know," Gus said, his head drooping into his hands.

"Gus, you cannot change what you are, only what you do," Bonnie told him.

"I just don't know if I can do that," Gus said.

Bonnie took his hands by the fingertips.

"Gus, you act like this tough guy who's not afraid of anybody or anything," Bonnie said. "All things are difficult before they are easy."

"Gus, You have to decide if living the rest of your life without your son and now your granddaughter is worth it," Bonnie said. "If it is, rip up his number on your kitchen wall and delete his contact info. There's no going back."

"Your son is reaching out. He has a whole life he's asking you to be part of. Maybe you see each other once a year and talk a few times on the phone. Or maybe it's more than that. But Gus, I know you have it in you because you took a gay kid who was a new co-worker and homeless and let him move in with you. I've seen you two together on Saturday here for breakfast. You like the kid and enjoy having him around."

"Every day, I look at his phone number on my phone and stare at the sticky note with his number on the kitchen wall," Gus said. "I want to call. Sometimes, I even start to dial the number."

"And then..." Gus mumbled.

"Were you afraid that Michael would reject you?" Bonnie asked.

Gus nodded several times.

"You don't have to worry about that now. He's reached out to you."

"Where are they now?" Bonnie then asked.

"At the Hampton Inn in Washington Township," Gus told her.

"I'll ask Joanne to get you a piece of apple pie with vanilla bean ice cream on top," Bonnie said. "After your dinner, you will eat it slowly, and then you are going to get into your pickup truck, turn right out of the diner, and take a right onto Academy Street. Then take a left onto Fries Mill Road until it ends at Route 42. Make a left and go down about a half-mile, and the Hampton Inn is on your right."

"I know how to get there," Gus snapped.

Bonnie's words were sharp and direct.

"If that's the case, then there's no excuse," Bonnie said. "Now eat your dinner, then the pie, leave Joanne a good tip, pay your tab, and drive there."

Gus saluted her. "Yes, boss. I didn't realize you were so bossy."

"With people I care about, I'm a dictator," Bonnie said, her eyes so deep, penetrating, and expressive.

Gus left Joanne a ten-dollar bill as a tip, much more than he normally would have, except when Bonnie waited on him.

As he walked to his truck, he spotted Bonnie getting into her red 2007 Hyundai Elantra, which she seemed to own forever. The car seemed like an oil change away from the junkyard.

Gus walked over to her car as she unlocked the driver's side door. He held the door open as she stiffly bent down and sat in the driver's seat. He closed the door once she was in and gave her something he rarely gave out—a smile.

"Bonnie, maybe..." Gus's voice trailed off.

"Gus, I accept your offer of a date," Bonnie answered immediately. "I hope you do a better job talking to Michael than you did trying to ask me out on a date."

Lashay had a long line to contend with the entire day at the outside Garden department. The constant churn kept her mind off the store closing, her impending homelessness, and her desire to be with Jack despite his recent stupidity.

I guess it didn't matter about the rumors of the store closing when people wanted their annuals, perennials, and bushes.

For some reason, Allegra stayed with her the entire day, entertaining customers and staying close to Lashay.

As Lashay watched these people, sometimes entire families, push their carts to checkout full of flowers, bushes, mulch, garden soil, and other garden supplies, Lashay felt a twinge of regret that she had never experienced the peacefulness and exhilaration of gardening and landscaping when she was part of a family. She knew it could be physically demanding but also extremely gratifying to decorate your home with flowers that bloomed in vivid purples and reds, to trim bushes into sculpted shapes, to plant vegetable gardens that fed the occupants, and to install ponds, gardens, and bird feeders.

Unfortunately, her life never made it that far. Lashay had lost everything and still fought to regain what so many others had. Her shift was almost over, and Lashay figured she had checked out at least 200 people. As the mid-May late afternoon heated up, the customer flow ebbed. She finally had a few minutes to catch her breath.

Unlike many employees, she was not one to stare at her phone at work. Instead, she people-watched in her department: a mother and teenage daughter picking out knockout roses, an older, 80-ish couple helping each other walk through the narrow paths as they searched for shepherd hooks, and a middle-aged man with a black beard headed toward his navel who loaded up bags of pea gravel with little effort.

Lashay watched these scenes unfold as she held Allegra in her arms. The Calico purred in a wave of contentment, sinking deep into her embrace.

She was caught unaware when a female voice said, "Hi, excuse me."

Lashay turned around to see Ava Snow standing on the other side of the checkout counter by the entrance.

Like in their first encounter, Lashay noticed how pretty Ava Snow was. Deep black hair that fell carefully on her shoulders framed her wide, chestnut brown eyes and full, rounded cheeks. She was at least four inches shorter than Lashay but thin and lean, with a baby bump that was more a speed bump than a fully developed mound.

"Oh, hi," Lashay said, turning on her best customer service smile.

"I felt like I needed to come back and talk to you about the cat," Ava Snow said.

With Allegra relaxing in her arms, Lashay said, "Would you like to hold her?"

Ava's face lit up, and she reached out her arms like she was receiving a baby.

"Thank you," Ava said as she cradled Allegra, who showed no signs of bolting.

"She's purring," Ava added.

"Were you able to check with the Clayton Animal Shelter?" Lashay asked.

Ava's face turned somber. "I was, and Cali was not returned to the shelter as my husband told me. Under intense interrogation, he admitted that he let Cali go in the cornfield near the lawyer's office on Delsea."

Ava's attention was diverted by Allegra meowing, and she used her right hand to stroke under her neck.

"She's your cat," Ava announced as if a peace treaty had been signed.

Ava offered to return her to Lashay, who waved her hand to indicate: *No, you hold her a while longer.*

"Are you married?" Ava asked.

"I was," Lashay said. "Years ago, but he we didn't want the same things. He wanted to beat me while I didn't want him to."

Lashay didn't know why she shared that piece of private information with a stranger. Working at HomeMaxx, Lashay had lost count of the times that a customer had confided something to her so personal that the customer had probably not even told the family.

One time in the Mantua store, a man about 80 confided, "My wife died six months ago, and sometimes I feel like killing myself." Lashay asked if she should call a family member for the man. He left the merchandise on the counter and walked out of the store.

Another time, a middle-aged man in the outside Garden department pushed a cart full of annuals up to checkout. Now, no one else was around or on the checkout line. As Lashay scanned the SKUs, the man leaned in and said in a plaintive voice, "You're the first person I ever told that I want to be a woman."

Lashay could think of no other response other than "thank you."

Now, Lashay was the oversharer. She didn't know why.

Ava responded with a heartfelt, "Oh my gosh, I'm sorry. I hope you got away from him."

Lashay just nodded, now on guard as to what she said.

"When I married Jacob," Ava began, "there were red flags. His father is very controlling and not really a nice person. He's tried to mold Jacob into that same kind of go-for-the-throat businessman."

"But there's a tenderness to Jacob." She went on. "He sometimes tries to suppress it, but it's there."

Lashay didn't know how to respond.

"Can I tell you something?" Ava asked.

"Between us, women," Ava said in a soft, conspiratorial tone.

"Yes," Lashay said.

"Last year, the company, Black Cobalt, bought this video game store company with about 25 stores in Pennsylvania and Delaware. His father wanted to, you know, extract all the value out of it and then close all 25 stores."

"What happened?" Lashay asked.

"Jacob loves video games," Ava said. "It's his true hobby or passion. He battled his father for two months, developing a new business plan for the stores and insisting they could be an asset to Black Cobalt."

"Did he convince his father?" Lashay asked.

Ava smiled. "He didn't. But Jacob went to others on the Board and convinced them. The stores have all been renovated and are now profitable with growing market share."

"That's terrific," Lashay said as Allegra decided to lay on the checkout counter, stretched out like a bikini model on a beach.

"Can you or your husband do anything to convince your father-in-law to let the store manager here, Tyler Rodgers, and my boyfriend, Jack, out of the non-compete clause so we can accept the jobs offered by Excell Hardware?"

"Your boyfriend is Jack?" Ava asked. "Jack Marsalis, I think, is his last name."

Lashay knew she was going to violate the no-sharing rule she had made with herself five minutes ago.

"I think Jack is my boyfriend," Lashay said. "We're still working that part out."

"But, I love him," Lashay said. "Just between us, women."

Ava grinned and said, "I heard Jacob talking to his father about him last night. Apparently, your boyfriend had called Bernard and asked him to allow you to take the Excell store manager job, and Jack would abide by the non-compete clause so my father-in-law could still have his revenge."

Lashay was shocked. Not that Jack would make that kind of gesture, but that he did.

"I think it's safe to say that he loves you, too," Ava said.

Ava gave Allegra a hug, and the cat responded with a head butt to her hands and a full-scale licking of Ava's fingers.

Ava turned her chestnut brown eyes on Lashay and said, "Thank you for taking care of our cat. Cali has been lucky enough to find new humans that love her. Maybe Jacob and I will rescue another cat after the baby is born."

"Best of luck with the birth and the baby," Lashay said.

Ava nodded, began to walk away, turned, and said, "Oh, and I'll talk to Jacob tonight so that the store manager, you, and your boyfriend can all work at that hardware place."

"After all," Ava added. "Us cat people have to stick together."

Chapter Twenty-Seven

"Not everything that is faced can be changed. But nothing can be changed until it is faced." James A. Baldwin

Gus was about ready to punch the clerk at the Hampton Inn. He didn't know Michael's room number and the clerk was quoting company policy about not giving our guest's room numbers.

Exasperated, Gus yelled, "I haven't talked to my son in over ten years. If he leaves before I do, it may be another ten years before we talk again. Or never."

"Room 402," the young man spilled.

Gus took the stairs to give him more time to think.

What should I say? How do I handle this?

Gus didn't have it in him to apologize. He found that more difficult than using his TV remote.

Second floor – *Am I disappointed in Michael because he's gay or because he didn't become the son I wanted?*

Third floor (huffing and puffing) – *A granddaughter. I can't wait to hold her.*

Fourth floor – *I better catch my breath before I knock on the door.*

Gus walked down the hall and stood in front of room 402's door for a minute. He heard muffled voices inside. He told himself to knock, but his hands would no longer obey his commands.

Gus froze.

The door opened. It was Noah's mother. *What was she doing here?*

"Mr. Gus," she exclaimed, hugging him. "Come in. Come in."

Gus stepped into the hotel room. It had a small living room and kitchen with a bedroom through a half-closed door. Noah's mother ushered him into the room. At a small round table sat Noah and Michael. Standing up holding a baby was a 30ish man, nice looking with a neatly trimmed beard and thick brown hair that was combed so that the waves all faced the same direction.

"Dad," Michael said. "You're here."

To Noah, Gus said, "I thought I kicked you out."

"My mother made tamales for all of us," Noah said. "I can never pass them up."

Gus forced a smile but was still too overwhelmed to speak or move.

Michael stood and stepped toward Gus. His features and body language said "welcome," and Gus realized nothing more was expected of him than acceptance.

"Dad, I want you to meet Max, my husband," Michael said.

The man with the thick hair stepped forward with the baby in his hands.

"Gus, it's a pleasure to finally meet you," thick hair said. Then, holding the baby directly in front of Gus, he said, "This is our daughter Aubrey Mae."

The baby was wrapped in a pink blanket with unicorns on the design. Her eyes were closed, and she made the slightest movements.

She's beautiful.

"You can hold her," Max said to him and began to hold the baby out toward Gus.

Gus remembered holding Noah's nephew Alex and how warm that made him feel.

This is my granddaughter.

Gus accepted the baby and took her in his arms. He held her against his chest, careful not to hold her too tightly.

She was so small and precious. Gus hadn't felt like this since he held Michael as a newborn. As he held her, Gus's attention was exclusively on the baby.

He suddenly remembered there were others in the room. As he looked up and glanced at their faces – Max, Noah, Noah's mother Antonella, and Michael – Gus realized that no words were necessary. Just acceptance.

He thought about Bonnie's advice at the diner, and Gus realized that his life was so much better with Michael, the baby, and Noah, too. Accepting Max and their lifestyle was the price he had to pay to become part of their lives.

"Max, nice to meet you," Gus said. "Does Michael still leave his socks all over the house?"

Max smiled and nodded his head. "Gus, Michael still has a definite sock problem. He likes to leave them in every room of our house."

The tension was broken. Gus had never felt this good in years. They all chatted while Antonella served tamales, and Gus learned about his son's life.

Michael now owned his own software company and worked from home and the office. He loved to cook, and Antonella promised to teach him how to cook Puerto Rican dishes. Max, an architect, was a huge baseball fan who dragged Michael to the Colorado Rockies games whenever possible.

Gus and Max talked baseball and even concrete since Max was an architect familiar with different building materials.

As they finished their meal, Gus found himself talking to Michael and getting to know his son again.

"Dad, we are visiting Aunt Lena and Aunt Patricia tomorrow," Michael told him. "I know you have work, but if you want to go with us..."

Gus looked over at Noah. "There's someone who works with me who can handle whatever comes up. I think I'll take my first day off in years."

"Besides, the store is probably closing in the next month or two," Gus added.

Gus wasn't sure what to do as he stood up to leave.

Michael came over to him and hugged him.

"Michael, I don't..." Gus started with no idea of what else to say.

"Dad, you don't have to agree with our lifestyle or lives," Michael said. "But I want you to respect my choices and put family before anything."

Gus nodded. He knew that Michael expressed his thoughts better than he could have.

Then, to Noah, Gus said, "See you later at the house."

"Of course," Noah said. As Gus turned to leave, Noah added, "And Gus, since Max brought it up, Michael isn't the only one with a sock problem. Since I clean up, I have found your socks all over the place."

"By the way, you're wearing two different socks," Noah pointed out.

The laughter carried down the hallway as Gus left.

Bonnie was right.

You cannot change what you are, only what you do.

Jack drove over to the Lost & Found Bookstore in Elk Township before it closed. He headed down Delsea Drive, turned right at the Heritage's convenience store, and then took Aura Road past the CVS and the Elk Township Municipal Building, the park, and Aura School. The bookstore was in a strip mall surrounded by a Christmas tree farm and a working dairy farm.

The shopping center had a bookstore on one end and a real estate company on the other. In between were a convenience store, a laundromat, and a pizza place.

Jack had never been a reader until he went to prison. With all that time on his hands, Jack started reading, and he found he enjoyed it. For some reason, other inmates didn't tend to bother you if you were reading. Jack liked military history, mysteries, detective procedurals, and biographies. Right now, he was reading *Judgment At Tokyo* by Gary Bass, which was about the war crimes trials held in Japan after World War II.

When Jack met Lashay and discovered she began reading for the same reason – downtime in prison – they began to recommend books to each other. They had just finished *Just Mercy* by Bryan Stevenson.

Jack met the owner, Nathan Jameson, a few years ago and hit it off. Nathan was 15 years younger than Jack, but they had similar sensibilities about the world. The bookstore also had a coffee shop, three private rooms for aspiring writers to work, and a book club room.

Jack's idea was to buy a few books for Lashay as an "I'm sorry."

Jack walked into the bookstore and was greeted by Heather Sandberg, the assistant manager. She was blonde, with crewcut hair dyed Carolina blue, a short, muscular frame, and piercings above both eyes on the left side of her nose and tongue.

"Jack, how's it hanging?" she asked.

"Hi Heather, how are you?" Jack responded as his eyes scanned the store for Nathan.

"If you're looking for Nathan, he's out on a case," Heather said.

Nathan also took on cases and clients where he needed to find something that was lost. It was the double entendre of the bookstore.

"You can help me, right?" Jack asked.

"What do you need?" Heather responded flatly.

Heather was an acquired taste. She never seemed to smile, had a mean resting face like Gus, allowed sarcasm to roll off her tongue, and was more a scowler than a talker.

And that was if she liked you. If she didn't, Heather would call someone out on whatever bullshit she thought that person would be trying to pull.

"I'm looking for a few books as a gift for someone," Jack told her.

"For that fine-looking Black woman you've come in here with?" Heather asked.

"Lashay," Jack said. "Can you suggest a few books?"

"Jack, you fucked up, didn't you?" Heather answered.

Before Jack could answer, she said, "Jack, if you screw up so bad she drops you, please let her know that I'm available."

"What happened to your girlfriend...?"Jack struggled to remember her name.

"Jocelyn," Heather said. "Yeah, she got a little rough in the sack, so I kicked her in her lady balls and sent her packing."

"Glad I haven't pissed you off," Jack said.

"Yet," Heather quipped.

"Let's do this, big guy," Heather said with a little enthusiasm as she punched him in his shoulder, and Jack tried to hide his wince.

After twenty minutes, Jack was forced to admit that Heather had a sandpaper personality, yet she was smooth as a book consultant. They had picked four books that Jack agreed Lashay would enjoy, including *The Year Of Yes* by Shondra Rimes and *On Her Own Ground* by C.J. Walker.

After ringing him up and giving Jack the "Friends of Nathan" 10 percent discount, Heather handed him his books in a Lost And Found Bookstore Gift Bag and said, "I don't say this often, but even though men suck, you are the best of the worst."

Jack shook his head. "Heather, if that's a compliment, you need to work on your positive feedback. If it's a diss, nice one."

When Jack got home and sat down at his dollhouse-sized kitchen table, he received a text from Lashay:

Come over to my place now. The door will be open. Bring work clothes for tomorrow. You'll be staying overnight...If you're good enough.

Jack read it twice and then a third time. His emotions swept through him like a hurricane making landfall. He couldn't decide what to do first. Gather his work clothes? Take a shower? Bring protection? Did he have protection? A quick survey of his one vanity drawer located two packs of condoms. What if she just wanted to talk?

Jack took a quick shower as if he were late for work, then debated: cologne or no cologne? As he decided against cologne, he started to think about his underwear. He had briefs that were from the Obama Presidency. He checked for holes, rips, and stains. He had only two more pairs to inspect before he found a presentable pair.

Jack breathed a sigh of relief when he found a grey pair of Jockeys that hadn't begun disintegrating. He trimmed his beard, brushed his teeth, flossed, and gargled. He carried his work clothes and boots in a paper bag and placed them on the passenger front seat. As he started the old, creaky

Nissan, he told himself to obey the speed limit.

It was almost ten o'clock at night, and the Franklinville Police had patrol cars on Delsea Drive to get speeders and people who had ingested too much alcohol. As he passed from Clayton to Franklinville, he passed two patrol cars in empty parking lots, waiting to pounce.

Jack put on his cruise control and set it at two miles above the speed limit, careful to go manual when the speed limit dropped near the paintball field from 50 to 40 MPH. Once in Newfield, he drove cautiously and finally pulled up to Lashay's mobile home.

Jack took a deep breath before getting out. He was unsure what was happening but was pretty sure what sleeping over meant.

Be cool, Jack. This woman has been through a lot. Don't be a typical man. Let her take the lead. Take your cues from her.

Jack tried the door handle, and it turned. He walked into a dark trailer with only a nightlight plugged into a socket near the hall as a directional guide. He locked the door before moving. He saw the bedroom door. It was partially open.

"Lashay," he called out in a whispered voice.

From the bedroom, he heard, "Jack, get in bed with me."

Conflict and contradictions pressed on Jack's psyche. He needed to proceed carefully, given what Lashay had suffered. Yet, he so wanted their first time – if this was even a time – to be so perfect and good for both of them.

Jack hadn't slept with a lot of women, but he knew enough that the first time having sex was too often like a practice session instead of the main event. Great sex was about knowing your partner's physical and emotional needs and channeling yours to mesh with your partner.

Jack had a girlfriend in college for all of their junior year. The first time they had sex, it was clearly a letdown for both of them. They were both inexperienced, so they practiced on each other and got better. By the end of the spring semester, they were in total sync and couldn't get enough of each other.

When she didn't return after the summer, Jack tried calling and eventually found out that her parents had both been laid off when their employer moved to China and she, Sheila, had to drop out and work in a factory that made timecards in Ohio.

Jack walked into the bedroom, and it was pitch black.

"You can wear pajamas if you want," Lashay said from the darkness.

"I'm naked," she added.

Jack put down the bag with his work clothes, removed them as quietly as possible, and folded them into a neat pile. He placed his bag and clothes pile against the wall.

Jack couldn't see Lashay in the darkness but could hear her breathing. Her breaths were soft and regular, and they were driving him crazy.

How many nights did he lay in his bed thinking of this moment? He hadn't conceived it playing out like this. In his mind, soft, symphonic music played in the background as he took her into his arms and...

Okay, be cool. Let Lashay take the lead.

Now naked and feeling the breeze from the ceiling fan blades whirling overhead, Jack pulled up the covers and slid in. Lashay had a queen-size bed, so he didn't immediately feel her beside him. He noticed she had soft, flannel sheets on the bed with flannel pillowcases on two pillows on his side.

Jack lay on his right side facing the middle of the bed when he felt her arms reach for his face. With her long, slender fingers on his flushed cheeks, Lashay kissed him hard for several minutes. Jack responded by kissing her back on her lips, neck, and ears.

Still, she said nothing.

Then, her hands guided his face to her stomach, even with navel. Jack carefully kissed her belly above and below her navel, and when he went below, her hands guided him lower.

When he began to use his tongue, Jack started slowly and then increased the pressure on her mound. Her body responded, and Jack went harder and quicker, allowing her response to dictate his movements.

Her pelvis began to move up off the sheets and then down like a wave cresting and falling. Her breath deepened and quickened, and as he felt her ready, Jack let her move her body up and down until she stopped, and he felt her whole body vibrate.

Still silent, Lashay inhaled fast, thready breaths, and her hands guided Jack to lay down on his back. Jack resisted the temptation to reach out to her and plunge himself into her.

Instead, he waited.

Carefully, almost cautiously, she straddled him, and then slowly, she sank on him so he was inside her. His pleasure center was off the charts, and he wanted to move up and down, but he did not.

Instead, Lashay put her hands on his chest and moved up and down, first bringing him to the edge of her skin and plugging herself onto him. She started slowly at first with long, unrushed, even gentle thrusts.

As Lashay pressed down on his chest, pushing herself up and then slithering down, her breathing became quicker and deeper. Jack fought the strong desire to match her rhythm but instead allowed her to control the pace.

Lashay would plunge onto him, pump five or six times, and then pull up and linger at his rim. Jack was ready to explode but held on as she slammed down on him, grunting now as her body rippled and quivered.

Jack could wait no longer, and he released; when she felt him do that, she went deep and placed her head next to his face.

It seemed like minutes, but it could have been seconds before their bodies relaxed. Jack felt her hair and smelled her Lashay-ness. He didn't want to let go and held her until she finally said, "I need to use the bathroom."

When she returned, Jack used the bathroom and returned to the bed, unsure where to lay. He decided to lay on his back even though he was a side sleeper. Lashay reacted by laying on his right arm and nestling on his chest. Their feet intertwined.

After they lay there in the dark, Jack wasn't sure if he should say anything.

It was five minutes before Lashay said, "Jack, thank you. I needed it to be like that to overcome my fear."

"I'm sorry it probably wasn't the experience you expected," she said.

Jack chose his words carefully.

"I'm fifty-one years old," Jack said, then paused.

"This is the best day of my entire life."

"I was thinking the same thing," Lashay said.

There was silence in the darkness, and Lashay announced, "This was the best day of your entire life."

Jack lifted his head from the pillow, "Screw you, Jones."

"I think you just did Marsalis."

Chapter Twenty-Eight

"**A**ll employees must know that violence in the workplace will not be tolerated and that appropriate action will be taken if threats of violence or violence occur." **HomeMaxx Employee Manual**

Tyler Rodgers thought this may be the toughest thing he had to do as a store manager. All employees on the weekday shift were coming in 15 minutes early to hear what he had to say.

Tyler was pretty sure everyone knew the content of the announcement. But thinking you know, and then actually hearing the words are two different psychological processes.

All HomeMaxx stores will be closing on July 1.

Black Cobalt sent him some talking points and recommended that all questions be directed to a new employee hotline, with an AI answering questions. No real person would be available.

Tyler tried not to think about his personal situation with Bernard Snow from Black Cobalt blocking his new job as Region Manager for Excell Hardware. The Excell VP, Sid Nelson, had been reassuring him that it would all work out. Nevertheless, Tyler was mired deep in sleep debt, as his mind went down an anxiety rabbit hole when the lights were out in their bedroom.

Pam reassured him that things would work out. Her theory was: "Because they always do." Tyler wasn't confident in that assessment, but he wanted to believe it.

On the positive side of the ledger, Jack had gotten Robbie Nowicki a job with a customer and friend, Luis, who told Jack that Robbie had already become one of his best workers cleaning offices at night.

Tyler's mother called him yesterday to thank him for Robbie's job. Despite his insistence that Jack deserved the credit, his mother's refrain was: "You're the store manager. You get the blame even if it's not your fault, so you get to take the credit."

Also, Lashay was off the banned list for non-compete clause so she could take the job at the Washington Township store of Excell Hardware. Of course, the problem was that Lashay wouldn't take the job without Jack.

It didn't take a genius to notice that Jack and Lashay had finally broken the barriers that kept them from developing a romantic relationship. When Lashay transferred from the Mantua store, it didn't take long for Tyler to notice that she and Jack had developed this non-verbal communication with their eyes and body language. It was like they knew from each person's non-verbal cues what the other person thought and felt.

Tyler was sure that he and Pam shared the same communication connectivity. Had a bad day at HomeMaxx or showing houses? They knew. Without words. Even when they fought, Tyler was always amazed at how they would look at each other for several seconds and broadcast either "I'm still furious with you" signals or, more often, "I'm sorry. Can we make up?"

It was almost time. Tyler stood up from his desk, holding the talking points from Black Cobalt in his right hand. As he stood behind his desk in his small office, which had concrete-block walls and a water-stained drop ceiling, Tyler visualized the faces of the employees he had worked with in the store.

Jack, Lashay, Luther, Ellen, Darla, Christine, Karen, Kelly, Harry...faces came at him, sometimes without names, just recollections. The bald guy from Lumber who wept during 9/11. The Rowan nursing student who kept diagnosing customers with or without their consent. The retired FBI agent who thought every customer was stealing. The runner-up to the Miss New Jersey pageant who attracted so much male attention that Tyler reassigned her to the office. The young guy with the amazing memory, who studied the products in the entire store and could tell any customer or employee where any product was located in the store. Or Skip, who knew more flooring than possibly any single human being. Customers came from as far as Pennsylvania to have Skip lay some of his knowledge about flooring on them. Tyler remembered how a stomach ache had him absent for a few days. Those days turned into weeks of chronic stomach problems. Skip finally went to the doctor. Pancreatic cancer took him within a few weeks.

Tyler thought of his two daughters. They had grown up so fast. Where had the time gone? Tyler remembered the first day the store opened. He had worked in the Mantua and Sicklerville stores as an assistant manager.

What pride he had felt when the Franklinville HomeMaxx store opened with him as the store manager. Where did the time go?

Tyler walked out of his office into the outer office and said," Everybody ready?"

The three women said in unison, "No," but they all followed him to the open area near the entrance door, where they stocked the pesticides.

As he walked through the Flooring and then the Window Treatments departments, Tyler assumed he would have to wait for everyone to assemble. He had even asked Jack to be his people wrangler and gather up those who were either afraid or to hear the announcement and too traumatized to hear the announcement.

When Tyler turned the corner near the checkout area, he saw that the employees had gathered in a semicircle. Tyler would make another one of these announcements for the next shift and contact anyone who just worked weekends, which was only a few people.

As Tyler approached the group, he heard nothing from the 30 employees. They stood in silence, and all eyes were on him.

Even Allegra the cat attended, relaxing atop a box of weed killer. He guessed that Jack and Lashay would take the cat with them when they left. Tyler found it ironic that after all these years of striving to improve sales at the store, the appearance of one cat did more for revenues than any sales promotion or gimmick.

As he stood before them, Tyler wondered what the store closing would do to many of them. Some, like recent college grads Justin and Trevor, wouldn't care because their parents would care for them financially. Others, like

Lauren Garcia and Christine Berrino, were single moms who were holding onto a thread.

Tyler had no idea what Gus would do. When Tyler approached him the other day to inquire about his future plans, Gus dismissed him with an "I'll find something. This place needed me more than I needed it."

Tyler doubted the accuracy of that statement. He did speak to Noah, who, he knew, had gone from homeless to Gus's roommate.

"I've applied to several auto repair shops in the area," Noah said. "Can I put you down as a referral?" he had asked.

"Yes," Tyler began, "And I will write you a recommendation you can use when you apply."

Before speaking, Tyler looked over at Jack, who gave him a subtle thumbs-up. Jack and Lashay were holding hands.

Right before he spoke, Tyler glanced at Darla Campanna, and he spotted anxiety and fear on her face. He had heard that the ex-husband had come around and threatened her.

Tyler cleared his throat.

"Good morning everyone. I'm going to get right to the point. All HomeMaxx stores, including this one, will close on July 1.

Tyler paused to gauge the reaction. He saw anxiety, fear, pain, disbelief, and acceptance of the inevitable.

"Black Cobalt will not pay any severance, and all employee health benefits will end as of June 30. The company 401k plan will be frozen for 90 days. All unused PTO days will not be paid. On June 1, a company specializing in bankruptcy liquidation will assist in the last month with product clearance."

Tyler had argued with Jacob Snow, the son, about the conditions of the store closure.

"The employees that have been here a long time deserve a severance," Tyler argued. "And not paying unused PTO days means employees will take them now in the next 45 days. We'll be shorthanded."

"I'm sorry, Tyler," Snow retorted. "This is the procedure. We've done this before."

"On June 1, the liquidation company will basically take over the sale of the products remaining in the store," Snow told him. "We don't really need a store manager after June 1 but have decided to keep you on till July 1."

"Am I supposed to say thank you?" Tyler snapped. "You are preventing me from taking a position at Excell Hardware?"

"That's not me," Jacob Snow answered, a tinge of regret seeping into his tone. "It's my father."

"I want to take my unused PTO immediately, "Harry said.

Tyler nodded. "I get it. All I ask is that we handle the PTO days with some order. I'll call each employee down to my office to discuss your unused PTO, if you have any."

The Franklinville HomeMaxx employees grumbled as a group, and Tyler let them express their disappointment and anger. The conditions of the store closure sent a crystal clear message: "We don't care about the employees of HomeMaxx."

After a few minutes of outbursts, Tyler raised his hands, trying to calm the group.

"I know how difficult this is," Tyler said, trying to regain control.

"If ownership will not say it, then I will," Tyler said. "It has been an honor to work with all of you, whether it's been for ten weeks or ten years. Your dedication to excellence and to our customers has made me proud to work with all of you. All the stores closing have nothing to do with what you did or didn't do. It's simply a matter of money."

Everyone had stopped grumbling, and their eyes were locked on him.

"The store has six more weeks before closing. Two more before the liquidation people arrive. All of you. You do what's best for you and your families. Once I get back to my office, Kelly will call you to meet with me about your concerns."

"Thank you," Tyler said as he started to return to his office.

"Tyler, can you hold up?" Jack said.

Jack turned around to face the other employees.

"I don't know about any of you," Jack said. "But we are damn lucky to have Tyler Rodgers as our store manager. He's had our backs and is more than just a boss. At one time or another, Tyler has come through for all of us, whether it's finding someone a ride to work who lost their license, getting them more hours to pay a debt, or even advising on their health benefits."

"I, for one, want to thank you, Tyler," Jack said.

Lashay followed with a thank you, then Ellen, Christine, Lauren, Harry, Noah, and even Gus.

As the employees said, "Thank you," Lashay turned to Jack and said, "The store is about to close, and you're still an ass-kisser."

Jack chuckled and then pointed to Tyler, where Allegra was now rubbing up against his leg, going inside one leg and then around another.

"Geez, Jack," Lashay mocked. "Now you even have the cat doing it."

Ava Snow worked in the spare room, which was her office for her graphic design business. The pregnancy had forced her to take more breaks, and even the expensive desk chair she had invested in felt uncomfortable.

There was a knock, and Jacob entered. When they first married, Jacob would barge into her office, sometimes when she was on a call with a client or in a flow state on a design.

Once, when his father was over their townhome, he opened the door and tried to talk to her.

"Excuse me," she said curtly. "I'm working. Please close the door."

She loved Jacob and saw in him qualities that he didn't even see in himself. When your father is Bernard Shaw, CEO of one of the largest private equity funds in the nation, it's natural to emulate that success. But Ava didn't want Jacob to be a clone of his father – controlling, greedy, manipulative, and vindictive.

Bernard Shaw was successful because he spotted opportunities and ex-ploited them and people. Jacob was a more critical thinker. He analyzed while his father bullied. Jacob planned for the long term, while his father always took the short-term gains. In the last year, Jacob had begun to challenge his father and his way of doing business.

But he was still his father's son.

Jacob dropping off Cali in the woods still upset her. Jacob and his father had played her. Unlike her father-in-law, Ava was in this relationship for the long haul. Supporting Jacob as he found his own way required patience, persistence, and, truth be told, the cunning to outfox Bernard.

"Almost done?" Jacob asked.

Ava didn't turn around from her computer. She had a MAC with two large monitors for design.

"Yes," Ava answered. "I'm just touching up this ad for a client."

"You know, my father would give you all the graphic design from all our companies if you'd accept them."

This had been a familiar disagreement. Ava did not want to work for Bernard or Black Cobalt because then they would control her. Truth be told, she was doing well without them.

Ava knew Jacob only brought this up because his father had asked him to.

"We are not doing this again," Ava said, swiveling in her chair to face him.

"Okay," Jacob answered, not pushing the issue.

"I need you to do something for me," Ava said.

"All right, Miss One-Way Street," Jacob joked.

Ava didn't smile back. She stood.

"You and your father need to release Jack Marsalis and Tyler Rodgers from those silly non-compete clauses."

"Ava, it's not me," Jacob pleaded. "It's my father. He was pissed that Marsalis showed him up in the store and then turned down his job offer. He thinks the store manager is weak and won't stand up to his employees."

Ava put her hands on her hips and stepped forward.

"Jacob, I love you," Ava began. "But if you think your father is in charge of us, our marriage, and our future, you are sadly mistaken."

"It's not like that," Jacob said, his hands out to the side with his palms up.

"You have to understand..."Jacob said.

Ava cut him off. "No, no, Jacob. Here's what you should know. If you love me, then you will do this. If you love your father and Black Cobalt, then you won't."

Jacob hesitated and asked, "Is this like a pregnancy hormone thing?"

Ava's face flashed fury.

"You have until tomorrow to get this done," Ava said.

Jacob mumbled, "But by tomorrow…"

Ava narrowed her eyes.

"Jacob, we've known each other since college. Do you think I'm bluffing? Remember when I broke up with you because you and your father tried to keep me from joining a pro-abortion protest on campus? You said it wasn't a good look for Black Cobalt."

"How long before we got back together?" Ava asked.

"Ava, it's my father," Jacob whined. "You know how he is."

"Yes, unfortunately, I do," Ava answered.

"Jacob, are you going to be Bernard Snow's clone or Jacob Snow, your own man?" Ava asked.

Gus walked down the hallway of the Hampton Inn to say goodbye to his son Michael, his granddaughter Aubrey, and his partner Max. They were leaving for the airport in an hour to fly back to Colorado.

Gus hated to admit it, but he had enjoyed his week with them. He loved his granddaughter and took every opportunity to hold her. He had never thought being a grandparent was a big deal, but now he knew how wrong he was.

To Gus, it was like having a second chance to be a better parent with a new person. He knew he had screwed up badly with Michael. Yet, once they had reconnected last week, it was like a second chance for all of them. Even though he found their lifestyle a violation of his values, Gus kept that opinion to himself. He didn't condone it or condemn it.

He had learned that balancing act from having Noah around. The kid signaled that Gus had gone too far by giving him this look, where he narrowed his eyes and furrowed his brow.

Gus knocked on the hotel door and heard a man's voice.

"Be right there," the voice said through the hotel door.

Gus assumed it was Michael, but when the door opened, it was Max, Michael's partner.

"Hi, Gus," Max said, smiling. "Michael and Aubrey are running late. They went antique shopping with Noah's mother."

Gus, feeling awkward, said, "I thought I'd say goodbye before you drove to the airport."

"You can come in and wait," Max said, standing to the side. "It's safe," he added, with a sly smile on his face.

Gus reluctantly walked in and immediately stood in the middle of the suit's small living room.

Max's phone dinged. He checked it and said, "They are five to ten minutes away."

Gus noticed their two pieces of luggage were sitting near the couch.

"Maybe I should wait in the lobby," Gus said, unsure what to say and how to act.

Over the last week, he hadn't really interacted with Max. Just Michael. Max always said hello and seemed gracious, but Gus still felt uncomfortable.

Max sat in the grey swivel chair and crossed his legs.

The silence was anguishing to Gus. He was never a big talker, but he hated awkward silences.

"Gus, we've enjoyed spending time with you and, for me, getting to know you," Max said.

Gus threw on his skepticism mask and said, "Really."

Max stopped the swivel and leaned forward, folding his hands. "Gus, you took in a gay kid whose father tossed him out of the house and who was homeless. You've decided to have a relationship with your son, granddaughter, and, I hope, me."

Gus nodded and then sat on a stool in the small kitchen, only four feet from the small living room.

"I don't know about that," Gus answered. "When the kid started working at HomeMaxx, I called him a different fruit name because...you know."

Max chuckled at that and said, "I get it. He's a fruit. A fairy. But Gus, we are not the stereotype. We are much more."

"Did you know I'm a lifelong Denver Broncos fan and have season tickets?" Max asked. "I have a black belt in karate and was middleweight boxing champ in my neighborhood's gym. I drink beer and fart and burp like real men, Gus."

"You have season tickets?" Gus said.

"And you are welcome to join us," Max answered.

Gus rubbed his chin stubble and asked, "What did your parents say when they found out, or did you tell them?"

Max leaned back in the swivel chair, doing a half circle.

"Gus, they are evangelical Christians. We were a church-going, God-fearing, commandment-keeping family," Max explained.

"So they, what banned you? Kicked you out? What do the kids say? Ghosted you?"

Max took a breath, exhaled slowly, and said, "Gus, they accepted me."

"Come on," Gus said. "Holly rollers, and they didn't freak out?"

"Were they hurt? Were they disappointed? Were they conflicted? Were they tempted to freak out, as you said? Yes. Ultimately, they accepted me as I am."

Gus shook his head in disbelief.

"Now, do they go around telling everyone in their church that their oldest son is gay? No. When my dad comes with me to a Broncos game, we talk football, not being gay. We both love puzzles and do Wordle daily and Connections. We both are self-proclaimed grillmasters, and we both love camping."

"I even got my dad to try bird watching," Max said. "He thought that bird watching was, you know, for ladies or gays. But after a few outings, he loves it like I do."

"I'm shocked," was all Gus could say.

"Hey, it's not all peaches and cream," Max said. "My dad's sister and brother-in-law are both members of that same church and refuse to accept or acknowledge us. We have a neighbor two doors to our left who calls our house "fairyland" loudly and to other neighbors. I could beat the shit out of him anytime, but I ignored him for now. If he does that as Aubrey gets older, we may have a confrontation."

"Does Michael like those things?" Gus asked.

"Yes, Gus," Max said. "Michael is a huge Broncos fan, is good with his hands like you, and is a talented furniture maker."

"Gus, I am not giving advice but stating a fact," Max began. "Michael was really hoping to restart a relationship. He was also hoping you would accept him. Be proud of him."

The hotel door opened, and Michael walked in with Aubrey in a carrier.

After some fast-paced small talk, Michael said, "We've got to return the rental car and catch our flight," Gus said goodbye to Aubrey with a soft kiss and a handshake with Max.

Gus faced Michael, who put out his hand to shake.

Gus hesitated, conflict erupting inside about what to do next.

He then decided.

Gus leaned in and hugged his son, saying softly in his ear, "Michael, I'm proud of you, and I love you."

Gus felt Michael's body shake and knew he was crying.

Gus did everything he could not to cry.

After all, he's a man. Men don't cry.

Chapter Twenty-Nine

"That's why they call it the American Dream because you have to be asleep to believe it." George Carlin

"Carlos, what will you do when the store closes?" Jack asked Carlos, owner and proprietor of Carlos's Authentic Mexican Food truck. It was parked in front of HomeMaxx as usual, and Jack and Lashay sat across from one another at the picnic table in front of the store near the three-deep line of stainless steel grills for sales.

Carlos handed them their lunch – one order of Pupusas and one of Gringas.

"Two new warehouses are opening on Route 322 in Logan Township," Carlos began. "I talked to the warehouse manager. He says that employees will have time to come out, buy from my truck, and eat lunch."

"Unlike the Amazon warehouses," Jack said. "Right, Carlos?"

"They are crazy there," Carlos answered, raising his hands as in prayer. "The employees there hardly have time to eat from a vending machine. A food truck. No way, Jose, as you gringos say."

"We'll miss you, Carlos," Lashay said as Jack handed her the Pupusas.

"You are my favorite customers, "Carlos answered, punctuating his claim with a smile as wide as his food truck.

"Carlos, we're on to you," Lashay replied. "You say that to all your customers."

"But I only mean it with you two," Carlos quipped.

"Carlos, I know I've asked this before but why don't you advertise your food and truck as Guatemalan?" Jack asked.

Suddenly the customer-facing smile that Carlos maintained faded. He said seriously, "Gringos know Mexican food, even if they only know it from Taco Bell commercials. That's why my truck decal is this silly display of sombreros, a cactus, a Mexican with a stupid mustache, a skull, a jalapeno, a Mexican blanket, and a margarita. It's what they expect. What they're comfortable with? To most Americans, Guatemala is just a small, poor country with cartels, drugs, gangs, and violence."

Jack shook his hand, and Lashay hugged him.

"Your secret is safe with us," Lashay told him.

It had been a crazy week at HomeMaxx. Store closing clearance sales, Memorial Day sales, and employees quitting or on PTO to use up their days. Irate customers because of long lines at the checkout counter and a lack of employees to answer any questions on the floor.

Everyone who stayed was working 70 hours.

We all will need the money, Jack thought.

Jack now took care of everything from Doors and Windows, Kitchen, Bath, Appliances, Plumbing, and Flooring. Lashay handled Outside Garden, Lawn Equipment, Chemicals, and sometimes even Paint.

For some reason, Harry had scheduled his 20 PTO days to run till the store closed, but every day, he would show up in Tools and help customers for several hours. After a week, customers began to recognize his pattern and would show up in the hours he was there. Jack heard there was even a subreddit page dedicated to Harry.

Kelly quit to work at Lowe's in Washington Township on the Black Horse Pike. Rumor has it that she now makes the announcements there. Lauren Garcia had quit to work at the Sherwin-Williams store on Egg Harbor Road in Washington Township. According to Harry, who had the latest news on the throuple, Kathy Marino, who had quit HomeMaxx right after the store closing announcement, had left her husband Ron for a Gloucester Township police officer who was currently on leave because he slipped on a wet spot at a WaWa convenience store near the slushy dispenser. Harry announced that the officer was on disability and suing WaWa for gross negligence.

Harry, of course, had even more late-breaking news.

"Apparently, Ron re-kindled his relationship with Lauren Garcia, now at Sherwin-Williams, and re-established the throuple with Shawna from Planet Fitness."

Gus had been in an uncharacteristic good mood despite the chaos because Noah explained to Jack that "Gus has reconnected with his son Michael and can't wait to visit his granddaughter Aubrey. Gus told me that he is going to a Broncos game in late September with Michael and Max."

Noah had come to Jack for some resume tips and employment advice.

"I have to pay Gus for rent and groceries," Noah insisted. "Gus says to not worry about it until I get a job, but I just won't do that."

It was easy to detect panic in the boy's voice.

Jack had an idea. He called Dave Maloney, owner of the Washington Township Excell Hardware store, where he had hoped to work until Bernard Snow threw a wrench in that plan. But Tyler said that some Excell executives were working on it, and Jack was optimistic something would break.

"Jack, no news on the non-compete clause yet," Dave Maloney had said.

"Thanks, Dave, but I'm calling about something else," Jack said.

"What's up?" Dave asked.

"There's a kid here, Noah, nineteen years old, who is one hell of an auto mechanic. Like all of us at HomeMaxx, he's going to need a job in about a month. I know your friends with Marty from Marlton Tire next to your store. Can you check to see if he has an opening?"

"That's easy," Dave said. "Marty comes over for coffee to talk Eagles and Phillies when I'm at the store. He's still hurting from COVID. He needs multiple people."

"Can you talk to Marty?" Jack asked. "The kid is a hard worker and a terrific mechanic. Jeez, we've had several customers who couldn't get their car started in the parking lot. Noah got every one of them on the road."

"You got it, Jack," Dave said. "And Jack, we're going to get you here to the store."

"Thanks, Dave," Jack replied. "That means a lot. But if it doesn't work out, you're still taking Lashay as the store manager, right? "

"Jack, we're going to get the Jack and Lashay package deal but if not, Lashay is in as store manager. We looked over her resume. She has so much finance experience she's perfect to handle the budget, the payroll, and the P&L sheets."

"I always hated finance crap," Dave admitted. "I love the store and the customers. Not the boring numbers stuff. Lashay is a natural at that."

That gave Jack an idea if everything worked out.

Since their first romantic interlude at Lashay's trailer, Jack and Lashay had spent the night together at his basement apartment on a Thursday. They were exhausted and fell asleep almost immediately after getting into bed.

When Jack woke up that morning with Lashay cocooned in his arms, he knew he wanted to live with her, be with her, even marry her.

Jack wondered if Lashay was thinking about what he was thinking about.

I'm wondering if she wants to find a place together.

"What's the latest on the apartment search?" Jack asked.

Lashay took a long sip of Diet Pepsi and said, "Not good. I have until July 1 to find a place, and hardly any places are available. Plus, everything is so damn expensive. And Jack, you may not know this, but I'm black."

Jack didn't respond right away. This was an issue that was a non-issue for Jack but he knew that Lashay had a radically different life experience than he had because he was white.

Jack disagreed with the "I don't see race or color" claim. That was bullshit to him. Of course, people saw color or race. It's how humans interact with their external world. Jack knew he had benefited from being white and a man in a multiplicity of ways.

"Why don't we move in together?" Jack asked, blurting it out rapidly.

He knew they hadn't discussed it in detail, and it was a big step in their relationship.

Lashay stopped eating. "Jack, I want that, too. You have to understand that being a black woman presents challenges. I've suffered from being black my whole life. You, Jack, will soon understand what I mean."

To Jack, it was like the external world had faded away. They sat on a picnic bench in front of the store, with customers coming in and leaving, Carlos selling food a few feet away, and cars zipping by at too high a speed in the parking lot.

Jack no longer heard and saw any of that.

"I want to understand," Jack said.

"I filled out an application at this new apartment complex in Williamstown by the high school, Lashay explained, "but the woman there said there might not be anything available for months."

Jack hesitated, allowing Lashay to finish the story.

"I thought there was something off about the woman and her story," Lashay said. "So, I completed another online application, this time changing my name from Lashay, an obvious black name, to Linda, an obvious white name."

"What happened?" Jack asked.

"The woman called me the next day and told me they had immediate availability," Lashay said, his voice exasperated and disappointed.

"I'm sorry, Lashay," Jack said.

"So I want you to know what you're getting into," Lashay cautioned. "You may find out what it's like to be black just by being with me."

"Can you handle it?" Lashay asked.

Jack reached for her hand, and Lashay met him halfway on the table.

"Lashay, it's been 20 years trying to rebuild my life from the dumpster fire I created," Jack said. "Here's the thing. Society doesn't just discriminate about color but also class. These politicians all talk with reverence about the American Dream. In reality, the people who live that dream are doing all they can to keep people like you and me, whether it's white, black, Hispanic, or gay, from attaining that same dream."

"You and I, we had that dream for a while or what we thought the American Dream should be," Jack said. "And then we got kicked to the trash pile. And you know what? No one offered us a helping hand to climb out. We did that. Both of us have worked so hard. And we found each other."

"Starting my life from now means nothing if it's not with you. So whatever shit I have to endure, I'm ready if it means sharing my life with you."

Lashay's blue eyes widened and sparkled.

"Sometimes, I still suffer from the trauma from my time on the streets and prison," Lashay said. "But lately, when you're next to me in bed, holding me, I realize that the journey was hard and harsh but worth it if it ends with you and me together."

"I love you, Jack," Lashay said.

Allegra jumped up on the wooden table as they held hands at the picnic table.

"Wow," Jack said. "She's never come out front before."

"She's a cat," Lashay said. "They sense things like the store is closing."

"Should we take her with us?" Jack asked.

"It'll make it even harder to find a place together. Many places don't take pets; if they do, the rent and security deposit are higher."

Allegra stretched out on the table and she rolled over as Lashay scratched her belly.

"You got the magic hands," Jack told her.

Jack got into scratching action as Allegra flipped to one side to face Jack.

"I guess you, me and Allegra can be homeless together," Lashay said.

Then, to lighten the mood, Jack said, "Dave Maloney from Excell has a sister who lives in Whitman and has a house with a mother-in-law suite they built for their mother, who passed away last year."

"I have to forewarn you," Jack chuckled. "At her age, Dave told me she farted all the time."

"In what way do you think that's any different than you, Jack?"

"In my defense, I have lived alone for almost 20 years," Jack answered.

"Is this why your landlords are selling their house," Lashay teased. "The odor was seeping upstairs into their living area."

They both laughed as Lashay said, "Let's go, Allegra. Lunch is over. Back to work."

Jack spotted her from the time she exited her blue Honda CR-V. He wasn't sure she'd show up. They had talked several times in the store and then on the phone. Jack was worried about meddling but wanted her to know the true story.

She was dressed in faded jeans rolled up above her ankles. She wore grey sneakers matched with a white crop top and a gold necklace. To Jack, she walked like Lashay and had her soft, smooth features and long, delicate fingers.

She walked up behind Lashay, who didn't see her. As she approached, Jack got up, as did Lashay.

"I'm going back to work," Jack said, gently picking up Allegra, who purred in his embrace.

"Lashay, we have the Outside Garden covered," Jack told her.

"Why, Jack, I'm heading over there right now," Lashay countered.

"I don't think so," Jack said.

From behind Lashay, a voice said, "Hello, Mom."

Lashay turned around. It was Tamara, her daughter.

"Tamara," was all Lashay could say.

Jack watched as both women stepped closer and then embraced.

"Thanks, Jack," Tamara said.

As Jack walked back inside with Allegra in his arms, he heard Lashay say, "Let's talk a walk. We have so much to talk about."

Tyler Rodgers had never spent so much time on the store floor since he was a young assistant manager. It was chaos out there. Too many customers hungry for liquidation deals that didn't exist, and not enough employees.

Tyler sat down at his desk for the first time all day, leaned back in his chair, and relaxed.

He still couldn't believe it was almost over.

The phone rang, and he was tempted not to answer it.

"Franklinville HomeMaxx," Tyler answered.

"Tyler, it's Jacob Snow," the voice on the other end announced.

Tyler wasn't sure if the younger Snow was calling to yell at him over the chaos at the store. Just in case, Tyler took a deep breath and engaged his core.

"Hello, how can I help you today?" Tyler asked.

"No Tyler, it's how can I help you," Jacob Snow replied.

"I don't understand," Tyler said.

"Tyler, I am calling to inform you that Black Cobalt will no longer enforce your non-compete clause," Jacob Snow announced. "You are free to take the job of regional manager at Excell Hardware. And that goes for Jack Marsalis as well."

Tyler was flabbergasted. Speechless.

"Are you there?" Jacob Snow asked.

"Yes, I'm sorry," Tyler stuttered. "I'm just surprised that Black Cobalt changed their mind on this," Tyler said.

"Truth be told," Jacob Snow began. "A valuable consultant to Black Cobalt recommended this course of action. My father objected, but I was able to persuade him."

"Thank you, Mr. Snow, "Tyler said. "Please thank your consultant. That person is clearly very smart about business and a good person."

"Yes, yes, she is," Jacob Snow replied. "Good luck, Tyler. I assume you'll take the job as soon as possible."

"This is just the best news," Tyler gushed. "I'll tell Jack."

"Thank you again," Tyler said.

The connection had already been severed.

Chapter Thirty

"Abuse is the weapon of the vulgar." **Author Samuel Griswold Goodrich**

Like everyone else who remained at HomeMaxx, Darla Campanna felt the last few weeks were exhausting. She handled the Returns /Customer Service Desk, which now had a line longer than that of the local Department of Motor Vehicles. People were angry. They had flocked to the store, thinking that a store closing was an invitation to the fire sale with bargain-basement prices. Instead, the deals weren't great; many of the employees had quit, so they received no help, and the checkout line was longer than the line in front of her desk.

"No, we are not selling refrigerators for ten dollars," Darla told one insistent woman. "Why do you think we do?"

"My sister-in-law said these store liquidations just want to sell everything at any price."

Darla looked her dead in her eyes and said, "Your sister-in-law may not be the retail genius you think she is."

To make her personal stress even more acute, Darla didn't know if she had a job at the Excell Hardware store in Washington Township because Black Cobalt was still blocking Jack from working there.

The only positive trend in her life was Edgar's dump truck business. The economy thrived despite higher inflation, insane home prices, and interest rates. New home builders were taking advantage of the chronic shortage of homes by building single-family homes, condos, townhomes, and apartments as fast as possible.

Edgar was now so busy as a dump truck driver that he was looking for a second driver. Darla knew that Gus had driven dump trucks and cement mixers throughout his career in concrete, and had endured an awkward conversation with the old goat to find out if he still had an active Commercial Driver's License (CDL).

He did, so Darla suggested to Edgar that he talk to Gus, who swore he would work at HomeMaxx until the last minute before it closed down for good.

Every morning when she arrived at work and every evening when she left, her hands trembled as she looked for her ex-husband, Clyde. He had threatened to kill her several times but had always been scared off by Gus and Jack arriving for work and leaving at the same time as her.

Tonight, Jack was called to Tyler's office, so he wasn't walking her out as usual. Thankfully, it was still light out in the early June evening, and the parking lot was full of rapacious customers desperately hoping to buy a washer/dryer combo for $20.

As Darla entered the parking lot, she cursed herself for parking far away from the entrance or exit doors. As she walked quickly toward her car, she watched any car that drove into the parking lot. She was looking for Clyde's rust-bucket Chevy Cruise.

She was only twenty feet away from her car and had hit the key fob to open the door when a red Ford F-250 drove by her.

Too late, she spotted the Chevy Cruze that was hidden by the Ford.

She tried to run, but he was out of the car and kicked the back of her right leg, sending her to the pavement sprawled out. Her head hit the asphalt hard, and she felt blood gush from her forehead.

Darla couldn't see much, her vision foggy from the fall, but she heard Clyde.

"You bitch, I'm gonna kill you."

She tried to move by crawling, but her body wouldn't obey her mind's red alert signal.

"You think I'm letting you live," Clyde screamed as he kicked her in the ribs.

She left out a welp and went limp.

Like it was in slow motion, she heard the click go off on the safety of his gun. She knew he was pointing the gun at her head. She was about to die. But her body was too injured to move.

She closed her eyes and waited.

Then she heard a body slam into another.

She forced her head to slide along the asphalt and saw him barrel into Edgar.

It was Jack.

Lashay ran from the Outside Garden department, leaving a customer who was just about to pay, into the parking lot toward Darla, her ex, and Jack. She spotted Gus lumbering toward the melee from the other end of the lot.

As she ran, Lashay thought about what Jack did to his friend, Dave Rendino, many years ago. As she came closer, she could see Jack just pummeling the limp man, landing blow after blow on his face.

"I fuckin' kill you," Jack yelled.

Lashay approached and thought about what she should do.

Do I physically jump on him to stop him from killing Darla's Ex?

Jack had the abuser on the ground on his back and was kneeling on him as he punched him in the face, neck, and forehead. Blood squirted in all different directions.

Gus had reached Darla and was helping her, while Lashay leaned over to Jack.

"Jack, Jack, Jack," she screamed.

He ignored her.

"Jack, are you going to make the same mistake and lose our chance at happiness?" She yelled at him.

Jack hesitated and stopped.

"You stopped him from hurting Darla," Lashay pleaded. "Now, think about our future."

Slowly, Jack stood, his hands bloody from pounding on Darla's Ex.

Then Gus was next to her.

"Get him the fuck out of here," Gus yelled. "The police are coming."

Go," Gus demanded and pushed Jack, who staggered but didn't move.

"Get him out of here," Gus said to Lashay.

"Now," he commanded.

Lashay grabbed Jack by the arm and pulled him, and he followed. Within 20 seconds, they were inside the store, and Lashay pushed her into the Men's Room to clean him up.

Jack wasn't talking, and she cleaned the blood off his hands and removed his bloody shirt. She desperately tried the lockers for an open one and found a black men's t-shirt that read, "Oh, Look, another F**k I don't give," and ordered him to put it on.

It was a size too small, but it would allow Jack to get out of the store without too much attention.

He sat down on the bench in front of the lockers.

"Thanks," Jack said.

"You saved me back there," he added.

"No, Jack," Lashay said, "I saved us."

The EMTs arrived first and began administering aid to Darla. They put her on a backboard and placed a neck collar on her. They had stemmed the bleeding on her head and bandaged her leg and arm wounds.

Another EMT vehicle pulled up and began to administer aid to Clyde, who was lifeless on the ground, lying on his back.

Three police cars pulled up, their sirens blaring, and they immediately began shouting orders to "get back" and "move back" as a crowd had formed.

Tyler was out now and trying to tell the police he was the store manager, but they just kept barking orders about staying back.

When a young police officer told him to get back right now, Gus said, "I'm the one who stopped this guy from killing this woman. Don't you want to talk to me? Or can I get back and then leave as ordered?"

The young officer spotted the gun on the ground — a Smith & Wesson and picked it up.

Gus muttered, "Great. First, I'm supposed to get back, but now I don't move."

Gus watched as both EMT vehicles left with Clyde and Darla.

Then, an older police officer, obviously the senior officer who was in charge, asked him his name and then said, "What happened here?"

While he waited for the police to do their thing around the area, Gus had crafted a believable story that omitted Jack pounding the living shit out of that asshole Clyde.

The senior officer listened to his story without interruption.

Clyde began by explaining that Clyde had abused Darla when they were married and had been showing up in the store parking lot, threatening her.

"So people in the store watched carefully when Darla left for the day in case that crazy Clyde showed up," Gus said.

"I saw him pull his car up to Darla, who was about to get into hers and point a gun at her. That gun," Gus said, pointing at the Smith & Wesson, which was now encased in a plastic evidence bag.

"What did you do then?" the officer asked.

"Punched him right in the face, and that knocked the gun out of his hand."

"The guy was pretty beaten up," the senior officer said. "And you don't have any blood on your hands, just your shirt."

Gus had anticipated this and put on his work gloves, smearing a little of Clyde's blood on them and his HomeMaxx work smock.

"He was going to shoot her, officer," Gus said. "No doubt about that."

"I had to keep hitting him because he kept trying to get his gun."

"Well, Mr. Burdette," the senior officer began. "Looks like you're a hero. You saved that woman's life."

"We'll get statements from the victim and the assailant tomorrow when they are able to speak," the senior officer told him.

The younger officer approached him and asked, "Hey, can we get any good deals in there now that the store is closing?"

That question piqued the interest of two other police officers, who awaited his answer.

"Nah," Gus answered. "This liquidation company is trying to rip people off. But if you need some drywall, pressboard, or two-by-fours, stop by the Lumber and Building Materials department in the next week, and I'll be happy to give you guys a sweet deal."

"Thanks. Thanks. Thanks," Gus heard as he walked back to the store.

Chapter Thirty-One

"As long as you're alive, you always have the chance to start again." Author Emily Acker.

So much had happened in the last two weeks that Jack's head was still spinning.

If you had asked him two weeks ago if he would be standing in the Excell Hardware store in Washington Township, ready to start his first day there, Jack would have called bullshit on that prediction.

After Jack had demolished Darla's ex-husband's face, Clyde spent several days at Jefferson Hospital in Washington Township. He was now sitting in the Gloucester County Prison unable to make bail.

Darla had been treated at the Jefferson Emergency Room and sent home. She didn't have a concussion but she did have a gash on her forehead that needed five stitches to close. Since Darla was already dazed by the time Jack showed up and tackled Clyde; she had nothing to report to the police other than his initial attack.

The police had no reason to doubt Gus, and Jack had thanked him several times.

Gus reacted with his characteristic grumbling.

"If I were a little younger, I would have beat you to Clyde, and then I'd have a murder charge. So, I figure you saved me. Stop thanking me, Jack. You've been hanging out with Lashay too long. You're turning into a woman."

When Jack found out that Jacob Snow had called Tyler and that they could accept the Excell Hardware jobs, he didn't know who was happier—him or

Tyler.

Jack had visited Darla at home, where she was recuperating.

"I want you to come and work with Lashay and me at the Washington Township Excell Hardware store," Jack had said. "Dave Maloney is losing his manager, assistant manager, and two employees. That means it's me, you, Lashay, and Ellen."

Darla relaxed on her sofa with a large bandage covering most of her forehead, cuts on both arms when she hit the asphalt, and an ankle brace because apparently she felt she had sprained her ankle.

"Jack, thank you so much," Darla said, her voice still wobbly due to her swollen lip.

Then she added, "You know I'm not used to saying that," Darla joked. "Jack, this is the second time you've saved me from Clyde."

"You have a good man in Edgar," Jack reassured her. "But if he goes off the rails, I'm happy to pound the shit out of him. Of course, I start charging for beating up husbands for the third time."

"Edgar's a charm," Darla said, wincing with pain in her ankle. "I've picked losers and made bad decisions my whole life and paid the price for it. I guess it's never too late to get your life together."

Jack stood to leave. "Darla, rest up and see if you are well enough to come in the following week."

"Screw you, Jack," Darla spit out. "I'll be there on day one."

They laughed.

"That made you feel better?" Jack asked.

"It's bad enough that HomeMaxx is closing," Darla began. "At least I still can follow my morning routine and curse you out as you arrive."

Jack chuckled.

"Always happy to oblige."

After that great news about Excell Hardware, Jack went home to meet his new landlords. The Szczesny's had already moved to Arizona, and there had been hugs, tears, and promises to see each other again.

He met the new landlords when their moving truck pulled up later that week.

He introduced himself to the couple. The husband was racetrack jockey short with a brown beard flecked with white and grey strands. The man met Jack's smile with a grimace. Behind him, his wife, several inches taller but with the same harsh features that defined the husband, forced a sideways, awkward grin.

"Jack Marsalis," the man repeated his name like he was taking attendance in homeroom. "Yeah, my mother-in-law is moving into your apartment on July 1, so you must be out by then."

While Jack processed and tried to refrain from punching the man in his face, the man went on.

"We'd appreciate it if you could vacate a few days early so we have time to, you know, clean and make upgrades."

Jack stepped a little closer to emphasize the size difference.

"The Szczesny's told me that they inserted a clause in the sale contract that I could stay until October 1."

The man scoffed at that.

"Yeah, they didn't read the contract that closely. I had my lawyer insert a clause that stated that we just had to give you 30 days' notice, and you have to vacate."

"Really," Jack responded. "So thirty days is July 15. So, actually, I don't have to be out until midnight on July 15."

"Technically," the man answered. "If you go by the strictest interpretation of the contract."

Jack looked at the man and woman before speaking. He didn't even know their names because they decided he was important enough to know that information.

"Let me give you both notice," Jack started, trying to throttle the anger flowing throughout his body.

"I will be moving out at exactly 11:59 PM on July 15. And not a moment sooner."

The woman now spoke, anxiety caught in her throat.

"But my mother will be here on June 30. What do we do with her?"

"You have two extra bedrooms upstairs," Jack said.

"What about her furniture?" the man asked.

"I don't even know you, and you didn't even have the decency to introduce yourselves," Jack said. "So what makes you think I give a shit about your problems?"

The woman moved beside her husband and said, "I'm sorry. I'm Rose Gold, and this is my husband, Martin."

"We obviously got off on the wrong foot," Rose said. "Mr. Marsalis, I wonder if you could move out by July 1 so my mother can move in?"

"No, I can't," Jack said abruptly. "With apartments so hard to find, what makes you think I can find a place in two weeks?"

"Well, if you don't," Marty chimed in. "We'll keep your security deposit."

Jack's anger had dissipated, and he now felt comfortable sticking it to this couple.

"I guess you didn't read the contract that closely," Jack mimicked what Marty had just told him. "I never had to give a security deposit because we got along and helped each other. I guess you two don't understand that concept."

As Jack turned to head back into his basement apartment, Lashay came out to meet him. She had stayed there the last few nights since she only had two weeks to vacate the trailer. They rented a storage unit down the street from the Excell Hardware store and moved her stuff to the unit daily. Noah helped them by driving Gus's pickup truck to the trailer and helping Jack and Lashay load up her belongings. That meant Gus had to drive Noah's Honda Civic home, and he whined about it like a five-year-old.

"Why does the kid's car smell like lamb?" Gus ranted. "The bearings are bad, the shocks are shot, and the valves are crying out for an overhaul. I can't hear myself drive."

As Lashay, dressed in sweatpants and a grey Breanna Stewart WNBA t-shirt, walked toward her, Jack thought the Golds would void their bowels.

Jack could read their wide eyes and shocked expressions.

A black woman is living downstairs.

"Lashay, these are the new landlords," Jack began in that fake customer service had used multiple times at HomeMaxx. "Rose and Marty Gold."

Lashay barely nodded.

"The Golds have given us good news," Jack said loudly and with faux enthusiasm.

You know how I said we had to be out by July 1? Guess what? Great news. The Golds here just informed me that we have until 11:59 PM on July 15. What a surprise!"

Lashay ignored them and said, "I made dinner. It's delicious. Come on."

Jack's smile could have blocked the sun as he walked toward the stairs.

"Nice to meet you, Golds," Jack hollered.

"Let me know what you'll offer me to leave by July 1?"

"Should have read that contract more closely," Jack said as he closed the door to his apartment.

As Jack scanned the Excell Hardware store, he was struck by its size compared to HomeMaxx. Like Home Depot and Lowe's, the average HomeMaxx was about 100,000 square feet.

This Excell Hardware store was about 15,000 square feet. At HomeMaxx, ceiling rafters were about 20 feet high, while at Excell, the ceiling height was 12 feet.

Lashay and Jack planned to collect Allegra's litter box, food, water bowl, and house and bring them to Excell until they found a place together.

During the crush of customers hunting for deals during the store liquidation, Allegra had been especially visible throughout the store, with so many more humans to visit.

Lashay had talked to Jack last week at the store.

"I want to take Allegra with us when we leave HomeMaxx on Friday,"

Lashay said.

Jack didn't think twice about taking Allegra. It was important to Lashay, and that was good enough for him. Besides, Allegra seemed to want to cuddle more with Jack than Lashay. He would kid her about it.

"We know who is her favorite," Jack always teased.

"I've had cats, and they are intuitive animals," Lashay said. "They often get close to humans who need the most help."

"Ha ha," Jack replied. "Allegra has good taste in humans, that's all."

But on their last day, Allegra was nowhere to be found. They looked for over an hour and couldn't find the cat.

Gus, who was one of the few HomeMaxx employees left, told them, "I saw her early this morning sitting on a stack of drywall. After that, no."

Lashay even tried to make a store announcement: "If anyone spots a Calico cat in the store, please let a HomeMaxx employee know immediately."

No one had seen her.

Jack and Lashay sat on the few patio furniture chairs that hadn't been sold yet and waited.

While they waited for news on Allegra or spotted her wandering the store greeting humans as usual, Jack looked over at Lashay.

"Strange that we won't be coming here on Monday," Jack said.

"This store saved me," Lashay said. "I had worked a lot of crappy server jobs before coming to HomeMaxx. It's like home. I feel comfortable here."

Touching his right hand and stroking his wrist, Lashay said, "It's where we met."

Jack leaned over to kiss her lightly on the cheek.

"You could get fired for that," Lashay teased.

"I'm counting on that," Jack volleyed the tease back to her.

Jack scanned the store one last time and noticed its remarkable features, which he had grown accustomed to seeing every morning.

After a while, you stop seeing and recognizing, and your brain doesn't register your environment anymore.

It just is.

Now, it was no more. Jack checked out the sealed concrete floor and the metal rafters supporting the roof, as well as the uneven lighting casting shadows in the store's nooks and crannies.

Jack could almost hear Kelly's announcements.

"Flooring department. Phone call on line two."

"Jack Marsalis, please report to Plumbing."

"Lashay Jones, please report to Paint."

Jack visualized Harry rushing up to him, out of breath, with eyes bulging with the information he was compelled to share.

"Jack, Jack, "Harry would beseech him. "Did you hear that Kathy, the new girl in Window Treatments, has an OnlyFans page?"

Jack thought about Gus doing the work of three people and yelling at HomeMaxx employees and customers. Or Darla's unique morning greeting.

Jack assumed that Lashay had similar feelings. The silence felt comfortable and cozy, even though customers, frantic for a deal, rampaged through the store like villagers with torches at a witch burning.

Jack looked over at Lashay, sure she was at the end of his journey. While starting his life over was agonizing, Jack thought it was worth the battle if Lashay was at the end of his rainbow.

I think I'm a better man than I was 20 years ago.

At least, I hope so.

Jack crossed his legs just as Lashay did, and they laughed. They held hands, took mental photos of the store that had been their lifesaver, and waited for Allegra, the cat, to appear.

As Lashay inspected her new work home at the Excell Hardware store, she felt a strong sense of claustrophobia. The high roof, expansive store footprint, and open space had been replaced by a smaller store crammed with narrow aisles and products stacked as high and deep as possible.

Jack and Lashay arrived at seven in the morning, an hour before the store opened. Ellen Cleary came after them, and they stood near the front checkout counter, waiting for the store owner, Dave Maloney, to show up.

The three of them didn't even talk but surveyed their new store.

The door opened, and in walked Darla Campanna.

Lashay had been told by Jack that she was still recuperating and would start work next week.

"Darla, good morning," Jack greeted her.

Darla, still wearing a forehead bandage and ankle brace and with a limp, offered them a huge smile.

"Screw you, Jack," Darla intoned like she had done for years at HomeMaxx.

Jack's face beamed, and he said, "The store has been christened. It feels like home."

The store owner, Dave Maloney, walked in after Darla. He wore dark blue shorts with a powder blue polo shirt. Lashay noticed sweat stains dotted the shirt, and she assumed he had just come from pickleball. Dave was always coming from or going to an athletic competition.

Lashay always found the store owner an intriguing contradiction. On the one hand, Dave was always friendly, outgoing, and sociable, but when he played any sport or game, his competitive fires burned white hot, and losing was akin to humiliation. Jack told her that years ago when Dave's daughter was about seven years old, he made her play the card game War over and over until he finally won.

Lashay, Jack, Ellen, and Darla stood along the checkout counter.

Dave's smile shone brighter than Lashay had ever witnessed. She knew it was because he could finally move full-time to Naples, Florida, and enjoy semi-retirement, where he would whip up on Sunshine State residents in tennis, pickleball, bocce, 5K runs, speedboat racing, and even bridge.

"Good morning, team," Dave began. "A new era of the Excell Hardware store is beginning in Washington Township in the great state of South Jersey."

Lashay gauged the faces of her three co-workers, Jack, Ellen, and Darla. Like her, they were excited about a new chapter in their lives.

Sure, it was a home improvement store like HomeMaxx, but they were more vested in the enterprise here. Dave was moving to Florida and promised a hands-off approach to running the store. Lashay believed they could do great things together.

"So with Jack as manager and Lashay assistant..." Dave started before he was interrupted by Jack.

"Dave, the manager of the store will be Lashay Jones. I will be the assistant manager with Darla and Ellen as assistants to the assistant manager."

"Jack, Jack," Lashay said, shocked and unsure how to respond.

Jack turned to her and said, "It makes sense. You have all the finance and budgeting experience needed as the store manager."

"But..." Lashay mumbled.

"This is what's best for the store and what's going to offer Dave here the best return on his investment in us," Jack said.

"Besides, what do you think? I'm a male chauvinist? I can't take orders from a woman," Jack cracked, his smile spreading from lips to cheekbones to forehead.

Lashay laughed, as did Ellen, Darla, and Dave. Lashay recalled the first day she worked at the Franklinville HomeMaxx, having just transferred from the Mantua store.

After being introduced to Jack and chatting with him that morning, she recalled what she first thought.

He's handsome and charming, and everyone who works at the store seems to follow his lead. But he seems full of himself, and he's white.

As she was suddenly store manager, Lashay thought about everything she had gone through to get to this point in her life. Daryll abused her and kicked her down the stairs. Getting more oxys any way she could and debasing herself to get more oxys. She had lost a daughter; she just got back and found this man who made the ultimate expression of love.

He put her needs in front of his.

Dave had been going over the details of the store, and Lashay had to force herself to pay attention. After focusing on Dave's explanation of locks, alarms, ordering, vendors, taxes, financial reporting, and their compensation, Lashay looked at her phone.

It was 7:59 AM. The store would open in a minute.

"I have to catch a flight to the Fort Myers Airport," Dave announced. "You don't need luck, but let's do something special here."

Dave high-fived everyone and walked out the door. As Lashay was about to lock it, Tyler Rodgers stood in front of her.

"It's 8 AM," he began, feigning ignorance. "Isn't your store open? I have purchases to make."

"Welcome," Lashay gushed. "You are our very first customer."

Tyler entered, and it was like they were at HomeMaxx, enjoying each other's company and ready to do their best job.

As Tyler spoke to Darla about her recuperation, Lashay wondered about Allegra. She had moved the cat's litter box, bed, food, and water bowls into the back room of the store here. She still hoped to find the cat.

To Lashay, Allegra wasn't just a cat. A pet.

No, she was somehow the catalyst for change.

Allegra couldn't save the store—its destiny was determined when Black Cobalt purchased it—yet her presence made the employees and customers feel better about life and themselves.

Allegra's appearance brought her and Jack closer. They had a common goal: to take care of Allegra. Lashay felt they were a family—her, Jack, and Allegra. When they found a place together, Lashay wanted to bring Allegra home.

Tamara had told her about Allegra that day at the picnic table at HomeMaxx and that she had been coming to the store for months to check out Lashay. Her mother.

"The cat somehow knew we were connected," Tamara had said. "I would stand near the refrigerators if you were working in the Lawnmower department, and Allegra would jump up on a shelf and then purr in my face and nudge me to pet her."

"I'd stand there for 30 minutes, and Allegra wouldn't leave my side," Tamara had added.

They had to keep looking for Allegra.

"Lookout everyone," Jack shouted mockingly, "the new evil region manager is visiting."

Tyler rolled his eyes at Jack and turned toward Lashay.

"Congratulations, store manager," Tyler shook her hand as he oozed sincerity.

"I know you'll do a great job," Tyler continued. "You'll have to watch out for the assistant manager. He's pretty shaky."

Ellen and Darla were behind the counter; Jack headed to the back stockroom while Tyler still talked to Lashay about the store.

"I'm going to have a monthly Zoom call with my store managers," Tyler told her.

Before Lashay could answer, the store door opened, and Robbie Nowicki and Luis, his new boss from the office cleaning business, walked in.

Robbie walked right up to Tyler and stuck out his hand.

"Mr. Rogers, thank you so much for my job at HomeMaxx," Robbie said.

"And for finding me this job with Mr. Luis," he added.

Tyler shook his hand and replied, "You're new job is thanks to Luis here and Jack. He's in the back. You should thank him."

Lashay waved him over and said, "Come on, Robbie. I'll take you back to Jack."

This was Noah's second week at Marlton Tire as an auto mechanic, and he already loved it. First, he had loved working on his cars with his father since he was a kid. When he was only five years old, his dad bought him a plastic auto mechanic kit with small plastic tools, and Noah would pretend he was helping his father fix a car.

Now, he was doing it for real.

He liked the boss, Marty, who could be abrasive to the mechanics—there were four mechanics who worked there. Noah had gotten used to Gus, whose natural resting state was either annoyed or angry – with either him or the customers.

The other nice part of the job was that Marlton Tire was only two doors from the Excell Hardware Store, so he could visit Jack or Lashay at lunch or after his shift.

Gus was working at HomeMaxx until the last day before the store closed, which was in a week. Being at different jobs made living at Gus's place easier because now they had something to talk about since they didn't work together anymore.

Gus was clearly happier after he made up with his son Michael and now had a granddaughter to pamper. Noah was shocked that Gus even liked Michael's partner, Max.

Gus and Noah sat at the kitchen table one morning before work, sipping coffee and eating a blueberry pound cake his mother had made.

"You know, kid," Gus began, slurping coffee between breaths. "I think Michael's partner, Max, is a good guy and smart, too. You know, for a gay guy."

Noah shook his head. "Yes, Gus. For a gay guy, he's smart and good,"

"Why do I think you're making fun of me?" Gus asked.

"That's because I am," Noah chirped.

Noah realized that Gus was still on his journey of understanding. Sadly, Noah's father hadn't even started to change his views. Noah still hadn't heard from him at all, but Noah's mother, sister Carmen, and her son, Noah's nephew, Alex, visited Noah and Gus several times a week.

Noah's mother still called him "Mr. Gus" and brought all kinds of Puerto Rican delicacies, which Gus devoured. Gus loved to play with Alex and enjoyed Carmen, who bonded with Gus on game shows. They'd watch reruns of Wheel Of Fortune at night and play against each other.

Noah thought something was going on with Gus and Bonnie, the server at the Silver Lake Diner. They ate there on Saturday morning as per Gus's routine, and Noah noticed something different, almost intimate, about the way they interacted. Plus, Gus had disappeared for several hours on successive Sundays with no explanation.

Noah hoped it was true because Gus, and probably needed Bonnie, needed that connection.

Noah, too, needed a connection, but with him being homeless, his new job at HomeMaxx, and his move-in with Gus, there was just too much going on in his life. It was like a plane that never landed or a train that never stopped at the station.

A few weeks ago, Noah stopped at the Playa Bowl on the Rowan University campus. Playa Bowl custom builds smoothie bowls with a variety of toppings. A bowl starts with a base made of house-made acai, pitaya, coconut, oatmeal, or chia pudding, and customers can add fresh fruit, seeds, nuts, granola, dried berries, and nut butter.

Noah's favorite was the Pua Vida, with blueberry flax granola, strawberry, blueberry, and honey. That's where Noah met Josh, a second-year Engineering student at Rowan. They hit it off and met up at LaScala Pizza, down from Playa Bowl, and across the street at Barnes & Noble for coffee and getting-to-know-you sessions.

Noah's Aunt Marie, much older than his mother, moved to New Jersey decades ago and went to Rowan to become a teacher when it was called Glassboro State College. In the late 1970s, it had about 1,500 students. Now, it had fifteen times that number.

Josh had shown Noah an article about Glassboro State. It read: "The Hollybush Summit took place in Glassboro, New Jersey, from June 23 to June 25, 1967. During these days, President Lyndon B. Johnson and Premier Alexei Kosygin met to discuss Soviet-American relations. This meeting was during the height of an accelerating arms race and against the backdrop of ongoing wars in the Middle East and Southeast Asia."

Josh told him, "The reasoning behind the selection of Glassboro for such a significant summit was because Glassboro lies halfway between New York City and Washington, D.C."

Aunt Marie said that in 1992, Henry and Betty Rowan gifted $100 million to the college, making it, at the time, the largest gift to an educational institution.

Noah explained to Josh that he couldn't come to Gus's house. Noah had nowhere else to go and didn't want to get kicked out by Gus. More importantly, he didn't agree with Gus, but he respected his wishes.

Noah had been invited to the Tylers Rodger's home for a barbecue on July 4th. His boss, now his former boss, had been thoughtful in inviting him since Noah had only worked there less than two months.

Noah knew that his former co-workers – Jack, Lashay, Ellen, and Darla – had started their first day at Excell Hardware a few doors away. He was happy for all of them.

"Noah, Marty wants you up front," Bobby, one of the other mechanics, said.

Noah, who had been rotating the tires on a Honda CR-V, said, "Just tightening the lugs on this last tire."

Noah finished and walked into the office, where Marty stood behind the counter, and a customer stood several feet away. Marty wore a Kelly green Marlton Tire polo shirt that stretched across his belly with considerable difficulty. He sported an 80s mustache, a haircut from a franchise salon, and a smile that could easily be mistaken for a smirk.

Despite that, Noah liked him. He was a decent guy who knew the business and didn't usually try to rip off customers.

"Noah, this gentleman here needs a new alternator and insists that you do the repair," Marty said, tossing his thumb toward the customer.

Noah looked over at a fifty-ish man, obviously Puerto Rican, with slip-on sneakers, baggy dad jeans, and a flannel shirt worn on an 85-degree day.

"Hi, sir," Noah said. "Can I help you?"

"Yes, ah, are you Noah Fernandez?" the man asked like he was reading from a script.

"I'm Noah," he answered.

"My alternator went bad on my Ford Fusion," the man responded. "I need you to put in a new one."

"I'd be happy to do that," Noah answered, still puzzled.

"But why did you ask for me? Noah asked.

"You were highly recommended," the man answered, still on a script.

"By who?" Noah asked.

"By a friend, Manny Fernandez," the man said.

Noah's father. He had to force himself not to cry.

Chapter Thirty-Two

"No matter how hard the past is, you can always start from now."
Seneca

Tyler Rodgers set up extra lawn chairs for the July 4th barbecue. This was the first big event for the renovated backyard. He and Jack had worked on the finishing touches last Saturday. Their daughters, Morgan and Taylor, had been home from college for six weeks with predictable outcomes. On some days, Tyler was so happy they were back home for the summer. Yet, on other days, he wished that college had year-round semesters.

Tyler had a better chance of communicating with either of them by texting than physically speaking to them when their faces were buried in their phone screens, and their thumbs were warping into overdrive.

Pam came outside from the kitchen French doors and said, "Twenty minutes, hon."

Tyler walked over to her and kissed her.

"No, buddy," Pam giggled. "We don't have time for that now."

"Wow, you went dark...fast," Tyler reproached her. "I was thanking you for doing so much work for this barbecue for the people who worked at HomeMaxx with me all these years."

"You're welcome," Pam answered. "I think it's nice that you're having this barbecue. After all, a lot of people have worked at HomeMaxx for 20 years."

Tyler nodded. "Ellen, Darla, Luther, and Harry. Jack and Lashay are about 15 years. Gus, ten, I think, and Noah, two months."

Tyler looked at the question on her face. Why someone who has only been at HomeMaxx for less than two months?

"He's a good kid, hard worker, who was homeless for a while," Tyler said.

Then, with a thumbs up, he said, "Plus, he's the one who fixed the rattle in your RAV4."

"What was it?" Pam asked.

"The heat shield was dangling, and he reattached it," Tyler said. "Now he's working at Marlton Tire on Greentree Road, so that's where our cars will be serviced from now on."

"It's going to be hot," Pam said. "Can you open the umbrellas on the three dining tables?"

Tyler gave her an AOK sign and said, "I can't thank you enough for finding an apartment for Jack and Lashay."

Pam nodded and said, "There's not much out there, and less available in their price range. Plus, you know."

Tyler just nodded as he raised one of the umbrellas.

"I've been a realtor for 20 years," Pam said. "I see racism all the time. It's not in your face like before, but it's there. In the shadows. You have to listen to the whispers."

"Lashay told me that now that she, Luther, and Tamara are coming to the barbecue, we can officially say we have three Black friends," Tyler said. "She said that we're two up on the bigots."

Pam chuckled and rearranged some of the chairs that Tyler had just put out on the lawn.

"You don't like my lawn chair strategy," Tyler said. "But here's something you will like."

"Does your next sentence end with a jewelry box," Pam chided him.

"Better than jewelry," Tyler crowed. "I talked to Katherine from the Sea Isle City house we rent every summer. She's agreed to a price. We are buying it in October."

Pam hugged him, "Tyler, that's great news."

Then, stopping mid-hug, Pam asked, "Wait. Did you negotiate a real estate deal?"

As Pam rearranged a few snack tables, she said, "Thank you, Tyler."

"I learned from the best," Tyler said. "You."

Gus's strategy was to get to the barbecue right at one p.m. so he could be the first one there. He didn't want people to make a big deal because he brought Bonnie with him as a date or friend.

He wasn't sure how to define their relationship, but he was sure he didn't want people making a big deal about it.

It had been a rough few weeks. Everyone else he knew at HomeMaxx had left for different jobs. Jack, Lashay, Harry, Ellen, Darla, even Noah. He couldn't blame them. But he was staying until the bitter end.

Working with those store liquidation people was rough; they were like vultures trying to eat the entrails out of the store. People came in looking for a bargain and got a higher price than normal, even though the product was listed at 80 percent off.

One customer wanted to buy an asphalt cold patch.

"Is this a good price?" the customer had asked.

"No, it's not," Gus had told him.

The customer left, and some store liquidation manager got in his face, yelling, "Listen, buddy, we're trying to sell all this shit. So say it's a great price."

Gus bumped his nose against the manager's and growled," Get this close to me again, and they'll find you under some asphalt cold patch one day."

A week before the store closed, Gus received an invitation from Rodgers to attend his barbecue. He wanted to ask Bonnie but couldn't find the words.

He asked Noah one night after work. The kid was covered in grease and smelled like decrepit tires from his new job at Marlton Tire.

"How do you people ask each other out?" Gus asked awkwardly.

Noah shook his head. "Gus, we're not aliens. The same way you people who think you're normal do. Say, 'Bonnie, would you like to go to a barbecue I'm invited to?'"

Gus took the kid's advice, but it took him three times at the diner before doing so.

After the second consecutive day of eating there, Bonnie said, "Gus, it's a pleasure to see you two days in a row. Anything going on?"

When Gus finally stumbled through asking Bonnie, she released a huge smile and said yes. Then she said, "Noah had stopped by to tell me you were going to ask me just in case you chickened out."

Gus's first reaction was to strangle the chicken-necked kid, but then he realized that Noah cared enough to do that. Speaking of the kid, Gus knew he was seeing someone. Noah thought he was so sly. He had been going out a lot and even stayed out a few nights on the weekend.

"What's up with you staying out all night?" Gus has asked him.

"I'm just hanging out with my cousin Jose, who lives in Berlin, and it's too late to drive home, so I crash on his couch," Noah said.

Gus didn't believe it for a moment. He didn't want another guy sleeping over but was happy he found someone. He'd never tell Noah that.

He liked having Noah at the house. The kid was neat and organized. He made coffee every morning and made breakfast for them, with his favorite being Huevos rancheros, which Gus refused to eat initially and now demanded.

Gus would never admit it to Noah, but he loved having his mother, Antonella, around, cooking delicious food – whatever it was — and dotting on him.

She had a saying for every life activity.

"Mr Gus," she would say, "Health is wealth."

"Mr. Gus, be the best version of you," she'd say.

Antonella would make dinner, Noah's sister Carmen would show up with baby Alex, and they'd eat until their plates were picked clean.

While Antonella and Noah cleaned up, Gus played with Baby Alex until Wheel of Fortune came on, and then Carmen and he dialed up the competitiveness.

"I've got to be me," Carmen would say, solving a puzzle on the show.

"Damn it," Gus would growl.

"Mr. Gus," Antonella corrected. "Alejandro must not learn such words."

Gus liked Tyler Rodgers, the HomeMaxx store manager. They weren't close because Gus wasn't really close with anyone. Gus respected him and knew that he cared about his employees and wasn't one of those profit-and-loss bosses who looked at you as an expense to be reduced if possible.

"Hi, I'm Pam Rodgers," an attractive blonde welcomed them.

"Hi, I'm Bonnie," Bonnie said, "I'm Gus's friend."

"Well, Bonnie and Gus, welcome," Pam said. "What can get you to drink? We have beer, wine, a mixed drink, soft drinks, water, lemonade."

Gus started to talk, "I'll have – " then pulled back and said to Bonnie, "Sorry, what would you like?"

Bonnie smiled at him. "I'll start with water and then start adding to the water later on."

They all laughed, and that relaxed Gus.

It didn't take long for others to show up to the barbecue. After Bonnie accepted Pam's offer to tour the home, Gus and Bonnie came through the kitchen French doors and bumped into Darla and her husband, Edgar.

Gus said loudly to Bonnie, "This is my new boss, Edgar. Edgar, this is Bonnie, my, ahh—" he paused as he looked at Bonnie for direction.

She nodded yes, and Gus finished, "Girlfriend."

After introductions, Darla jumped in with, "Bonnie, do you know what Gus's nickname was at HomeMaxx?"

"No," Bonnie answered. "I 'm guessing it wasn't Mr. Cool, Calm, and Collected."

They elicited a laugh from several people close by.

"We called him Bumble, the nickname Yukon Cornelius gave the Abominable Snow Monster in Rudolph The Read-Nosed Reindeer," Darla announced.

While others laughed, Gus decided to join them, understanding that this was a joke among friends. His skin had gotten a little thicker recently.

"Ready for your first day of work next Monday?" Edgar asked.

After working with the Gloucester County Prosecutor on Clyde's case, Gus had talked to Edgar, who said he had a good problem to solve. Business was good—too good—and he needed another driver. Edgar had a second dump truck as his spare.

"Would you be interested in driving with me after HomeMaxx closes?" Edgar had asked.

Gus picked up on the "with me" instead of "for me," and while he didn't know Edgar well, his reputation as a fair guy was well-known. At 65 years old, Gus's body was breaking down after all those decades of concrete work. It was back-breaking work.

Edgar was upfront with him and said there would be times when Gus would only drive a few days of the week and other times when he'd work a 12-hour day. If it had been before he met Noah and his family, reconciled with Michael, and started a relationship with Bonnie, Gus would have turned him down.

Now, Gus had a richer life with people who cared about him and people he cared about.

Gus had driven Edgar's Kenworth T-880 dump truck with a PACCAR Automated 12-speed transmission. The truck drove smoothly, and it was obvious that Edgar took care of his equipment.

The pay was much more per hour than he made at HomeMaxx, and since he now had Medicare, he didn't need employer insurance. Besides, HomeMaxx's health benefits package sucked, and he had been taking his blood pressure and statin pills every two days instead of daily to save the tremendous costs of the drugs.

Gus decided he would still do concrete sidewalks and patios for people, and Noah had already agreed to be his assistant. There, he received cash he didn't report, and he sometimes made more on a weekend job than he did at HomeMaxx for the week.

While Edgar bored Bonnie with the ins and outs of driving a dump truck, Gus talked with Darla.

"How are you healing up?" Gus asked her.

She still had a bandage on her forehead and gauze on her right forearm.

"I'm almost there," Darla said. "I still have a headache sometimes, but I'm working at Excell Hardware and don't notice any major issues."

Silence hung awkwardly between them until Darla said, "Thank you, Gus, for coming to help me. I know Jack got there first, but you wanted to save me. And thank you for telling the police it was you, not Jack, who beat the shit out of Clyde."

"You're welcome," Gus said, nodding and adding, "With Jack's prior record, who knows what could have happened? Besides, we all want Clyde to go to prison for a long time."

"The prosecutor, Mr. Hogan, says Clyde could get 15 years for attempted murder and more on the gun charge," Darla said.

"I've lived in fear of that man for years," Darla went on. "I always thought he'd show up and shoot me dead. Sometimes at night, when I'm lying in bed, I'd see Clyde holding a gun pointed at my head. The hatred in his eyes and the gunbarrel pointed right at me still haunts me."

"I get that," Gus replied, then grunted, "Don't worry, Darla. You can call me. Any time. I'll be there to protect you."

Darla nodded, and her eyes moistened.

"Gus Burdette, I always told people that you're a teddy bear underneath that gruff exterior."

Gus made a valiant effort to smile.

"Don't tell anyone, okay? Our secret."

When Noah got out of the Toyota Corolla passenger seat, his body was all static electricity with nerves.

"Noah, are you going to be okay?" Josh asked him as he exited the driver's side.

Noah nodded three times quickly.

"You don't have to go through with this," Josh assured him. "I don't want Gus to throw you out of the house."

Noah nodded again, but not moving away from the car door.

Josh walked over to Noah and held his hand.

"Noah, just introduce me as your friend," Josh advised. "We don't hold hands and no PDA. This barbecue is full of suburbanites who are heteros.

We're guests. We make these people comfortable. And you decide that if someone asks you if you're in a romantic relationship, how to answer. I'll take my cue from you."

Noah swallowed and nodded as they walked along the driveway toward the side paver path that led to the backyard and the barbecue.

As they opened the gate to the yard, he was greeted by Mr. Rodgers, whose smile was broad and genuine.

"Noah, glad you could make it," Mr. Rodgers said, then to Jonah, "Hi, I'm Tyler Rodgers."

"Mr. Rodgers, I'm Josh, a friend of Noah's. Nice to meet you," Josh said, extending a hand coupled with a friendly smile.

"It's Tyler to both of you," Mr. Rodgers began.

He had probably suffered a lifetime of Mr. Rogers jokes, Noah assumed. "And that's my wife, Pam, over there. I think Noah, you'll recognize your former co-workers from HomeMaxx."

As Noah and Josh mixed with Luther, Harry, Ellen, and Darla, Noah relaxed. Josh seemed comfortable meeting people and comfortable in his own skin, which is one attribute that Noah admired and envied in him.

After a few minutes, Gus approached them. Noah felt a lump of stress and anxiety stick in his throat. He thought he was having trouble breathing.

"So Noah, who is this?" Gus asked, that twisted sarcasm in his tone.

Noah was afraid Gus would start calling Josh fruit names or worse.

"Gus, this is my friend, Josh," Noah answered nervously.

Josh extended his hand and offered a smile.

Gus didn't move at first, staring at Josh's hand.

Then Gus grabbed Josh's hand hard and shook it vigorously. He leaned in a little closer to Noah, and Josh then put his arms around Josh's shoulders, and said, "Well, Josh, Noah's friend. Glad to meet you. Josh, I would be very upset if I found out that Noah was treated badly."

Josh didn't flinch at Gus's intimidation.

"Gus, so would I," Josh answered.

Gus laughed. "Noah, I like this kid."

Noah took a breath of air into his lungs for the first time since he exited the car.

Once Noah and Josh were introduced to Mr. Rodgers's daughters, Morgan and Taylor, the four of them formed a circle and bathed in millennial humor.

The two daughters were funny, fun-loving, and easy to get along with.

Unlike the older people at the barbecue, the four of them talked openly about him and Josh being gay.

Noah felt his phone vibrate in his pocket. He pulled it out. It was a FaceTime request from Michael, Gus's son. Since Gus refused to buy a smartphone and used an old flip phone, Michael resorted to calling Noah, who didn't mind because he liked Gus's son.

Michael's face appeared on his phone screen.

"Hi, Michael," Noah said.

He saw that Michael was at home with Max and Aubrey in the background. Max waved.

"Noah, hi. You're at the barbecue. I'm sorry. But I have important news for my Dad."

Noah walked across the lawn as he talked to Michael.

"No problem," Noah answered. "Your Dad is right here with Bonnie."

Michael purred. "Bonnie, huh? Very nice."

"Gus, Michael is on the phone," Noah said as he approached Gus and Bonnie, who were talking with Harry.

Gus was always flustered by FaceTime, saying, "Where do I look?"

Noah would answer, "At the screen."

Noah had to hold the phone for Gus, or he would move out of the picture.

"Hi, Michael," Gus said.

"Dad, I know you're at that barbecue with Bonnie. Hi, Bonnie. But I have something to show you."

"Hi, Michael," Bonnie interjected.

"Make sure my Dad invites you when he comes to Colorado to visit in September," Michael said.

"Thanks, Michael," Bonnie said as she yielded the screen to Gus, whose eye still wandered.

"Dad, here we go," Michael said, excitement rising in his tone.

Max brought over Aubrey in his arms, and Michael stood close and said to the screen, "Okay, Dad. I hope she says it."

Noah watched as Max and Michael cooed at the 14-month-old, "Hi Aubrey, Aubrey, hello. Aubrey."

At first, the baby just smiled and flailed with her hands as Max and Michael continued.

Then: "DaDa."

Again: "DaDa."

Max and Michael unleashed smiles of overwhelming pride.

"Did you hear?" Michael said.

Gus hadn't reacted to "DaDa" with the enthusiasm that Noah had expected, but then again, Gus's face was not a reliable indicator of what he was thinking. Gus generally possessed a "you talkin' to me" visage.

"Michael, Max," Gus began, dialing up the excitement. "That's incredible. You guys must be so happy."

"We are," Michael said, then he whispered something to Max.

"Watch what we are trying to teach Aubrey to say," Max said.

Noah watched as Max and Michael faced Aubrey in Max's arms and both men then cooed, "PopPop. PopPop. Can you say PopPop?"

Aubrey excited about the attention, replied with a "DaDa."

"We're working on it," Michael said to the screen.

Noah watched Gus closely. The man was struggling to keep from tearing up. Bonnie apparently noticed it, too, because she took his hand.

Gus managed to say, "That's so nice of you both."

"We'll let you go," Michael said. "Love you, Dad."

Michael and Max held Aubrey's arms in a waving motion.

"Love you all, too," Gus replied.

Noah was ready to end the call, but Michael said, "Not so fast, little bro. We expect to come in September, too."

"Are you sure?" Noah asked.

"Noah, you are family now," Michael said as they waved goodbye.

As Noah realized he had gained a second family, he felt a paw grab his left shoulder.

It was Gus.

"He's right about that, you know. You're family."

Before things got sappy, Gus added, "Now stop hanging out with us old people and get over there with people your age."

Noah headed back over to Josh, Morgan, and Taylor. As he rejoined their group, all laughing at something Josh had said, Josh looked over at him.

"Are you okay?" Josh asked. "You seem emotional."

"No, No," Noah answered. "Things couldn't be better."

Jack and Lashay arrived later than everyone else because they waited for Tamara to arrive at Jack's place in Clayton. She was going to ride over with them. Since Tamara had re-entered Lashay's life, Jack wouldn't have said that the reunion was all peaches and cream, but progress had been made.

Tamara had strong feelings of abandonment. It turned out that her father, Daryll, had moved to Arizona after getting out of prison and had never been heard from again. After several attempts on Tamara's part to connect with her father via his social media, she was blocked by him.

She got the message. Go away.

Lashay was dealing with her guilt issues at not trying to reconnect with Tamara after getting out of prison. One night, Lashay said to Jack, "I'm not ready to share my past with Tamara yet."

Jack replied, "Got it. Your story to tell if and when you want to."

Jack felt both women were wise to move slowly in reconnecting. Jack genuinely liked Tamara. Like Lashay, she was smart and hard-working. She had graduated from Rutgers in Camden as a registered nurse and worked at Inspira Hospital in Mullica Hill as a pediatric nurse.

She lived in the Meadows condo complex on Fries Mill Road in Washington Township and was on a break from dating after several disastrous online dating episodes.

When Jack, Lashay, and Tamara showed up after parking down the street because all the close spaces were taken, Pam greeted them with that same smile she had plastered on her real estate FOR SALE signs.

She hugged all three of them as they entered through the front door. Lashay and Tamara enthusiastically accepted an offer of a house tour. Jack walked into the backyard, and even though he had helped renovate it, he was still impressed with the additional design work Tyler and Pam had done. The four chaise lounges featured a sleek, protective powder-coated aluminum frame with subtle weathered gray teak and plush azure blue cushions you could sink into and drift off.

Tyler greeted him.

"Thanks for showing up," Tyler kidded.

"I was going to rearrange my sock drawer," Jack teased. "But I decided to come here instead."

"The backyard looks incredible," Jack added.

"It was hard getting good help, but I managed to coax the lazy workers to get it all done," Tyler chided him.

"Seriously, Jack. Thank you. You did an amazing job. We are going to pay you back later on."

"Tyler," Jack answered, in that "what did you do" voice.

"What do you want to drink?" Tyler asked.

"Beer," Jack answered.

"We have Bud Lite on tap and Corona bottles."

"Bud Lite," Jack said, "And a glass of Pinot Noir for Lashay with a little ice."

"Coming right up," Tyler said as he toiled behind the bar.

As Pam returned with Lashay and Tamara after the tour, Tyler said, "It's a great time for a toast."

Jack got Tamara a White Claw and watched as Tyler stood on a stool.

"Hey, everyone, can I get your attention?" Tyler announced.

As conversations slowly ceased and eyes turned toward Tyler, he addressed the crowd.

"Thank you all for coming," Tyler began. "First, I want to thank my wife Pam for organizing this barbecue. On our first date, I took Pam to a Mexican restaurant in Berlin, and then we played a round of mini-golf. She crushed me in mini-golf. On our second date, I took her to Dave & Buster's in Philly, where she proceeded to beat me at every arcade game we tried. Now, after 25 years of marriage, I can finally admit that Pam is pretty much better at everything than I am."

Laughter made Tyler pause.

"I need to thank my daughters, Morgan and Taylor, for another successful year at college. And after they graduate next May after we paid for their college tuition and room and board, I have to warn you girls – Payback is a bitch."

Again, laughter, with Morgan and Taylor booing their dad in jest.

"Finally, Pam has given many of you a tour, whether you want to or not, and you've seen our new backyard setup. We could not have accomplished all that without the help of one man. That man is Jack Marsalis."

People applauded politely for Jack, with the Rodgers girls, Noah and Josh, adding whistles and "Woo, woo, woo" to the toast.

Jack held up his beer to say thank you.

Tyler added: "Most people here worked at the Franklinville HomeMaxx for years. Or your spouse or family member did. It was a special place. To me, and I think to many of you, we were more than co-workers. We shared our lives with each other. Our dreams. Our accomplishments. Our disappointments."

Tyler drew a breath: "Remember when Ellen's daughter, Claire, was on Jeopardy and finished in second place? Or when Luther won $5,000 on a scratch-off? Or when Harry stopped gossiping. Only kidding. Harry, you never did stop, did you? How about when Jack walked in every morning and wished Darla good morning and added a sarcastic comment, and Darla would answer with a 'screw you, Jack.' Those were the days."

"Now, I'm spreading rumors at Home Depot," Harry yelled out.

"And I'm still telling Jack to screw himself, only at Excell Hardware now," Darla chimed in.

"Who could forget the sounds of The Bumble emanating from the lumber department when Gus lost his temper?" Tyler started again.

"It was scary," Ellen admitted. "And daily."

Jack looked at Gus, afraid he might get upset, but Gus nodded his head and Jack could see that he tried to soften his mean, resting face.

"In recent months," Tyler continued, "we welcomed Robbie, who transformed our parking lot with carts all over into a neat, organized area That made it look like we knew what we were doing."

When he came in, Jack spotted Robbie with his mother, Elaine, near the grill. They both smiled, and Elaine mouthed thank you to Tyler and then looked at Jack.

Tyler continued his speech. "After going through about 20 Lumber department associates to work with Gus, we found Noah. We knew he was a keeper after he didn't quit on the first day. Noah was a hard worker who has moved onto Marlton Tire where he is an excellent auto mechanic.

"And then we made the best deal possible for the store about two years ago when Lashay transferred to our store. Lashay transformed the outside Garden department, and, truth be told, Jack, too. And, she brought us our lucky charm, Allegra, the Calico cat that captured the attention of the local media and would have saved the store if it hadn't been for Black Cobalt."

Boos began to grow in depth and volume as Tyler mentioned Black Cobalt. Tyler raised his full beer glass.

"I want to toast all of you here today and, especially, those who worked at HomeMaxx. We shared a past. We're together in the present. And in the future, I wish you all health, happiness, and prosperity."

Everyone drank, and there was a collective "Here, here."

Once the toast was done, people roamed the yard, forming temporary groups. Jack helped Pam with the barbecue, grilling the staples—hot dogs, hamburgers, chicken, sausage, and veggies—while Tyler kept glasses full and guests engaged.

Jack and Lashay sat and ate while Tamara headed over to join the young group of Morgan, Taylor, Noah, and Josh. Jack watched as they shared photos and videos from their phones.

Jack chatted with as many people as he could, assuming he would not see them again.

When he saw Harry, Jack asked, "So Harry, what gossip do you have from the Turnersville Home Depot?"

Harry looked around as if Home Depot spies had infiltrated the barbecue.

"Jack, you won't believe what's going on there," Harry began in his conspiratorial voice. "The one assistant manager is sleeping with a male and female employee from the Window Treatments department."

Jack looked at Lashay and feigned shock.

"Harry, I'm going to miss you," Jack told him.

Jack talked with Luther, who was getting ready to leave.

"Luther, you didn't bring your lovely wife?" Jack said as a statement and a question.

Luther, with his car keys already in his hand, answered. "Jack, my wife knows that white people's barbecues are boring as hell."

Jack looked over at Lashay, who nodded her head.

"You two suck," Jack said.

They laughed, and Jack said, "Luther, enjoy retirement, brother."

"Thanks, Jack," Luther said. "Take care of my girl here," pointing to Lashay. "If I were 20 years younger, I would have stolen her away from you."

Jack nodded. "I'm sure you would have. And I will."

After desserts were served—cheesecake, watermelon, and apple pie with vanilla ice cream—Jack and Lashay sat next to one another in the shade as the afternoon sun dipped in the sky.

Jack and Lashay sat in comfortable lawn chairs a few feet from the crowd. They didn't speak. They felt an early July breeze, dry for South Jersey, blowing across the yard in puffs, grazing their skin.

Lashay felt comfortable here. Here, she was a manager, a co-worker, a mother, a friend, and a lover. She wasn't that one black friend that white people could point to. No one watched to feel her hair, and nobody told her that they liked hip-hop.

She thought people were inherently tribal. Too often, tribes are based on race or ethnic background. Sometimes, a tribe develops in the workplace, on a baseball team, or in a hospital.

Soon, the differences within that tribe dissipate, and the tribe becomes a complete unit where the whole, instead of the parts, define the tribe.

As Lashay felt the breeze tickle her skin, Pam approached them with a full wine glass in one hand and a paper in the other.

"Jack, Lashay," Pam said, extending the paper so either of them could take it.

"Is this our notice of dismissal," Jack asked, "Did your husband already fire us from Excell?"

Pam went along with the joke. "He wanted to, but I talked him out of it. "

"It's your rental lease to sign," Pam said. "I found you a place on Hurffville Crosskeys Road next to the Virtua medical building. It's called Woodmont Square. It's a two-bedroom, and pets are allowed, so you can bring Allegra."

Jack got out of his chair and hugged her.

"Pam, I don't know how to thank you. You're the best," Jack said.

"No, Jack. I should be the one thanking you. You did most of the work in this backyard and on earlier home renovations," Pam said.

"Pam, thank you so much," Lashay said, standing up, although she didn't know Pam very well.

Pam embraced her with a hug.

"Did you have any problems with, you know," Lashay hesitated.

"You mean with Jack being a dickhead," Pam chided.

Lashay laughed and replied, "Yeah, that."

Jack feigned surprise and indignation.

"Hey, that's Mister Dickhead to you two," Jack shot back.

"Original, Jack," Pam retorted. "You're going to have to up your game with two classy ladies like us."

"Thank you again, Pam," Jack said as Lashay added, "You're a lifesaver."

"Anything for you two," Pam said. Someone called her name from behind her, and Pam said, "Excuse me."

When Jack and Lashay sat down, they looked at each other with an "I guess we're doing this" look.

Jack sipped a sweetened iced tea while Lashay let the ice melt in her red wine.

"Jack, can I ask you something," Lashay asked.

"Sure."

"Before you got screwed by your friend Dave," Lashay began, putting air quotes around the word friend. "You lived a typical comfy white suburban life. Good job, wife, nice house in the suburbs, and white friends. You probably never had to worry about money as a kid and an adult."

"What's the question?" Jack asked.

"Would you be the Jack Marsalis I know now if your life didn't go into the toilet and you've been fighting for years to crawl out?"

"Wow," Jack said. "Saving the tough questions just before we move in together."

Lashay turned her body toward Jack. She waited patiently for an answer.

"I thought about that question a lot," Jack answered. "I always cared about my employees and not just the job or the company I worked for. At home, I realized a few months after I was married that she and I had very different ideas about life. To her, things were important. So was status. People, not so much. We would have broken up even if I hadn't trusted Dave Rendino and still kept my job."

Jack swallowed hard. "In prison, I read a lot. As I've said before, you keep your head buried in a book, and people generally leave you alone. Anyway, I came across this quote from Helen Keller that I still retain. It goes, 'Character cannot be developed in ease and quiet. Only through experience of trial and suffering can the soul be strengthened, ambition inspired, and success achieved.' In my case, that's true."

Lashay said, "When I came to the Franklinville store from Mantua, Luther and I were the only black employees," Lashay explained as she sipped her red wine, now watered down by the melting ice cubes.

"On my second day at our store, Luther approaches me and says, 'They are a good bunch of white people working here. But if you have a problem, see Jack Marsalis right away. Jack sets the tone. The workers here follow Jack, and let me tell you, Jack doesn't put up with any crap from anyone, regardless of who you are, what you look like, or what you believe.'"

Jack shifted in his lawn chair. Nearby, people laughed, ate, drank, played cornhole, told jokes and stories, discussed their futures, and did their best to put forth their best version of themselves.

Jack said, "A month after you arrived at the store, Ellen Cleary came to me and said, 'Jack, why don't you ask her out?'"

"What did you say?" Lashay asked.

"I told her that love isn't something you find," Jack said. "No. It finds you."

"Who would have ever guessed that I found the love of my life working in a home improvement store," Lashay said.

"Being with you makes everything I went through worth it."

"We are getting awfully mushy," Lashay kidded.

"I set up dinner with Tamara for next Thursday at the Lake House," Lashay added. "I never did thank you for Tamara."

Jack nodded, leaned over, and kissed Lashay on the cheek. Then, the barbecue guests began clinking their glasses and facing Lashay and Jack.

Lashay and Jack didn't disappoint, leaning in to kiss for a full five seconds, eliciting a "woo hoo" from everyone.

They kissed again to more noise from the guests. As Jack and Lashay separated, Jack said, "Hey, is it okay if I start calling you Shay as a nickname?"

Lashay replied with a severe stinkeye.

"Is it okay if I start calling you jackass as a nickname?" Lashay answered.

"Okay, Shay,"

"Jackass."

"Shay."

"Jackass."

"I can do this all night," Jack said.

"I know what else we could do all night," Lashay said with a devilish smile.

"That sounds amazing," Jack said.

"Jack, on the way back to your place," Lashay began. "Can we swing by the store and look again for Allegra?"

Chapter Thirty-Three

"We need each other, deeper than anyone ever dares to admit even to themselves.." Patch Adams

The cat felt that his home was disappearing. The humans who walked around each day became fewer and fewer, and his two humans were around less and less. He felt that the time had come to move along. She needed a new home somewhere close by because she knew the area.

She left the building she had lived in comfortably for multiple nights and days and moved back into the trees next to the cornfield. Since it was hot during the day and cooler at night, she relaxed in a thicket of trees surrounded by reddish barbed bushes.

She hunted at night and found plenty of prey: rabbits, squirrels, birds, and chipmunks.

There were no other cats wandering in her territory, so she felt safe enough to explore. At night, she could see the lights of a building across the blacktop where dangerous machines could kill.

After a few more days and nights, she watched carefully before crossing to the other side. She had watched the patterns and realized that there were fewer machines crossing.

Once across, she moved cautiously to the building. It was long and white, built low to the ground. She walked around the building, taking notice of any entrances and exits. As she moved to the rear of the building, a door was propped open. She heard the whir of machinery inside.

She approached carefully, crouching low to the ground. She waited a few minutes, motionless and focused on the open door.

Then, in a flash, she was inside the building.

Head Nurse Dotty McBride made her rounds of the Manor Life Nursing Home like she did every weeknight. It was two hours after dinner, and many of the patients were already asleep, and others were halfway there.

As she walked down the second hallway, nicknamed Pine Barrens, Dotty heard laughter coming from Mrs. Whipple's room. That surprised her. Mrs. Dorothy Whipple was 82 years old and afflicted with Parkinson's disease. Most days, she lay immobile in her bed or her chair, the vacant, faraway look on her face.

Now, she was laughing.

Dotty headed into her room and saw the woman sitting up in bed.

A cat sat on her lap, and the woman's shaky hand caressed the cat's coat.

Dotty immediately recognized the cat. It was the Calico from HomeMaxx, which was now closed across the street.

Allegra was her name.

The woman she met from the store, Lashay, had stopped at the nursing home the other day, searching for the cat.

"She has left her home, food, litter box, and cushy pillow," Lashay had told her, clearly upset.

Lashay said she was moving in with a co-worker soon and wanted Allegra to live with them.

At the time, Dotty hadn't seen the cat.

Until now.

Mrs. Whipple was hugging the cat, and the Calico responded by purring even louder.

"Can I keep her?" Mrs. Whipple asked.

Dotty didn't answer right away. She just watched.

Allegra's presence, her closeness, and her intimacy helped Mrs. Whipple.

Dotty wondered if somehow she could convince the administrators to allow the cat to visit patients regularly.

But even if she gained approval, the cat couldn't stay at the nursing home. It wasn't sanitary and safe.

Then she thought of Mr. Whiskers, her 18-year-old Tabby, who had recently died.

If I get approval, what if I kept Allegra at home with me and brought her a few times a week?

As Dotty McBride watched Allegra's presence energize Mrs. Whipple, she realized that this cat was somehow special. At HomeMaxx, it brightened the days of the customers and almost saved the jobs of the employees.

Here, at the nursing home, Allegra could help a group of older people who had been locked away and had been largely forgotten.

What was the greater good? Bring a little sunshine into the lives of older, infirmed people trapped in a nursing home. Or does the cat live as a house cat for the rest of its life?

Dotty McBride decided to take Allegra home with her and talk with the administrators.

She would call her Mrs. Whiskers.

About The Author

Frank Racioppi is a South Jersey-based author who publishes his daily podcast e-publication —*Ear Worthy* — on several platforms, including Blogger, Substack, ManyStories, Medium, Tumblr, and Vocal.

Frank lives with his partner Linda; cats named Moogie and Tinker Bell, and two squirrels named Bonnie and Clyde, who always try to steal the birdseed from his bird feeders!

He is also the author of five non-fiction books, four novels, and two short-story collections.

Hit Pause For Life is a collection of essays about our heroes, our homes, and our culture, with essays ranging from a profile of a retired teacher who teaches English as a second language for immigrants to the top ten Billboard songs on August 22, 1964.

A Suburban Prison recounts the history of the American suburbs and their present-day condition from a scholarly and humorous perspective.

Stop For My School Bus...Or Else peers into the dystopian world of the school bus driver, where parents are always right, being on time is being early, and squirrels have the right of way!

The COVID Hotel is a memoir that recalls how a holiday cruise from Rome to Barcelona was detoured into a nightmare of 18 days of COVID quarantine in another country.

Ear Worthy is a deep dive into the podcasting industry, with sections on podcast trends, interviews with influential podcasters, and podcast reviews and recommendations.

Away From Home is a novel about four homeless house cats, a lovable golden retriever, and a parakeet caring for nursing home residents who join together to battle the 2017 raging forest fires of Northern California to find "their new home?"

For The Love Of Books is a romance novel set at one of New Hampshire's most scenic and famous lakes. Two people on vacation must decide if their love of reading is enough to begin and sustain a relationship.

Cardinal Rules is a carefully assembled collection of short stories, including *Book Club Confessions, The Man Who Hated Google, The Ill-Fated Man, Unforgettable, and Wingspan.*

The Deep World is a fantasy novel that introduces us to teenagers Colin, Madison, and David and warriors Dimiseus, Ahuic, and Mahmoud. While we sleep and dream, we are all transported to The Deep World, an ethereal universe where the primal forces of Evil and Good are locked in an eternal battle for supremacy in the physical world.

Least Best Employee (Subtitle: How to Survive Corporate Life) is the all-too-familiar story of a long-term employee at a large corporation who becomes a casualty of relentless cost-cutting and shareholder value initiatives. The weapon of choice to terminate this manager, Mark Rossi, is the annual employee review.

Tales of South Jersey is a collection of short stories set in South Jersey, celebrating the land of blueberries, Pine Barrens, WaWa, and Wildwood.

Starting From Now is a novel about redemption, set in a fictional home improvement store in Franklinville, NJ, called HomeMaxx. Long-time employees Jack Marsalis and Lashay Jones try to ignite a romantic relationship that may be smothered by the secrets both carry with them.

You can find his books on frankracioppi.com, or in select independent bookstores.